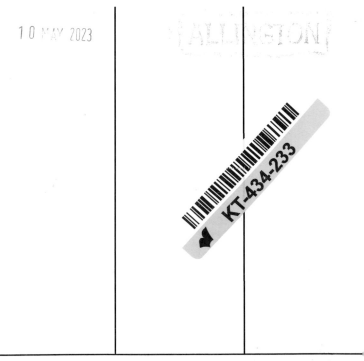

Books should be returned or renewed by the last
date above. Renew by phone **03000 41 31 31** or
online *www.kent.gov.uk/libs*

Praise for *If There's No Tomorrow*

'Thought provoking and powerful'. Erin Watt, #1 *New York Times* bestselling author

Praise for *The Problem with Forever*

'Armentrout is consistently stellar, but this book blew me away, completely. Gripping from page one, I—quite literally—couldn't put it down until I'd reached the end, and when I did, I wanted to be able to start all over again for the first time.'

— Christina Lauren, *New York Times* bestselling author

'Heartbreakingly real—a remarkable novel about the power of first love and the courage it takes to face your fears. I carried the book everywhere until I finished it, but I'll carry the story with me forever. Jennifer L. Armentrout truly blew me away.'

— Kami Garcia, #1 *New York Times* bestselling coauthor of *Beautiful Creatures* and author of *The Lovely Reckless*

'An achingly real masterpiece from Jennifer L. Armentrout. Heart wrenching, heart warming, heart everything.'

— Wendy Higgins, *New York Times* bestselling author

'We fall in first love with Armentrout's characters, she leads us to the front porch and we await our kiss and everything that comes after...we are left breathless and a little haunted and wanting more.'

— Danielle Page, *New York Times* bestselling author

'The intensity between Mouse and Rider is palpably sizzling...Romance aficionados [will] lose themselves in Mouse and Rider's smoldering glances and steamy kisses.'

—*Kirkus Reviews*

'Armentrout's effort to gradually coax her protagonist from her shell via a supportive, loving community succeeds, and readers looking for an inspirational comeback story will find

ALSO AVAILABLE FROM
JENNIFER L. ARMENTROUT

The Problem With Forever

IF
THERE'S
NO
TOMORROW

JENNIFER L.
ARMENTROUT

YOUNG
ADULT

HQ
An imprint of HarperCollins*Publishers* Ltd
1 London Bridge Street
London SE1 9GF

This paperback edition 2017

1
First published in Great Britain by
HQ, an imprint of HarperCollins*Publishers* Ltd 2017

A catalogue record for this book is available from the British Library.

ISBN: 978-1-84845-687-7

MIX
Paper from responsible sources
FSC™ C007454

This book is produced from independently certified FSC™ paper to ensure responsible forest management.

For more information visit: www.harpercollins.co.uk/green

Printed and bound in Great Britain by CPI Group, Croydon CR0 4YY

I couldn't move, and everything hurt—my skin felt stretched too tight, muscles burned like they'd been lit on fire, and my bones ached deep into the marrow.

Confusion swamped me. My brain felt like it was full of cobwebs and fog. I tried to lift my arms, but they were weighed down, full of lead.

I thought I heard a steady beeping sound and voices, but all of it seemed far away, as if I was on one end of the tunnel and everything else was on the other.

I couldn't speak. There…there was something in my throat, in the *back* of my throat. My arm twitched without warning, and there was a tug at the top of my hand.

Why wouldn't my eyes open?

Panic started to dig in. Why couldn't I move?

Something was wrong. Something was really wrong. I just wanted to open my eyes. I wanted—

I love you, Lena.

I love you, too.

The voices echoed in my head, one of them mine. Definitely mine, and the other...

"She's starting to wake up." A female voice interrupted my thoughts from somewhere on the other side of the tunnel.

Footsteps neared and a male said, "Getting the propofol in now."

"This is the second time she's woken up," the woman replied. "Hell of a fighter. Her mother is going to be happy to hear that."

Fighter? I didn't understand what they were talking about, why they thought my mom would be happy to hear this—

Maybe I should drive?

Warmth hit my veins, starting at the base of my skull and then washing over me, cascading through my body, and then there were no dreams, no thoughts and no voices.

YESTERDAY

CHAPTER ONE

THURSDAY, AUGUST 10

"All I have to say is that you almost had sex with *that*."

Scrunching my nose, I stared down at the phone Darynda Jones—Dary for short—had shoved in my face five seconds after walking into Joanna's.

Joanna's had been a staple in downtown Clearbrook since I was knee-high to a grasshopper. The restaurant was kind of stuck in the past, weirdly existing somewhere between big-hair bands and the rise of Britney Spears, but it was clean and cozy, and practically everything that came out of the kitchen was fried. Plus it had the best sweet tea in the entire state of Virginia.

"Oh man," I murmured. "What in the world is he doing?"

"What does it look like?" Dary's eyes widened behind her white plastic-framed glasses. "He's basically *humping* a blow-up dolphin."

I pressed my lips together, because yep, that was what it looked like.

Whipping her phone out of my face, she cocked her head to the side. "What were you thinking?"

"He's cute—*was* cute," I explained lamely as I glanced over my shoulder. Luckily, no one else was within hearing range. "And I *didn't* have sex with him."

She rolled dark brown eyes. "Your mouth was on his mouth, and his hands—"

"All right." I threw up my hands, warding off whatever else she was about to say. "I get it. Hooking up with Cody was a mistake. Trust me. I know. I'm trying to erase all of that from my memory and you're not helping."

Leaning over the counter I was standing behind, she whispered, "I'll never let you live that down." She grinned when my eyes narrowed. "But I understand. He has muscles on top of muscles. He's kind of dumb but fun." There was a dramatic pause.

Everything about Dary was dramatic, from the often abhorrently bright clothing she wore to the super-short hair, cropped on the sides and a riot of curls on the top. Right now her hair was black. Last month it was lavender. In two months it would probably be pink.

"*And* he's Sebastian's friend."

I felt my stomach twist into knots. "That has nothing to do with Sebastian."

"Uh-huh."

"You're so lucky I actually like you," I shot back.

"Whatever. You love me." She smacked her hands down on the counter. "You're working this weekend, right?"

"Yeah. Why? Thought you were going to DC with your family this weekend."

She sighed. "A weekend? I wish. We're going to DC for the *whole week*. We leave tomorrow morning. Mom can't wait. I swear she actually has an itinerary for us, like which museums she wants to visit, the expected time in each one, and when we will have our lunches and dinners."

My lips twitched. Her mom was ridiculously organized, down to labeled baskets for gloves and scarves. "The museums will be fun."

"Of course you think that. You're a nerd."

"No point in denying that. It's true." And I had no problem admitting it. I wanted to go to college and study anthropology. Most people would ask what in the hell would you do with a degree in that, but there were a lot of opportunities, like working in forensics, corporate gigs, teaching and more. What I wanted to do actually involved working in museums, so I would've loved a trip to DC.

"Yeah. Yeah." Dary hopped off the red vinyl bar stool. "I got to go before Mom freaks. If I'm five minutes past my curfew, she'll call the cops, convinced I've been abducted."

I grinned. "Text me later, okay?"

"Will do."

Waving goodbye, I grabbed the damp rag and ran it along the narrow countertop. Pots clanged together, echoing out from the kitchen, signaling it was close to shutting down for the night.

I could not wait to get home, shower off the scent of fried chicken tenders and burnt tomato soup, and finish reading the latest drama surrounding Feyre and the fae courts. Then

I was moving on to that sexy contemporary read I'd seen people talking about in the Facebook book club I lurked in, something about royals and hot brothers. Five of them.

Sign me up for that.

I swore half the money I made waitressing at Joanna's went to buying books instead of filling my savings account, but I couldn't help myself.

After wiping around the napkin dispensers, I lifted my chin and blew a strand of brown hair that had escaped my bun out of my face as the bell above the door rang and a slight figure stepped inside.

I dropped the lemony-scented rag with surprise. A breeze could've knocked me flat on my face.

For the most part, the only time anyone under the age of sixty came into Joanna's was on Friday nights after the football games and sometimes Saturday evenings during the summer. Definitely *not* on Thursday nights.

Joanna's made its bread and butter off certified AARP members, which was one of the reasons why I started waitressing here during the summer. It was easy and I needed the extra money.

The fact that Skylar Welch was standing just inside Joanna's, ten minutes before closing, was a shock. She never came in here alone. *Never.*

Bright headlights pierced the darkness outside. She'd left her BMW running, and I was willing to bet she had a car full of girls just as pretty and perfect as her.

But nowhere near as nice.

I'd spent the last *million* years harboring a rabid case of bitter jealousy when it came to Skylar. But the worst part was that she was genuinely sweet, which made hating her a crime against humanity, puppies and rainbows.

Tentatively walking forward like she expected the black-and-white linoleum floor to rip open and swallow her whole, she brushed her light brown, blond-at-the-end hair over her shoulder. Even in the horrible fluorescent lights, her summer tan was deep and flawless.

"Hey, Lena."

"Hey." I straightened, hoping she wasn't going to place an order. If she wanted something to eat, Bobby was going to be pissed, and I was going to have to spend five minutes convincing him to cook whatever she wanted. "What's going on?"

"Nothing much." She bit down on her glossy bubblegum-pink lip. Stopping next to the red vinyl bar stools, she took a deep breath. "You're about to close, aren't you?"

I nodded slowly. "In about ten minutes."

"Sorry. I won't take long. I actually wasn't planning to stop here." I silently added a sarcastic *Really?* "The girls and I were heading out to the lake. Some of the guys are having a party, and we drove past here," she explained. "I thought I'd stop by and see if...if you knew when Sebastian was coming home."

Of *course*.

I clenched my jaw shut. It should've been obvious the moment Skylar walked through those doors that she was here about Sebastian, because why else would she be talking to me? Yeah, she was sugary sweet, but we didn't operate in the same circles at school. Half of the time I was invisible to her and her friends.

Which was okay with me.

"I don't know." That was a lie. Sebastian was supposed to come home from North Carolina on Saturday morning. He and his parents were visiting his cousins for the summer.

A twisty pang lit up my chest, a mixture of yearning and panic—two feelings I was well acquainted with when it came to Sebastian.

"Really?" Surprise colored her tone.

I fixed a blank expression on my face. "I'm guessing he'll be back this weekend sometime. Maybe."

"Yeah. I guess." Her gaze dropped to the counter as she fidgeted with the hem of her slinky black tank top. "He hasn't… I haven't heard from him. I've texted and called, but…"

I wiped my hands along my shorts. I had no idea what to say. This was so incredibly awkward. Part of me wanted to be a total bitch and point out that if Sebastian wanted to talk to her, he would've responded, but that just wasn't me.

I was the kind of person who thought things but never said them.

"I think he's been really busy," I said finally. "His dad wanted him to check out some of the universities down there and he hadn't seen his cousins in years."

Someone out in the BMW slammed on the horn and Skylar looked over her shoulder. My brows rose while I silently prayed that whoever was in the car stayed in that car. A moment passed, and Skylar tucked bone-straight hair behind her ear as she turned back to face me. "Can I ask you one more thing?"

"Sure." Not like I was actually going to say no even

though I was picturing a black hole appearing in the diner and sucking me into its vortex.

A faint smile appeared. "Is he with someone else?"

I stared at her, wondering if I lived through a different history of Sebastian and Skylar.

From the moment she moved to Clearbrook, population *meh*, she'd attached herself to Sebastian. Not that anyone would blame her. Sebastian came out of his mom's womb stunning and charming everyone around him. Those two got together in middle school and had dated all through high school, becoming the King and Queen of Coupledom. I'd resigned myself to the fact I'd have to force myself to attend their wedding at some point in the future.

But then spring happened...

"*You* broke up with *him*," I reminded her as gently as I could. "I'm not trying to sound like a bitch, but what does it matter if he's with someone else?"

Skylar curled a slender arm across her waist. "I know, I know. But it matters. I just... Have you never made a huge mistake?"

"Tons," I replied drily. The list was longer than my leg and arm combined.

"Well, breaking up with him was one of my mistakes. I think, at least." She stepped back from the counter. "Anyway, if you see him, can you tell him that I stopped by?"

That was the last thing I wanted to do, but I nodded because I would tell him. Because I was *that* person.

Eye. Roll.

Skylar smiled then. It was real, and made me feel like I should be a better person or something. "Thanks," she said.

"I guess I'll see you at school in a week or so? Or at one of the parties?"

"Yep." I fixed a smile on my face that felt brittle and probably looked half-crazed.

Wiggling her fingers goodbye, Skylar turned and walked toward the door. She reached for the handle but stopped and looked over her shoulder at me. A strange look crossed her face. "Does he know about you?"

The corners of my lips started to turn down. What was there to know about me that Sebastian didn't already know? I was legit boring. I read more than I actually talked to people and was obsessed with the History Channel and shows like *Ancient Aliens*. I played volleyball, even though I really wasn't that good at it. Honestly, I would've never started playing if it hadn't been for Megan conniving me into it when we were freshmen. Not that I didn't have fun, but yeah, I was as stimulating as white bread.

There were literally no hidden secrets to uncover.

Well, I was scared to death of squirrels. They were like rats with bushy tails, and they were *mean*. No one knew that, because that was super embarrassing. But I doubted *that* was what Skylar was talking about.

"Lena?"

Jarred out of my thoughts, I blinked. "What about me?"

She was quiet for a moment. "Does he know you're in love with him?"

My eyes widened as my mouth dried. I felt my heart stutter and then drop to the pit of my stomach. Muscles locked up in my back and my gut churned as that wall of panic slammed into me. I forced out a wheezing-sounding laugh.

"I'm…I'm not in love with him. He's like a…like a *brother* I never wanted."

Skylar smiled slightly. "I'm not trying to get up in your business."

Sort of sounded like she was.

"I saw the way you would look at him when we were together." There was no bite to her tone or judgment. "Or maybe I'm wrong."

"Sorry, you're wrong," I told her. I thought I sounded pretty convincing.

So there *was* something that I thought no one knew about me. One hidden truth that was just as embarrassing as being afraid of squirrels but completely unrelated.

And I'd just lied about it.

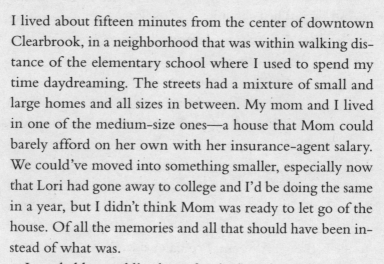

CHAPTER TWO

I lived about fifteen minutes from the center of downtown Clearbrook, in a neighborhood that was within walking distance of the elementary school where I used to spend my time daydreaming. The streets had a mixture of small and large homes and all sizes in between. My mom and I lived in one of the medium-size ones—a house that Mom could barely afford on her own with her insurance-agent salary. We could've moved into something smaller, especially now that Lori had gone away to college and I'd be doing the same in a year, but I didn't think Mom was ready to let go of the house. Of all the memories and all that should have been instead of what was.

It probably would've been for the best for all of us if we had moved, but we hadn't, and that was a flood under the bridge now.

I pulled into the driveway, passing the used Kia that Mom had parked on the side of the street. I turned off the engine and breathed in the coconut-scented interior of the decade-old silver Lexus that had once belonged to Dad. Mom hadn't wanted it, and neither did Lori, so I ended up with it.

It wasn't the only thing Dad had left me.

I grabbed my bag off the passenger seat and climbed out of the car before quietly closing the door behind me. Crickets chirped and a dog barked somewhere on the mostly silent street as I looked over at the larger house next to ours. All the windows were dark and the limbs of the thick maple in the front swayed, rattling the leaves.

A year from now I wouldn't be standing here, staring at the house next door like a bona fide loser. I'd be away at college, hopefully at the University of Virginia, my top choice. I was still going to carpet-bomb other colleges in the spring just in case I didn't get in on early admission, but either way, I would be gone from here.

And *that* would be for the best.

Getting out of this town. Moving away from the same old same old. Putting much-needed distance between the house next door and me.

Tearing my gaze away from the house, I walked up the flagstone sidewalk and went inside. Mom was already in bed, so I tried to be as quiet as possible as I grabbed a soda from the fridge and made my way upstairs to take a quick shower in the hallway bathroom. I could've moved into Lori's bedroom at the front of the house after she left for college. It was larger and had its own bathroom, but my bedroom had privacy and it had an amazing second-story deck that I wasn't willing to give up for a multitude of reasons.

Reasons I didn't want to think about too much.

Once inside my bedroom, I set the soda on the nightstand and then dropped the towel by the door. I pulled my favorite sleep shirt of all time from the dresser and slipped it over my head. After turning on the lamp on the nightstand and flooding the bedroom with soft buttery light, I picked up the remote and clicked on the TV, turning to the History Channel with the volume on low.

I glanced at the scribbled-on world map tacked to the wall above my desk. The map to everywhere I planned on eventually visiting. The red and blue circles drawn all over it brought forth a grin as I grabbed a massive red-and-black hardcover from my desk, which was pretty much used only to stash books now. When we first moved in, Dad had built shelves lining the wall where the dresser and TV were, but those bookshelves had been overflowing for years now. Books were stacked in every spare place in the room—in front of my nightstand, on both sides of the dresser and in my closet, taking up more room than the clothes did.

I'd always been a reader and I read a *lot*, usually sticking to books with some sort of romantic theme and a classic happily-ever-after. Lori used to make fun of me nonstop for it, claiming I had cheesy taste in books, but whatever. At least I didn't have pretentious taste in books like she did, and sometimes I just wanted to…I don't know, *escape* life. To delve headfirst into a world that dealt with real-life issues to open my eyes, or a world that was something else, something completely unreal. One with warring faes or roaming vampire clans. I wanted to experience new things and always, *always*, reach the last page feeling satisfied.

Because sometimes happily-ever-after existed only in the books I read.

Sitting down on the edge of my bed, I was just about to crack the book open when I heard a soft rapping coming from the balcony doors. For a split second, I froze as my heart rate spiked. Then I hopped to my feet, dropping the book on my bed.

It could be only one person: *Sebastian*.

After throwing the lock, I opened the doors and there was no stopping the wide smile from racing across my face. Apparently there was also no stopping my body either, because I propelled myself through the threshold, arms and legs moving without thought.

I collided with a taller and much, much harder body. Sebastian grunted as I threw my arms around his broad shoulders and practically face-planted on his chest. I inhaled the familiar fresh scent of detergent his mom had been using since forever.

There wasn't a moment of hesitation from Sebastian as his arms swept around me.

There never was.

"Lena." His voice was deep—deeper than I remembered, which was strange, because he'd been gone for only one month. But a month felt like an eternity when you saw someone nearly every day of your life and then suddenly didn't. We'd kept in touch over the summer, texting and even calling a few times, but it wasn't the same as having him *here*.

Sebastian hugged me back as he lifted me up so my feet dangled a few inches off the floor before he settled me back down. He lowered his head as his chest rose sharply against mine, sending a wave of warmth all the way to the tips of my toes.

"You really missed me, huh?" he said, fingers curling through the wet strands of my hair.

Yes. *God*, I did miss him. I'd missed him way too much. "No." My voice was muffled against his chest. "I just thought you were the hot guy I waited on tonight."

"Whatever." He chuckled against the top of my head. "There was no hot guy at Joanna's."

"How do you know?"

"Two reasons. First, I'm the only hot guy that ever steps one foot into that place and I wasn't there," he said.

"Wow. Real modest, Sebastian."

"I'm just speaking the truth." His tone was light, teasing. "And second, if you thought I was someone else, you wouldn't still be attached to me like Velcro."

He had a point.

I pulled back, dropping my arms to my sides. "Shut up."

He chuckled again. I always loved his little laughs. They were infectious, even when you were in a bad mood. You couldn't help but smile.

"I thought you weren't coming back until Saturday," I said as I stepped inside my bedroom.

Sebastian followed. "Dad decided I needed to be back for the scrimmage game tomorrow night, even though I'm not playing. But he'd already worked everything out with the coach. You know how Dad is."

His father was the stereotypical football-obsessed father who pushed and pushed and *pushed* Sebastian when it came to playing ball. So much so that I was downright shocked when Sebastian announced that they would be out of town while there was football practice. Knowing his dad, I bet he had Sebastian up every morning at the butt crack of dawn running and catching.

"Your mom's asleep?" he asked as I closed the balcony doors.

"Yeah..." I turned around and got a good look at him now that he was standing in the light of my bedroom. As embarrassing as it would be to admit, and I would never admit it, I completely lost my train of thought.

Sebastian was... He was effortlessly *beautiful*. It wasn't often you could say that about a guy...or about anyone, to be honest.

His hair was a shade somewhere in between brown and black, cropped close on the sides and longer on the top, falling forward in a messy wave that nearly reached dark brown eyebrows. His lashes were criminally thick, framing eyes that were the color of the deepest denim jeans. His face was all angles, with high cheekbones, a blade of a nose and a hard, defined jaw. A scar cut into his upper lip, just right of a well-formed Cupid's bow. It had happened our sophomore year during football practice, when he'd taken a hit that had knocked his helmet off. His shoulder pads had caught him in the mouth, splitting the upper lip.

But the scar fit him.

I couldn't tear my gaze from his basketball shorts and a plain white T-shirt as he glanced around my bedroom. When he was younger, back in middle school, he'd been tall, all arms and legs, but now he'd filled out in every way, with muscles on muscles and sculpting that rivaled Greek marble statues. Years of playing football would do that to a body, I imagined.

Sebastian wasn't simply the *cute* boy who lived next door anymore.

We'd been doing this for *years*, ever since he figured out it was easier than going to my front door. He'd head out his back door and come into our backyard through a gate, and then it was a short walk up the steps that led to the balcony deck.

Our parents knew he could get to my bedroom this way, but we'd grown up together. To them—and to Sebastian— we were like brother and sister.

I also suspected they didn't know the visits occurred at night. *That* hadn't started until we were both thirteen, the first night my Dad was gone.

I leaned against the door, biting the inside of my cheek.

Sebastian Harwell was one of the most popular guys in school, but that wasn't surprising. Not when he was gorgeous. Talented. Funny. Smart. *Nice.* He was in his own league.

He was also one of my best friends.

For reasons I didn't want to examine too closely, he made my bedroom appear smaller when he was in it, the bed too tiny and the air too thick.

"What in the hell are you watching?" he asked, keeping his voice low as he stared at the TV.

I looked at the screen. There was a guy with bushy, crazy-looking brown hair waving his hands around. "Um...*Ancient Aliens* reruns."

"All righty, then. Guess it's less morbid than the forensics show you watch. Sometimes I worry..." Sebastian trailed off as he faced me. His head tilted to the side. "Is that…my shirt?"

Oh. Oh my *God*.

My eyes widened as I remembered what I was wearing: his old freshman practice shirt. A couple of years ago he left it over here for some reason or another, and I kept it.

Like a stalker.

My cheeks flushed, and the blush raced down the front of my body. And there was a whole lot of body on display. The shirt hung off one shoulder, I had no bra, and I fought the urge to tug on the hem of the shirt.

I told myself not to freak out, because he'd seen me in bathing suits a million times. This was no different.

But it was.

"It *is* my shirt." Thick lashes lowered, shielding his eyes as he sat on my bed. "Wondered where that went."

I didn't know what to say. I was suddenly petrified, plastered to the door. Did he think my wearing his shirt to sleep was weird? Because yeah, it was kind of weird. I couldn't deny that.

He threw himself down on the bed, then immediately sat up. "Ow. What the hell?" Rubbing his back, he twisted at the waist. "Jesus." He picked up my book and held it out. "You're reading this?"

My eyes narrowed. "Yeah. What's wrong with that?"

"This thing could double as a weapon. You could hit me over the head with this thing, kill me and then end up on one of those shows you watch on Investigation Discovery."

I rolled my eyes. "That's a bit excessive."

"Whatever." He tossed the book to the other side of the bed. "Were you getting ready for bed?"

"I was getting ready to read before I was rudely interrupted," I joked. Forcing myself away from the door, I slowly dragged my way over to where he was now stretched out on his side, lying there like it was *his* bed, cheek resting on his fist. "But someone, no names mentioned, is now here."

His lips kicked up at the sides. "Want me to leave?"

"No."

"Didn't think so." He patted the spot next to him. "Come talk with me. Tell me everything I've missed."

Ordering myself not to act like a complete dork, I sat on the bed, which wasn't easy because of the shirt. I *so* did not want to flash him. Or maybe I did want to flash him. But he probably didn't want that.

"You haven't missed much," I said, glancing at my bedroom door. Thank God I'd closed it already. "Keith's thrown a couple of parties—"

"You went to them without me?" He pressed his hand to his chest. "My heart. It hurts."

I grinned at him as I stretched my legs out, crossing them at the ankles. "I went with the girls. I didn't go by myself. And so what if I did?"

The grin went up a notch. "Did he have any down by the lake?"

Shaking my head, I tugged on the hem of my shirt as I wiggled my toes. "No. Just at his place."

"Cool." When I looked over at him, his lashes were lowered. His free hand rested on the bed between us. His fingers were long and slender, skin tan from being outside all the time. "You do anything else? Go out with anyone?"

I stopped moving my toes, and my head swung back toward him. That was a random question. "Not really."

An eyebrow rose as his gaze lifted to mine.

I quickly changed the subject. "By the way, guess who stopped in at Joanna's tonight, asking about you?"

"Who wouldn't stop by asking about me?"

I shot him a bland look.

He grinned. "Who?"

"Skylar. Apparently she's been messaging you and you've been ignoring her."

"I haven't been ignoring her." He reached up, knocking the flop of hair off his forehead. "I just haven't been responding."

A frown turned down the corners of my lips. "Isn't that the same thing?"

"What did she want?" he asked instead of answering.

"To talk to you." I leaned back against the headboard and grabbed the pillow, thrusting it into my lap. "She said... She asked me to tell you that she was asking for you."

"Well, look at you, doing as you're told." He paused, his grin increasing. "For once."

I chose to ignore that comment. "She also said she thought breaking up with you was a mistake."

His head jerked back and that grin faded. "She said that?"

My heart started pounding in my chest. He sounded surprised. Was that a happy surprise or bad one? Did he still care about her? "Yeah."

Sebastian didn't move for a second and then shook his head.

"Whatever." His hand moved lightning fast, snatching the pillow out of my lap. He shoved it under his head.

"Help yourself," I muttered, tugging the shirt back up my shoulder.

"Just did." He smiled up at me. "You have another freckle."

"What?" I turned my head to him. Since I could remember, my face looked like it got hit with a freckle cannon. "There is no way you can tell if I have another freckle."

"I can tell. Lean over. I can even show you where."

I hesitated, eyeing him.

"Come on," he coaxed, hooking his finger at me.

Inhaling a shallow breath, I leaned toward him. Hair slipped over my shoulder as he lifted his hand.

That grin was back, playing over his lips. "Right there…" He pressed the tip of his finger to the center of my chin. I sucked in air. His lashes swept down. "That's a new one."

For a moment, I couldn't move. All I could do was sit there, leaning toward him with his finger touching my chin. It was crazy and stupid, because it was just the softest touch, but I felt it in every cell of my body.

He lowered his hand to the space between us again.

I exhaled a shaky breath. "You are… You are so stupid."

"You love me," he said.

Yes.

Madly. Deeply. Irrevocably. I could come up with five more adverbs. I'd been in love with Sebastian since, jeez, since he was seven and brought over the black snake he'd found in his yard as a gift. I don't know why he thought I wanted it, but he'd carried it over and plopped it down in front of me like a cat bringing back a dead bird to its owner.

A really, truly weird gift—the type of gift one dude would give another dude—and that pretty much summed up our relationship right there. I was in love with him, painfully and embarrassingly so, and he mostly treated me like one of his guy friends. Had since the beginning and always would.

"I barely tolerate you," I said.

Rolling onto his back, he stretched his arms out above his head, clasping his hands together as he laughed. His shirt rose, revealing his flat lower stomach and those two muscles on either side of his hips. I had no idea how he got them.

"Keep lying to yourself," he said. "Maybe one day you'll believe it."

He had no idea how close to the truth he was.

When it came to Sebastian and how I felt about him, all I did was lie.

Lying was another thing Dad had left me.

It was something he'd also been so, *so* good at.

CHAPTER THREE

It was too early for this crap.

Standing behind Megan, I was hoping I could just blend into the wall and be forgotten. Then I could lie down and take a nap. Sebastian had stayed till three in the morning, and I was way too tired to do anything remotely physical.

Coach Rogers, also known as Sergeant Rogers or Lieutenant First Class Jerk Face, crossed his arms. His face held a permanent scowl. I'd never seen him smile. Not even when we made it to the playoffs last year.

He was also the ROTC drill instructor, so he treated us like we were in boot camp. Today was going to be no different.

"Hit the bleachers," he ordered. "Ten sets."

Sighing, I reached up and tugged on the tail of my hair, tightening the ponytail as Megan bounced around, facing me. "Whoever finishes last has to buy the other a smoothie after practice."

The corners of my lips turned down. "That's not fair. You're going to finish first."

"I know." Giggling, she tore off toward the indoor bleachers.

Reaching down, I tugged on my black practice shorts and then resigned myself to death by bleacher.

The team hit the metal seats. Sneakers pounded as we worked our way up. At the top row, I smacked the wall as expected. If we didn't do it, we'd be starting all over. Back down I went, gaze focused on the rows in front of me as my knees and arms pumped. By the fifth round, the muscles in my legs burned, along with my lungs.

I almost died.

More than once.

Once it was over, my legs felt like jelly as I joined Megan on the court. "I'd like a strawberry banana smoothie," she said, her face flushed pink. "Thank you."

"Shut up," I muttered breathlessly as I glanced over to the bleachers. At least I wasn't last. I twisted back to her. "I'm getting McDonald's."

Megan snorted as she fixed her shorts. "Of course you are."

"At least I'm eating eggs," I reasoned. I'd probably have a hell of a lot toner legs and stomach if I got that smoothie after practice instead of the Egg McMuffin and hash brown I was planning to do bad, bad things to.

She wrinkled her nose. "I don't think those kind of eggs count."

"That's sacrilegious to even utter."

"I don't think you know what that word means," she replied

"I don't think you know when to shut up."

Tipping her blond head back, Megan laughed. Sometimes

I wondered how we'd become such close friends. We were polar opposites. She didn't read unless it was flirting tips in *Cosmo* or the weekly horoscopes in the magazines her mom had around the house. I, of course, read every book I got my hands on. I was going to be applying for financial aid, and she had a major college fund. Megan ate McDonald's only if she'd been drinking, which wasn't often, and I ate McDonald's so much I was on a first-name basis with the lady who worked the window in the morning.

Her name was Linda.

Megan was more outgoing than me, more willing to try new things, while I was the person always weighing the pros and cons before doing something, finding more cons than there were pros to almost *every* activity. Megan seemed years younger than seventeen, oftentimes acting like a hyper kitten climbing curtains. She was downright goofy half the time. But what seemed like cluelessness was only surface deep. She was an ace at math without even having to try. On the outside, she appeared to take nothing seriously, but she was as bright as she was bubbly.

We both planned—or hoped—to get into UVA, prayed that we'd get housed together and strived to give Dary the hardest possible time, with love, every day of our lives.

Deciding I was going to order two hash browns and eat them right in front of her face, I cut in front of her as we walked to where our captain was waiting.

Practice was grueling.

Since it was preseason and a Friday, it was all calisthenics. Lunges. Squats. Suicide sprints. Jumps. Nothing made me feel more out of shape than these kinds of practices. I was dragging ass by the time we wrapped up, sweating in places I didn't even want to think about.

"Seniors, I need you guys to stick around for a few minutes," Coach Rogers called out. "Everyone else can head out."

Megan shot me a look as we lumbered to our feet. My stomach ached a little from the sit-ups, so I concentrated on not bending over and crying like a teething baby.

"Our first game is a couple of weeks off, as is our first tournament, but I want you all to make sure you realize how important this season is." Coach straightened his cap, pulling the bill down. "This isn't just your final year. This is the time that scouts will be coming to the tournaments. Many of the colleges here in Virginia and surrounding states are looking for freshman players."

Pressing my lips together, I loosely crossed my arms. A volleyball scholarship would be sweet. I wanted one. Was going to gun for it, but there were better girls on the team, including Megan.

The likelihood of both of us landing positions at UVA was slim.

"I cannot stress how important your performance will be this season," Coach droned on. His dark gaze lingered on me in a way that made me feel like he'd noticed just how crappy my sprints had been. "You're not going to get a do-over. You're not going to get second chances to impress these scouts. There isn't a next year."

Megan's gaze slid toward mine and her brows lifted about an inch. This was a wee bit dramatic.

Coach went on and on about good life choices or something, and then he was done. Dismissed, our group made our way toward the remaining burgundy-and-white gym bags.

Megan bumped her shoulder into mine as she reached to grab her water from the top of her bag. "You kind of sucked today."

"Thanks," I replied, mopping the sweat off my forehead with the back of my hand. "I feel so much better after hearing that."

She grinned around the rim of the bottle, but before she could respond, the coach yelled out my last name. "Oh crap," Megan whispered, widening her eyes.

Swallowing a groan, I pivoted around and jogged over to where he was standing near the net we often had to repeatedly jump in front of. When Coach used your last name, it was a lot like your mom using your full name.

Coach Rogers's neatly trimmed beard was more salt than pepper, but the man was fit and more than intimidating. He could run those bleachers in half the time Megan could, and right now he looked like he wanted to order me to do another set of ten. If he did, it would be RIP Lena.

"I was watching you today," he said.

Oh no.

"Didn't look like your head was in practice." He crossed his arms, and I knew I was in for it. "Are you still working at Joanna's?"

Tensing because we'd had this conversation before, I nodded. "I closed last night."

"Well, that explains a lot. You know how I feel about you working when you have practice," he said.

Yes, I did know. Coach Rogers didn't think anyone who

played sports should work, because work was a *distraction*. "It's just during the summer." That was kind of a lie, because I planned to work weekends during the school year. I needed to keep my McDonald's fund fluffy, but he really didn't need to know any of that. "I'm sorry about practice. I'm just a little tired—"

"A lot tired by the looks of it," he cut in with a sigh. "You were forcing yourself through every set."

I guess I wasn't going to get credit for that effort.

He lifted his chin and stared down his nose at me. Coach was a beast during practice and the games, but most days I liked him. He cared about his players. *Really* cared. Last year, he organized a fund-raiser for a student whose family lost everything in a house fire. I knew he was against animal cruelty, because I saw him wearing ASPCA shirts. But right now, in this moment, I did not like the man at all.

"Look," he continued, "I know things are tight at home, especially with your father... Well, with all of that."

Clenching my teeth until my jaw ached, I fixed a blank expression on my face. Everyone knew about my dad. It sucked living in a small town.

"And you and your mom could use the extra cash—I get that—but you really need to look at the big picture here. Take these practices more seriously, dedicate more time, and you can up your playing this year. Maybe catch the eye of a scout," he said. "Then you get a scholarship. Less aid. That's what you need to be focused on—your future."

Even though I knew he meant well, I wanted to tell him that my mom and I *and* my future were really none of his business. But I didn't say that. I just shifted my weight from one foot to the next, picturing the greasy hash brown in my head.

Oh my God, I was going to smother that baby with ketchup.

"You have talent."

I blinked. "Really?"

His expression softened a bit as he clapped a hand down on my shoulder. "I think you have a shot at landing a scholarship." He squeezed gently. "Just keep your eye on tomorrow. Work for it, and there'll be nothing standing in the way. You understand?"

"I do." I glanced over to where Megan waited. "A scholarship would be... It would help a lot."

A *way* lot.

It would be nice not to spend a decade or more after college working myself out of student-loan hell I'd already been warned about.

"Then make it happen, Lena." Coach Rogers dropped his hand. "You're the only person standing in your way."

"I don't care what you say, Chloe was the better dancer!" Megan shrieked from where she was perched on the edge of my bed. I expected her hair to rise and turn into snakes at any given moment, to snatch out the eyeballs of anyone who disagreed with her.

Okay, maybe I was reading way too much fantasy lately.

"We seriously can't be friends if you disagree!" she added vehemently.

"It's not a question of who is a better dancer, but I personally think you're going with the 'blondes have to stick together' route." Abbi was sprawled on her belly on top of my bed. Her hair was a mess of tight, dark curls. "And honestly, I'm Team Nia."

Megan frowned as she threw up her hands. "Whatever."

My phone rang on my desk, and when I saw who it was, I sent the call to voice mail without even thinking twice.

Not today, Satan.

"Y'all really need to stop watching reruns of *Dance Moms*." I turned back to my closet and restarted my search for a pair of shorts to wear on my shift. Smothering a yawn, I wished I had time for a nap, but Megan had come over after practice and I had only about an hour before I had to head to work.

"You look tore up from the floor up," Abbi commented, and it took me a moment to realize she was talking about me. "Did you not sleep last night?"

"Wow. Thanks," I responded, frowning. "Sebastian came home last night, so he stopped over and stayed for a while."

"Ooh, Sebastian," cooed Megan, clapping her hands. "Did he keep you up all night? Because if so, I'm going to be upset that you didn't mention this earlier. I'm also going to want details. *All* the dirty, juicy details."

Abbi snorted. "I seriously doubt there is any juicy or dirty details."

"I don't know if I should be offended by that statement or not," I said.

"I just can't see that happening," Abbi replied with a lopsided shrug.

"I don't know how you spend so much time with him and not want to jump on him like a rabid mountain lion in heat," Megan mused. "I wouldn't be able to control myself."

I leaned my head back. "Wow." My friends were kind of weird. Specifically Megan. "Aren't you back with Phillip?"

"Kind of? Not sure. We're talking." Megan giggled. "Even if I were back with him, it doesn't mean I can't appreciate that fine specimen of a guy living next door to you."

"Have at it," I muttered.

"Have you noticed how hot people flock together? Like all of Sebastian's friends—Keith, Cody, Phillip. All of them are hot. It's the same with Skylar and her friends. Kind of like birds migrating south for the winter," Megan continued.

Abbi murmured under her breath, "What the hell?"

"Anyway, I'm not ashamed of my not-so-friendly thoughts toward Sebastian. Everyone has a crush on him," Megan said. "I have a crush on him. Abbi has a crush on him—"

"What?" shouted Abbi. "I don't have a crush on him."

"Oh, I'm sorry. You have the hots for Keith. My bad."

I twisted halfway to see Abbi's reaction to that and I was not let down.

Abbi lifted up onto her elbows, turning her head toward Megan. If looks could kill, Megan's entire family would've just died.

"I might seriously hit you, and since you weigh, like, eighty pounds wet and I have about a hundred on you, I'm going to snap you like a KitKat bar."

I grinned as I turned back to my closet and dropped to my knees, rummaging through the books and jeans on the bottom of the narrow closet. "Keith's cute, Abbi."

"Yeah, he's hot, but he's also the school bike and everyone has had a ride," she commented.

"I haven't," Megan said.

"Me neither." Finding the cutoffs, I snagged them off the floor and rose. "Keith has been trying to get with you since you developed breasts."

"Which was, like, the fifth grade." Megan laughed as Abbi threw my poor pillow at her. "What? It's the truth."

Abbi shook her head. "Y'all are crazy. I don't think Keith is into girls darker than your lily-white asses."

I snorted as I dropped into the desk chair. The back bumped into the edge of the desk, rattling the stack of books. "I'm pretty sure Keith is into girls of all skin tones, shapes and sizes and then some," I said, bending over and grabbing the pens and highlighters that had fallen from the desktop.

Abbi huffed. "Whatever. We are not talking about my nonexistent attraction to Keith."

I turned to Abbi. "You know, Skylar stopped into Joanna's last night and asked if Sebastian knew I was in love with him." I forced out a casual-sounding laugh. "That's crazy, right?"

Megan's blue eyes widened to the size of planets. Not Pluto...more like Jupiter. *"What?"*

Abbi was also paying attention. *"Details,* Lena."

I filled them in on what Skylar had to say last night. "It was just really weird."

"Well, obviously she wants to get back with him." Abbi looked thoughtful. "But why would she ask you that? Even if it was true, why would you admit that to her, his ex-girlfriend?"

"Right? I was thinking about that earlier." I toed myself around in a slow circle on the chair. "I've been around her a lot because of her dating Sebastian, but it's not like we're friends. I wouldn't admit my deepest secrets to her."

Abbi tilted her head to the side and looked like she wanted to say something but kept quiet.

"Oh! I almost forgot," Megan exclaimed as she dropped her feet to the floor, clearly on to the next topic. Pink flooded her heart-shaped face. "I heard that Cody and Jessica are seeing each other again."

"Not surprised." Cody Reece was the star quarterback. Sebastian was the star running back. Friendship made in football heaven right there. And Jessica was, well… She wasn't particularly the nicest person I'd ever met.

"Didn't Cody try to get with you at Keith's party back in July?" Abbi asked, rolling onto her back.

I shot her a death glare more powerful than the Death Star's laser. "I had forgotten all about that, so thanks for bringing *that* back up."

"You're welcome," she quipped.

"I remember that party. Cody was super drunk." Megan started twisting her hair in a rope, which she'd loved doing since we were kids. "He probably doesn't even remember hitting on you, but you better hope Jessica doesn't find out. That girl is territorial. She will make your senior year a living hell."

I wasn't really worried about Jessica, because, logically, how could she be that upset over Cody hitting on me at a party when they weren't even together? That didn't even make sense.

Megan cursed, jumping to her feet. "I was supposed to meet my mom ten minutes ago. She's taking me back-to-school shopping, which really means she's going to try to dress me like I'm still five." She picked up her purse and then her gym bag. "By the way, it's Friday, and don't think I've forgotten my weekly reminder."

I sighed heavily. Here we go...

"It's time for you to get a boyfriend. Anyone really, at this point. And a real one, too. Not a book boyfriend." She walked to my bedroom door.

I threw up my hands. "Why are you so obsessed with the idea of me having a boyfriend?"

"Why are you so obsessed with me?" mimicked Abbi.

I ignored it. "You do remember that I had one, right?"

"Yes." She raised her chin. "*Had*. As in past tense."

"Abbi doesn't have a boyfriend!" I pointed out.

"We're not talking about her. But I know why you aren't interested in anyone." She tapped the side of her head. "I *know*."

"Oh my God." I shook my head.

"Heed my words. Live a little. If you don't, when you're thirty and living alone with a ton of cats and eating tuna fish for dinner, you'll regret it. Not even the *good* tuna fish. The generic kind steeped in oil. All because you spend every waking minute reading books while you could be out there, meeting the future daddy to your babies."

"That's a little excessive," I murmured, side-eyeing her. "And what's wrong with generic tuna fish in oil?" I looked over at Abbi. "It tastes better than when it's soaked in water."

"Agreed," she replied.

"And I'm really not interested in meeting my future baby daddy," I added. "I don't even think I want kids. I'm seventeen. And kids weird me out."

"You disappoint me," Megan stated. "But I still love you, because I'm that good of a friend."

"What would I do without you?" I gave myself a twirl in the chair.

"You'd be a basic bitch." Megan gave me a cheeky grin.

I pressed my hand to my heart. "Ouch."

"I've got to go." She wiggled her fingers. "Text ya later."

Then she flounced out of the room. Literally. Head back, arms flailing and prancing like a show horse.

"Talk about basic." Abbi shook her head as she stared at the empty doorway.

"I will never understand her fascination with my single-ness." I looked at Abbi. "Like, at *all*."

"Who knows with her." Abbi paused. "So... I think my mom is screwing around on my dad."

My jaw dropped. "Wait, *what*?"

Abbi stood and planted her hands on her hips. "Yeah. You heard me right."

For a moment I didn't know what to say and it took a couple of seconds to get my tongue to work. "Why do you think that?"

"Remember how I was telling you that her and Dad had been arguing more lately?" She walked over to the window that overlooked the backyard. "They try to keep it quiet so my brother and I don't hear it, but it's been getting pretty heated and Kobe is having nightmares now."

Abbi's brother was only five or six years old. Rough.

"I think they've been fighting over her working so late at the hospital and, you know, *why* she's working so late. And I mean *late*, Lena. Like, how often are there call-ins that make other nurses stay? Is my dad that stupid?" She turned from the window, came back over to the bed and plopped down on the edge. "I was still up when she came home Wednesday night, four hours after her shift would've ended, and she looked a hot mess. Her hair was sticking up in every direction, clothes all wrinkled like she rolled out of someone's bed and came home."

My chest squeezed. "Maybe it was just a rough night at work for her."

She shot me a bland look. "She smelled like cologne, and not the kind my dad wears."

"That's not…good." I leaned forward in the chair. "Did she say anything to you when you saw her?"

"See, that's the thing. She looked guilty. Wouldn't look me in the eye. Couldn't get out of the kitchen quick enough, and the first thing she did when she got upstairs was shower. And the whole showering thing might not be abnormal, but when you add all of that together…"

"Damn. I don't know what to say," I admitted, twisting my shorts in my hands. "Are you going to say anything?"

"What would I say? 'Oh, hey, Dad, I think Mom is slutting around on you, so you might want to check on that'? I don't see that ending well. And what if, by a snowball's chance in hell, I'm wrong?"

I cringed. "Good point."

She rubbed her hands over her thighs. "I don't know what happened between them. They were happy up until about a year ago and it's just all gone to shit." Pushing her curls out of her face, she shook her head. "I just needed to tell someone."

I toed my chair closer to her. "Understandable."

A brief smile appeared. "Can we change the subject? I really don't want to deal with this longer than five minutes at a time."

"Sure." I got that more than anyone else. "Whatever you want."

She drew in a deep breath and then seemed to shake out all those thoughts. "So… Sebastian came home early."

That wasn't necessarily the conversation I wanted to go back to, but if Abbi wanted to use me as a distraction, I could be that for her. I shrugged and let my head fall back at the same moment my stupid heart did a giddy little flip.

"Were you happy to see him?" she asked.

"Sure," I replied, going for my usual bored tone when talking about Sebastian.

"Where's he at now?"

"At the school. They've got a scrimmage game tonight. He's not playing, but they've probably got him practicing."

"You're working this weekend?" she asked.

"Yeah, but this is my last weekend for a while, since school starts. Why? You want to do something?"

"Of course. Better than being stuck on babysitting duty at home and listening to my parents bitching at one another." Abbi nudged my leg with her sandaled foot. "You know, I hate to even point this out, but do you think Skylar might've had a point asking—"

"About me and Sebastian? No. What? That's stupid."

A doubtful look crossed her face. "You don't love Sebastian at all?"

My heart started pounding in my chest. "Of course I love him. I love you and Dary, too. I even love Megan."

"But you didn't love Andre—"

"No. I didn't." Closing my eyes, I thought about my ex even though I really didn't want to. We'd dated almost all last year, and Abbi was right: Andre was awesome and nice, and I felt like a jerk for ending things with him. But I tried, really tried, even by taking it to the next level—*the* level— but my interest just wasn't there. "It wasn't working out."

She was quiet for a moment. "You know what I think?"

I let my arms fall to my sides. "Something wise and sage?"

"Those two words mean the same thing, idiot." She kicked my leg again. "If you're not being entirely honest with yourself about Sebastian, then applying to UVA is a smart idea."

"What does he have to do with UVA?"

She tilted her head to the side. "Are you saying it's a coincidence that the one school that's not high on his list is the one school you're gunning for?"

Stunned into silence, I wasn't sure what to say. Abbi had never insinuated that I was interested in Sebastian beyond being friends before. I was confident I'd kept that embarrassing yearning desire well hidden, but obviously not as well as I believed. First Skylar, who really didn't know me, and now Abbi, who did?

"UVA is an awesome school and has an amazing anthropology department." I opened my eyes and my gaze fixed on the cracked plaster of the ceiling.

Abbi's voice softened. "You're not...hiding again, are you?"

The back of my throat burned as I pressed my lips together. I knew what she was talking about, and it had nothing to do with Sebastian. It had everything to do with the missed call earlier. "No," I told her. "I'm not."

She was quiet for a moment and then said, "Are you really going to wear those shorts to work? You look like a low-rent Daisy Duke in them."

At Keith's. You coming out?

The text from Sebastian came just as I was pulling into my driveway after my Friday shift. While I normally didn't pass up an opportunity to hang with Sebastian, I was feeling a little weird after the whole conversation with Abbi. Plus I was exhausted, so I was ready to climb under the covers and lose myself for a little while in a book.

Staying in tonight, I texted back.

He promptly replied with the smiling poop emoticon.

Grinning, I replied with Turd.

The triple dots appeared and then, You going to be up later?

Maybe. I climbed out of the car and headed toward the front door.

Then maybe I'll swing by.

My stomach dipped as it twisted. I knew what that meant. Sometimes Sebastian snuck over *really* late, usually when something was going down at home he didn't want to deal with…that something usually being his dad.

And I knew, I knew deep down, that even with all the years he'd been dating Skylar, he'd never done that with her.

When something was troubling him, he sought *me* out, and I knew I shouldn't have been thrilled about that, but I was. And I held that knowledge close to my heart.

I followed the low hum of the TV, passing through the small entry room that was overflowing with umbrellas and sneakers and the small table piled with unopened mail.

The glow of the TV cast soft, flickering light over the couch. Mom was curled up on her side, one hand shoved under a throw pillow. She was out cold.

Stepping around the love seat, I grabbed the afghan off the back of the couch and carefully draped it over Mom. As I straightened, I thought about what Abbi had told me earlier. I had no idea if her mom was cheating on her dad, but I thought about my mom and how she would've never cheated on Dad. The mere thought almost made me laugh, because she loved him like the sea loved the sand. He'd been her universe, her sun that rose in the morning and the moon that took over the night sky. She loved Lori and me, but she had loved Dad more.

But Mom's love wasn't enough. My and my sister's love was never enough. In the end, Dad still left us. All of us.

And, God help me, I was a lot like my father.

I looked like him, except I was more of an…average version. Same mouth. Same strong nose that was almost too big for my face. Same hazel-colored eyes, more brown than any other interesting shade. My hair matched his, a brown that sometimes turned auburn in the sunlight, and it was on the long side, falling past my breasts. My body was neither thin nor overweight. I was somewhere stuck in the middle. I wasn't tall or short. I was just…

Average.

Not like my mom, though. She was stunning, all blond hair and flawless skin. Even though life had gotten way harder in the last five years, she persevered and that made her all the more beautiful. Mom was strong. She never gave up, no matter what, even if there were moments where she looked like she just might want to pack it all in.

For Mom, our love was enough to keep going.

Lori got the blessed side of our genetics, taking after Mom. Blonde bombshell to the max, with all the curves and pouty lips to back it up.

But the similarities ran deeper than the physical for me.

I was a *runner*, too, and not the healthy kind. When things got too rough, I checked out, just like Dad had. I made an art form of looking toward tomorrow instead of focusing on today.

But I was also like my mother. She was a *chaser*. Always running after someone who didn't even realize you were there. Always waiting for someone who was never going to come back.

It was like I ended up with the worst qualities of my parents.

Heaviness settled in my chest as I went upstairs and got ready for bed. This November would be four years since Dad left. I couldn't believe it had already been that long. Still felt like yesterday in a lot of ways.

Throwing back the covers on my bed, I started to climb in but stopped when my gaze fell on the doors leading out to the balcony. I should lock the doors. Sebastian probably wouldn't stop by, and besides, even if he did, that…that wasn't good.

Maybe that was why no one else interested me.

Why Andre hadn't kept my interest.

Scrubbing my hands down my face, I sighed. Maybe I was just being dumb. How I felt about Sebastian couldn't change our relationship. It *shouldn't*. Putting a little distance between us, setting up some boundaries, wouldn't be a bad idea. It was probably the smartest and healthiest thing to do, because I didn't want to be a runner or a chaser.

I was moving off the bed before I realized what I was doing.

I walked over to the doors and unlocked them with a soft click.

CHAPTER FOUR

I half awoke to the feeling of my bed shifting and the soft whispering of my name.

I rolled onto my side and winced as I blinked open my eyes. I'd fallen asleep with the lamp on and I could feel the hard edges of the book now pressing into my back. I wasn't really thinking about the book, though.

Sebastian was sitting on the edge of my bed, his head tilted to the side and a small grin on his lips.

"Hey," I murmured, staring up at him with sleepy eyes. "What...what time is it?"

"A little after three."

"Are you just getting home?" Sebastian didn't really have a curfew. I did during the school year, but as long as he was scoring touchdowns, his parents pretty much let him come and go as he pleased.

"Yeah. We got into a mad game of badminton. Loser out of five games has to wash the cars."

I laughed. "Seriously?"

"Hell yeah." The grin kicked up a notch. "Keith and his brother versus me and Phillip."

"Who won?"

"Do you really need to ask that?" He reached out, gently shoving my arm. "Phillip and I did, of course. We made that birdie our bitch."

I rolled my eyes. "Wow."

"Anyway, our win involves you."

"Huh?" I squinted at him.

"Yep." Lifting his hand, he knocked a hank of hair off his forehead. "I plan on getting the Jeep as dirty as humanly possible, and I mean I want it to look like one of those abandoned cars on *The Walking Dead*. So how about we ride out to the lake this week and mess my baby up."

Grinning, I pressed my face into the pillow. Sebastian wanting me to go to the lake with him shouldn't mean anything, but it did. It meant too much. "You're terrible."

"Terribly adorable, right?"

"I wouldn't go that far," I murmured, sticking my arm under the blanket.

Sebastian leaned onto his side, stretching his legs out on top of the covers. "What did you do with your night? Read?"

"Yeah."

"Such a nerd."

"Such a jerk."

He chuckled. "How was practice today?"

Wrinkling my nose, I groaned.

"That bad?"

"Coach thinks I shouldn't work," I told him. "Not like

it's the first time he'd brought it up, but he brought up Dad, and that just…well, you know."

"Yeah," he replied quietly. "I know."

"He did say he thought I had a chance at landing a scholarship if I focused more on playing."

Sebastian flicked my arm. "I've told you a million times you've got skill out on the court."

I rolled my eyes. "You have to say that because you're my friend."

"Because I'm your friend, I'd tell you if you sucked."

I laughed softly. "I know I'm not terrible, but I'm nowhere near as good as Megan or half the team. There's no way a scout is going to pay attention to me. And that's okay," I quickly added. "I'm not banking on that kind of scholarship anyway."

"I feel you." His grin started to slip away. His expression turned pensive, and as I watched him, the last of the sleepiness faded away.

I gripped the edges of the blanket, tugging it to my chin. A heartbeat passed. "What's going on?"

Scrubbing a hand down his face, he exhaled heavily. "Dad…he really has his heart set on Chapel Hill."

From previous experience, I knew to proceed with caution with this conversation. He wouldn't talk about his dad a lot, and when he did, he quickly reached the point where he would just shut down about the whole thing. I always thought he needed to talk about it. I totally got the irony of that, since I wouldn't talk about my dad, but whatever.

"Chapel Hill is a really good school," I started. "And it's

really expensive, right? If you get in on a scholarship, that would be pretty amazing. You'd also be close to your cousins."

"Yeah. I know that, but…"

"But what?"

He rolled onto his back and thrust his hands under his head. "I don't want to go there. I don't really have a good reason. The campus is freaking cool as hell, but just not into it."

Knowing that Sebastian was as close to Keith and Phillip as he was to Cody, I figured maybe it had something to do with them. "Where do the guys want to go?"

"Keith and Phillip are hoping to get on at West Virginia University. Phillip really wants to play ball for them. Thinking Keith wants to go there because of the parties." He paused. "I think Cody is set for Penn State."

For years, WVU had been the number one party school in the United States, and I was sure it was still up in the top five, so it would be a great fit for Keith. "Do you want to go there?"

"Not really."

I wiggled down, getting comfortable. "Where do you want to go?"

"I don't know."

"Sebastian." I sighed. "You have to know. This is our senior year. You don't have much time left. Scouts are going to be coming to the games and—"

"And maybe I don't care about the scouts."

I snapped my mouth shut, because there it was, the thing I'd been sensing about Sebastian for the last year.

He turned his head toward me. "You don't have anything to say to that?"

"I was waiting for you to elaborate."

A muscle worked in his jaw as he stared back. "I... God, even in the middle of the night, in your room, I still don't even want to say it. It's like my father is going to pop out of the damn closet and lose his mind. Instead of Bloody Mary, he'd be Bloody Marty."

I drew in a deep breath. "You don't... You don't want to play college ball, do you?"

His eyes closed and several moments stretched out between us. "It's crazy, isn't it? I mean, I've *always* played ball. I don't even remember a time when I wasn't being carted off to practice or seeing my mom cleaning grass stains out of my pants. And I *like* playing it. I'm good at it." He said it without an ounce of arrogance. It was just the truth. Sebastian had a God-given talent for playing football. "But when I think about another four years of getting up at dawn, running and catching...another four years of Dad basing his entire existence on how the game goes...I want to turn to drinking. Hell, maybe even crack and meth. *Something.*"

"We don't want that," I said drily.

He flashed a brief grin and then it disappeared. Our gazes met and held. "I don't want to do it, Lena," he whispered this to me, a secret he couldn't speak loudly. "I don't want to spend another four years doing this."

My breath caught. "You know you don't have to, right? You don't have to go to college and play ball. There's still time to get other scholarships. A ton of time. You can do anything. *Seriously.*"

He laughed, but there wasn't an ounce of humor to it. "If I decided not to play ball, my father would stroke out."

I squirmed closer so our faces were inches apart. "Your dad will be fine. Do you still want to study recreational science?"

"I do, but not for the reasons Dad thinks." He bit down on his lower lip, slowly letting it pop out. "He has this plan for me. I'd play college ball, then be drafted—second pick. Not first. He's realistic." His grin was wry as his gaze slid to mine. "I'll play a couple of years and then move on to coaching or working with the teams, putting to use the recreational science degree."

The all-American dream right there. "And what is your plan?"

His eyes were wide, the blue startling and vibrant. "Do you know how much you can do in recreational science? I could work in hospitals, with vets or even in psychology. It's not all about sports injuries. I want to actually *help* someone. I know this sounds stupid and cliché."

"It's not stupid or cliché," I insisted. "Not at all."

A half smile formed. After a moment, some of the light faded from his eyes and he said, "I don't know. He would flip out. It would be like the end of the world."

I had no doubt in my mind that Sebastian was correct in that assumption. "But he'd get over it. He has to."

His lashes lowered. "He'd probably disown me."

"I don't know if he'd go that far." My gaze flickered over his face. "It's your life. Not his. Why would you do something that you weren't really into?"

"Yeah." A brief smile appeared and then he shifted back so he was facing me. "You still hoping for UVA?"

Clearly he was officially done with the conversation. "Yeah."

"Can I ask you a question?"

"Sure."

"It's kind of random."

I grinned. "You're always random."

He nodded in agreement. "Why did you and Andre break up?"

Blinking, I wasn't sure I heard him correctly. I started to respond but laughed.

He nudged my leg through the blanket with his. "Told you it was out there."

"Yeah. Um…I don't know." Holy crap, wasn't like I could tell him the truth. *It didn't work out because I was in love with you. That* wouldn't go over well.

Sebastian opened his mouth, then closed it. When I peeked at him, his lips were pressed in a hard line. "He didn't do something, did he? Like mess around on you or hurt—"

"*No.* Oh my God, no. Andre was practically perfect." My eyes widened as what he said really sank in. "Wait. Did you think he did something?"

"Not a hundred percent. If I had, he wouldn't be walking right now." I raised an eyebrow. "I just never knew why you guys broke up. One second you two were together and then you…you just weren't."

I let the blanket slip down my shoulders. "I just wasn't into him the way I should've been, and it made me… uncomfortable."

His chest rose with a deep breath. "Know the feeling."

My gaze shot to his. He was staring at my ceiling. "You know I'm going to ask this… Why did Skylar break up with you? You've never told me."

"You've never really asked." His eyes shifted back to me. "Actually, come to think of it, you never really asked about anything that has to do with Skylar."

My mouth opened, but I didn't say anything, because, come to think of it, he was right. I didn't ask about Skylar, because I just didn't want to know. Supporting him hadn't meant I needed to know all about their relationship.

"I...I figured it wasn't any of my business," I answered lamely.

His brows pinched together as his lips turned down at the corners. "I didn't know there was anything between us that wouldn't be each other's business at this point."

Well...

"Skylar broke up with me because she felt like I wasn't giving the relationship my all. She thought I cared more about ball and my friends than her."

"Well, that's kind of lame."

"Kind of the same reason why you broke up with Andre, right? You weren't into him. Probably weren't giving it your all."

I pursed my lips. "Whatever. We're in high school. Exactly how much work do we have to put into relationships?"

"Don't think you should ever have to 'put in work' in a relationship," he replied. "I think it should come naturally."

I wrinkled my nose. "Aren't you so deep with all your worldly experience," I teased.

"I *am* experienced."

Rolling my eyes, I kicked his leg from under the cover. "Was it true? That you cared more about your friends and football than her?"

"Partly true," he answered after a moment. "Well, you know the football part wasn't."

Mulling it over, I wasn't sure how to feel about that. Since I was one of his friends, was he saying he cared about me more? A second later, I realized that was a stupid thing to question and I sort of wanted to punch myself.

"I'm going to stay here for a little while," he murmured, lifting his hand. He caught a strand of hair that had fallen across my cheek. As he tucked it back behind my ear, his fingers dragged over my skin and my breath hitched in my throat. A wave of shivers skated across my skin as he drew his hand back. "You okay with that?"

"Yes," I whispered, knowing he hadn't seen my reaction. He never did.

Resting his hand between us, he shifted closer, and I felt his knee press against mine. "Lena?"

"What?"

He hesitated for a moment. "Thank you."

"For what?"

The corners of his lips picked up. "For just being here, right now."

Closing my eyes against a sudden rush of tears, I spoke the truest thing I could've. "Where else would I be?"

"So my mom made me write down this list of the top ten things I want to do with my life, since she thinks it's completely ridiculous that I'm about to enter my senior year and I don't know what I want to do yet," Megan said, nursing her third glass of sweet tea as she rooted around in a basket of fries. "Which is hilarious considering my mom is like the official hot-mess express, ticket for one."

"Does she not realize you don't have to declare a major right off the bat?" Abbi was sketching what appeared to be a rose garden on her napkin. "Or you could change it later on?"

"You'd think she'd know that, being an 'adult,'" Megan said, curling her fingers in air quotations. "You'd also think she'd cool it, since I ended junior year a half a point away from a 4.0. I'll do fine no matter what I choose to study in college."

From behind the counter at Joanna's, I grinned as I folded my arms and leaned against the countertop. Luckily, the diner was virtually dead, since it was Saturday night. There were only two tables set, and both parties had already handled their checks. Bobby was somewhere out back smoking half a pack of cigarettes, and I had no idea where Felicia, the other waitress, was. "So did you make a list?"

"Oh, yes. Yes, I did."

Abbi snuck a fry. "Can't wait to hear this."

"It was the best list ever." She popped a fry in her mouth and wiped her fingers on a napkin. "I listed amazing careers such as hooking, stripping, dealing drugs…and not the small stuff. I'm thinking *heroin*. Oh, by the way, I heard Tracey Sims is on the brown sugar."

"Okay." Abbi twisted on the stool, angling her body toward Megan's. "I don't know if you're talking about heroin or the actual sugar."

"Heroin. You've never heard it called that?"

I shook my head. "I haven't, but where did you hear that?"

"You know how my cousin used to date her?" She picked

up two fries and made a cross out of them. "He told me she's using. That's why they broke up."

Abbi frowned. "Are you serious?"

I pushed away from the counter. "God, I hope not."

Megan nodded. "I'm serious."

"That's so…so sad," I murmured, glancing up as the door opened. I almost couldn't believe what I saw. It was Cody Reece and crew, including Phillip, glued to the phone in his hand. Why were they here? None of them usually hung out in Joanna's unless they were with Sebastian.

"It is. I mean, that's some hard-core stuff right there," Megan continued, smacking her fry cross off the edge of the basket. Sprinkles of salt hit the counter. "Just can't even imagine actually taking a needle and injecting something into me. And if it's going to cause me to pick at my face, *so* not volunteering as tribute."

"I hope it's not true. Tracey is nice." Abbi's eyes widened as she glanced over her shoulder, just as Phillip spotted Megan.

He raised his finger to his mouth as he crept forward, looking ridiculous as he walked on the tips of his sneakers, which made him about six foot twelve or so. With his dark brown skin and a flirtatious grin that had gotten him in trouble more than a time or two with Megan, he was just as crazy-smart as she was. Grinning, he stopped right behind Megan.

"Come to think of it, there are a lot of things I wouldn't volunteer for," Megan continued, dropping the fry cross into the basket. "There are a lot of things I don't—" She squealed as Phillip circled his arms around her.

"Hey, babe." He rested his chin on her shoulder. "Miss—"

"What are you doing here?" Megan asked the question of

the century as she elbowed him hard enough that he grunted. "Seriously? Are you stalking me or something?"

"Maybe." He let go, leaning against the counter as he grinned at us. "Hey, if you don't want me stalking you, don't check into every place you visit."

I snorted.

She narrowed her eyes at him. "I'm not talking to you right now. Do you remember that?"

Dark skin around his eyes crinkled as he smiled. "You didn't have a problem talking to me last night."

"That's because I was bored." Looking up at me, she brushed her thick braid over her shoulder. "Can't you make him leave?"

"No." I laughed.

Abbi helped herself to another fry as she leaned forward. "What does your shirt say?" She squinted. "'Ain't no party like a George Washington party, because a George Washington party don't stop…until the colonies are free and the world recognizes them *as a sovereign nation*'—oh, what the hell?" Laughing, she shook her head. "Where did you find that shirt?"

"Found it on the street, by a Dumpster."

I rolled my eyes as the other guys took the booth in the back. "What do you want to drink?"

"Grey Goose."

"Ha ha," I replied drily. "What age-appropriate drink do you want?"

"Coke is fine." Phillip smacked his hand on the counter as he changed focus. "Megan, my love…"

Shooting Abbi a look, I pivoted around and grabbed him

his drink from the soda station. Then I picked up the pitcher of ice water and made my way over to the table.

I hadn't seen Cody since the night at Keith's party. Heat was already creeping steadily into my cheeks, but I squared my shoulders. "Hey, guys."

Cody looked up first. The other two guys had their heads bowed, watching something on their phones.

"Hey," he said.

Plastering a smile on my face, I ordered myself to not think about that party. I had to admit that Cody was definitely good-looking, which led to my bad life choices that night. He had a head full of wavy blond hair and an easy smile that he broke out frequently, complete with perfectly straight, blindingly white teeth and a cleft chin. He looked like he belonged on the beaches of California, hauling a surfboard behind him, instead of in Nowhere, Virginia.

And Cody *knew* he was good-looking. That knowledge was etched into that smile he gave so freely. "So what are you guys doing here?" I asked as I poured their water.

"Is that a question you ask all your customers?" Cody threw his arm along the back of the booth.

"Yes. Always." Ice clinked off the glasses. "My version of great customer service."

"We're bored. Plus Phillip saw that Megan was here." Cody swiped the glass of water. "Wanted to see her."

I glanced over at the counter, where Phillip looked like he was serenading Abbi and Megan.

"And I wanted to see you."

My head swung back around and I raised a brow. "Are you high?"

"Not at the moment." He winked. "Why is that hard to believe? I like you, Lena. And I haven't seen you in a while."

"I've been around, working." I stepped aside as Phillip joined them, scooting in beside Cody in the booth. I quickly took the others' drink orders. "Do you guys need menus?"

"I do." Cody gave me *that* smile, and my expression turned bland. "I like choices," he added. "Lots of choices."

Thinking that sounded like a really poor sexual innuendo, I shook my head and walked away. "Someone kill me now," I said to the girls as I grabbed a stack of menus.

"Hey, don't leave yet." Megan twirled on the stool. "While you were busy adulting and I was busy ignoring Phillip, Keith texted Abbi and asked her out."

"Oh, really?" I cradled the menus to my chest.

"To his party tonight," Abbi clarified.

"He wants to get with you," I reminded her, backing away.

Abbi rolled her eyes. "He can want whatever he wants, but that is never going to happen."

"Famous last words," muttered Megan, and then I heard her say, "We should go. I haven't been to Keith's in a couple of weeks."

"I don't know." Abbi stared down at the napkin she'd been doodling on. "I have a feeling if I agree, you're going to embarrass me."

"Never," gasped Megan.

"Well, you guys figure that out." I turned away and brought the menus to the guys, placing one in front of each of them. Then I filled their drink orders and brought them over. "You guys know what you want yet?"

"I do." Cody's brown eyes twinkled as Phillip chuckled,

and I prepared myself, knowing it had nothing to do with the menu. "What if I wanted a piece of you for dinner?"

I cocked my head to the side, not entirely surprised. Cody was... Well, he was just *Cody*. It was hard to take him seriously and he could be, as my mom would put it, crude as hell. "That had to be the absolute stupidest thing I've heard in the seventeen years of my life and I don't even know what human being would be impressed by that statement."

"Daaamn." Phillip drew the word out, chuckling.

Cody leaned forward, completely unfazed. "I have better one-liners saved up. Want to hear them?"

"No. Not nearly buzzed enough for that."

"Come on," Cody insisted. "Trust me, it's a true talent I have."

"Well, you keep living the best life you can, and I'll keep waiting for you to give me your orders."

"Ouch." He clasped his hand on his chest, falling back against the booth. "You wound me. Why so mean?"

"Because I just want to take your orders so I can go back to pretending to work when I'm really just reading," I replied, smiling as sweetly as I could.

Cody laughed as he reached over, snatching the phone out of one of his friends' hands. "Well, let's not keep you from working too hard."

The guys finally gave me their orders, and I walked back the short hall, past the restrooms and through the double doors into the kitchen. I found Bobby in the back, tugging a hair net on, smashing his man bun. I turned in the orders and then wheeled around, heading back to the counter.

"You guys need anything else?" I asked the girls as I picked up the empty fry basket.

Abbi shook her head. "Nah. I'm probably heading out of here soon."

"Are you walking home?" Looking over her shoulder at the guys, Megan sighed as she eyed Phillip. "Why does he have to be so good-looking?"

"You have the attention span of a gnat. You ask me if I'm walking home and then immediately start talking about Phillip." Abbi rested her head on the countertop. "Your ADD has ADHD. And yes, I was planning to walk home. I live, like, five blocks from here."

Megan grinned as she faced her. "You do realize I *actually* have ADD, right?"

"I know." Abbi raised her arms but kept her head down. "We *all* know that. You do not need to be a professional to know that."

"Did I ever tell you about that time when my mom was convinced I was one of those indigo kids?" Megan picked up her braid and started fiddling with the ends. "She wanted to get my aura tested."

Slowly, Abbi lifted her head and looked at her, her lips slightly parted. "What?"

Leaving them to that conversation, I took that basket to the kitchen and checked the guys' orders. When I stepped back out into the hallway, I spotted Cody in the hallway leaning against the wall across from the restrooms.

My steps slowed. "What's up?"

"You got a second?"

I eyed him warily. "Depends."

After running a hand through his shaggy blond hair, he then dropped his arm. "Look, I actually did want to see you."

"Uh, for what?" I crossed my arms and shifted my weight from one side to the next.

"I needed to talk to you about Sebastian."

My brows lifted with surprise. "Why?"

"Sebastian and I are good friends, but I know you guys are closer. You're like his sister or something."

Sister? Seriously?

"Anyway, I wanted to ask you something." He looked away. "Has Sebastian said anything about not wanting to play ball to you? Like I said, he and I are close, but he won't talk to me about something like that."

I stiffened for a fraction of a second and then folded my arms. There was no way in hell I was going to betray Sebastian's confidence. Not even to his friend. "Why would you think that?"

He then tipped his head back against the wall. "He's just… I don't know." Cody dropped his arm from his head. "He just doesn't seem into it. Like he'd rather be anywhere but at practice. Couldn't seem to care less about the upcoming season. When he's on the field, he's only half-there. He's got talent, Lena. The kind of talent he doesn't even have to work for. I've got this feeling he's going to throw it all away."

Biting the inside of my cheek, I searched for something to say and finally settled on, "It's only football."

Cody stared at me like I'd grown a third hand out of the center of my forehead that then flipped him off. "Only football? You mean it's only his *future*."

"Well, that sounds a little dramatic."

He raised a brow as he pushed off the wall. "Maybe I'm just imagining things," he said after a moment.

"Sounds like it," I replied. "Look, I've got to check on your order, so…"

Cody studied me a moment and then gave a little shake of his head. "So, you're done doing the small-talk thing. Gotcha."

Heat invaded my cheeks. Was I as transparent as a window?

"I'll leave you be." Shoving his hands into his jeans, he pivoted around and walked back to the front of the diner, leaving me standing there, staring after him.

I wiped my oddly damp palms along my apron as I exhaled roughly.

By the time I'd grabbed the food and delivered it to the guys' table, Abbi and Megan were ready to leave.

"You guys heading out now?" I asked.

"Yep." Abbi slung her bag over her shoulder. "Friends don't let friends walk home by themselves. Especially if said friend is likely to take rides with strangers."

Megan rolled her eyes. "So, I saw Cody come from the back. Were you talking to him?"

I nodded as I picked up the cleaning rag. "He wanted to talk about Sebastian."

"Uh-huh," Megan murmured. "You know what I was thinking?"

Abbi's expression said it was anyone's guess.

Megan raised both brows and lowered her voice. "I wonder what Sebastian would think if he ever found out his best girl friend totally made out with his best guy friend. *Drama*."

I sucked in a sharp breath. Drama llama, indeed. But I

was hoping God liked me enough that I never had to cross that bridge.

The girls left and I turned my attention to the book I had stashed behind the counter, choosing not to dwell on what Megan said. If I did, I would probably break out into a cold sweat or something.

I'd made it about a page before I felt my phone vibrate in my back pocket.

I took one glance at it and I was no longer thinking about Sebastian and football or Cody and secrets.

I saw who the text was from.

I didn't read further.

I deleted it without reading.

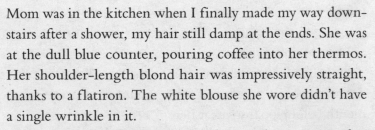

CHAPTER FIVE

Mom was in the kitchen when I finally made my way down-stairs after a shower, my hair still damp at the ends. She was at the dull blue counter, pouring coffee into her thermos. Her shoulder-length blond hair was impressively straight, thanks to a flatiron. The white blouse she wore didn't have a single wrinkle in it.

"Morning, hon." She turned, a faint smile curving up her lips. "You're up early."

"Couldn't sleep in." I'd had one of those annoying morn-ings when I woke up at 4:00 a.m. and thought in detail about everything in the world. Every time I tried to go back to sleep, something else would pop up in my head, from catch-ing the eye of a college scout to what Cody had said Satur-day night. If Sebastian didn't want it, was he really throwing it all away?

"You feeling okay?" she asked.

"Yeah, just some insomnia this morning. I have practice

later, so figured I'd just get up." I walked to the small pantry and opened the door, scanning the shelves. "Pop-Tarts?"

"Out of them. I'll pick up some on my lunch break. It's going to be a cereal day for you."

I grabbed the box of generic corn flakes and went to the fridge. "I can grab some later."

"I don't want you doing that." She eyed me over the rim of the thermos. "I don't want you to use the money you make on Pop-Tarts. We have money for groceries, hon."

She gave me a half grin. "Generic Pop-Tarts, though."

"I know we have money for that, but if you don't like them—"

"Because they're literally one of the worst things you could put in your mouth," she cut in and then paused, her gaze glancing to the ceiling. "Well, there are worse things."

"*Ew.* Mom!" I moaned.

"Uh-huh." Mom moved over to the table but didn't sit.

She was quiet as I shoved a few spoonfuls of cereal in my mouth before looking up at her.

Mom was staring out the small window over the sink, but I knew she wasn't seeing the backyard. Not that there was much to see. It was just grass and secondhand patio furniture we rarely used anymore.

When Dad had been here, they would sit out there late at night through the summer and straight up to Halloween, staying up and talking. There used to be a fire pit, but it had fallen apart a few years ago, and Mom had kept it another year before throwing it away.

She kept holding on, even long past the point things were rotten out and decayed.

Lori and I used to sit up on the balcony and eavesdrop, but I think they knew we listened, because they only ever talked about boring stuff. Work. Bills. Vacations planned but never taken. Renovations on the dull blue counters in the kitchen that never happened.

Looking back, though, I could pinpoint the month when things began to change. It had been August, and I was ten. It was when their conversations out on the patio had turned to hushed whispers that ended with Dad storming inside, slamming the screen door shut behind him, and then Mom chasing after him.

Mom was always chasing after Dad.

I liked this Mom better.

Bitter-tasting guilt swallowed me up in one gulp, and I lowered my spoon. It was terrible thinking that, but it was true. This Mom made dinner when she could and asked about school. She joked around and spent the evenings eating ice cream on the couch with me while watching *Dance Moms* or *The Walking Dead*. The old Mom was always at dinners with Dad, and when she was home, so was he, so she was with him.

The old Mom had been all about Dad, every second of every day.

Now the grin had faded from her face, and I wondered if she was thinking about Dad, thinking about her life when she wasn't an insurance agent living paycheck to paycheck, didn't spend the nights alone.

My spoon clanged off the bowl. "You okay, Mom?"

"What?" She blinked a couple of times. "Yes. Of course. I'm fine. Why do you ask?"

I studied her for a few seconds, unsure if I should believe her. Mom looked okay—looked like she did yesterday and the day before—but there were faint lines around the corners of her mouth and eyes. Her brow creased where it hadn't before, and her eyes, the same hazel as mine but more green, appeared haunted. "You looked sad."

"Not sad. Just thinking about things." Clasping the back of my neck, she bent down and kissed my forehead. "I won't be home until late tonight, but I will be home for dinner tomorrow. Thinking about making spaghetti."

"And meatballs?" I asked, hopeful for those homemade balls of grease and goodness.

She pulled back, wiggling her brows. "Only if you do the laundry. There's a pile of towels that need your love and attention."

"Done." I hopped up out of my seat to take my bowl and spoon to the sink. I rinsed them out and placed them on the counter above the broken dishwasher. "Anything else you need me to do?"

"Hmm." She headed into the living room, slinging her purse over her shoulder. "Clean the bathrooms?"

"Now you're taking advantage of my kind offer."

Mom grinned back at me. "Just do the towels and you'll get meatballs."

I was *way* too excited about those meatballs.

"And I'll pick you up low-fat Pop-Tarts," she added.

"You do that and I will never speak to you again!"

She laughed as she grabbed her gray blazer from the banister. "You kind of have to talk to me. I'm your mom. You can't escape me."

"I will find a way to escape if you walk through these doors with low-fat Pop-Tarts."

She laughed while opening the front door. "Okay, okay. They'll be full of all the sugar and fat you can want. See you tonight."

"Love you." I moved to close the door, but I leaned against the frame, watching her teeter down the driveway in heels.

Chewing on my lower lip, I shifted my weight, trying to work out the weird unease stirring in the pit of my stomach. Mom said she was fine, but I knew she wasn't. She might never be, because, deep down, even though she was right here, her heart was still chasing after Dad.

I kept my head in the game during the different drills we had to do and while we practiced techniques, which meant I didn't get a Coach Rogers lecture afterward. I left practice feeling a million times better than I did on Friday.

At home, I washed off the layer of sweat and then ate a lunch of microwavable bacon and another round of cereal. I was walking into the living room just as my phone rang on the coffee table. I groaned when I saw who it was. I sent the call to voice mail without hesitation, picked up the remote and settled on the ID channel.

With the *Dangerous Women* marathon playing in the background, I sat back on the couch and picked up my book. I'd finished the first one in a series last night and had made it through only the first couple of chapters of the second, but I couldn't wait to fall back into the world of the Night Court and High Fae.

And Rhysand.

Couldn't forget about him.

I curled up on the corner of the couch about to get my reading on, when there was a knock on the door. For a minute I considered ignoring it and getting lost in the pages of the book, but when there was another knock, I sighed, got up and made my way to the front door. I peered out the window and my stomach dropped all the way to my toes when I saw who was there.

Sebastian.

Unable to fight the stupid grin spreading across my face, I opened the door. "Hey."

"You busy?" He placed one hand on the doorframe and leaned in. The movement caused the old, faded gray shirt to stretch across his biceps in a way that drew my gaze.

"Not really." I stepped back to let him in, but he stayed at the door.

"Perfect. I was going to head out to the lake and get my car dirty as hell. You game?" He winked, and dammit all to hell, he actually looked good doing it. "It'll be fun."

I'd forgotten about his badminton win. "Sure. Let me get my keys." I toed on a pair of old sneakers and grabbed my phone and bag before following Sebastian outside. "What are you planning to do?"

"You know the dusty roads leading out to the lake area?" he asked. "Figured that should do enough damage."

I got in the passenger side as he got behind the wheel. "Not sure how I'm supposed to help."

He shrugged with one shoulder as he turned the key. "Just wanted your company."

My stomach fluttered, and I sat back, buckling myself in

as I desperately ignored the feeling. Bright sunlight streamed through the windshield. Sebastian reached behind him, snagging his baseball cap off the floor, and pulled it on, tugging the bill down low, and I…I *sighed*.

I couldn't help it.

Boys in baseball caps were my weakness, and Sebastian rocked the look. Something about that old, worn cap showcased the chiseled line of his jaw.

Ugh.

I closed my eyes and told myself to stop looking at him. Just in *general*. Maybe for the rest of my life? Or at least for the next year or so. That sounded like a valid plan.

I really needed to get a grip.

I rolled my eyes and turned down the radio for a distraction. "I haven't been to the lake since Keith attempted to make water skis out of snow skis."

Sebastian laughed deeply. "God, when was that? In July? Seems like forever ago."

"Yeah." I sat back, fiddling with the hem on my shirt. "It was right before you left for North Carolina."

"Can't believe you haven't headed out there since. Is it because going to the lake is only fun when I'm with you?" he teased, reaching over to flick my arm. "You know, you can just admit it."

"Yeah. That's exactly it." I knocked his hand away and crossed my ankles. "The girls aren't huge fans of the lake." That wasn't a lie at least. "So do you think Megan and Phillip are going to get back together?"

"God only knows. Probably. Then they'll break up again.

Then get back together." He grinned. "I know he wants to get back with her. He's pretty open about that."

"That's cool," I murmured.

He quirked a brow at me.

"Most guys don't want to admit stuff like that to their dude friends," I reasoned.

"And you'd know this because you're a guy?"

"Yes. I'm secretly a guy."

Sebastian ignored me. "I think when most guys are really into a girl, they don't care who knows. They're not ashamed of it."

I was going to have to take his word on it.

The lake was about twenty minutes outside town, near Keith's family farm, after a series of gravel and dirt roads. From what I knew, it was actually on the outskirts of Keith's family property, and his family owned it. But they didn't really police it, so people could use it however they saw fit.

Sebastian turned onto the private access road. The wheels bumped over the uneven terrain and dust plumed into the air, coating the Jeep within moments. "Keith is going to be so ticked at you." I laughed as I peered out the window. "But he'd totally do the same thing."

"Hell, he would've taken his car *mud-bogging* and then brought it to me. I don't feel bad at all."

After hitting every barely accessible road for about an hour, my butt hurt and the Jeep was completely unrecognizable. I figured we'd start heading back, but then I caught a glimpse of the lake through the trees.

Yearning sparked in my chest. I thought about going home to the empty, quiet house that sometimes reminded me of a set of bones that had no skin or muscle. It was just an outline of a home. No filler.

Guilt churned my stomach. The house *did* have filler. It had my mom, and my sister when she was home, and my mom did everything and more to make it a home…but sometimes there was no denying what was missing.

Mom lived a… She lived a half life.

She worked all the time, came home, worked some more, ate dinner and went to sleep. Rinse and repeat the next day. That was her half life.

"Can we stay for a little while?" I asked, shoving my hands between my knees. "Or do you have somewhere to be?"

"Nope. Got nothing else to do. Let me hit these roads a couple of more times, and we'll head down to the dock."

"Awesome," I murmured.

I stayed quiet as Sebastian drove down a few more roads before he pulled off on the shoulder, by some bushes. I unbuckled my seat belt.

"Stay put for a second," he said before I could open the door.

I watched him with raised brows as he hopped out and jogged around the front of the Jeep. He opened my door and bowed with flourish. "Milady."

I snort-laughed. "Seriously?"

He extended a hand toward me. "I'm a gentleman."

I took his hand and let him help me out of the Jeep. I started to hop down when his other hand landed on my hip. Surprised by the contact, I jerked forward and my foot slipped on the wet grass.

Sebastian caught me, his hand sliding off my hip and

wrapping around my waist. He drew me to him, against his chest. Air punched out of my lungs at the unexpected move. Our bodies were sealed together.

My throat dried instantly as I slowly lifted my head. I couldn't see his eyes, since they were hidden behind the bill of the cap. My heart was pounding so fast I wondered if he could feel it.

We were *that* close.

"Having trouble?" He laughed, but something sounded off about it. It was deeper than normal, and his laugh sent a series of tight shivers down my spine. "I don't know if I can trust you to walk to the docks."

"Oh, come on." I started to step back, needing the space before I did something incredibly stupid, like, say, stretching up, grabbing his cheeks and bringing his mouth to mine.

Then Sebastian smiled. It was his only warning.

He dipped slightly, hooked his arm behind my knees, and a second later I was up in the air, my stomach folding over his shoulders. His arm clamped down over my hips, holding me in place.

Shrieking, I grabbed the back of his shirt. "What are you doing?"

"Helping you get to the docks."

"Oh my God!" I yelled, clasping the back of his shirt. My hair fell forward like a thick curtain. "I can walk on my own!"

He pivoted around and started walking. "I don't know about that."

"Sebastian!"

"If you were to fall and get hurt, I would never forgive

myself." He stepped over a fallen tree limb. "And then your mom would be upset with me. Your sister would have to come home, and she actually *scares* me."

"What?" I shrieked, smacking his back with my fist. "Why does Lori scare you?"

He picked up his pace, taking long, unnecessary steps that caused me to bounce. "She's intense. Her glare alone can shrivel up parts of me I prefer not to be shriveled."

I lifted my head. I could barely see the Jeep anymore. I slammed my fist into his kidney, causing him to grunt, and he returned the gesture by putting an extra little hop in his step.

"That wasn't nice."

"I'm going to *physically hurt you*."

"You'd do no such thing."

Shade gave way to sunlight and the rocky dirt and broken twigs turned to grass. The scent of wet soil grew stronger. "You can put me down now."

"Just one more second."

"What—"

Suddenly he threw his other arm out and spun around as he belted out, *"I believe I can fly. I believe I can touch the sky—"*

"Oh my God!" A laugh burst out of me even though there was a good chance I was going to puke all over his back.

"I think about it night and day!"

"You're so stupid!" I choked out another laugh. "What is wrong with you?"

"Spread my wings and something, something away!" He stopped suddenly, and I slid off his shoulder. With impressive ease, he caught me, pulling me down the front—the *entire* front— of his body.

I wobbled backward and plopped down in the plush grass, planting my hands in the warm blades. "You...you are not right."

"I think I'm pretty amazing." He dropped down beside me. "Not everyone gets to hear my hidden talent."

"Talent?" I gasped, looking over at him. "You sounded like a polar bear getting murdered."

He threw his head back and laughed so hard his baseball cap fell off. "You're just jealous you don't have the voice of an angel."

"You're delusional!" I swung my arm out.

He was wicked fast, catching my wrist effortlessly. "No hitting. *Jesus.* You're like a five-year-old."

"I'll show you a five-year-old!" I tried to yank my arm free, but he pulled forward at the same time, and I was off balance. Somehow, and I don't know and would never understand how, I ended up half on top of him, half on the grass. My legs tangled with his, I was nearly in his lap, and we were eye to eye.

Except he wasn't staring at my eyes.

At least it didn't seem that way. It felt like his gaze was focused on my mouth, and my stomach hollowed. Time seemed to stop and I became aware of every part of him that was touching me. His arm still circled around my waist, and his hard thigh pressed against mine. His thin shirt was under my palm, and I felt his hard chest under that.

"I'm delusional?" he asked, voice raspy.

I shivered. "Yes."

He lifted his hand, and I held my breath as he caught the hair in my face and carefully, so gently, brushed it back from my face. He left his hand curled around the nape of my neck.

Seconds passed, only a few heartbeats, and he made a sound I'd never heard before. It was raspy and low and seemed to come from deep within him. And I was moving without thinking, lowering my head, my mouth...

And I kissed Sebastian.

CHAPTER SIX

The kiss was so light, like a whisper against the lips, I almost didn't believe it had happened, but it had, and his arm was still around me, his hand still on the nape of my neck, tugging on the strands of my hair.

His mouth was still close to mine, so close I could feel every breath he took against my lips, and I wasn't sure I was breathing, but my pulse was thrumming wildly. I wanted to kiss him again. I wanted him to kiss me back. That was all I ever wanted. But surprise held me immobile.

Sebastian's head tilted to the side and his nose brushed mine, and I knew I was breathing then, because I sucked in a shallow breath. Was he going to kiss me? Harder this time? Deeper?

He suddenly jerked his head back, and before I knew what was happening, I was on my butt, in the grass beside him. We weren't touching anymore. I started to speak, to say what, I don't know. My brain had completely stopped working.

And then it struck me—what had happened.

Sebastian hadn't kissed *me*.

I kissed *him*.

I kissed him and…and for the tiniest moment in the history of all histories…I thought he was going to kiss me back. That was how it felt.

But he hadn't.

He'd *dumped* me onto the grass beside him.

Oh my God, what had I done?

My heart lodged somewhere in my throat as a thousand thoughts rushed through me all at once. I opened my mouth even though I had no idea what to say.

Sebastian jumped to his feet, his face pale and jaw hard. "*Hell*. I'm sorry."

I snapped my mouth shut. Had he just apologized for *me* kissing *him*?

He swiped his hat off the ground and pulled it down on his head. He wasn't looking at me as he took a step back. "That wasn't— It wasn't supposed to happen, right?"

Slowly, I lifted my gaze to his. Was he seriously asking me that? I had no answer, because it wasn't like my lips had slipped and fallen on his. Drawing in a shallow, burning breath, I focused on the bright green grass. My fingers curled into the blades as his words sank in.

A sharp slice of pain lit up the center of my chest, flowing into my stomach like a thick oil spill, coating my insides.

"I, uh, I forgot I'm supposed to meet up with Coach before dinner," he said, turning sideways. "We've got to head back."

That was a lie.

It had to be.

He wanted to escape. I wasn't stupid, but damn, that hurt, because I couldn't remember a time when he'd ever wanted to run away from me.

The pain in my chest moved up my throat, choking me. A prickly heat hit my face as deep-rooted embarrassment welled up.

Oh God.

I was going to face-plant in the lake and just let myself sink under.

Numbly, I pushed to my feet and wiped the grass off my shorts. We didn't speak on the way back to the Jeep, and oh *God*, I wanted to cry. The back of my throat burned. My eyes stung. It took all my willpower not to break down right there, and my heart ached in a way that was far too real for it not to have cracked open.

Once inside, I buckled myself in and focused on taking deep, even breaths. I just needed to hold it together until I got home. That was all I needed to do. Once I got there, I could curl up in bed and sob like an angry baby.

Sebastian turned the Jeep on and the engine rumbled to life. The radio kicked in, a low hum of words I couldn't make out.

"We're...we're okay, right?" he asked, his voice strained.

"Yeah," I said hoarsely, and cleared my throat. "Of course."

Sebastian didn't respond, and for a few seconds I could feel his gaze on me. I didn't look at him. I couldn't, because there was a good chance I would start crying.

He shifted the Jeep into Drive and pulled off onto the road. What in the world had I been thinking? Never once had

I acted on anything I felt for Sebastian. For the most part, I played it cool. But now I'd *kissed* him.

I wanted to rewind time.

I wanted to rewind time to feel those brief seconds again because I was never going to get the chance to feel that again.

I wanted to rewind time and *not* kiss him, because it had been a big, huge mistake.

I knew that our friendship, our relationship, would never be the same.

By Wednesday morning, my temples ached and my eyes hurt, but I actually hadn't cried yet. I thought I would, especially when I'd barely been able to force down the bread-and-onion-filled meatballs at dinner last night. Mom had noticed, but I sidestepped her questions by saying I wasn't feeling well after the early practice in the morning. Later I couldn't even read. I just lay in bed, curled on my side, and stared at the balcony doors, pathetically waiting for him to show up, for him to text—for something. *Anything.* And there was nothing.

Normally that wouldn't have been a big deal. We didn't talk every day during the summer. But after what had happened at the lake? It was different.

The burning in my throat and the stinging in my eyes were there, but the tears never fell. Sometime in the middle of the night, I realized I hadn't cried since…since everything with Dad. Somehow that made me want to cry even more. Why couldn't I let myself cry?

All I managed to do was give myself one hell of a headache.

Thank God I didn't have practice on Thursday, because I

would've ended up with another well-deserved lecture. After Mom left, I crawled back in bed and stared at the cracked ceiling, replaying everything from the lake, right up to the moment things went south.

The moment I kissed Sebastian.

Part of me wanted to just pretend it didn't happen. That had worked before.

I still pretended my Dad didn't exist.

But when I woke up on Thursday morning after no late-night visits from Sebastian and no missed texts, I knew I had to talk to someone. I didn't know what to do or how to handle this, and it wasn't likely to suddenly come to me. So I'd texted the girls that morning, saying I needed to talk to them. I knew they'd understand the urgency when they saw I didn't give a reason.

Abbi and Megan came as soon as they could, and I knew Dary would've, too, if she'd been in town.

Megan sat on my bed, her long legs tucked under her and her blond hair loose, falling over her shoulders. Abbi was in my computer chair, looking like me—like she just rolled out of bed and grabbed a pair of oversize sweats and a tank top.

I'd already given them the rundown of what had happened, assisted by the package of Oreos Megan had brought along. I may have eaten three or five while I talked. Okay, ten. Even so, I was still planning on murdering the leftover spaghetti and meatballs after they left.

"I just want to say, I've always known you had a crush on Sebastian," Megan announced.

I opened my mouth, not sure how her weekly lecture

about finding my future baby daddy could have anything to do with me having a crush on Sebastian.

Megan continued, "Since I've suspected you've had a huge obsession with him for a while now, I kept giving you my weekly lecture in hopes you'd admit it."

I did not understand her thought process. At all.

"Obviously, I guessed it, too," Abbi said. "I mean, the last we talked, I even said something."

"It's no big surprise you broke up with Andre," Megan added. "You wanted to really, really like Andre, but you couldn't, because you really, really like Sebastian."

True. I had wanted to really like Andre, and I *had* liked him. It just… My heart wasn't there, and it was probably the dumbest reason ever for sleeping with him, but I thought that if we took our relationship to the next level, then maybe it would change how I felt. It hadn't and that had been the wake-up call to end the relationship.

I started walking back and forth in front of the closet. "Why didn't you guys say something if it was that obvious?"

"Figured you didn't want to talk about it," Megan said with a shrug.

Abbi nodded. "You don't like to talk about anything, really."

I wanted to deny that, but…it was true. So damn true. I was the same way with Sebastian. I was a listener, not a talker. I could spend hours thinking about something but never giving voice to any of the thoughts.

"But let's move past that for now. I'm so confused," Megan said. "You said he made this noise—and I know what kind of noise you're talking about. And that he held you. Kind of sounds like he was into it."

My hands opened and closed at my sides. Full of restlessness, I continued to pace in front of my bed. "I don't get it either. I mean, I really don't know what I was thinking. Everything was fine. He was being his normal self and we were fooling around—"

"Fooling around?" Megan asked, and when I shot her a look, she threw up her hands. "Look, I'm just trying to make sure I have the full picture here."

"Not the way you're thinking," I replied, rubbing my temples. "I went to hit him on the arm, you know, just being stupid, and he caught my wrist. The next thing I knew, I was in his lap and we were...just *staring* at one another."

"And that's when you kissed him?" Abbi crossed her legs. "Just one kiss?"

Covering my face with my hands, I nodded. "It was just a quick kiss on the lips. I'm not sure you could even consider it a kiss, really."

"Quick or not, a kiss is a kiss," Abbi said.

"I don't know about that." Megan dug out an Oreo from the package beside her. "There are different levels of kissing. There's a quick peck on the lips, and then there's a longer closed-mouth one, and then there's— Wait, why am I explaining different kisses to you two? No one in this room is a member of the hymen parade. You know the different types of kissing."

"Oh my God," I groaned, dropping my arms.

Abbi rolled her eyes as she shook her head. "I can't *even*

with you most of the time, but hymen parade? That's...
There are no words."

After popping the entire cookie in her mouth, Megan
talked around it. "So you kissed him briefly, no tongue, and
then freaked out?"

I started pacing again. "Yes. That's about it."

She picked up her napkin and wiped the little black crumbs
off her lips. "Did he kiss you back?"

"No," I whispered. "I thought he was going to, but he
didn't."

Abbi raised her eyebrows. "What did he do? Just lie there?
While you were in his lap?"

Cringing, I nodded again. "Pretty much."

The girls exchanged looks, and Megan went for another
cookie. "I'm not exactly surprised you kissed him. Not when
you've been lusting after him since you realized boys had a
pe—"

"I know when I started liking him more than just a friend,"
I cut in. "I don't even know what happened exactly."

"Probably because you were cataloging every second instead of actually experiencing it." Abbi leaned back in my
chair. "That's what you usually do. Overthinking and obsessing while something amazing is happening."

I wanted to deny that, too, but she was right. I did that.
A lot. "Maybe that happened, but seriously, can we pick another time to point out my character flaws?"

Abbi flashed a brief grin. "Sure."

"Maybe you just caught him off guard," Megan said. "That
could be why he freaked out."

"You think that's the reason?"

"Maybe. I mean, you guys have been just friends forever. Even if he's into you, it probably caught him off guard." She brushed her hair over her shoulder. "Did you say anything to him afterward? Wait, don't even answer that. I already know. You said nothing."

My lips pursed.

She lifted her hands. "I'm not trying to be ignorant. I'm just pointing out if you didn't do anything or say anything, there's a chance *he* thinks that *you* think you made a mistake." She glanced over at Abbi. "Right?"

"Well…" Abbi leaned into the arm of the computer chair. "Okay. You know I love you, right?"

Oh, this was going someplace I wasn't going to like. "Yeah?"

"I'm just going to throw something out there. Just something to consider," she said, clearly choosing her words very carefully. "You kissed Sebastian. Let's assume it wasn't just a friendly kiss. Like, let's leave kissing on the mouth to people interested in being more than friends."

"Agreed," Megan chimed in. "Because that would just be super confusing."

"So you kissed him and he knows it's not because you like him as a friend. There are two possibilities. One being what Megan said—he was caught off guard and just reacted weird and is now hiding in a corner somewhere."

I couldn't picture Sebastian hiding in a corner over anything.

"Second option is that you kissed him and *he* didn't think that felt right. And when it got awkward, he got away as quickly as possible. Now he's hoping you forget about it."

Ouch.

I walked over to the balcony doors. "Like he wished I hadn't done it?"

"Well, okay…" She bit down on her lower lip. "He's not with anyone. Neither are you." Abbi's voice was soft as she continued. "You both have a ton in common. You're both attractive—"

"I'd do you," commented Megan.

"Thanks," I said, laughing hoarsely.

"And you both know so much about each other. I just have to think that if you kissed him and he realized he really liked that and wanted that, he would've kissed you back. Or he would've said something other than that it shouldn't have happened."

Chest squeezing, I pulled the curtain back and peered outside. A breeze stirred the limbs on the ancient maple.

Abbi had a point. Sebastian *had* said it shouldn't have happened.

"Because there really isn't a reason for you two to not be together," she added. "And I have to think that if he was into you…he wouldn't have said it shouldn't have happened."

Acids churned in my stomach and the hurt spread inside. How could it feel so real, like my chest was being cracked open? I drew in a shaky breath. "What should I do?" I let the curtain fall back in place and faced them.

Megan's fair brows rose. "I would've already texted him and asked him what the hell was up."

Trepidation exploded in my gut as I considered doing that. "I might be too much of a coward for that technique."

"You're not a coward, Lena," Abbi reassured me. "I get

why you haven't. He's one of your closest friends. This is super tricky."

Tricky didn't even cover it.

"I think it's probably smart if you do say something," Abbi continued. "Maybe just text him and ask if everything is okay. That is pretty low-key."

Even thinking about doing that made me want to hurl. "I feel like an idiot."

Megan frowned. "Why?"

"Because...because I shouldn't even be focused on this stuff." I walked over to the bed and plopped down next to Megan. I fished out another cookie, but my throat thickened with that burn again. "I mean, there are more important things I could be stressed over."

"Like what?" Megan challenged. "World peace? Politics? The nation's debt? I don't know. I'm sure there is more stuff. You watch the news. I don't even know what channel the news comes on."

Smiling faintly, I shook my head. "I should be thinking about my senior year. I have almost all AP classes this year and our volleyball schedule is going to be brutal. I need to get scholarships—"

"You know what, that's all bullshit." Megan twisted toward me, her cheeks flushing red. "So what? You're thinking about a guy and talking to us about a guy. I know you think about other things. Abbi knows that. You don't need to walk around all day long talking about all the serious important things to prove you're not boy crazy. And screw the whole 'oh my God, she's boy crazy' thing, because we can't win. Us girls. We can't."

"Oh no." Abbi grinned. "Someone's about to rant."

"Damn straight I am. See, if we think about guys, other people—usually other girls, because let's be real, girls can be bitches—say we're shallow. We're not well-rounded, whatever the hell that's supposed to mean. And if we say we don't worry about a guy that we like, then we're accused of lying. Or being weird. And if we focus on other things, then we're pretentious. We literally *cannot win*. It's like we're not allowed to have feelings or think about our feelings. It's bullshit."

"I don't say this often," Abbi said seriously, "but she has a point."

"Of course I do!" She threw up her hands. "And all that could still be said about girls who like girls. Just flip *boy crazy* with *girl crazy*. It's messed up. You think about what's going on with Sebastian because he's *important* to you, but so is school and volleyball, so is work and, yeah, even the nation's debt."

I laughed.

Megan drew in a deep breath. "I like thinking about boys, Phillip in particular, and I'm actually smarter than most people, especially those people who'd call me boy crazy. I can think about boys all I freaking want and still have a life outside of doing so, so screw that. Don't get down on yourself because, for right now, you're focused on what is important to you at this moment in your life. That happens to be a guy. Tomorrow it could be something else."

Staring at her, sort of shocked, I started to smile. "Wow, Megan. I kind of want to have you repeat that whole rant and record it."

She rolled her eyes. "Don't, because it won't be as good the second time around."

Abbi rolled her chair over to us. "I'm going to say it again—Megan's right."

I flopped backward on the bed, almost landing on the package of Oreos. I stared up at the ceiling as the tightness in my chest eased a little. Sadness still lingered like a shadow, as did a whole truckload of confusion over Sebastian, but it had lessened. Because of them. Because of my girlfriends. "Guys," I said, "I actually feel a little better. That means I may not eat all seven leftover meatballs while curled up on the couch, sobbing."

Abbi coughed out a laugh. "That's good to hear."

"Can I have a meatball?" Megan asked, nudging my arm with her hand. "I feel like I could use some meat with all the sugar I just consumed."

Abbi sighed.

"Okay. I'm about to sound super cheesy," I warned, not moving. "But we're going to be best friends forever, aren't we? Because I have a feeling this won't be my only episode of pure, unedited stupidity."

Megan giggled. "That was cheesy, but yes, yes, we are."

"Don't forget Dary," Abbi said, knocking her foot against mine. "The four of us will always be the four of us. No matter what."

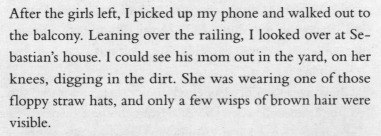

CHAPTER SEVEN

After the girls left, I picked up my phone and walked out to the balcony. Leaning over the railing, I looked over at Sebastian's house. I could see his mom out in the yard, on her knees, digging in the dirt. She was wearing one of those floppy straw hats, and only a few wisps of brown hair were visible.

Her entire body shook as she jabbed the spade into the landscaping surrounding their patio. Several bright blue and red peonies were still in their cartons beside her. My gaze flipped to their brick patio, and their fire pit sat in the middle. It hadn't fallen apart like ours had.

Sebastian's mom was quiet. Out of all the years I'd known him, and all the times I'd been in and out of their house, well over a thousand times, I'm sure, I'd probably held just a handful of conversations with his mom.

She was always kind, always said hello, asked how I was

and how my mom was or how Lori was doing at college, but that was it.

Sebastian's dad did all the talking.

Exhaling heavily, I looked down at my phone. This whole time, Abbi and Megan had suspected what I felt for Sebastian was more than a friend thing. I knew Dary probably also guessed it. The fact that they'd kept it to themselves and hadn't pushed me on it was huge. They knew me too well.

I backed away from the railing and plopped down in my chair, planting my feet on the edge of the seat. With my phone clutched in my hands, I considered my options.

I could ignore it and pretend it never happened. That had been my MO for, like, forever. I would swear to myself that I would take care of things tomorrow. But I knew how I operated. Tomorrow was always full of possibility and potential for me, but when it came, I pushed things off until another day.

I couldn't do that.

Chewing on my lip, I opened up my texts and found the last one from Sebastian, the one from the past Friday. My stomach took a tumble as I typed out the words Is everything okay between us?

Several moments passed before I worked up the nerve to hit Send, and when I did, I almost immediately wished I hadn't. I couldn't take it back, though, so I stared at my message for twice as long. I knew football practice was over. Sometimes he hung out with the guys afterward. Other times he came straight home.

When he didn't immediately respond, I rested my forehead on my knees.

I was still a little surprised by the fact I had texted him.

My natural response would've been to do nothing, let Sebastian eventually come to me or let it work itself out. But I just couldn't do that.

I considered going next door to see if he was there, but I'd *just* texted him, so maybe that was a wee bit much. Unable to sit, I got up and walked out onto the balcony and started down the steps. I stopped halfway down, unsure of what I was doing.

I looked to Sebastian's yard again. His mom was almost done with the flowers. Only the bright pink ones were left in their cartons. I pivoted, went back up the stairs, went inside, then went downstairs to heat up some meatballs. I ate four of them while perched on the arm of the couch, watching the news.

When I'd finished, Sebastian still hadn't texted back.

Back upstairs, stomach painfully full, I stood in the middle of my room with my phone in hand. Too much restless energy was buzzing around in me to sit down and read. Maybe I could clean something.

I was *that* desperate to distract myself.

I set my phone on the nightstand and moved over to my closet. Jeans and books were scattered everywhere. Half of the shirts and sweaters were hanging partway off their hangers.

Yeah, I wasn't that desperate.

I closed the door and pivoted to face-plant on my bed, which did nothing to help my stomach.

I groaned and muttered, "I suck," into my sheets.

My phone chirped and I launched to my knees. In an instant I'd snatched my phone off the nightstand. Air caught in my lungs. Sebastian had responded. *Finally.*

Yeah. Why wouldn't it be?

"Why?" I whispered when I really wanted to scream it at the top of my lungs. "What do you mean *why*?"

I started to respond with exactly that, but I stopped, my fingers hovering over the screen. My heart was racing like I was running sprints.

I could be up front and point out exactly why I was asking that question. I could say a million things, to be honest. Ask what he thought about me kissing him, or ask why he'd then freaked out. I could ask him if he wished I'd never done it. I could even text him and tell him that when I kissed him, it felt like coming home.

I didn't type any of those things.

My phone dinged again.

Everything is okay with you, right?

No. It wasn't.

I'd been in love with him since I could remember, and now I was afraid our friendship was ruined and everything was going to be awkward as hell from here on out.

I didn't type any of those things either.

Instead I typed, Yeah. Of course. Then I tossed my phone onto the pillow. Groaning again, I fell backward onto the bed.

"I'm such a coward."

I was so ready for Feyre to kick some serious ass.

I slapped the hardcover shut and pressed my forehead

against the smooth cover. My heart pounded in my chest. The last five chapters had been a nonstop heart attack, and I prayed that the third book was already out. If not, I was going to pitch myself off the balcony.

Lowering the book to my lap, I shifted my weight in the old Adirondack chair. It wasn't exactly the most comfortable, but with the throw pillow under my butt and my legs resting on the railing, it made for a perfect little reading spot.

A warm breeze swept through the balcony, moving over my bare legs and lifting the thin wisps of hair around the nape of my neck. Another book rested on the floor beside my chair. This one was the contemporary.

I couldn't think of a better way to spend the Saturday before school started than doing nothing but reading and eating.

I switched my hardcover for the paperback with a shiny gold crown on it and rested it in my lap as I quickly checked Facebook on my phone. No private messages. I had a few notifications from Snapchat, so I watched one of the football players drunkenly stumble down a sidewalk last night. Another snapped a pic of himself eating breakfast. There was a snap from Dary of the Washington Monument, followed by a series of street signs. She had this thing with street signs.

I moved on to Instagram, scrolling mindlessly through selfies and end-of-the-summer beach pics. I was about to close the app when I started to recognize a theme from everyone's recent pictures. All the girls were in bathing suits. Guys were in swim trunks. Everyone was holding red plastic cups. And all the pictures were all at night.

Keith.

He must've had a party last night.

My thumb stopped moving as I saw a pic posted by Skylar.

My heart dropped, and all I could think was that I was stupid, so stupid.

She was sitting on the edge of one of those rattan lounge chairs, her hands planted behind her. She had on a royal-blue two-piece that showed off her banging body. Sitting across from her was Sebastian. He was smiling. *Both* were smiling. They…they looked amazing together.

I stared at the picture for God knows how long. *Too* long.

Why oh why was I following her?

I knew the answer. I'd started following her years ago because she was dating Sebastian and apparently I was into self-punishment. I even liked her pictures just to prove that I wasn't a jealous bitch.

But I was a jealous bitch of the highest order.

I couldn't stop what I did next. I quickly went to Sebastian's account to see if there were any pictures from last night, but the last post was from three weeks ago. He wasn't big on social media, sporadically popping on and off.

Now I wanted to pitch myself off the balcony for a totally different reason.

Sebastian had texted a few times since Thursday, but I hadn't seen him since the kiss. There was no fooling myself. Things had changed. When Sebastian was home, even when he was dating Skylar, I saw him nearly every other day, if not every day. The only time I didn't was when he wasn't home.

So he was avoiding me.

I cursed under my breath, tapped out of the app and dropped my phone on top of the book on the floor. Edgy anxiety churned my stomach, and I shook my head as I stared at the large maple in the backyard. Was he back with Skylar, a handful of days after I kissed him? Did it even matter?

It shouldn't, but it did.

Disgusted with myself, I opened up the paperback, needing to lose myself in something unrelated to me.

I'd made it a couple of pages before I heard footsteps on the stairs leading up to the balcony. I lifted my chin and I froze when I saw the top of Sebastian's head, torn between wanting to dive back into my bedroom and rush him with my arms spread wide.

I did neither of those things.

Heart thumping heavily in my chest, I slowly closed the book as he crested the last step. All the air leaked out of my lungs.

Oh, come on.

Sebastian was shirtless. It wasn't the first time I'd seen him half-clothed, but each time was *like* the first time.

Chest defined, stomach chiseled like he was cut of marble and hips lean. He wasn't overly muscled. Oh no, he was just a prime example of how football could do a body good. And he was wearing a baseball cap. Backward.

I just imploded into mush and goo.

I hated him.

One side of his lips quirked up as he swaggered across the small balcony.

"Hey, nerd."

For a moment, I couldn't respond. I was thrust back to the lake, me in his lap and his mouth oh so briefly on mine. Heat flushed my cheeks and spread lower, much lower.

Oh my God.

I needed to get control of myself and go about things as if nothing had happened. That was what he was doing. I could do it, too. I had to, because if I couldn't, how could we be friends?

He looked up and his gaze met mine for a second before flickering away. I thought I saw a faint pink infuse his cheeks. Was he blushing? Maybe he wasn't as good at pretending as I thought he was.

Clearing my throat, I cradled the book to my chest. "Hey, dumbass, did you forget to get dressed before you walked out of the house?"

His eyes glimmered as they moved back to me. His shoulders loosened. "I was just so excited to come visit you that I didn't want to waste time finding a clean shirt."

"Uh-huh."

"I thought about texting you." He leaned against the railing, next to my feet. "But figured you were out here."

"Am I that predictable?"

"Yes."

"Well then," I muttered, searching for something to say. "Did…did you have practice this morning?"

Sebastian nodded. "Yeah. Till twelve. Than I took a nap when I got back."

"Late night?" I asked innocently enough, but my pulse was spiking.

He shrugged one broad shoulder. "Not really," he answered, and I tried to determine if that was code for getting back with Skylar or hooking up with someone else.

But really it was just two words that didn't mean anything.

"Keith ended up getting plastered and setting off a stash of fireworks." He folded his arms, drawing unneeded attention to his chest. "I'm still surprised he didn't blow off a couple of fingers. Or a hand."

"Me, too, actually."

"Anyway, I'm over here for a reason. He's having a barbecue today. Actually, his older brother is. Only a few people are going to be over there," he said. "You should come with me."

My heart started dancing all over the place, screaming, *Yes, yes, yes!* My brain recoiled and immediately told my heart to shut the hell up, because my heart was stupid and it made me do stupid things. "I don't know…"

"Come on." He grabbed my foot. I tried to pull it away, but he held on, wrapping his fingers around my ankle. I refused to read anything into that. "We haven't had the chance to see each other the last couple of days and I just got back last weekend."

Yeah, and I kissed you and obviously you weren't into it. He was acting normal, totally normal, though. So much so I almost wondered if I'd hallucinated the lake.

"Spend time with me. Quality charbroiled-cheeseburgers time."

I dropped my book in my lap and grasped the arms of my chair. "I'm not hungry."

"Turning down grilled cheeseburgers? Now I know you're just being difficult."

My eyes narrowed as I tried to pull my leg free again. Sebastian dipped his chin. "I'll drive and you'll have fun.

All you have to do is get your pretty butt out of that chair and I'll handle the rest."

I froze, eyes wide.

He thought I had a pretty butt?

The grin on his face spread, and a second later his fingers danced over the bottom of my foot. I immediately shrieked. "Stop! Stop it!"

His fingers hovered over my foot as he raised his brows. "Are you going to come out with me?"

I was breathing heavy, paranoid that he was going to start tickling my feet again. "You're not playing fair here."

"Why play fair when I can just tickle you into doing what I want?" he replied, placing one finger on the center of my foot. My whole leg jerked. "So, what's it going to be, Lena-bean?"

"Lena-bean?" I shouted, fingers digging into the arms of the chair. When was the last time he called me that? Before I needed to wear a bra? "I'm not ten years old, Sebastian."

His lashes flicked down, shielding his eyes. "I know you're not ten anymore." His voice deepened. "Trust me."

My lips parted as his words cycled over and over in my head. His gaze flickered up and met mine. There was no dancing in my heart, only a wild beating I felt in every single part of my body.

Why didn't you kiss me back?

"Come with me," he said again. "Please?"

I closed my eyes. I wanted to go, but...if I did, I needed backup. "Can I see if Megan and Abbi can go?"

"Hell yeah," he replied. "Keith will be ecstatic to hear that. You know he's—"

"Trying to get with Abbi. Yes." I inhaled deeply, opened my eyes and then nodded. "Okay."

"Perfect." He flashed a wide smile and then lowered my leg back to the railing. His fingers lingered for a few seconds and then he let go. "Knew you couldn't resist me."

Deciding to pretend I hadn't heard him say that, I dropped my legs to the floor and swiped up my books and phone. "Give me a few minutes." I rose and stepped over to the door, feeling my cheeks heat. "Got to let Mom know."

"Get a swimsuit," he ordered, pushing off the railing and dropping into my chair.

I thought about Skylar in her bikini and decided I would accidentally forget mine.

After placing my books on the bed, I quickly texted Abbi and Megan and then dropped my phone in my purse.

Downstairs, I found Mom in the kitchen. Papers were spread out in front of her, some loose and others stapled. Her blond hair was pulled up in a high ponytail and she had reading glasses on, perched at the end of her nose.

"Whatcha doing?" I asked as I stopped in front of the chair beside her.

"Looking over the new underwriting laws." Mom looked up. "Basically spending my Saturday in the most boring way possible. What about you? You're not working this weekend, right?"

"Nope." I smoothed my palms over the back of the chair. "I was thinking about going to a barbecue with Sebastian."

"That sounds fun." Mom rested her chin in her palm as she stared up at me. "Kind of sounds like a date."

"Mom," I warned.

"What?" She widened her eyes. "I would a hundred percent support that—"

"Oh my God," I groaned, throwing my hands up as I glanced toward the stairs, praying that Sebastian would decide to make himself known. "It's not like that. You know that."

"A mother can hope and dream," she replied. "He's a good boy, Lena."

"Abbi and Megan will probably be there. So will other people." I pushed away from the chair. "Sorry to ruin your dream."

"Damn." She sighed pitifully. "I was thinking about knitting little baby booties for your and Sebastian's first child."

"Oh my *God*." I gaped at her, horrified but not surprised. My mom wasn't right sometimes. "You're ridiculous and I'm surrounded by ridiculous people."

"Why be surrounded by anyone else?" She grinned as she fixed her gaze on the mass of papers in front of her, and I shook my head. "When do you think you'll be home?"

"Not before dinner. Maybe this evening?"

"Sounds good to me. At least I don't have to make dinner tonight." That was Mom, always looking on the bright side of things, even when it was impossible. "By the way," she said, looking up again, pinning me with that mom look I only ever saw when she was going to say something she knew I didn't want to hear.

I knew it had to be about Dad.

I tensed.

"You need to start answering your phone, Lena. This has been going on too long."

Folding my arms across my chest, I inhaled through my nose. "Not nearly long enough."

"Lena," she warned. "You are beautiful, loyal to a fault, but what happened between your—"

"Mom, I promise I'll answer the phone. Okay?" I *so* did not want to have this conversation right now. "But I have to get going. Sebastian is waiting for me."

She looked like she wanted to say more but tipped her head back. "Okay. Have fun, but be careful."

Bending over, I kissed her forehead. "Always."

"All I'm saying is that it's a double standard." My feet were on the warm dashboard of Sebastian's Jeep. The air conditioner was cranked on high, but it was barely beating the heat out of the interior. "You can drive around shirtless, but if a girl drove around wearing a bikini top and no shirt, people would lose their ever-loving mind."

"And all I'm saying is that I would a hundred percent support the idea of girls driving around in bikinis," he replied, one hand resting on the steering wheel, the other thrown over the back of my seat. The baseball cap was turned forward, blocking the sun, and he was still shirtless in his swim trunks and Nike sandals.

Behind my sunglasses, my eyes rolled. "Of course."

"Look, guys don't care about that kind of stuff. We would not be against equal-opportunity nudity. Ever." He slowed as we neared the exit off the interstate. "That's girls hating on girls."

I turned my head slowly in his direction, but he was focused on the road.

"I could easily see a girl calling another girl a slut for driving their car wearing a bikini top and then telling a guy who's doing it shirtless that he's hot."

Sebastian had a point, but hell would freeze over before I admitted that. I pulled my feet off the dashboard and shifted in my seat as I watched the trees blur past. Abbi and Megan were coming out, catching a ride with Megan's cousin Chris, who played football with Sebastian.

I had a feeling the little barbecue was going to turn into a massive party before the night was over. Wouldn't be the first or last one to go from a small get-together to a gloriously out-of-control rager within hours. *Especially* when it involved Keith.

Sunlight filtered through the trees crowding the narrow, curvy back road. Whoever built this road must've followed a snake or something.

Leaning my head back against the seat, I watched the taller maples and ferns give way to apple orchards. They went on as far as the eye could see, lined up in rows, on every hill, and Keith's family owned most of them.

I'd been down this road so many times with Sebastian and with my friends, and it struck me then that this would be the last Saturday before our last year of school. I wouldn't have another Saturday like this ever again, and in a year, Sebastian and I wouldn't be riding down this familiar road in his Jeep. He wouldn't be randomly appearing on the balcony, and Dary wouldn't be popping into Joanna's to rub my bad life choices in my face.

I sucked in a shaky breath as my chest burned.

Oh God, I suddenly wanted to cry like a baby. And I

shouldn't cry now, because everything that was about to change was good. I would go off on my own, and if I was lucky, Megan and I would both be accepted at UVA, and she would still remind me every Friday that I was going to grow old alone, surrounded by cats, eating cheap canned tuna. Dary would point out all my future terrible choices through FaceTime. Abbi would be going to a college not too far away and we'd be able to see each other on the weekends.

Sebastian would go to whatever college offered him a full ride to play ball if he stuck with football, and let's be honest, he would. And we'd stay in touch. We'd call each other and those calls would eventually give way to texts, and those messages would become more sporadic until we talked only when we were both home for the holidays.

We would grow up and grow apart, and that was terrifying, but for right now, right this second, we had tomorrow. We had next week. We had the whole year. Practically forever, I told myself.

I didn't have to face the inevitable yet.

Sebastian tapped his fingers off my knee, surprising me. I looked at him.

"You doing okay over there?" he asked.

"Yeah," I said hoarsely. I cleared my throat.

A concerned expression settled over his features. "What were you thinking about?"

I shrugged. "I was just thinking about how this time next year we'll both be at college. That this is the last summer before school, you know?"

Sebastian didn't respond. He was staring at the road, his

jaw a hard line. It got like that when he was mad or had something to say that he was keeping quiet about.

I started to ask him what he was thinking about, but he said, "You're always going to be a part of my life—you know that, right?"

Not expecting that statement, I didn't know how to respond.

"Even if we end up at different colleges," he continued like there was a chance that we'd be at the same place in a year. "We're not going to become strangers." It was almost like he could read my mind. But he just knew me so well. Too well. "That's never going to happen to us."

I wanted to tell him that happened to everyone no matter their best intentions. My sister swore she'd stay in contact with all her friends who went to different colleges, but she was now a junior and had all new friends and a new boyfriend.

When people left you and they didn't see you every day, they stopped wanting to see you. I, more than anyone, knew that was the truth.

Even if they said they loved you.

"We're always going to be friends." His eyes briefly searched my face. "No matter what."

Holy crap, was I just friend-zoned?

Yep. That was what it sounded like.

Breathing past the burn, I ignored the hollow achy pain in my chest as I smoothed my hands over my shorts. "Aye, Captain."

His lips twitched into a small grin.

"Is Skylar going to be at Keith's?" I regretted asking as soon as the words were out of my mouth.

"Don't know." The response was clipped, which was very unlike him.

I nibbled on my bottom lip as he slowed down, hanging a right onto the road that led to Keith's monstrosity of a house adjacent to the miles of orchards. The home was on a massive farm, and it was the kind of house no one needed unless they were polygamists and had fifty children.

His family had money. They'd run the orchards for generations, and I figured Keith would take over the family business at some point, though I knew he planned to go to college and play football like Sebastian. From what I heard, he'd already been accepted to WVU. He had the size to play college-level defense.

The paved driveway was already lined with cars, a few of which I recognized. I didn't see Skylar's BMW or, thank God, Cody's SUV. "A small party?"

Sebastian chuckled. "Yeah, that was the plan."

"All righty, then."

He parked the Jeep behind a Honda, leaving enough space between the vehicles to get out later. I grabbed my purse off the floor and then climbed out. We hoofed it the rest of the way, bypassing the double glass doors and following the large river-rock pathway that led around the side of the house. With each step, the sound of laughter and shouts grew louder, along with splashes of water. I could smell meat grilling, making my empty stomach grumble happily.

Sebastian was right: I would never turn down grilled cheeseburgers.

"Hey." Sebastian nudged my arm with his. "Whenever

you want to leave, let me.know, okay? Don't roam off with someone."

"I'm pretty sure I can catch a ride home with anyone. No need to worry."

"Not worrying. I'll just take you home when you're ready."

He slung his shirt over his shoulder. I guess putting it on would take too much effort.

To the outsider, Sebastian could come across as bossy, but he was just the type of guy who didn't bring someone to a party and then leave it to them to find their own way around or home.

"Maybe I don't want a ride home with you." I swung my purse. "I'm sure there are a ton of people who'd give me a ride."

"Wouldn't that be stupid, since we live next door to each other?"

"Don't question my logic." I stepped around Sebastian, I walked in front of him. "And seriously, I don't want to stay out forever."

"I don't either—"

"Dammit!" I shrieked as he kicked the bottom of my foot just as I raised it. Swinging around, I smacked him with my purse.

Laughing, he blocked the hit with his arms. "Watch your step there."

"Jerk," I muttered, turning back around.

"I'm not planning to stay out late either," he continued. "Got practice tomorrow morning, one-on-one with the coach." He paused. "And Dad."

I cringed for him. "How has your dad been?"

"There's not even enough time in the day for that conversation," he replied, and before I could push that further, he caught my hand, stopping me. I faced him. "I'm not staying out late because of practice and because—" those vivid blue eyes fixed on me "—I need to talk to you."

My heart lurched. I wanted to pull my hand free and run screaming into the orchards…but that would be weird. "What do you want to talk about?" I asked even though I knew what it was about.

"Stuff."

I arched a brow. "Can't we talk now?"

"No. Later," he said. He let go of my hand and walked around me. "After I've had a drink."

CHAPTER EIGHT

"My man!"

Keith jumped from the deck, landing in front of us like Tarzan, if Tarzan wore...oh my God, *Speedos*? Keith was a big guy—big like a bear, broad shouldered and tall. Speedos shouldn't be in the same zip code as him.

"You brought Lena!"

Sebastian halted to a stop in front of me. "What in the hell are you wearing?"

I tried not to look down, but it was like I was compelled by some dark magic and couldn't help myself. I saw... I saw *too* much. I took a step back, but it was too late. Keith darted around Sebastian, and a second later my feet were lifted off the ground and I was being squeezed to death. I squeaked like a chew toy.

"It's been forever since I've seen you." Keith moved his shoulders, swinging my legs to and fro. "How long has it been?" he asked, and I could smell the beer oozing out of his pores.

"I don't know," I gasped out, my arms pinned. "A month or so?"

"Nooo!" he drew the word out. "It has to be longer than that."

"Put her down," Sebastian barked. "Jesus, you're practically naked, man."

Keith threw his head back and laughed and then twirled, spinning me along with him. Without any warning, he let go and I stumbled back. Sebastian's hands landed on my shoulders, steadying me. "You guys like my swim shorts?" He put his hands on his hips and widened his stance, and *oh my God*, my retinas were burning. "I can move more freely and I think it makes my ass look *amazing*. Plus the green matches my eyes, don't you think?"

"Yeah," I whispered, slowly shaking my head.

Sebastian reached under the bill of his cap and rubbed his forehead. "I'm officially scarred for life."

"More like blessed. You're both officially *blessed* for life." Keith smacked his hands down, one on each of our shoulders. He steered us through the open gate. "Hamburgers are almost ready. We're about to throw some dogs on the grill in a few. Drinks are in the coolers."

Keith's place was always the spot to party. Fall through spring, there were bonfires every weekend in the fields beyond manicured lawns, and during the summer, everyone was gathered around the pool as large as the first floor of my house. And that wasn't including the sand-colored brick patio surrounding it. A dozen lounge chairs dotted the patio, most of them occupied by faces I recognized from school. A few waved when they spotted us.

His parents had to have dropped some major money on the backyard—the kind that could've paid off Mom's mortgage. Besides the pool and patio, there were flower gardens and benches everywhere, a horseshoe pit behind the pool house that was bigger than some people's apartments and a badminton net strung up.

I hadn't been back since the party in July.

"Hey." Keith ran a hand over his buzzed head, drawing my attention. "Is your girl Abbi coming out?"

"Yeah." I pictured Abbi's face when she saw what Keith was wearing and nearly laughed out loud. "She'll be here soon, and she's going to be so happy to see you."

She was *so* going to kill me.

"Awesome," he replied, appearing a little too pleased by the whole idea. "Glad you made it out here. Was beginning to think you no longer wanted to be friends with me."

I shook my head. "I still love you, Keith. Just been busy."

"You can never be too busy for me." Keith started walking backward, making his way to where his older brother, Jimmy, was standing in front of the grill.

His brother looked over and then burst into laughter. "Holy shit, you're wearing them."

Keith stuck out his rear, shaking it at his brother. "I don't think I'll ever take them off."

"God help us," muttered Sebastian.

Wiping the beads of sweat off my forehead with the back of my hand, I peered up at Sebastian. It was so hot I was already beginning to regret the whole no-bathing-suit thing. "He's *your* friend."

"Yeah." Chuckling, he stepped around a colorful potted plant.

Glancing at the double glass doors leading into the back of the house, I thought I saw movement inside. "Do you think Keith's parents are here?"

"God, I hope so." Sebastian eyed the pool. "Nothing's more hilarious than his father coming out here and challenging everyone to a horseshoe tournament."

I dropped my purse by several others and said, "I can't believe his parents are cool with these parties. I mean, my mom is pretty chill, but I'm also not throwing parties every weekend."

"Guess Keith and Jimmy lucked out in the parental department." He angled his body toward mine. The cap hid the upper half of his face. "Before we were interrupted by the disturbing sight of Keith, I—"

"Yo! Seb." Over his shoulder, I saw Phillip pop up from one of the loungers, his dark skin glistening in the sunlight. "When did you get here?"

"Just a few seconds ago," Sebastian answered as he turned.

Phillip swaggered over to where we were standing. He clapped a hand on Sebastian's shoulder as he nodded in my direction. I wiggled my fingers at him.

The two started talking about the scrimmage game and their first game of the season next Friday while I stood there singing "It's a Small World" in my head. Eventually Keith returned to deposit a red plastic cup in my hand and another in Sebastian's.

"Only one," he said, sipping at the foam. "Got to drive back tonight."

Keith snorted. "Pansy ass."

"Whatever." Unbothered, Sebastian grabbed some plates and we got down to eating cheeseburgers. "You see the quarterback for the Wood team? He can throw…"

I zoned back out of the conversation, sipping my beer until I saw Chris coming around the corner of the house. Slipping away from the guys, I met Megan and Abbi at the gate.

"Thank God you two are here," I said. "They're talking about football. Nothing else but football. That's it. *Only* football."

"No bathing suit?" was the first thing out of Megan's mouth. She was wearing cutoffs and a bikini top. Half her face was covered by black oversize sunglasses. "You and Abbi have no concept of how to dress when you come to a party that involves a pool."

Abbi's curls were sectioned into two pigtails. "Heads up, she's been bitching the whole ride out, about everything and everyone."

"It's been a long day." She snatched my cup out of my hand and lifted it to her mouth, downing at least half of it in one impressive gulp. "First off, that jerk over there," she said, extending her finger—middle finger—in Phillip's direction, "didn't text me back last night, and I know he was here and so was Meg, and you know how Meg has been obsessed with him for, like, two years."

I pursed my lips. I didn't think Meg Carr had been obsessed with anyone, but I wisely remained silent. Abbi didn't.

"Do I need to remind you that you guys are actually broken

up? I mean, you said you were talking, but that doesn't mean anything." Abbi leaned into me, resting her arm on my shoulder. "So what's the point?"

"There's a point. I'm getting to it." Another deep gulp of my drink. "He says he wants to get back with me, and I'm entertaining the idea. But if he wants to get back with me, he should at least be responding to my texts."

Abbi looked at me.

I kept quiet.

"Then my dumbass cousin over there—" her middle finger went toward Chris, who was with Sebastian and the guys "—who, mind you, I love deeply, was texting Mandi like crazy on the way over here. And I'm pretty sure he's already half-lit. I thought we were all going to die a horrible death."

My stomach dropped slightly. Mandi was friends with Skylar. If Mandi was seeing Chris, which was a new development, then she'd be here tonight. So would Skylar, because those girls traveled in packs.

So did I, but whatever.

"That last part is true," Abbi confirmed. "I thought we were going to die, too."

"Finally, Mom wanted me to go out to dinner with her new boyfriend tonight. Who, by the way, is maybe only ten years older than me, and that's gross."

I glanced over at Abbi. She was grinning slightly, despite what she suspected her family was going through.

"So I had to explain to her that this was my last weekend before my senior year and the last thing I wanted to do was spend it with her and the guy who'd be replaced by a newer, shinier version next month."

"Uh-oh," I murmured.

She lifted my cup again. "That went over well, but I'm here, so I win." She raised the cup in a toast and then offered it back to me.

"You can have it." I waved it off. "Seems like you need it more than I do."

"Thank you." Megan popped forward, kissing my cheek. "You're my very best friend."

Abbi cocked her head to the side. "What about me?"

"You just said I was being bitchy. You've been downgraded to second place," Megan replied over the rim of the cup.

I laughed. "So Dary is in third place?"

"When is Dary getting back?" Megan asked, looking around.

"Tomorrow," Abbi reminded her.

Her face fell. "I miss her. We should take a ton of selfies and continuously bombard her with them."

I laughed. "I'm sure she'll appreciate that."

"But first, how are things with Sebastian?" Abbi asked, nodding in his direction.

"Fine," I replied quickly. "We'll chat later about it. Okay?"

Abbi looked like she wanted to protest, but she let it go. I wanted to enjoy myself for a little bit before I started stressing over what Sebastian wanted to talk about.

We spent way too long taking random selfies with everyone at the pool and all around the property, sending them to Dary from all our phones. Her initial amused responses had died, and knowing her, she was probably getting super annoyed by the twentieth selfie, which kind of made it all the more entertaining.

Later, Keith did a grab-and-twirl with Abbi, who appeared horrified by his outfit, but I could tell she was also reluctantly amused by it. She wiggled free, groaning about how much of an idiot he was while smiling. Megan eventually roamed off, joining Phillip and another guy on the other end of the pool.

"Is she really thinking about getting back with him?" I asked Abbi.

"Who knows?" She sighed. "God, I hope not. They're like the Selena Gomez and Justin Bieber of Clearbrook."

"Except no one wants them to get back together?"

A loud laugh burst out of Abbi. "So true."

Looking around the backyard, telling myself I wasn't looking for Sebastian, I spotted Cody by the grill, cup in hand and surrounded by the rest of the guys. "When did he get here?"

"Who— Oh. No idea." Abbi straightened her hot-pink sunglasses. "A lot of people have just randomly shown up. It's crazy."

We walked over to the cooler. Abbi grabbed a soda as I fished a water bottle out of the ice. "So Sebastian says he wants to talk to me later."

"About?" She popped the lid on her can.

"I have no idea. Usually he's not so evasive. But I'm thinking it's about the obvious, you know?"

Abbi was quiet for a moment and then she said, "You saw Skylar's Instagram post from last night, right?"

Knots filled my stomach. "Yeah."

"Maybe he's planning to get back with Skylar," she said, and I sighed. "He might want to tell you they're getting back together. I hate to say that, but after the whole kissing thing, he probably thinks he should say something to you about it," she said, pushing her sunglasses up as a cloud covered the sun.

"Well, he and Skylar do make the perfect couple." I glanced at the guys. Keith was thrusting his hips and smacking the air with one hand.

"You and Sebastian would make a perfect couple."

I suddenly wanted to throw myself under the bushes. "I don't want to think about this anymore. It's annoying—I'm annoying myself. For real." I turned to Abbi. "I'm literally driving myself crazy."

"Then you should find some hot dude to pass the time with until you leave for college."

"Now you sound like Megan," I said. "But maybe I will find someone to pass the time with. Preferably a hot dude who likes to read and is interested in history."

"That sounds like relationship material. I was just talking about Netflix and chill." Her tone was dry. "Let's not get ahead of ourselves."

I laughed as I took a sip of water.

Abbi turned as Megan danced her way over to where we stood. She stopped in front of us, shoving her sunglasses up. "Guys, you're not going to believe what I just heard."

"What?" I asked, happy for the distraction.

Excitement buzzed in Megan's voice. "Griffith and Christie just left with Steven to meet up with some shady-ass dudes from the city to buy coke."

I lowered the water bottle. I was *so* not expecting that to be what she was going to tell us.

"Not surprising," muttered Abbi. "Didn't they do that

in July? Christie got all kinds of messed up. Keith almost called 911."

Megan's mouth dropped open. "You knew about this? Is it something regular they do?"

"Regular enough that they're going to get it now, apparently," she shot back.

I was still stuck on the whole randomly-leaving-to-buy-coke thing, like they were going to the store to pick up some chips and dips.

Jesus, that seemed hard-core.

I wasn't naive, but I was surprised that *they* were the ones going to get stuff. Really, I would have been surprised if *anyone* I knew was doing coke or heroin.

"Well, hell." Megan looked down at her red cup. It had been refilled. "Phillip is thinking about trying it tonight. Like, he almost left with them. Can you believe that?"

Abbi curled her lip. "Idiot."

"Right?" Megan took a drink. "I'm going to go yell at him. Be back later."

My brows rose as I watched her walk away. "That's… Wow."

"Do you think Keith does it?"

I tucked my hair back behind my ear. "I didn't even know *they* did, so I have no idea."

"Well, that would explain the Speedo," she said with a heavy sigh. "You would have to be high to think that was a good idea."

I giggled. "So true."

"Hey." Sebastian's voice was in my ear a second before his arm curled around my shoulders. A puff of air left me.

His warm, hard chest pressed against my back. A tight wave of shivers wound down my spine as heat blasted my face. "Where've you been?"

Abbi stared at me, brows arched.

I quickly focused on the pool. "I've been right here. Where've you been?"

"Everywhere," he replied, and he turned me around. The baseball cap was on backward again. Our faces were inches apart, nearly as close as we were at the lake. So close I could smell the faint trace of beer on his breath. "So, I have this idea. It involves me. And it involves you…getting wet."

My mouth dropped open as my mind belly flopped into the gutter.

Oh my God.

"Really?" Abbi chirped. "I cannot wait to hear more about this idea."

Oh. My. *God*.

He grinned as he reached over and plucked the sunglasses off my face. He put them on top of his head. "Well, I'm more of a show versus tell kind of person."

All I could do was stand there and stare at him, because I felt like I'd slipped into some alternate reality—the kind that existed in the super-adult romance books I read, where public declarations of love were abundant and happy endings were promised. I couldn't look away from his heavily lidded eyes, which were so blue they almost seemed unreal. We were so close I could see the one tiny freckle he had under his right eye.

"What are…?" I whispered, completely losing my voice.

Sebastian dipped his chin as he slid his arms down my

back, hooking me around the waist. He drew me up against him, and my heart was beating at a near-deadly pace.

This was actually happening. Surrounded by our friends, this was actually *happening*.

His head tilted to the side, and our mouths were lined up. "Lena, Lena, Lena."

My eyes drifted shut, and I felt his warm breath on my lips. Every muscle in my body tightened. I was breathless with anticipation, want and need.

It was happening and this time it would end differently.

CHAPTER NINE

My hands landed on his chest and slid up to his shoulders. Shouts of laughter and beats of music sounded miles away. Sebastian shifted against me, dipping down and sliding an arm under my legs. He lifted me up, and my eyes popped open.

Sebastian kissed the tip of my nose.

Then I was flying through the air, so suddenly that I was too shocked to scream.

I hit the cold water butt-first and my lungs locked up as I dropped under the surface, arms flailing. I sank like a water buffalo. My feet hit the bottom of the pool, and I stayed there for a second in disbelief.

What had just happened? Oh my God.

I thought he was going to kiss me, but it was just a game. It was something Sebastian would do to his *friend*. He was just messing around, like nothing had gone down between us on Monday, and I...I was a complete idiot.

And I knew how it must've looked to everyone standing

around us. Me with my eyes closed and my hands on his shoulders.

I was such a *fool*.

And I was going to drown.

Lungs burning, I pushed off the floor of the pool and broke the surface, sputtering water as I cursed, "You *asshat*!"

"Hey, I was just helping you out." Sebastian stood at the edge of the pool, a smug smile on his striking face. "You looked like you needed cooling off."

"I don't think that was the kind of wetness Lena was hoping for," Abbi replied drily.

Sebastian's head swung in Abbi's direction, and Megan, who had appeared beside Abbi while I was drowning in my own dumbness, choked on her drink and whirled around, marching away from the pool. Her hand flapped at her face.

I sank back under the surface, imagining myself strangling Abbi. I was *so* going to kill her.

More embarrassed than I'd been in a very, very long time, I swam over to the shallow edge and then rose, dragging myself out of the water. Sebastian walked around the pool, a beach towel in his hand.

"You look so cute wet," he said.

"Shut up." I climbed the wide steps.

"I kind of like you this way."

Bending over at the waist, I brought my hair over my shoulder and wrung it out. Fat drops of water splashed and pooled under my waterlogged flip flops. "I kind of want to hit you."

"You're so aggressive."

I pulled at my T-shirt, but it was no use. It clung to my upper body. All I could be thankful for was that my shirt wasn't white and my shorts weren't loose enough to slide off. "I'm about to get real aggressive up in your face."

He tipped his head back and laughed loudly. "I might actually like that."

"Oh, you're not going to like it." Stretching up, I grabbed my sunglasses off his head and put them on. "Trust me."

Keith strolled by. "You really know how to get a girl wet, Seb."

My face caught aflame as I balled my hands into fists.

"Yeah, neither of you have a *clue*," Abbi shot back.

Keith's dark brows flew up. "Oh, baby, I would get down on my knees right here and now if you'd let me prove to you just how good I am at getting girls—"

"That's all I need to hear to know you have no idea what you're doing." Abbi raised her hand, silencing him. "If you did, you wouldn't have to announce it."

"She has a point," Sebastian commented.

Keith laughed as he reached out, yanking on Abbi's pigtail. "I can totally prove you wrong. Give me five minutes."

"Five minutes?" She snorted.

Snatching the towel out of Sebastian's hand, I shoved past him and walked over to where the patio led to the pool house and the horseshoe pit to avoid doing something like, say, punching him in the throat.

"That was kind of stupid, wasn't it?"

I twisted around and saw Cody standing there, a bottle in his hand. Why couldn't I just hide in my corner and marinate in my foolishness alone? Was that too much to ask?

"Yeah," I muttered.

"You look pretty pissed over it," he remarked.

I took a deep breath and lifted my gaze. "Has anyone ever told you that you're very observant?"

He laughed softly, raising the bottle. "Hey, I'm not the one who threw you into the pool like a basketball."

Wrapping the towel around my shoulders, I mentally counted to ten. Cody hadn't done anything wrong. "So, what are you up to?"

"Nothing really." He took a swig from the bottle. "Trying to decide if I feel up to staying here or heading elsewhere."

While I wasn't in the mood for conversation, I wasn't doing anything else. Abbi was still arguing with Keith, and Sebastian was with Phillip and Megan, by the lounge chairs. "What else do you have planned?"

"No idea. Just not really feeling it today, you know?" Crossing his legs at the ankles, he leaned against the side of the pool house, looking out toward the pool. "You're missing a friend, aren't you?"

I nodded. "Dary. She's doing the family thing in DC."

"Sounds like fun." He didn't sound like he believed that. "How late are you planning to be here?"

Dusk was settling, so I knew it had to be past eight. I'd already stayed later than I'd anticipated. "Not much longer." I pretty much just wanted to go home and eat the Pop-Tarts Mom had picked up.

"You're obviously not feeling it either." He shifted his body toward mine. "We could steal Sebastian's keys and go for a ride."

I swallowed my snort. "Yeah, I don't think that would be wise."

"What?" A playful grin tugged at his lips. "It would be fun."

"Uh-huh." I kicked off my flip-flops, hoping the stone walkway was baked with enough heat that they'd dry. "First off, pretty sure you're not going to be able to steal the keys that are currently in the pocket of his shorts."

"You have such little faith in me," he replied. "I have sneaky fingers."

"I'm sure you do, but since I've heard you're back with Jessica, I seriously doubt she will be happy to hear that we stole Sebastian's car together," I told him. "And I really don't want that kind of drama."

"Damn, news travels fast, huh?" Cody shook his head. "Jessica can be...feisty."

"That is a really tame description of Jessica," I said, laughing a little. "Not trying to be mean or anything."

"Nah, I get you." He nudged my arm slightly. "We're about to get company."

I didn't get a chance to glance over my shoulder.

"Hey," Sebastian said from behind me. "Am I interrupting something?"

Tensing, I refused to let myself turn around and look at him. "Cody and I are talking."

"I can see that." Sebastian moved to stand beside me, so close I could feel the warmth radiating off his body. "About what?"

"We were plotting nefarious things," Cody answered.

Sebastian snickered. "Do you even know what *nefarious* means?"

"Damn, Seb." Cody coughed out a laugh. Stepping to the side, he tipped his bottle at me. "Have fun with all of that." He then pointed at Sebastian with the mouth of the bottle. He grinned. "Good to hear you got extra practice tomorrow with the coach. You've been gone all month. Don't want to be holding the team back."

"You don't have to worry about me holding anyone back," Sebastian replied.

"Sure, sure," Cody said as he pivoted and walked away.

I glanced at Sebastian. "That was kind of rude, don't you think?"

"Not really. Figured I'd come over here and save you from being stuck in a conversation with him."

"I don't recall sending up an SOS signal."

"Wow." He moved in front of me just as the twinkling lights strung along the trees blinked on. His brows were furrowed together. "That was a little—"

"I'd proceed with caution with what you're about to say," I warned, staring up at him. "Choose your words wisely."

He opened his mouth and then snapped it shut. Turning sideways, he whipped off his baseball cap and thrust his fingers through his hair before he pulled the hat back on. "Are you ticked off because I interrupted you guys?"

Oh. Yeah. *That* was the reason. I could feel my cheeks heating up, and I was grateful that the outdoor lights weren't that bright. Frustration swept over my skin like an army of fire ants. "Whatever."

"Wait." He laughed, but that sound was hoarse. "Are you, like, *interested* in Cody?"

"What?"

"Are you into Cody?" he repeated.

I tugged the towel closer. I could *not* have heard him correctly. I'd just kissed him and he was asking me this? "Why would it matter if I was?"

He looked like I'd admitted to dropping out of school to pursue a career as a professional street performer. "Cody is a player, Lena. He's been with half the school. He's back with—"

"I know what he is, but what I don't know is why you care," I shot back, struggling to keep my voice low.

Sebastian stared down at me, disbelief etched into his face. "You've never been interested in him. Ever. And now you are?"

Okay, so I wasn't interested in Cody whatsoever, but this conversation was ridiculous. "Why are we talking about this? Weren't you hanging all over Skylar last night?"

Sebastian's chin jerked to the side. "What does that have to do with the conversation we're having?"

The breath I took scorched a hole into my chest, and I could taste the metallic bitterness and rancid jealousy, feelings that had existed beneath the surface for far too long. Feelings I'd hidden and pretended didn't exist for years. But now it was like I was stripped bare, my skin flayed open, and there was just no more hiding.

He rubbed his palm across his chest, right above his heart. "I actually cannot believe we're having this conversation."

I jolted. "You can't believe we're having this conversation?

You started it and, you know what, I don't want to talk to you right now. I'm mad at you."

"Mad at me?" His brows flew up. "About what?"

Dropping the towel, I looked down at myself pointedly. A small puddle of water had formed under me. I knew in the back of my head that being pissed at him for throwing me into the pool had nothing to do with the actual act. Hell, he'd done that before. I'd actually pushed *him* into Keith's pool a few times. But I wanted to be mad, because being mad was better than being embarrassed and hurt and *disappointed*.

"You're seriously mad at me for that?" He stepped back. "What the hell? Are you—"

"I kissed you!" The moment I said those words, a knot formed in the back of my throat.

His jaw tightened as he lowered his head toward mine. "What?"

"I kissed you on Monday, and I...I didn't mean to. It happened and before...before I could say *anything*, you practically ran away. And I thought you were going to kiss me when you threw me in the pool," I said, breathing heavy and feeling a little sick. "That's what I thought you were doing."

In the failing light, his eyes looked like the ocean at night, a dark and deep endless blue. "Lena, I thought—"

"Sebastian!"

He jerked back at the sound of Skylar's voice and then he looked over his shoulder, chest rising and falling deeply.

Oh for crap's sake...

She was coming down the walkway, clad in a strapless dress that skimmed the top of her thighs. She was walking so fast her hair lifted off her shoulders. It looked like she was prowling down a runway. "There you are. I've been looking everywhere for you."

Pressing my lips together, I fought the urge to point out that we weren't exactly hidden and were not hard to find, so she seriously didn't need to look *everywhere*.

Skylar had that Miss America smile on her face as she walked up to us. She placed her hand on Sebastian's arm, and I focused on the ground. "Can we talk for a second?" she asked.

I briefly squeezed my eyes shut, knowing he was going to say yes and it was time for me to end this conversation before any more serious damage was done. I shoved my feet into my flip-flops. "I've got to go over…there."

Sebastian turned to me. "Lena—"

"See you in a bit," I cut in, forcing a smile at Skylar.

She smiled back, and I think she said something, but I didn't hear her over the roaring in my ears as I hurried back toward the pool, immediately tracking down Abbi.

"You okay?" She was sitting on the edge of a lounge chair. Keith was leaning back in it, and at some point he must've decided the Speedo had to go, since he was now wearing shorts and a T-shirt. It was a definite improvement.

"Yeah." I cleared my throat. "Totally fine."

She looked doubtful as she glanced back toward the pool house. She opened her mouth, but I cut her off. "We'll talk tomorrow."

"Okay." She patted the space next to her. "Sit with me."

I sat on the edge of the chair, with my back to the pool house, and I didn't look over my shoulder. Not once. And as

I sat there, listening to Keith and Abbi attempt to outsnark each other, I told myself that everything that had happened with Sebastian wouldn't matter. Tonight sucked. But tomorrow would be a better day.

Tomorrow had to be.

TODAY

CHAPTER TEN

SUNDAY, AUGUST 20

I couldn't move, and everything hurt—my skin felt stretched too tight, muscles burned like they'd been lit on fire, and my bones ached deep into the marrow. I never knew pain like this before. I could barely breathe around it.

My brain felt like it was full of cobwebs and fog. I tried to lift my arms, but they were weighed down, full of lead. Confusion swirled inside me.

I thought I heard a steady beeping sound and voices, but all of it seemed far away, as if I was on one end of the tunnel and everyone was on the other end. I couldn't speak. There... there was something in my throat, in the *back* of my throat. My arm twitched without warning, and there was a tug at the top of my hand.

Why wouldn't my eyes open?

Panic started to dig in. Why couldn't I move? Something

was wrong. Something was *really* wrong. I just wanted to open my eyes. I wanted—

I love you, Lena.

I love you, too.

The voices echoed in my head, one of them mine. One of them definitely mine, but the other—

"She's starting to wake up," a female said from somewhere on the other side of the tunnel.

Footsteps neared and a male spoke. "I'm adding propofol now."

"This is the second time she's woken up," the woman replied. "Hell of a fighter. Her mother is going to be happy to hear that."

Fighter? I didn't understand what they were talking about, why they thought my mom would be happy to hear this—

Maybe I should drive?

The voice again, in my head, and it was mine. I was sure it was mine.

Warmth hit my veins, starting at the base of my skull and then washing over me, cascading through my body, and then there were no dreams, no thoughts and no voices.

TUESDAY, AUGUST 22

Nausea churned my stomach.

It was the first thing I noticed when the suffocating, blanketing darkness eased off again. I was sick to my stomach, like I could vomit, if there was actually anything in my stomach. *Everything* hurt.

My head throbbed, along with my jaw, but the worst pain

was coming from my chest. Each breath I took scorched my lungs and didn't seem to really do anything for me. I had to take more breaths to get enough oxygen. There was unnatural tightness, like rubber bands had been stretched around my chest.

Struggling to make sense of what was going on with my body, I willed my eyes open. Nothing happened at first, like they were sewn shut, but I worked and worked at it until I peeled them open.

Bright light blinded me, forcing me to lose all progress and close my eyes again. I wanted to shrink back from it. I shifted slightly, then stopped when darts of pain shot up and down my body.

What was wrong with me?

"Lena?" The voice moved closer. "Lena, are you awake?"

I knew that voice—it belonged to my sister. But that didn't make sense, because she should be at Radford. At *college*. I think.

I had no idea what day it was. Saturday? Sunday?

Cool fingers touched my arm. "Lena?"

Trying again, I opened my eyes, this time prepared for the light. My vision cleared, and I saw a drop ceiling, like the kind in my classroom. Lowering my gaze, I looked to the right and I saw Lori sitting in one of the two chairs next to me.

It was her.

But it *wasn't*.

My sister looked horrible, and she *never* looked bad. She was genetically predetermined to always look amazing, even in the mornings, but right now her hair appeared unwashed and was pulled up in a haphazard bun. Her eyes were blood-shot and the skin under them puffy and pink. The gray Radford University shirt was wrinkled.

"Hey," she whispered, smiling, but something was off about the smile. It was weak and strained. "You're awake, sleepyhead."

Had I been sleeping a long time? Felt like it. Like I'd been sleeping for days. But this wasn't my bed or my bedroom. I wet my lips. They felt dry, as did my mouth and throat. "What...?" I ran out of air, and the words were hard to force out. "What is...going on?"

"What's going on?" she repeated, and then closed her eyes tight. The skin puckered at the corners. "You're in the intensive care unit in Fairfax. At INOVA," she said softly, opening her eyes and glancing at the door.

"I...I don't understand," I whispered hoarsely.

Her gaze darted back to mine. "What?"

Getting the words out was exhausting. "Why am...I in the ICU?"

Lori's eyes searched mine. "You were in a car accident, Lena. A really—" Her breath caught and she breathed deeply. "A really bad car accident."

A car accident? I stared at her for a moment and then shifted my gaze from her, back to the drop ceiling and the too-bright lights. A second passed and I turned my head slightly, wincing as stabbing pain ricocheted from one temple to the next. The walls were white, lined with boxes and containers marked as hazardous material.

The tugging feeling at the top of my hand made more sense. It was an IV. I was most definitely in a hospital, but a car accident? I searched my head, but it…it was full of shadows with memories cloaked behind them.

"I…I don't remember a car…accident."

"Jesus," Lori murmured.

The door opened, and I saw Mom. A tall, thin man followed her, wearing a white lab coat. Mom halted almost immediately, clasping her hands together against her chest. She looked as bad as Lori.

"Oh, baby," Mom cried, and then she was lurching forward, rushing to the bed.

A memory floated to the surface. Words—words that had been spoken to me. *Do you love me enough to carry me inside my house, pass my mom and tuck me into bed?*

Someone had said that to me—outside, in the driveway of Keith's house. The voice came back out of the darkness, eerily familiar. *But only after we stop at McDonald's so I can get chicken nuggets.*

Chicken nuggets?

The memory floated away as soon as it formed, and I couldn't place the voice or tell if it was even real or just from a dream.

"Thank God." Mom bent over, carefully kissing my forehead and then my nose and then my chin. "Oh, thank God. Thank God." She kissed my forehead again. "How are you feeling?"

"Confused," I forced out. Really, extraordinarily confused.

"She doesn't remember." Lori rose, smoothing her hands over her hips. "She doesn't remember the car accident at all."

"That's not uncommon with these types of injuries along with heavy sedation," the man in the white lab coat said. "Her memory will most likely come back either completely or with a few patches once we get everything out of her system."

Heavy sedation?

Mom took Lori's place, sitting the closest to the bed. She picked up my hand, the one with the IV. "This is Dr. Arnold. He was the one who…" Lowering her chin, she shook her head as she drew in what sounded like a halted breath.

I knew whatever she couldn't say was pretty serious, and as I stared at her, I saw her in my mind, sitting at the kitchen table, poring over contracts. She'd been wearing her reading glasses, and she'd told me that when my phone rang again, I had to answer it. And she'd said something else.

Be careful.

Always.

When had that been? Saturday. Saturday before—

Dr. Arnold sat on the edge of the bed, crossing one knee over the over. "You are a very lucky young lady."

Focusing on him, I decided I was going to have to take his word for it, because I had no idea what was going on.

Mom squeezed my hand, and when I glanced at her, she looked like she was on the verge of tears. Her eyes were just as puffy and red rimmed as Lori's.

The doctor reached to the front of the bed and lifted a chart up. "Other than tired, how are you feeling?"

I swallowed and it was like sandpaper rubbing together. "Tired. And I…I don't feel good."

"That's probably the leftover effects of the sedation," he said, running his fingers along the center of the chart. "We've got you on some strong pain relievers right now, so that can also make you feel a little sick. That said, how is the pain?"

"Um…my head hurts." I glanced at Mom, and she smiled reassuringly. "My chest hurts. Everything…hurts."

"You took quite a beating," Dr. Arnold replied, and my eyes widened. A beating? I thought it had been a car accident. Before I could ask, he continued. "You suffered a concussion, but there's been no evidence of swelling of the brain. As long as that remains true, we're going to be out of the woods in that area." He scanned the chart. "You might've figured out that your left arm is fractured. It's going to be in a cast for anywhere from three to six weeks."

I blinked slowly. A cast?

But my arm *couldn't* be fractured. I had practice and games coming up.

I lifted my left arm and it throbbed dully. Yep. There was definitely a cast around my forearm. My gaze flickered back to the doctor. Nothing about this felt real.

"I…I can't be in a cast. I play…volleyball."

"Honey." Mom squeezed my hand gently again. "There is no need to worry about volleyball right now. That is the last thing you should be stressing over."

How could I not stress over it? It was my senior year. Coach thought I could catch the eye of a scout, and Megan would be so ticked off if I couldn't play.

Dr. Arnold closed the chart. "You've had some very serious injuries, Lena, including trauma to your chest, which caused a bilateral pneumothorax."

I stared at him blankly. Pneumo-what?

He smiled faintly, obviously reading my confusion. "It basically means you had air in your chest cavity, which put pressure on the lung and prevented it from expanding. Oftentimes it's single sided and the puncture is so minor that all we need to do is get the air out."

I had a feeling, based on how my sides felt like they were packed in Ace bandages, that wasn't what had happened here.

"In your case, you broke ribs on both sides, puncturing your thorax on both sides, so both of your lungs collapsed and were unable to compensate. I cannot stress how serious of a situation that is. When we have two lungs down, we often aren't having a conversation with the patient later."

Mom lifted her other hand, smoothing it over her face. She stopped with her fingers covering her mouth.

The doctor draped one arm over his knee. "We had to go in and do surgery on both sides." He gestured to the location on his body. "To remove the air and seal off the leaks."

Holy.

Crap.

"We wanted to give your lungs time to recover, so we've had you heavily sedated and let the machines do the breathing for you, but we didn't have to keep you under very long. You were ready to wake up yesterday." Dr. Arnold smiled again.

I had a vague recollection of hearing people talk about me waking up, but there was something else existing on the fringes. Other people talking. Someone screaming—no, the screaming wasn't from the hospital.

"As I said, you're a very lucky young lady. We were able to remove the ventilation tube, but we're going to hold you in the ICU for another day or two, since your blood pressure is a little low. We want to keep an eye on that."

I understood what he was staying and it made sense, but a huge part of me couldn't believe it.

"Once we think you're ready, we'll move you into recovery so we can monitor for infection and inflammation. We'll get you started on breathing exercises later today, and by tomorrow we'll have you out of this bed, walking for a little bit."

I could barely process this.

"If all goes well, which I believe it will, you'll be back home by the beginning of next week."

Beginning of next week?

"You're going to be bruised and sore for some time, and I think volleyball is going to be sidelined for quite some time."

My heart sank. No. I had to play. I could—

"But you should heal a hundred percent and there should be no long-term effects within reasonable exceptions. But we'll tackle more of that later." Dr. Arnold stood, and I wondered what he meant by *within reasonable exceptions*. "The seat belt saved your life. If the others were wearing—"

"Thank you," Mom cut in quickly. "Thank you so much, Dr. Arnold. I cannot express how grateful I am—how grateful we are—for all that you've done."

Wait a second. There was something missing here. Something more important than volleyball and chest tubes. How did I get here? What happened?

"Others?" I gasped out, glancing at Lori.

My sister paled as she plopped down in the chair beside where Mom stood.

Dr. Arnold's face went expressionless, like he'd slipped a mask on. He said something about how long I would be expected to be in the hospital and then hightailed his butt out of there.

I shifted my gaze to Mom. "What...what did he mean about others?"

"What's the last thing you remember?" my sister asked when Mom didn't answer.

Mom glanced at her sharply. "Not now, Lori."

"Yes." I took a shallow breath. "Yes. Now." I tried sifting through the gaps and the empty parts. I remembered talking to Mom on Saturday, telling her I— "I went...to Keith's party." Closing my eyes, I ignored the throbbing ache in my head. "I remember..."

"Remember what?" Mom whispered, slowly sitting back down.

My jaw pounded as I ground my teeth together. The pool party. Sebastian. Thinking he was going to kiss me again. Being thrown in the pool. Talking—no, *arguing*—with him afterward, then... "I remember sitting down with...with Abbi by the pool and... I don't remember anything else."

I love you, Lena.

I love you, too.

Who had said that? Abbi? Megan? It was one of them. I lifted my hand in frustration, wincing as the IV tugged at my hand.

Mom caught my hand, carefully lifting it to her lips. She pressed a kiss against my knuckles. "You've just had a lot of information dumped on you right now. You should be resting so we can get you out of here and back home. We can talk about this later."

What had the doctor said? The seat belt had saved my life, but the *others*—he made it sound like the others hadn't... *Oh my God.* There were others in the car with me.

"No." The beeping in the machines picked up, matching my heart rate. Trying to sit up, I felt like I was being dragged down through the bed. "I want to know…about this… I want to know what…happened right now."

Tears filled Mom's eyes. "Baby, I don't think we should talk about this right now."

Someone screamed—Megan?

"Yes," I gritted out. "Yes, we should."

Mom closed her eyes briefly. "I don't know how to tell you this."

"Just say it," I pleaded as my heart thudded so fast I thought it would rip through my chest. Was it Megan? No. Abbi? I couldn't breathe. Sebastian? Oh God, Sebastian had given me a ride to the party in his Jeep. Oh God.

I tipped my head back, struggling to get enough air in my lungs.

Mom carefully lowered my arm. "You weren't in the car by yourself."

Oh God. Oh God.

Pressure clamped down as my gaze moved frantically from Mom to Lori. My sister looked to the small window, squeezing her eyes shut. "You were in the car with Megan and… and her cousin Chris. Phillip and Cody were with you, too." Lori blinked as she faced me, and then I saw them—the tears streaming down her cheeks. "I'm sorry, Lena. They…they didn't make it."

CHAPTER ELEVEN

"No," I whispered, staring at Lori. "No. That's...that's not right."

Dropping her head, she placed her hands over her face. Her shoulders shook, and a tremor coursed through my body. My heart was racing as I struggled to get in enough air. "No," I said again.

"I'm sorry," she replied.

I flipped my gaze to Mom. "She's wrong. Right? Mom, she...she has to be wrong."

"No, baby." Mom still held my hand—held it tight. "They...they passed away."

Shaking my head slowly, I pulled my hand free. I lifted my left arm. A sharp stabbing sensation radiated all the way up to my shoulder. "I don't...understand."

Mom took several deep breaths and seemed to collect herself. The sheen of tears glistened in her eyes as she leaned over, resting her hands beside my hip. "Do you not remember anything about the car accident?"

I tried in that moment, really tried, but all I could grasp were pieces of conversations. Something about chicken nuggets, and I…I could, if I tried really hard, remember standing in the driveway of Keith's, looking at Cody and thinking something and saying—

Maybe I should drive?

That had been me. I had asked that question. I knew I had. The feeling of unease surfaced, of hesitation and concern. I saw myself stopping at the back passenger door of an SUV—of Chris's SUV. *Maybe I should drive?*

No. *No.*

I shut my eyes tight as a knot of emotion expanded in my chest. I didn't understand. I'd been sitting with Abbi. Sebastian had driven me to the party. How had I ended up in the car with them? How had Megan—

I couldn't think of that. I just couldn't do it. "What happened?" I rasped out. "Tell me…everything."

Several moments passed. "The police…a deputy knocked on the door at eleven o'clock. I was still up. I was in the kitchen, and when I looked outside and saw him, I knew something had happened. The police don't show up—" Mom cut herself off, and I opened my eyes. Her lips trembled. "He told me that you had been in a very bad car accident and had been medevaced out to INOVA. That I needed to get to the hospital immediately."

"She called me when she left. I drove up here, overnight." Lori scrubbed a hand over her forehead. "They didn't tell us anything at first. We heard that there were two patients brought in here. Both were in surgery."

I shifted my legs under the thin blanket. "Two? Is—"

"It was Cody," Lori said, shaking her head as she looked up at the ceiling. "He passed away last night."

Last night? Sunday? "How?"

"We don't know exactly. I haven't spoken to his parents since they were called to his room," Mom answered, her gaze searching mine. "All I know is that he had severe head trauma. I don't think…" She exhaled roughly. "I don't think they ever expected him to wake up."

No. He couldn't be gone. I remembered talking to him at Keith's. He'd been joking about stealing Sebastian's keys and going for a ride. There was no way he was…he was dead. Cody was…was the quarterback. He'd be playing in Friday night's game alongside Chris and Phillip. Rumor had it Cody would play for Penn State. He was just talking to me, wasn't he? Joking and messing around.

But if Chris and Phillip were with us, too, that meant… that meant they didn't…

My mouth moved, but I couldn't find words. I couldn't find the courage in me to ask what I needed to. I couldn't face what I wanted to know. A knot formed in the back of my throat as I kept moving my lips, but there was no sound.

Mom touched my right arm, the pressure light, and she blew out a shaky breath. "Megan and the others died… They think they died on impact. None of them were wearing their seat belts."

"How?" I asked, and I didn't even know why I was asking. I had enough answers to understand what she was saying. Cody was gone. Phillip and his stupid, stupid shirts were gone. So was Chris.

And Megan... We were going to go to college together. Maybe even to play college volleyball. She was one of my closest friends, my loudest and most spontaneous friend. She couldn't be gone. That was not how these things turned out.

But she was.

They were all gone.

Wetness gathered under my eyes. "How?" I repeated.

Mom didn't answer. Lori did, and she did so without looking at me. "The news said they were ejected. The SUV sideswiped a tree and then flipped over a couple of times."

The news? This was on the *news*?

I had no idea what to think except this couldn't be real. Pressing my head back against the pillow, I ignored the flaring pain that shot down my spine. I wanted to get out of the bed. I wanted to get out of this room, away from Lori and Mom.

I wanted to be back home where everything was normal and right. Where the world was still revolving and everything was fine. And alive.

Mom said something, but I didn't hear her as I closed my blurry eyes. Lori responded, but her words made no sense to me. I counted to ten, telling myself that when I opened my eyes, I would be in my bed at home and this—all of this—would be a nightmare. Because it couldn't be real. This couldn't have happened.

Megan was still alive. Everyone was still alive.

"Lena?" Mom's voice intruded.

No one had died. Megan was fine. So was everyone else.

I was going to wake up and everything was going to be normal and okay.

Mom spoke again, and no matter how hard I tried, I wasn't waking up.

This wasn't a nightmare I could wake up from.

"I don't want…to talk anymore," I said, voice trembling. "I don't…want to."

I was greeted with silence.

So I lay there, keeping my eyes tightly squeezed shut as I told myself over and over that this wasn't real. None of this was real.

This couldn't have happened to us, because they didn't deserve this.

No way.

A second passed, maybe two, and I…I shattered like I was nothing more than spun glass. There was a sound that reminded me of a wounded, dying animal, and it took me a moment to realize that it was me making it. It was me who was crying so hard I couldn't catch my breath, couldn't breathe around the pain engulfing every sense. The tears stung raw areas on my face and clogged my throat, and I couldn't stop.

"Baby. Sweetie," Mom said, her hands on me. "You need to calm down. You need to take deep, even breaths."

But I couldn't, because they were dead, and it was like a violent summer storm erupting inside me, unpredictable and severe. The tears kept coming and they didn't stop until there were strange voices in the room followed by a stinging warmth in my veins, and then there were no more tears.

There was nothing.

★ ★ ★

Much later, Mom touched my arm again, and when I opened my eyes, I was still in the ICU room. The antiseptic smell still clogged my nostrils. Machines still beeped. I was here, and there was no escaping what that meant.

Mom was staring at me, her eyes no longer filled with tears. I didn't think she or my sister had moved one spot while I lay in that bed. The sedative, whatever it was that they'd added to my IV, was sluggishly leaving my body.

"I need to ask you something," Mom said after a couple of moments.

Lori rose from the chair and walked to the foot of the bed. "Mom, not now."

Mom ignored her as she focused on me. "They're saying that there was alcohol involved. That the driver—that Cody was possibly intoxicated."

My brows furrowed together. Cody had been driving? That didn't make sense. I didn't think he'd driven to Keith's party, because he'd talked about taking Sebastian's Jeep, unless… "Whose…car were we in?"

"Chris's," answered Lori. She folded her arms across her chest.

"And…and Cody was driving his car?" None of this made sense.

She nodded. "It was in the news that alcohol was suspected. They even mentioned the party at Keith's house. Apparently the police went there that night. It's been…"

To Keith's? I lifted my good arm and the IV tugged. I dropped it back to the bed. Why would he have been driving Chris's car?

Then I remembered what Abbi and Megan had said when they'd gotten to the party. They'd believed Chris had already been drinking, and I hadn't...I hadn't even thought about it. There hadn't even been a flicker of concern or a question of what the hell was he doing driving to Keith's like that. I'd been...more concerned with what was going on with Sebastian.

"Were they drinking?" Mom asked.

I'd seen Cody with a drink—a red plastic cup and a bottle. I remembered that. I remembered... I remembered thinking—

I wasn't so sure if he was fine or not, but the guys were staring at me and Megan was pushing me, going on and on about the ten-piece nugget meal she was going to murder. Maybe I could talk to Abbi and catch a ride with whoever she was going home with, but she was in a pretty deep conversation with Keith, oddly enough, and I had a feeling she wasn't planning to leave anytime soon. There was this tiny voice in the back of my head, coming from the center of my stomach, but I...I was being stupid.

I had gotten in the car.

"Mom, she doesn't remember the accident. How can she answer that question?" Lori pointed out, but did I really not remember?

Mom stared at me, her chest rising and falling rapidly, and she just lost it. Her face bleached of all color and she started to stand but immediately sat—fell—back into the chair. "What were you thinking, Lena?"

I opened my mouth, my mind running a million miles a minute. I didn't know what I was thinking. I didn't understand. Oh God, this couldn't be happening. This wasn't supposed to happen.

"Mom," Lori said, coming back around the bed.

"You got into that car. That is what happened. You got into that car, and that boy, they said he'd been drinking. The police said they could smell it on all of you. And you—you could've died. *They* died." Mom rose suddenly and stayed up this time, balling her fist to the center of her chest. "I love you and I am counting every lucky star in the sky right now that you're alive, but I'm so disappointed. I raised you... your father and I raised you...to never, ever get behind the wheel after drinking or get into the car when someone had been drinking."

"Mom," whispered Lori, her cheeks wet again. So were mine.

"Did you know he was drunk?" Mom demanded, her voice thready.

Maybe I should drive?

"I don't know." My voice shook as another memory poked free. *Seriously. I'm fine. I've driven this road a million times.* I knew that voice. That was Cody—no, that *had* been Cody. But it couldn't be, because he wouldn't have driven drunk with us in the car, because who would do that? *Chris had earlier and you didn't even care*, whispered a tiny voice in the back of my head. But this was different. I wouldn't have gotten in the car. I knew I wouldn't have. And I wouldn't have let him drive.

That wasn't who I was.

I wasn't that kind of person.

I *wasn't*.

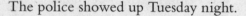

CHAPTER TWELVE

The police showed up Tuesday night.

And that was how I realized that it was Tuesday, three days past Saturday. Three days since my friends had...had died and I'd been asleep. I'd been alive and been asleep.

The cops walked into my hospital room, two of them, and icy fear pooled into my stomach. I was petrified, my wild gaze darting from my mom to the two men in light blue uniforms and weird hats. A nurse was with them, and before they could even introduce themselves, she warned, "You got about ten to fifteen minutes before we need to give her another round of meds. She does not need to be upset right now."

The older trooper removed his hat and nodded, revealing graying sandy-colored hair. "We won't take up a lot of time."

The nurse shot them another stern look before leaving the room.

I swallowed as the old man introduced himself to me and Mom.

"I'm Trooper Daniels. This is Trooper Allen." He gestured at the younger dark-skinned man, who'd also removed his hat. "We are investigating the crash from Saturday night and we have some questions if you're up for it."

"I don't know if she's ready." Mom looked at me wearily. "She only just woke up this morning and found out about her friends…"

Trooper Allen bowed his head. "We are truly sorry for your loss." He held his hat at his waist, just below his navel. "We have a few questions that we hope you'll be able to answer so we can fill in some gaps."

I didn't want to do this. The tears were already snaking back up on me, but I cleared my throat. I didn't think I really had a choice. "Okay."

"Okay." Trooper Daniels moved to the side of the bed. "We need to know everything that you remember. Do you think you can do that?"

Closing my eyes, I wanted to be anywhere other than I was, and I didn't want to talk about what I was starting to remember, but this was the *police*.

So I did.

As I spoke, I started crying again, because the look on Mom's face screamed disappointment and hurt. The cops had little to no reaction as they peppered the room with brisk questions.

"Was alcohol being served at this party?"

"Were Keith's parents home at the time and were they aware that you were drinking?"

"Do you remember seeing Cody drinking?"

"Was Chris too intoxicated to drive his own vehicle?"

"How much did you have to drink?"

Some of these questions I suspected they already knew the answers to, but they were checking my answers to see if they matched. When they stopped, I felt like I had to say something. The words were crawling up my throat.

"We... I didn't think anything would happen," I whispered, voice and soul and heart and everything about me feeling frayed and broken. "We didn't think."

"People so rarely do nowadays," Trooper Daniels responded, voice heavy. "Especially kids your age. We see it far too often."

And that was...*that*.

Especially kids your age. Like it was nothing at the end of the day. They left the room, and all I could do was stare after them. The room was left in silence. This horrible, nerve-stretching silence. I closed my eyes, because I couldn't bear to look at Mom, to see what I knew she was thinking.

I was *that* person.

Reckless.

Irresponsible.

At fault in every sense of the word.

The meds they administered into the IV made everything... easier and I was just able to lie there. I didn't hurt. I didn't have to talk. Lori and Mom were silent, sitting in their chairs, watching reruns of some show.

My brain didn't shut down as I lay there.

But I didn't think about that night.

I couldn't think about that.

As I lay there, feeling like I was floating a good foot or two off the bed, I remembered a different night.

The last time we all were at the lake, back in July.

It had been the weekend of the Fourth of July, and we'd all been together—all of us. Someone had carted out an old charbroil grill, and Sebastian had the back of his Jeep open and the music turned up high.

I sat with Abbi, Dary and Megan as Keith attempted to use snow skis on the lake. Everyone was laughing except Abbi. Her eyes... Her eyes were wide as she murmured over and over, "He's going to kill himself. We're all about to watch him die."

But Keith hadn't died.

He'd fallen and yelled that he'd broken his butt or something. He'd dragged himself out of the lake, holding up his swimming trunks. Phillip and Chris had been waiting for him. I didn't remember seeing Cody there.

And in my memory, I'd been busy watching Sebastian, who was standing on the dock, talking to another guy. I'd watched him a lot that night, because I knew he was leaving soon, so my gaze kept finding him.

I wanted to change what I did that night. I wanted to look away from him. I wanted to watch Phillip and Chris. I wanted to turn my head to the right and look at Megan. I wished I'd listened more closely to what she was chattering on about, because now I couldn't remember. But I knew she looked happy and she was smiling.

And when she got up to join Phillip by the lake's edge, I wanted to call her back. And I wanted to follow them, forever hold the sight of them standing side by side, but I didn't. I stayed where I was while someone across the lake let off fireworks.

I tried to change my memory.

But then there had been Sebastian. As the sky lit up and the air echoed, he'd draped his arm over my shoulders. Another firework had shot into the air on a smooth whistle, exploding into a shower of bright red sparks. The entire right side of my body had been warm and pressed against Sebastian. I'd rested my cheek in the crook of his shoulder as the sky flashed, because there was nothing awkward between us then, and I remembered thinking that...that life couldn't be any better than right then, that moment.

And I had no idea how right I'd been.

Wednesday morning Mom broke the news. "Your father is on his way."

"Why?" I asked, staring at the ceiling.

"He's your father," she responded, sounding tired.

That wasn't much of an explanation. He was my father, but he sure as hell hadn't done a lot of fathering. Why start now?

A horrible thought formed: if I'd been in the hospital since Saturday night, in the ICU, and it was now Wednesday, was he just now on his way?

Sounded so much like Dad that I wanted to laugh but couldn't.

"He's driving from Seattle," she explained, obviously thinking the same thing I had. "You know how he is. Refuses to fly. He should be here tonight, tomorrow morning by the latest."

I didn't know my father anymore, and right now I really didn't have the brain space to figure him out. I didn't want to see him, but I also didn't have anything to really say about it.

I just wanted to be left alone with my memories instead of everything that had changed. I didn't want these new memories erasing everything.

Mom and Lori were taking shifts staying with me. One would drive the forty-some-minute ride home, check the house, shower and grab fresh clothes. The other stayed. Mom didn't bring up what we'd talked about with the cops.

During one of Mom's trips home, Lori told me that the accident happened just three miles from Keith's parents' house. We hadn't even made it to the highway, which was a twisted blessing. The curvy road leading to the farm was rarely traveled by anyone beyond those who were going to Keith's house. If we'd gotten on the highway, we could've hit someone else.

Killed more people.

Killed people other than ourselves.

In those hours, when Lori or my mom was quiet, or when the nurses were checking my vitals, thoughts of Megan and the guys consumed me even though I tried to shut it all down. I wanted to ask questions. How was Abbi doing? Had someone called Dary or had she come home Sunday to this? What did Sebastian think? How was Coach... How was Coach handling the loss of Megan? I was replaceable on the team. Megan wasn't. School had started the day I woke up. How was everyone else doing?

In the ICU, they allowed only family to visit. That would change once I was moved into recovery. From what I heard,

INOVA had an open visiting policy. People could come at any time, even overnight. But for now, I was grateful it was only Lori and Mom.

Seeing my friends would make me think about what had happened, beyond the surface level. And I couldn't. Doing so would make it all too real, too painful, and while I was in the hospital, away from that life, I tried to pretend I was in here for anything other than the reason I was.

"Mr. Miller has been amazing with Mom," Lori said late Wednesday evening while Mom was in the cafeteria, wherever that was located. Mr. Miller was Mom's boss, the insurance-agency owner. "He gave her this week and next off without making her use her vacation. He rolled over all her unused sick time."

"That's nice," I murmured, staring out the small square window. I couldn't really see anything other than the sky.

Lori sat on the other side of the bed, her arms propped on the mattress, by my legs, which were currently encased in some kind of bizarre pressure cuffs. Something to do with circulation and preventing blood clots.

"Sebastian texted me," she announced.

I closed my eyes.

"He's been asking about you. Every day." She laughed hoarsely. "You know, when I went home on Monday for the first time, I swear he must've been waiting by the window for Mom or me. He came barreling out the door before I even got out of my car. He's been really worried. So have Abbi and Dary."

My chest squeezed. I didn't want to think about them. I didn't want to think about Sebastian or Abbi and Dary worrying about me when Megan was gone. When his friends, his close friends, were also gone. I didn't want to *think*.

Lori exhaled raggedly, and a moment of silence passed. "Megan and Chris's funeral is tomorrow. Their family has decided to hold them both at the same time."

I stopped breathing.

Her *funeral* was tomorrow? It seemed so quick. Like it was over already, before it even began. And her family wasn't just...wasn't just burying her; they were also burying Chris. I couldn't even... I just *couldn't*.

"Phillip's funeral is on Friday and Cody's is on Sunday. His is taking longer because..." She trailed off.

I opened my eyes. The sky was a deeper shade of blue. It was almost night. "Why?" I croaked out.

Lori sighed again. "They had to do an...an autopsy on him, since he was driving. They didn't perform one on the rest. It wasn't necessary beyond taking blood samples."

Autopsies and blood samples.

Was that all they were now?

"The school is letting students attend the funerals if they want. The absence won't be held against them."

That was...nice of the school. I imagined there would be a lot of people at the funerals. The guys were super popular. So was Megan. A stupid thought flickered through my head: How would they play football Friday night? It was their opening game. They would be missing three...*three* starting players.

I bet they had a team of grief counselors at the school. A sophomore had died last year from cancer and there'd been extra counselors brought in.

"Mom is going to Megan's funeral tomorrow," Lori said, and I stiffened. "I don't know if she's going to tell you ahead of time. She didn't want me telling you about the funerals, but I thought you should know."

I didn't say anything.

Several minutes passed. An eternity it seemed, but not long enough.

"You don't have to talk about it now. You don't even have to think about it," my sister said quietly. "But you're going to have to, Lena. At some point, you're going to have to face what happened. You just don't have to right now."

Thursday morning they moved me into general recovery. There was less serious-looking equipment in this room and more chairs. In my new room, they had the top of my bed inclined to help with breathing, and after I went through several rounds of breathing treatments, they had me up, walking back and forth in the hallway outside. The nurse walked alongside me, holding the back of my gown closed.

Walking was exhausting.

According to the doctor, I wouldn't be fully healed for about two weeks, and during this time I would tire out easily, but I had to keep moving to make sure I didn't end up with fluid in my lungs or a blood clot.

Before the accident, I would've been scared witless of fluid in my lungs or a blood clot. I'd think every pain in my leg or half breath was a harbinger of death. I'd be Googling the symptoms nonstop.

Now?

I...I just didn't care.

As I shuffled down the hall, I thought about how a blood clot would be quick. Wouldn't it? Like the very second it broke loose, it would be over.

Just like the moment the car hit the tree. It was over for Megan and Chris and Phillip. There one second, and gone in the next heartbeat.

Lori would be heading back to Radford that weekend, since Dr. Arnold was pretty positive I'd be released on Sunday, Monday by the latest.

Life would go back to normal for the most part.

But it wouldn't.

Life would never be normal.

Mom told me she'd gone to Megan's funeral.

"It was lovely, the way they handled it with her and Chris." She'd paused. "When you're ready, we can visit their resting place."

That was all she'd said about it.

Now she was sitting in the chair by the window. The glass was spotted, like it hadn't been cleaned in a while, and for some reason I was fascinated by that. It was a hospital. How could there be dead flies on the windowsills?

Mom hadn't asked me what I was thinking when I got into the car. After the outburst in the ICU, she was a pillar of strength. Blond hair smoothed into a coiffed ponytail. Black yoga pants defuzzed. The swelling in her eyes hadn't gone down, though, and I had this sinking suspicion when she drove home or when I slept, she let the control crack.

She was crying a lot.

Like she had in the months after Dad had left us.

"I checked in with the school on the way here," she told

me, closing the magazine she'd been skimming. "They're aware that you won't be starting until the third week." She shoved the magazine into her tote. "I'm sure you're ready to get back to it."

I didn't care about going to school. How was I supposed to care about that when Megan wasn't going back? When Cody and Phillip and Chris were also gone? Nothing about that seemed fair.

Nothing about the accident was.

Like how…how did I survive? Because out of everyone, it shouldn't have been me.

"The teachers have been amazing," she continued. "They've been collecting work. I believe Sebastian will be bringing it over to the house tomorrow."

Sebastian.

How could I see him again?

How could I see Abbi or Dary again, because I knew… I remembered enough to know that I…I shouldn't have gotten in the car. I shouldn't have let Megan. I should've—

Shifting in my bed, I looked up at the ceiling and blinked rapidly. Wetness gathered in my eyes. How was I supposed to walk into that school when everyone else was dead? When Megan wouldn't be waiting at my locker for me to head to volleyball practice? When she wouldn't be giving me my weekly Friday lecture in the most obnoxious way possible?

When I didn't answer, Mom looked over at the books Lori had brought for me. They sat on the little stand. "Have you already read them?" she asked. "If you give me a list, I can grab the ones you haven't read."

I hadn't touched the pile of books. I wasn't sure if I'd read them or not. Drawing in a shallow breath, I focused on the TV. Mom had turned it on a national news channel. "The books are fine."

Mom didn't respond for a long minute. "You're able to have visitors now. I know—"

"I don't want visitors."

Mom frowned. "Lena."

"I don't want...anyone here," I repeated.

"Lena, I know Abbi and Dary are planning to come see you. So is Sebastian." She scooted forward, keeping her voice low. "They've been waiting until—"

"I don't want to...see them." I turned my head toward her. "I just don't."

Her eyes widened. "I think it would be very good for you to see them, especially after—"

"After Megan died? After Cody and the guys died?" I snapped as my pulse picked up. The stupid heart monitor matched its tempo. "You think it would be good for me to see my friends, knowing...that I let everyone get in the car and they died?"

"Lena." Mom rose, coming closer to the bed. She put her hand on the headboard and leaned over me. "You weren't the sole person responsible that night. Yes, you made a se-verely bad choice, but you are not the sole—"

"I wasn't drinking," I said, and watched the blood drain from my mom's face. "I remember that. I had...a few sips earlier in the night. If they tested me...when I came in, they would've seen I...I wasn't drunk. So I...I was sober. I could've driven." My voice cracked. "I *should've* driven."

Mom slowly pushed away from the bed and sat down

heavily in the chair. "Then why didn't you?" Her voice was thick.

"I don't know." I clutched the edge of the blanket, causing my left arm to ache. "I guess I…I didn't want to…"

"Want to what, Lena?"

The next breath I took hurt. "I didn't want to…to be the person who makes a big deal out of things."

"Oh. Oh, baby." Mom placed her hand over her mouth and then closed her eyes. "I don't know what to say."

Probably because there was nothing to say.

I remembered standing outside the car now. I remembered watching Cody reach for the door handle and miss. And I remembered asking if he was okay and then caving to the pressure around me.

I *remembered*.

A knock interrupted us. Mom tensed, dropping her hand. I looked over, and I…I felt nothing and everything in one instance.

Dad stood in the doorway.

CHAPTER THIRTEEN

I hadn't seen Dad in four years.

The last time had been in the kitchen, sitting at the table. He and Mom had been waiting for me and Lori to get home from school, and I think I'd known what was happening the moment I'd walked into the kitchen. Mom had been red eyed.

Lori hadn't seen it coming.

Dad now looked… He looked older, but good. There were more lines around his eyes and the corners of his mouth, and his hair was more salt-and-pepper than brown, but he looked like life was going smoothly for him in Seattle.

Dad used to be a developer. His company—Wise Home Industries—was responsible for more than half of the homes built in the last two decades. Then the housing market slammed face-first into rock bottom and Dad had to make cuts and the jobs slowed before stopping, and then he had to close the business. Money stopped flowing in. Things got tight.

And he couldn't handle it.

He'd bailed on Mom and us, moved to Seattle of all places, to find himself or some crap. The last I heard, he'd started working for some advertising firm.

I thought I'd feel something stronger than mild annoyance or surprise. I'd spent years ignoring his phone calls. Years being ticked off at him. And now I was just empty. Probably had something to do with the painkillers pumping through my system.

His hazel eyes shifted to Mom before settling on me. A lopsided smile formed as he shuffled over to the bed. He cleared his throat as he stared down at me. "You look… You look…"

Like I'd been in a car accident? Like I'd had two collapsed lungs, a swollen jaw and face, and a fractured arm? Like I went to a party and made a series of really bad decisions I couldn't even begin to unravel in my head? Like I'd basically let my friends die?

Exactly how did I look?

He stopped beside my bed, his posture stiff and unnatural. "I'm glad to see you."

What was I supposed to say to that?

Rising from her seat, Mom leaned over and kissed my forehead. "I'm going to grab something to eat." She straightened, sending a pointed look in my father's direction. "I'll be back in a little while."

Part of me wanted to demand that she stay because *she* wanted Dad here, not me, but I let her go. Dealing with my dad was nowhere near punishment enough for everything that had happened.

Dad nodded at her and then walked around the bed to sit in her chair. If Lori was here, she would be coming out of her skin with excitement to see him. They still talked. Not often, but they did.

He lowered his clasped hands to his knees as his gaze traveled over me. Several moments passed. "How are you feeling?"

I started to shrug, but my ribs protested. "Okay, I guess."

"Kind of hard to imagine that you feel okay after everything," he said, stating the obvious. "Your mother said you should be going home this weekend and that the doctor expects you to heal up without any complications."

"That's...what he's been saying." I slipped a finger under the cast, trying to get at an itch.

Dad was quiet for several moments. "I don't know where to start, Lena. Getting that phone call from your mother was one...was one of the worst things to happen. I know you've been through a lot and I don't want to add to it."

"Then don't," I said, voice low and hoarse.

"But what happened could've been avoided," he continued as if I hadn't spoken, and he was right, so right, but I didn't want to hear *him* saying it. "This wasn't just an accident. You kids made some—"

"Are you...seriously going to lecture me?" I coughed out a hard laugh and then winced. "For real?"

Shoulders tensing, he took a visible deep breath. "I understand. I get it, Lena. I haven't been around, but I've been calling you. I've been trying to—"

"You left and we didn't hear from you for *two years*." How

could he ignore that tiny little fact? And waltz back into my life with a phone call?

"I'm sorry," he was quick to say, and maybe he even meant it, but right then and right now, that apology was as empty as our house. "But I am still your father, Lena."

"Yeah, you're my father, but I stopped thinking of you that way the...moment you walked out that front door and disappeared for two years." My ribs ached with each word. "How...can you say anything to me?"

The centers of his cheeks flushed. "Lena—"

"I don't want to...do this right now," I told him, clamping my eyes shut and wishing, no, *praying*, that he'd disappear. That all of this would just disappear. That I could walk out of this room and disappear. "I don't want to talk. I'm...tired and I...I just want to be left alone."

Dad didn't respond, and I turned my cheek to the other side, keeping my eyes closed until I heard his footsteps, until I was sure he'd left the room like I knew he would.

And I knew I wouldn't see him again.

I'd dozed off after Dad had left and timed meds had been shot into my IV. I had no idea if Mom or Lori had come back in the room after that or if they'd spent time with him. I'd almost guarantee that Lori had, and despite my own personal issues with him, I didn't hold that against her. Just because our relationship had shattered, didn't mean their relationship had to end.

I had no idea how long I slept. I knew it wasn't long. Sleeping in a hospital was nearly impossible. There were so many noises. Machines kicking on and off. Footsteps out in the hall.

Distant conversation. Codes being called out. I only ever slept a few hours, and when I woke this time, I came to thinking about the time Megan had attempted to reenact a routine she'd seen performed on *Dance Moms* in my living room.

She'd sprained her ankle.

And broken the vase on the coffee table.

Coach had been so ticked off. She was out of several games, and I could barely keep a straight face while he yelled at her.

Megan was such a dork.

Heaviness settled in the center of my chest and it had nothing to do with my screwed-up lungs or aching ribs. Seconds ticked by as I lay there and slowly I realized I wasn't alone.

Over the scent of cleaning supplies and that weird antiseptic hospital scent, I smelled something fresher. Not my mother's vanilla perfume or the raspberry lotion Lori wore. This smelled like the outdoors, like pine and cedarwood.

Air lodged in my throat, and my eyes flew open. I turned my head just the slightest, and there he was, sitting in the chair by the spotted window.

Sebastian's face was turned to the side. He was looking out the window, and all I could see was his profile, but it was enough to tell me everything. Faint stubble covered the hard line of his jaw. His elbow was on the arm of the chair, his chin in his palm. He was paler than I was used to seeing him. His hair was a mess, falling onto his forehead.

What was he doing here?

I'd told Mom I didn't want visitors, I wasn't ready to see him or Abbi or Dary or anyone, really.

I didn't make a sound, but he turned his head in my direction. Deep shadows were carved into the skin under those beautiful eyes the color of a sky at night, and those eyes were full to the brim. They looked *haunted*.

Our gazes met and held. For a second, he didn't move. I wasn't even sure he breathed. He just stared at me like he never expected to do so again…and I guessed he hadn't, for a period of time.

Sebastian's gaze moved, searching my face, lingering on the swollen and bruised side. He opened his mouth, but there were no words. He didn't speak for a long moment, and I almost wished he wouldn't. That he'd stay quiet, because hearing his voice would remind me of before, of every stupid thing I'd worried about right up to Saturday night. Of every dumb moment I'd wasted. Remind me of why I'd left that party.

"What are…you doing here?" I whispered.

His eyes drifted shut and his features tightened as if he were in pain. A moment passed before his eyes opened, and there was a rawness to them I'd never seen before. "God," he rasped out. "Part of me wants to ask you what in the hell kind of question that is, but all I can think about is that you're actually talking. That you're still here."

Every muscle in my body tensed. Dull pain flared across my ribs. "I…I told Mom I didn't want to see anyone."

"I know you did." Sebastian leaned forward, gripping his knees. "Why?"

"Why?" I repeated, incredulous.

"How could you even think for one second that I would not come here the moment I could? Abbi and Dary might back off, but there is no way in hell that, after what happened, I wouldn't be here." He scooted to the edge of the chair. "I wanted—no, I *needed*—to see you for myself, to prove that you really were alive. That you're going to be okay."

My pulse started racing. "You know that I'm okay. I'm the only person who is okay."

"Okay?" His face contorted and then smoothed out. "You didn't stub your toe, Lena. Both of your lungs collapsed. Your arm is broken. You look like hell and you—" His voice cracked. "You could've died. Instead of going to the funeral of a girl I've known for years today, I could've been going to *your* funeral."

That shut me up.

"I watched one of my friends be buried today. Tomorrow I will watch them bury one of my best friends," he continued, his voice thick and lips thinning out. "On Sunday, I will see *yet* another one of my friends buried. Within three days, I will have watched four of my friends be buried."

Oh God.

"I will never listen to Megan again and try to figure out what the hell she's ranting about," he said, and my throat constricted. "I will never listen to Cody giving me crap about playing ball. I won't ever sit in class and watch Chris cheat on his exams, wondering how he never gets caught. I won't get to chill with Phillip and play 'Madden' again." His voice shook, and I wanted him to stop. "I never got to say goodbye to any of them Saturday. I didn't get to say goodbye to you that night."

Oh God.

"You know what? Losing them is something I cannot even process right now. Hell if I ever will be able to. But losing you?" His back straightened and his jaw flexed. "I would never get over that."

Squeezing my eyes shut, I breathed around the razor-edged knot in my throat. "I can't do this."

"Do what?" he asked.

"You…" I sucked in a sharp breath. "What happened, it's…it's my fault."

"What?" He sounded astonished. Dear God, he actually was shocked. "You weren't the one driving, Lena. You didn't get behind that wheel drunk."

"That doesn't…matter," I whispered back.

"Lena—"

"You don't get it." I lifted my good arm, placing my hand over my eyes. I didn't want to cry in front of him. I didn't want to cry again. "I don't…want to talk anymore."

A couple of moments passed and he said, "We don't have to."

I squirmed restlessly. Something was building inside me. Something ugly and messy and too raw, too powerful. "Can you just leave?" I asked, begged really. "Please?"

His gaze held mine for a moment and then he stood, and I wanted to sink through the bed, sink down into nothing.

Sebastian didn't leave, though.

He wasn't my father.

He wasn't *me*.

Grabbing the chair, he picked it up and planted it right by the top of my bed and then he sat down. My heart pounded. He rested his right arm on the bed beside mine and then leaned over, stretching his left arm so his fingers caught the limp strands of my hair, brushing them back from my face as he said, "I'm not leaving. You can get mad. You can get upset, but I'm staying right here, because whether you realize it or not, you shouldn't be alone. I'm not going anywhere."

CHAPTER FOURTEEN

Sebastian stayed even though we didn't talk. He'd turned on the TV and he watched the news. I didn't look at him, but every so often, I could feel his gaze on me. I waited for him to say something, to ask questions, but he didn't. And he was there when the nurses came into the room and forced me out of the bed to walk.

Horrified that he was about to witness the absolute struggle it was to get out of bed only to moon whoever was in the room, I locked up when the nurse helped me sit up.

A frown creased the nurse's brow when I didn't budge. "Are you in pain?"

Mouth clamped shut, I quickly shook my head. I could feel Sebastian's gaze boring holes into my back.

The nurse seemed to know what the holdup was. "Do you mind going to the nurses' station down the hall and grabbing us a cup of ice?" she asked him.

"No problem." Sebastian popped to his feet, and I stared at the floor until I heard him leave the room.

"Thank you," I whispered.

"No need to thank me," she replied, getting a firm hold on my uninjured arm. "Is he your boyfriend?"

I shook my head as I slipped out of the bed. "Just...just a friend."

It used to hurt to say that. People often assumed that we were together, something that always secretly pleased me to no end, but I felt nothing as I got my feet into the slippers and started walking. No excitement. No sweet anticipation that usually turned bitter. No sadness because it wasn't true.

I was... I was just empty.

The nurse held my gown closed as we walked up and down the hall. After a couple of passes, my knees weren't as wobbly and I was definitely breathing better than before. I could've kept going, but the nurse escorted me back to the room.

Sebastian was still there, sitting in the chair. He stood as I neared the bed, a pale yellow plastic cup in his hand. "I have the ice."

"Perfect," the nurse replied, still gripping the back of my gown. "Can you put it on the table?"

As Sebastian turned to do just that, the nurse held my gown as I climbed onto the bed. It was on an incline, so I was sitting up. Keeping my attention trained on my hands, I could feel Sebastian moving closer as the nurse pulled out the inhalers for the treatment.

Sebastian stayed through that, too.

Then after the nurse left, he was still there when my mom returned. I pretended to sleep while they talked in hushed tones about nothing. I eventually fell asleep, listening to voices that should've been as familiar as breathing to me but sounded like strangers now.

I learned Friday afternoon that there was no football game, when Sebastian showed up about an hour after school let out.

Unlike the day before, there was a tiny spark of *something* inside me when Mom looked up over at the door and I saw Sebastian. I guessed that was an improvement from feeling nothing at all.

Sebastian looked better.

He still hadn't shaved, but the deep shadows under his eyes had lessened and there was more color to his skin.

He did all the talking then—about school and the two classes we shared this year, about Abbi and Dary. Talked about everything except for the accident or the funerals. I didn't do much talking. I just lay there, staring at the TV.

He came by again Saturday afternoon, and there was another spark, that warming in my chest I wanted to grasp ahold of, but it…it didn't feel right to do so.

I might've said a total of five sentences total.

I didn't have it in me to talk, to put voice to everything that was inside my head or what I was feeling…and what I wasn't.

Sebastian also showed up on Sunday, his face clean shaven, wearing black trousers and a white button-down. He had the sleeves rolled up and was carrying a flat brown paper bag. I knew where he'd come from.

"You're looking a lot better," he said, sitting in the chair by the window. The paper bag dangled between his knees. "Where's your mom?"

I drew in a shallow, uneven breath. "Home. She's…she's coming soon."

"Cool." Those deep blue eyes caught mine for a moment. "You think you're getting out tomorrow?"

Shifting on the inclined bed, I nodded.

His thick lashes lowered as he lifted his bag. "I meant to give this to you yesterday. Left it in the Jeep without think-ing." He reached into the bag, then pulled out a large square that I quickly realized was a giant card.

My dry lips parted. "What…what is that?"

A lopsided grin appeared. "It's a card. Pretty sure it's made it through the whole entire school."

A card.

A card for me.

I lifted my gaze to Sebastian. He was holding it out to me, but I couldn't make myself move. I couldn't take it. It wasn't right. Jesus Christ, it was so not right.

Sebastian stared at me a moment. Silence stretched out and then his chest rose with a deep breath. He placed the bag on the window ledge and moved closer to the bed.

"Everyone has been thinking of you." He carefully opened the jumbo-sized card, holding it in front of me. "They miss you."

My gaze flickered over the card. I could see signatures all along the card, underneath doodled hearts and bubbly "Get well soon" messages. I saw "We love you" written in cur-sive and in block letters. Guilt churned in my stomach, fill-ing my veins with battery acid.

Didn't they know?

"I miss you," Sebastian added quietly.

Slowly, I lifted my eyes to him, and emotion clogged the back of my throat. They missed me and they wanted me to get better, but they didn't know that I could've—I should've—changed what had happened.

Sebastian closed the card, clearing his throat as he stepped back. "I'll put it on your table, okay?" Not waiting for my answer, he propped it up on the small table by my bed.

I peeked at him. He was quiet as he moved the chair closer to my bed and sat, resting his arms on his legs, and he had this look on his face, like he didn't know what to say or do and he was trying to figure it out.

"You…you don't have to stay here," I told him, returning to staring at my hands. "I know I'm not much company."

"I don't want to leave," he replied and then exhaled roughly. "Do you want… Do you want to talk about it?"

My entire body stiffened. "No."

Sebastian was quiet for a long moment again. "Dary and Abbi really miss you. They're trying to give you space, but—"

"I know," I interrupted. "I'm just… I don't want them to have to come here. Hospitals suck."

"They wouldn't mind."

I knew they wouldn't. "It doesn't matter. I should be home tomorrow."

He shifted in the chair, leaning back. "Cody's funeral was today. They had it at the big church off of Route 11. You know the one? Where we used to do the whole trick-or-treat thing at," he explained. "The place was packed. Standing room only. I mean, all the… All the funerals were that way, but you know Cody." He laughed hoarsely. "He would've loved it. You know, all those people."

Pressing my lips together, I nodded. Cody would've... He would've been reveling in the attention.

"His parents..." Sebastian trailed off, clearing his throat. "You know his younger brother, right? Toby? He's what? Twelve? Thirteen? God. He's a spitting image of Cody. And he was... He was pretty upset. They had to take him out halfway through the service. He's gonna be..."

Hands clenching, I glanced over at Sebastian. He was staring into the space in front of the bed, his jaw tight and his mouth strained. "He's going to be what?"

His chest rose with an audible breath. "He's gonna be okay. Eventually."

I didn't reply, even though I wanted to agree. I wanted Toby to be okay, but how could we know if that would happen? He'd lost his older brother. How does one just get over that? How does that pain ever lessen, even over the years? How is the hole in your life, the place another person belonged in, ever filled up again?

How do you move on?

CHAPTER FIFTEEN

Walking through my bedroom door Monday morning was harder than I could have ever anticipated.

Mom was already inside, fluffing several extra firm pillows she'd bought, building a pillow fort at the head of the bed. Per the doctor's orders, I was supposed to sleep in a recliner for the first three days, since my breathing hadn't exactly returned to normal, but since we didn't have a recliner, the pillow fort would have to do.

I knew she'd been able to use sick time for the days off, but we didn't have a lot of extra money to be going out and buying pillows. I'd offered to pay for them out of the small fund I had saved up, but Mom had refused. Dr. Arnold said I could return to waitressing once I was cleared by my general doctor, but he'd said volleyball was going to be up in the air for a while, obviously, with the arm injury.

I wasn't sure how I was supposed to go back to Joanna's.

I wasn't sure how I was supposed to go back to volleyball.

I wasn't sure how I was supposed to go back to *anything*.

Mom straightened and looked over her shoulder. "You okay?"

No.

I was still standing in the doorway, stuck, as my gaze flickered across the room. Everything was like it was before, except on my desk was a stack of textbooks and binders. Sebastian must've brought them over. I'd have the rest of this week to get caught up on what would be two weeks of missed classes.

I also wasn't sure I had it in me to walk into this bedroom.

My room was still the same, while nothing else was, and it didn't feel right walking into it when I could still see Megan the last time she was here, sitting cross-legged on my bed, twisting her long blond hair between her hands or tossing a volleyball against the wall as she talked about Phillip. I could go further back in time, seeing her when she was thirteen, going through the stacks of my books, searching through the adult books, looking for the dirtiest scenes to read out loud to Dary, whose face would turn the color of a radish. I could hear Megan and Abbi arguing about which dancer was the best on *Dance Moms* or whose mother they'd pick to win a street fight. My lips started to turn up at the corners.

I didn't even get to go to Megan's funeral.

Closing my eyes, I planted my right hand on the doorjamb as I swayed slightly.

"Lena?"

"Yeah," I bit out, swallowing. "I'm just..."

I didn't know what I was anymore.

I was at home. I was alive and I was at home.

No one else in that car was.

They all were in the ground.

"You're probably exhausted. You need to be resting, not standing." Mom tugged down the comforter on my bed. "Come on. This is where you need to be."

Mom fussed over me until I got in bed and she had the covers over my legs. Then she fussed some more, bringing up a glass of water and a can of soda, along with a bowl of chips. Only after I was surrounded by everything I could possibly need did she leave the bedroom and return with something else in her hand.

"I didn't want to bring this into the hospital, especially since you weren't up to seeing anyone." She walked over to the bed and held out her hand. "The police brought it by on Wednesday when none of...none of the other families claimed it."

It was my cell phone.

"I've kept it charged for you. I think you've got quite a few messages on there." She glanced down at it. "I have no idea how it stayed in one piece."

Slowly, I took my phone out of her hand and turned it over, screen up. How had my phone survived that crash? The vehicle had rolled, and I'd...I'd been holding that phone when Cody hit the tree.

I remembered that.

I'd been texting Abbi.

I stared at my phone, barely aware of Mom saying she was going downstairs to make some calls. The phone wasn't at all damaged. Not a single crack in the screen or anything. How was that possible?

I saw the missed texts, phone calls and social media noti-fications. There were so many—*too many*. I bypassed them all and opened up my texts, then scrolled until I saw Abbi's name. I didn't read her messages. I zeroed in on the message box, on the half-complete message.

Caught a ride with Megan. Didn't want to bother

"Oh my God," I whispered, dropping my phone on the bed like it was a bomb waiting to go off.

My text was still there, waiting to be sent. A thought left unfinished. A message that never made it to the intended. That could've been the last thing I ever typed. Probably should've been, but a strap only two inches wide had saved my life.

I smoothed my hand over my hair, pushing the strands back from my face. I sat there for several minutes, not mov-ing. I needed to do my breathing treatments soon. The in-haler was on the nightstand. Throwing the covers off my legs, I carefully scooted over the bed. Standing made my ribs feel like someone was taking a vise grip to them, but I ignored the pain as I walked the short distance to my desk and picked up my laptop.

Back on my bed, I cracked open my laptop and went straight to Google to type in the local newspaper's name. The website popped up and it took no amount of time to find what I was looking for.

Articles on the accident.

The first one, the day after the accident, had a picture of the SUV. I clapped my hand over my mouth as I stared at the image. It had been taken that night. There was a red-and-blue glare to the picture.

How could they be allowed to post a picture like that?

The vehicle had been smashed to the point it was almost unrecognizable. The roof caved in, doors peeled off. Windows broken out. One side looked like it had been peeled open. A yellow tarp covered part of the windshield.

Chris had been sitting up front.

Jerking my hand back from my laptop, I sat there for a second, wondering how I'd even survived the crash. How had a seat belt saved me from *that*?

Names had not been released when this article was printed. Families had still been waiting for their lives to be shattered. Two patients had been transported by air to INOVA. Alcohol was suspected as a preliminary cause.

Clicking back, I scanned the headlines and stopped on the one that read Four Local Students Die in Alcohol-Related Accident. It was from Tuesday.

I read the article numbly, as if I were reading about strangers instead of my friends. They listed them out by name. Eighteen-year-old Cody Reece. Eighteen-year-old Chris Byrd. Seventeen-year-old Megan Byrd. Eighteen-year-old Phillip Johnson. My name wasn't listed. I was referred to as a seventeen-year-old minor listed in critical but stable condition.

All except for one had been ejected from the vehicle, and another had been partially ejected. I thought about the tarp over the front passenger side…and I didn't want to think about it anymore.

I kept scrolling and I kept reading. Preliminary toxicology

reports indicated that the driver—Cody—had a blood-alcohol level two times the legal limit. On Tuesday, nearly a week ago, they'd been awaiting a full toxicology report, and I...I saw Cody in my head, reaching for the door handle and missing. I heard him saying as clear as day, as if he were sitting next to me, *Jesus. Are you serious? I had one drink.* And I didn't want to read anymore, but I couldn't stop.

I skimmed the article announcing that Clearbrook High had forfeited the game against Hadley this past Friday night out of respect for the massive loss to the football team. They talked about the boys, about their records on the field. How Cody had been hoping to attend Penn State and Phillip had been planning to go to WVU, the same for Chris.

Another article was posted yesterday, announcing a vigil to be held at Clearbrook High this Friday night, after the football game, when Clearbrook would kick off their "bitter-sweet" season. But that article mentioned something else— *charges.*

Charges against— Oh my God. I read the lines twice, stunned and sick to my stomach.

An investigation of the accident is currently pending. Local authorities have revealed that all the occupants in the car were minors and had left the residence of Albert and Rhonda Scott. At this time, it is believed that both adults were home while the party was being held at their residence. If charged, they could be found guilty of endangering minors, furnishing alcohol to minors, reckless endangerment and criminal negligence.

Holy crap.

That was Keith's parents, and I knew they'd been home. I'd seen them inside the house, in the kitchen. And that hadn't been the first party they'd been well aware of.

Dazed, I got to the end of the article and I...I did something I knew I shouldn't do, but I did it anyway. I started reading the comments on the article that had announced their names. The first comment simply said "Prayers." Second comment read "What a waste of potential. RIP." Third comment was "Seen that Reece boy play. What a damn waste. Surely heading for the NFL."

"This is why you don't drink and drive. What a damn shame."

"Driving that road sober is scary, let alone drunk? Idiots."

The comments just...just went downhill from there. People, complete strangers, commenting as if they knew them— knew *us*. Strangers saying horrible, horrible things as if they didn't care that Cody and Phillip's friends, or Megan and Chris's family, could be reading these.

"They made stupid decisions. They died. End of story."

"Why are we having a vigil for four dumbasses who got behind a wheel of a car drunk?"

"Well, that's four people we don't have to worry about repopulating the earth."

"The parents of the party host should be charged with murder!!!"

"Does it make me a bad person to be grateful that they didn't kill anyone else?"

"Thank God they didn't kill anyone else. Dumbasses."

On and on the comments went, hundreds of them. Hun-

dreds of strangers weighing in, their comments stuck in between the "prayers" and the "poor parents."

"Lena?" Mom filled the doorway. "What are you doing?"
Her gaze moved from my face to my laptop. She quickly
stepped around the bed, looking down at the screen. She
snapped forward, grabbed the computer out of my lap and
closed it as she backed away.

I stared up at her, shaking. My entire body was trembling.
My face was wet. I hadn't realized I'd started crying. "Have
you read those comments?"

"No." She placed my laptop on the desk. "I caught a
glimpse of some of them and I didn't need to read any more."

"Do you know…what they've been saying?"

"It doesn't matter." She sat on the edge of the bed, beside
me. "It doesn't—"

"That's what they think about them!" Pointing at my computer, I struggled to get in deep, even breaths. I knew I
needed to calm down. "This is how they're going to be remembered, isn't it?"

"No. That's not how they're going to be remembered."
Mom eased her arm around my shoulders. "Because that's
not how you're going to remember them or how their families will remember them."

But that wasn't true, because the whole world would forever see them differently. That was all Megan, Cody, Phillip and Chris were now. Four lives reduced to blood-alcohol
levels and bad choices. That was who they were now.

Not football stars.

Not undecided college majors.

Not a badass on the volleyball court.

Not a friend who'd drop everything and listen to you whine about a boy.

Not a guy who worried enough about his friend's future to ask questions.

Not a guy who had the worst taste in shirts.

Not the kind of people who could always make you laugh no matter what.

Instead they were two times the legal limit of alcohol.

They were reckless and irresponsible.

They were people removing themselves from the gene pool.

They *brought* this onto themselves.

They were *dumb* kids who made *dumb* decisions who *died*.

They were a lesson to others.

That was all they were now.

Their entire lives were now a fucking after-school special on the dangers of drinking and driving. That was it.

And I hated it.

Because it was right.

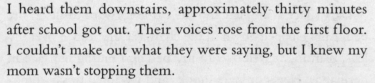

CHAPTER SIXTEEN

I heard them downstairs, approximately thirty minutes after school got out. Their voices rose from the first floor. I couldn't make out what they were saying, but I knew my mom wasn't stopping them.

Panicked, I rose from the bed and glanced at the balcony doors. Could I make a run for it? That was almost laughable. My ribs would fall out of my body if I tried to run, and where was I going to go? I was stuck.

Abbi and Dary were coming.

Every muscle in my body tensed as their footsteps pounded up the stairs. Pain flared across my ribs, no longer dulled by the potent pain meds the hospital had administered. They'd given me a prescription, but I hadn't taken it yet.

I dropped the binder full of homework and catch-up assignments, the pressure in my chest increasing.

Abbi was the first through the door. She stopped just inside my bedroom. Dary was behind her, but Abbi didn't move for what felt like forever. Like she couldn't come into my room, because the room represented everything that was no longer there. Just like I had felt.

Her curls were smoothed back into a high, tight bun. The dark skin under her eyes was puffy. Dary finally edged in around her, into the room, and she looked just as...shattered.

Her wild black hair was gelled back. The white-framed glasses did nothing to hide how swollen her eyes were. Normally Dary was wearing something bizarre. Today she just had on jeans and a loose V-neck shirt. No bright colors. No funky dresses or suspenders.

"You look like crap," Abbi said finally, her voice hoarse.

My mouth was dry. "I feel...like crap."

Dary's face crumpled and she came forward to sit on my bed. Abbi plopped down in the chair as Dary leaned over my legs, planting her elbows in my bed and hiding her face in her hands. Her shoulders shook, and I wanted to say something, to offer comfort.

"I'm sorry." Dary's voice was muffled. "I told Abbi I would keep it together."

"She did." Abbi pulled her legs up, wrapping her arms around her knees. "She promised me."

"I just... I've missed you." She pushed her glasses up to her head and wiped under her eyes as she straightened. "And when your mom said you didn't want visitors, I had to wait to see you—to make sure you're okay."

"And I'm trying not to be pissed off about that," Abbi said, resting her chin on her knees. "But it sucked real bad having to get updates through Sebastian."

"I'm sorry." I leaned back, careful to not let the pillows slip too far down. "Sebastian kind of...forced his way in."

"You wanted space. I'm trying to understand that, but..." Dary dragged the backs of her hands under her eyes. "It was just really hard." There was a pause. "Everything has been really hard."

"It has," I admitted softly.

"How are you feeling?" Dary asked, dropping her hands as she sat up straight.

"Better. Sore."

She slipped her glasses back on. "What about your chest? Your lungs? Is that what the inhaler is for?" She glanced toward where it sat next to the pile of textbooks.

I nodded. "Yeah. The doc thinks everything will heal fine, but I have to use the inhaler a couple of times a day for the next week or so."

"What about the arm?" Abbi asked.

Lifting my left arm, I winced. "Should heal fine. Hopefully, I get the cast off in a couple of weeks."

Abbi stared at my arm. "So...what's going to happen with volleyball?"

"I don't know." I shifted against the pillows. "I haven't really thought about it."

"When I broke my arm, I had that cast for, like, six weeks." Dary frowned. "God, I remember getting poison ivy somehow under my cast that summer. Ugh. It was torture."

I glanced over at Abbi. She wasn't looking at my cast anymore but at the foot of the bed. "Are...are you guys okay?"

Abbi laughed, but it was without humor. "I don't know what that question even means anymore."

"It's just…" Dary closed her eyes and shook her head. "Megan was nuts—nuts in the best way. It's just so weird not having her here, not hearing her voice or seeing her get excited about seeing a cat in a yard or something. It's just… Nothing is the same."

"Do you remember the car accident at all?" Abbi asked suddenly.

A tremble coursed through me. "Only a little bit. Like flashes of conversations."

"Your mom said you had a concussion and that you were having trouble remembering," Dary said.

I nodded.

"So you don't remember it all?" Abbi asked again, and my gaze flicked to hers briefly.

"Not much," I said, and hated myself for it. "But I…I remember that I was going to text you and let you know that… I was leaving."

"I didn't get the text." Abbi lowered her feet to the floor.

"I didn't get…a chance to send it."

Dary closed her eyes. "I know you don't remember, but do you think they…that they suffered?"

Smoothing my hands along the comforter, I let out a shaky breath. "I don't think so. I don't think Cody did either."

"He never woke up," Abbi stated quietly.

I shook my head, at a loss for what to say as I glanced between them. The lack of Megan was a heavy, tangible presence in the room.

They stayed for a bit, Dary sitting on my bed, Abbi in the computer chair. They talked about school and about Megan—about the songs played at her funeral. They talked about the charges that Keith's parents could be facing and how he was handling it all. Dary did most of the talking.

I went through the motions, nodding and answering when I needed to, but I wasn't there, not really. My head was a hundred miles away. It was close to dinner when they got up to leave and Dary hugged me goodbye.

Abbi hugged me just as carefully as Dary did. "I know you need some time, some space," she said, pressing her forehead against the side of my head. Her voice was low enough so only I heard her. "I know this has been hard for you, but it's also been hard for us. Don't forget that. You need us right now." Her voice cracked, and over her shoulder, I saw Dary bow her head. "We need you right now."

I heard the knob turning and I looked over. A shadow was on the other side of the balcony doors. Putting the inhaler aside, my heart skipped a beat. The door opened, and Sebastian came in, closing the door behind him.

Sebastian was dressed for bed, wearing flannel bottoms and a white tank top. He looked good. He always looked good, but I almost didn't want to acknowledge that. Like I shouldn't be able to do that anymore.

Like I'd lost that right.

"I didn't text you," he said, walking over to the bed and sitting down. "I figured you wouldn't answer it."

"Then why did you come over?"

His lips kicked up at the corners. "You know why."

I raised a brow. Before I could respond, he started moving. Turning sideways, he scooted up the bed and shifted onto his back. We were shoulder to shoulder. Hip to hip.

The acute sense of awareness that always accompanied this kind of closeness was there. A shivery wave that rippled over my skin. It didn't… It didn't feel right. That *aware* feeling. Like I shouldn't feel those things after what had happened. It wasn't right.

"What are you doing?" I asked.

"Getting comfortable," he replied, grinning at me. "I plan on being here awhile."

My mouth dropped open. "Not sure if you realize this or not, but I tire out really easily right now. Supposed to be resting—"

"Do you remember when you were eleven and had mono?" he asked suddenly.

I frowned. Of course I remembered. The fever had been the worst part for me. I'd felt like my head was going to explode. I was pretty sure I'd caught it from Dary.

"Our parents wanted us to stay away from each other. Dad was afraid I'd catch it and I'd miss Little League practice." He laughed quietly. "Anyway, you were upset because you were lonely and being all kinds of whiny about it—"

"I wasn't being whiny," I argued. "I was stuck in my bedroom by myself for days, and if I wasn't sleeping, I was bored."

"You were sick and you didn't want to be alone." He paused, waiting for me to look at him. "You wanted me."

My brows lifted as heat hit my face. Was he on drugs? "I didn't want *you*, per se. I just wanted someone—"

"You've always wanted me." He cut me off, his gaze meeting mine. "Not just anyone, but *me*."

Lips parting, I could only stare at him for several seconds. The night of the party came back. Us by the pool. Me thinking he was going to kiss me. Us arguing that night. And I thought about the Monday before that night, at the lake. I'd kissed him, but I hadn't allowed myself to think about any of that, because it didn't seem fair.

"So, you not wanting me here has nothing to do with you being tired. I know why you don't. Or at least I think I understand part of it, and we'll talk about the you-wanting-me part later," he replied, loosely folding his arms across his chest. "But for right now, I want to know how things went with Abbi and Dary."

We were going to talk about the me-wanting-him part later? That was a later I was going to make sure I wasn't around to see.

"I'm not leaving." He nudged my knee with his. "Get talking."

After a few moments, I shifted my gaze to the TV. Deep down, I knew I could make him leave. If I told him I really didn't want him here, he would go. He wouldn't be happy about it, but he'd leave. But as I stared at the TV, I knew I didn't want him to leave. I didn't want to be alone. I wanted my friends.

I wanted him.

"It was good seeing them," I admitted, voice hoarse. "How did you find out they were here? Were you watching the house?"

"Maybe." He chuckled again. "No, they told me today at school that they were coming over and forcing their way in if necessary. They've really missed you, Lena. This past week has been really hard on them."

"I know."

He was quiet for only a moment. "Megan was their friend, too."

Guilt was a snake twisting up my insides. "I know that, too."

"I know you do, but something is going on in your head."

Running my hand over the comforter, feeling like there was so much I wanted to say but didn't know how to. "There's a lot of stuff in my head right now."

"Understandable," he murmured. "There's a lot going on in my head right now. It's weird. Like I'll wake up thinking about something Cody had said to me. Or some dumbass ignorant thing I said to him."

I closed my eyes, feeling my throat burn.

"In class today, someone said something hilarious, and my first thought was I couldn't wait to tell Phillip. That he'd get a kick out of the joke. Then I remembered I couldn't tell him," Sebastian said. "I walked into the lunchroom yesterday looking for you."

I didn't know what to say.

"I miss them, Lena." His shoulder pressed lightly into mine. "I miss you."

Opening my eyes, I let myself lean into him. "I'm here, though."

"Are you really?"

I blinked. "Yeah."

Sebastian was quiet for a long moment. "It's good to talk about them, you know? At least that's what the grief counselors have been saying."

Talking about Megan and the guys hurt like a gunshot blast to the chest, so I couldn't imagine how it felt good.

When I didn't answer, he asked the same question Abbi had: "Do you remember the accident?"

I gave the same answer I'd given the girls. "Only bits and pieces."

He nodded slowly. "Do you… Do you know why you left with them without coming to me?"

A sixth sense told me he wanted to talk to me about something…about something I'd been super avoiding. I wasn't sure how to answer that question. The reasoning now seemed so stupid. So incredibly dumb. But I was tired of saying "I don't know" and exhausted with telling half truths and lies. "You were with Skylar and I…I just didn't want to bother you." When I peeked over at him, he was looking at me like he had no idea what I was talking about. "I didn't see you after she showed up. I didn't want to come looking for you. I figured you guys wanted…private time or something."

An emotion I couldn't quite decipher flickered on his face, and he turned his head. A muscle along his jaw flexed. "Hell," he muttered, thrusting his fingers through his hair. His fingers scrunched. "I don't know why you think Skylar and I needed private time, but I would've appreciated the interruption. I thought you were just having fun."

Under the covers, I crossed my ankles. "Okay."

"No. Seriously." He dropped his hand and his hair flopped back onto his forehead. "Skylar wanted to talk to me about… about getting back together. I spent that entire time with her trying to explain that getting back together wasn't going to happen. She was really upset. Crying and everything."

Surprise shot through me. "You're not back with Skylar?"

"No." He laughed. "When we broke up in the spring, it

was over. Done. Not going back there. Nothing against her, I still care about her, but that's just not going to happen."

There was the part of me, the old part, that wanted to dissect every single word he'd just said. *Everything* he had been saying. That old part of me wanted to figure out if he was telling the truth or downplaying what was happening so he didn't hurt my feelings.

The new part of me didn't do that now.

Sebastian had no reason to lie about this.

"When I was talking to her, I got a text message from Abbi, when she was looking for you and Megan." This time, he scrubbed his hand over his jaw. "Some of the people leaving the party had seen the accident, recognized Chris's SUV and came back to the party, since the road was blocked. That's when I knew something had happened. I tried calling you. Texting you."

The missed calls and texts sat unread and unchecked on my phone.

He exhaled roughly. Several heartbeats passed. "How are you really doing?"

That simple question cut straight through me, wrecked into the walls, opening up a tiny crack. "I don't want to go to school next week," I whispered. "I don't know if I can see everyone when I'm…"

"When you're what?"

When I'm responsible for my friends' deaths.

Thinking those words caused my heart to jump a beat and my throat closed up. I wasn't ready to go back to school. And I wasn't ready to talk about the agony and the pain, and all the *guilt.* I wasn't ready to put those messy, bitter emotions to words. I didn't know how to admit to my friends that I loved, to the boy that I'd been in love with all this time, that I could've stopped what had happened. That I could've done better.

"All right," he said. "We don't have to talk anymore."

A knot formed. "Thank you."

"Things will eventually be better." Reaching between us, he found my left hand and carefully threaded his fingers through mine. "You know how I know?"

"How?" My eyes were getting too heavy to keep open.

He squeezed my fingers. "You left the balcony door unlocked."

CHAPTER SEVENTEEN

Tuesday afternoon I sat in the middle of my bed, staring at my phone. Mom was downstairs, attempting to handle the few accounts she was able to access from home. She'd told me this morning that she had talked to Dad. It was the first time she'd brought him up since he'd been at the hospital.

She'd told me that he was going to make an effort to be more *present*, whatever the hell that meant.

I wasn't expecting anything to be different. Dad would sporadically call and I wouldn't answer. Nearly dying changed a lot of things, but not that.

Glancing at the space on the bed beside me, I thought about last night. I had no idea what time Sebastian had left, because I'd fallen asleep by then. All I knew was that when I woke up this morning, he was gone.

Things will eventually be better.

Would they? When I first woke up this morning, before

the fog of sleep completely cleared, I could almost believe that they would. Until I shifted and pain shot across my chest.

I'd thought that maybe things were better, until I remembered that my friends were dead.

Until I remembered that I could've kept them alive.

Sucking in a sharp breath, I winced as a burning sensation arced across my ribs. I swallowed hard, growing uneasy and restless.

Coach Rogers had called this morning. I hadn't known it was him until Mom brought the phone to me, and at that point there was no way I could turn the call down.

I had taken it with a trembling hand, my stomach knotted in dread. Coach was strict. Girls had been kicked off the team for far less than what I'd been involved in.

I rubbed my hand over my forehead. Coach had asked how I was feeling and I told him I was getting better. He'd asked about my arm, and I said that it could be several weeks before I got the cast removed.

He was up front about my position, and I was surprised when he told me that he expected to see me at the practices and at the games. I was shocked when he said I still had a spot on the team.

That was *not* how I'd expected the call to go.

Coach was going to move in one of the girls from the junior team and play it by ear. I thought I might've said okay.

He didn't ask about Megan or the guys.

Part of me wondered if my mom had said something to him, because how could he not bring up Megan? She was such an important part of the team, better than our captain. Megan would land a spot on a college team.

Would *have*.

Megan would have landed a spot. The call ended with Coach telling me to take care of myself and that he expected to see me next week. When I hung up, Mom took the phone and I just sat, staring at my own phone, knowing there were unopened texts and unheard voice mails. But I couldn't think about those—I could think only about what Coach had said.

He wanted me on the team, but I...I couldn't picture myself doing it. Traveling with the team and sitting on the bench, pretending like I hadn't started playing volleyball because of Megan. Pretending that it was okay that she was no longer there.

My gaze fell to the knee pads in my closet, and I knew right then.

I slipped off the bed and shuffled over to them. I braced my bad arm against my ribs as I bent down and snatched them off the floor. I tossed them into the back of the closet, beyond the books and the jeans. I closed the door and stepped back.

I wouldn't need them again.

Saturday morning Lori sat on the kitchen table, her feet on the seat of a chair. If Mom was home, she'd be losing her mind, but she was out running a thousand errands. Normally Lori didn't come home on the weekends, since it was quite the hike from Radford to Clearbrook, but Mom didn't want me left alone, afraid my lungs would deflate or something.

Two weeks from sustaining a life-threatening injury and, for the most part, my body was starting to feel normal. I was winded easily and my ribs and arm ached nearly every second of the day, but the bruises on my face had faded and my jaw no longer hurt.

And I was alive.

I was currently walking circles around the kitchen table, partly because I was now supposed to be up and moving as much as possible and partly because I was having a problem staying seated. Walking jarred the ribs, but it was the kind of pain I was getting used to.

Lori was peeling an orange and the citrusy scent filled the kitchen. "So, did you know Dad is still in town?"

I stopped, halfway between the fridge and the sink. Mom had mentioned that she'd talked to him, not that he was still in town. I'd assumed he'd gone back to Seattle. "What?"

"Yep." She dropped the peel on a paper towel beside her. "He's staying at one of the hotels that have suites. You know, the kind for, like, extended stays or something."

"How long is he staying?"

A shrug. "Don't know. I'm meeting him for dinner tonight. You should come."

I laughed and immediately regretted it. The laugh hurt. "I'll pass. Thanks."

Lori rolled her eyes as she carved out a slice. "That's not nice."

Walking again, I ignored that comment. "How does he afford to stay in a hotel? That's got to get expensive."

"He's doing okay," she replied. "And he's been saving up money. You'd know that if you actually talked to him."

"Oh, so he's doing well enough to afford to stay in a hotel for an extended time?" Irritated, I stopped at the fridge and grabbed a soda. "That's *swell*."

Lori popped the final piece of orange in her mouth and looked at me. "And Mom isn't doing that bad either."

"It hasn't been easy," I shot back. "You know that."

I walked into the living room and turned on the TV. Easing down on the couch, I started flipping through the channels. Lori followed me into the living room, but before she could sit, there was a knock on the front door.

"I'll get it." She pivoted and disappeared into the small foyer.

It couldn't be Sebastian. He'd come over every night—Every. Night.—since Monday, but he should still be at football practice. Every. Night.

"She's in here," I heard Lori say.

A second later, Dary came through the archway into the living room. "Hey." She waved. "I'm bored."

My lips twitched into a small grin that felt weird, and I realized that I hadn't smiled since…since that Saturday night. "So you decided to come over?"

"Yep." She sat down in the armchair. "I'm so bored I thought I'd come over and—" she squinted at the TV "—watch the Battle of Antietam with you."

Lori snorted as she sat down on the couch. "You're gonna wish you stayed home."

"Not likely." Dary curled her legs under her. "Mom wants to organize closets. You might think I'm exaggerating, but no, I'm not. She was waiting with a *list* when I got home. So, I lied and told her that I had to help you with schoolwork. I walked over here, which, by the way, why is it so damn hot in September?"

"Global warming." Lori picked up the remote and muted the TV. "Where's Abbi?"

I winced. Abbi had stopped by only once since Monday, on Wednesday. She hadn't stayed long, leaving Dary here. She hadn't texted or called.

"She's with her parents," Dary said. "They're doing something today."

I said nothing to that because I knew it was a lie. Her mom always worked Saturdays at the hospital, and the way things had been going for her parents, I doubted they were having a family day.

The banana I ate earlier soured in my stomach. Abbi didn't want to see me and there were so many reasons why she probably felt that way. I couldn't blame her for any of them.

"Are you starting school on Monday or Tuesday?" Dary asked.

"I saw the doc yesterday. He wants me to come back in Monday morning, and if everything checks out fine like he thinks, I'll start on Tuesday."

Dary ran her hand through her short hair. "I bet you're ready to get back to school."

"Not really," I murmured. A ball of dread formed.

She frowned. "Really? I'd be going stir-crazy by now and you actually like school."

I was going a little stir-crazy and I did like school, but school meant I had to face everyone and—

"Everyone is excited to see you," Dary said, obviously reading my hesitation. "So many people have been asking how you're doing. A lot of people have been thinking about you."

I took a sip of my soda as I thought about that card Sebastian had brought me. It was still on my desk, in its brown bag. "It just won't... It won't feel the same without them there." I admitted a tiny truth of what I'd been thinking. Just like I had with Sebastian on Monday night, telling him I didn't want to go back to school.

Dary lowered her gaze and her shoulders rose with a deep breath. "It's not. It's really not, but...it's getting easier."

It was?

She drew in another breath, and when she spoke, her voice shook. "Anyway, are you caught up on schoolwork?"

Welcoming the change of subject, I relaxed. "Pretty much. It's just mostly reading assignments and quick worksheets."

"That's good. At least you don't have to be overwhelmed with trying to get caught up." She rested her elbow on the arm of the chair. "So how are things going with Sebastian?"

Lori snorted yet again. "He practically lives here now."

I shot her a dark look. "No, he doesn't."

"I thought it was bad before," my sister continued, ignoring me. "Like having a damn brother in the house. But now he's here all the time."

Dary laughed.

"You're not even here all the time," I pointed out. "You don't know what you're talking about."

"Isn't it time for you to do your inhaler?" she quipped, grinning.

I rolled my eyes. "I don't even know why you're asking me how things are going with Sebastian."

Dary was the one to make the piglet noise now. "Come on, Lena. Just because I wasn't home for a week doesn't mean

I don't know about the kiss and the argument at the…" She stopped for a second, and I stiffened. She recovered with a shake of her head. "Abbi filled me in."

It was probably a good thing that Abbi wasn't here, because I sort of wanted to smack her upside the back of the head.

"Wait." Lori sat forward, staring at me. "You *kissed* Sebastian?"

I opened my mouth.

"Yeah," Dary answered for me. "At the lake, supposedly."

"About damn time." Lori sat back, grinning. "Oh my God, wait until I see him again. I'm so—"

"Don't say anything to him. Please, Lori. It was a… I don't know. It wasn't supposed to happen. He didn't kiss me. It was just a random thing that kind of happened—"

"Kissing someone is not something that just happens, you know." Lori tilted her head to the side. "Pretty sure you know that."

"Abbi said you two kind of got into it after he threw you in the pool or something? You were supposed to tell her about it later." Dary planted her cheek on her fist. "What did you guys get into it about? And come on, I know you admitted to Abbi and…and Megan that you *like him* like him, and we all already knew that."

"Nothing really." I sighed, eyeing the room for an escape. It felt weird, wrong even, talking about Sebastian after what had happened. But both of them were staring at me and waiting like it didn't feel weird to them at all. "When he threw me in the pool, I thought he was going to kiss me. I got mad and walked away. I was talking to…to Cody," I said, losing my breath at the sharp slice of pain in my chest.

"And he came up, and I don't even know how we started arguing. He said something. I said something back, and then I admitted that I thought he was going to kiss me, but then Skylar came over, and I walked away."

I paused, glancing at Dary. "He told me that he and Skylar aren't back together."

"Doesn't appear to be to me. He doesn't hang with her at school," she said, looking to the ceiling. Her lips pursed. "I've seen her going up to him, though. He doesn't look thrilled, you know? Like he's being polite but is in desperate need of his best friend forever, also known as Lena, to swoop in and rescue him."

She grinned when I shook my head.

"Wait a second. Let's back up a second. You kissed him, right?" Lori asked. "Does Mom know? Because if you think she doesn't know he sneaks into your bedroom at 1:00 a.m., then you got another think coming."

My eyes widened. "She knows about that?"

Lori laughed like she thought I needed to be patted on the head. "I think she has her suspicions."

Oh.

That probably wasn't good.

"You two are going to get married one day and it's going to be so cute it's gross," Dary announced.

"I don't know about that," I protested, lifting my good arm. "Can we not talk about this?"

"I did have another reason for coming over." Dary straightened her glasses. "I was wondering if you wanted to go to the cemetery… I can drive your car." She glanced over at my sister. "Or maybe Lori can drive us?"

I blanched as pressure clamped down on my chest. Go to the cemetery? To see Cody's and Phillip's graves? Megan's and Chris's? The soil would still be disturbed. Grass wouldn't have grown over it.

"I don't know." Lori was watching me. "It's pretty hot outside and that's a long walk at the cemetery. I don't think she's ready for all of that."

Dary appeared to accept the excuse, which was partly true, at least.

She stayed for a couple of hours longer and then left, promising to text me later.

"Thank you," I said to Lori after she'd shut the door. "For the cemetery thing."

She nodded absently, her face pinched. "You aren't ready to do that, and I'm not talking just physically."

I picked up a throw pillow and clutched it to my chest, knowing she was right.

"You won't even talk about Megan or the guys." She walked close to the couch. "You won't talk about the accident or anything. I knew you wouldn't want to go to their graves."

Graves. I hated that word. It was cold and barren.

"You know you've got to eventually." Lori sat next to me and kicked her bare feet up on the coffee table. "You need to. It's closure. Or something."

I nodded. "I know. I just..." A knot twisted deep in my stomach. "Can I ask you something?"

"Sure."

"Do you think what happened is really an accident?"

Her brows knitted. "What do you mean?"

"It's hard to explain but…is it really an accident? I mean, Cody was… He was drinking and driving." I held the pillow close. "If he'd survived, couldn't he be charged with vehicular manslaughter or something?"

"I guess."

"Then how is it really an accident?" And shouldn't I be charged with something because I hadn't been drunk? I didn't voice that. "To me, an accident is something that couldn't be prevented. This could've been."

Lori tipped her head back against the cushion. "I get what you're saying, but I…I don't know what to say. He didn't intend to lose control and wreck. He didn't intend to kill anyone and hurt you, but he did. Actions have consequences, right?"

"So does inaction," I murmured.

She was quiet for a moment. "Mom told me."

I tensed.

A heartbeat passed. "She told me they checked your blood-alcohol level when you came into the hospital, when they did the rest of the tests. The doctors said you weren't drunk. There was nothing in your system."

Closing my eyes, I swallowed hard.

"What happened, Lena?" She twisted toward me, drawing one leg up. "You can talk to me, you know? I'm not going to judge you. It will help you to talk."

I opened my mouth. The desire to tell her was almost overwhelming. But she *would* judge me. She had to.

So I said nothing.

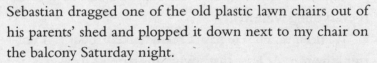

CHAPTER EIGHTEEN

Sebastian dragged one of the old plastic lawn chairs out of his parents' shed and plopped it down next to my chair on the balcony Saturday night.

We were sitting side by side. His feet on the top of the railing, mine on the bottom because it put too much pressure on my ribs to lift them that high.

It had been hot during the day, almost like we were still smack-dab in the middle of August, but at night it had cooled down significantly. That was how the weather was here. One day it was like summer refused to let go, the wind hot and the air humid, and later that night, fall would steadily creep in, bringing with it colder wind and dying leaves, turning the world orange and red. By the end of the month, pumpkins would start popping up on front porches. In two months, talk of Thanksgiving and Christmas would fill the air. Life was ultimately moving on, not at a snail's pace but at a rapid clip that happened so fast it seemed slow.

"Don't you have something more interesting to do tonight?" I asked. He'd shown up about a half an hour ago. A month ago he would have been at Keith's on a Saturday night. Or out at the lake with Phillip and Cody. But he was here, sitting on my balcony.

"Not really."

I shifted the pillow behind me. "I guess there aren't many parties going on right now."

"There are some. Not at Keith's, obviously." He flicked at the bottle of water between his knees. "But this is where I want to be."

My heart swelled in response, but I ignored the pleasant trilling the sensation induced and popped a hole in it. "How is everything with Keith?"

"It's been rough. He hasn't really talked about it. I don't think he can. At least that's what his parents' lawyers have probably advised." He took a drink from his bottle. "I don't know what his parents are going to do. There's talk that Phillip's family is planning to sue Keith's. That they've been in talks with the other families. I wouldn't be surprised if you end up getting a phone call from them."

Watching the leaves fall from the limbs in the night breeze, I shook my head. "I don't want to be a part of that."

"I didn't think you would. I know Keith feels like shit for it. Feels responsible."

I toyed with the cap on my soda. "But is he responsible? I mean, his parents knew about the parties there. We all know that. They never had a problem with it. But they didn't make anyone drive drunk." I stopped, wondering why I was saying any of this. Probably trying to make myself feel better. "I don't know what I'm saying. I'm just thinking out loud."

Truth was, a month ago I never would've even thought about any of this. Going to parties, having a drink or two and leaving—it was just the norm. I never thought this would happen, and I knew how stupid that sounded. How incredibly naive that belief was. How ultimately tragic.

Sebastian didn't respond for a long moment, so I looked over at him. He was staring up at the dark night sky blanketed with stars. "You know what I think?"

"What?" I whispered, almost afraid to know.

He tipped his head in my direction. "I think all of us are responsible."

Turning my head toward him, I stilled and was unable to look away.

"It's just something I've been thinking about a lot lately. I went to that party. I drank and I planned on driving you home. Didn't cross my mind that I would be putting you in danger— putting myself in danger."

"You didn't get drunk, though," I pointed out. "I've never seen you get legit drunk and then try to drive."

"I haven't, but is there really a difference?" he asked. "Two beers? Three? Just because I think I'm fine and I act right doesn't mean I wasn't affected and didn't realize it. Not to sound like a damn commercial, but it only takes a couple of seconds, right?"

"Right," I murmured.

"And I bet Cody thought he was fine. He didn't think for a second that getting behind that wheel would end that way."

He hadn't.

My chest ached and it had nothing to do with my injuries. Cody had believed he was okay to drive. So had Chris and Megan and Phillip.

"He's fine. Come on." Megan took my hand and leaned in, whispering in my ear, "I want chicken nuggets and sweet-and-sour sauce."

Swallowing hard, I let the memory slip away, but the meaning lingered. None of them thought for a second there'd be a problem with Cody driving, because all of them had been drinking. But me? I'd known differently.

But Sebastian was right, in a way. We all were responsible, in varying degrees. We'd all been so incredibly careless, time and time again. It was just no one thought about these kinds of things until they happened, until it was too late. But at the end of the day, I was just as responsible as Cody. Maybe not legally. But definitely morally.

And I didn't know how to live with that.

"Dary texted me earlier."

I raised a brow. "Why? She was over here today."

"I know." Sebastian placed the bottle back between his knees. "But she's worried about you."

"She shouldn't be." I leaned to the side as the twinge in my ribs increased. "I'm fine."

Sebastian laughed softly under his breath. "You're far from being fine, Lena."

"What's that supposed to mean?"

"It means that pretending you're straight in the head doesn't mean you actually are."

Brushing hair back from my face, I watched a star disappear behind clouds. "Are you now thinking about a career in psychology or something?"

He chuckled this time. "Maybe. I think I'm pretty good at it."

I snickered. "Whatever."

He stretched over, caught a strand of my hair and tugged gently. "Are you able to drive to school this week?" he asked. "I was talking to Dad about it, and he said one of the guys he knows at the plant had a collapsed lung. Just one. They didn't want him driving until it was fully healed."

"Yeah, I hadn't gotten that far in my planning yet. I'm hoping they'll be okay with me driving."

"What about the arm, though? It's just your left arm, but add that with the lungs, maybe you shouldn't." He dropped his arm and lifted his gaze skyward. "I live right next door. I can drive you until you're fully healed."

"That's not necessary. I'm sure I'll—"

"I don't know if it's necessary or not, but I want to give you a ride until you're a hundred percent."

I looked over at him. Our eyes met and held. "I'm fine. I can drive."

"Or maybe you're not. Maybe your reflexes are slow because your ribs are killing you. Or maybe you have trouble breathing and an accident happens." He shifted toward me, and even though we were in separate chairs, there was suddenly very little space between us. "I almost lost you once. I don't want that to happen again."

My breath caught and it had nothing to do with the current state of my crappy lungs. "How will I get home, though? Don't you have football practice? I don't have volleyball practice," I added, lifting the arm in a cast. "I'm out."

"I've got almost an hour between when school ends and

practice begins." Sebastian didn't question the whole volleyball thing. And Coach was probably expecting me on Tuesday, but that wasn't going to happen. "I have time to get you home. I want to do it," he added, voice lower. "And why wouldn't I? If this was the other way around, you'd insist on driving me."

He was right, but it would never be the other way around, because he wasn't as stupid as me. Arguing over this was dumb, though. He lived next door. He was still, no matter what, my…my best friend. Though maybe not once he knew about the part I played in the accident.

He did that thing that drove me crazy: biting his lower lip and then letting it go slowly. "There's something we need to talk about."

"Is there?" I was staring at his mouth, thinking about how his lips had felt against mine.

His head tilted to the side. "There are a lot of things we need to talk about."

Yeah.

Things I was sure I didn't want to delve into.

Pulling away, I carefully leaned back in the chair. "I'm getting tired and I—"

"Don't do it," he demanded softly. "Don't shut me out."

My heart dropped. "I'm not shutting you out."

"Yes. You're shutting Abbi and Dary out, and the only reason you haven't completely shut me out is because I'm not letting you."

"You're kind of annoying," I admitted in a mutter.

He dropped his feet onto the floor and placed his bottle by his chair. "I have to say something to you. You don't have to respond. You don't have to tell me anything. All you need to do is listen while I clear something up."

"I'm going to be honest right now," I said, facing him. "I have no idea where you're going with this."

A lopsided smile appeared. "You will in a few moments."

I waited.

His gaze locked on mine. "When did we meet? At six? Seven?"

"Eight," I answered, wondering what that had to do with anything. "We moved into this house when I was eight, and you were outside, in the backyard throwing a football with your dad."

"Yeah, that's right." His lips curved up at the corner. "You were out on this balcony watching me."

I gaped at him. "You saw that?" We'd never talked about that. Why would we? So I never knew he saw me. It had been the next day when he came over, asking if I wanted to ride bikes with him.

"I saw you." He reached over, tapping his finger off my arm. "I also heard your dad telling you to get your butt back in the house and start unpacking. I think you responded by telling him unpacking boxes violated child labor laws."

I couldn't fight the grin. "I might've said something like that."

"That's when I fell in love with you."

Jerking slightly, I blinked once and then twice. "Wh-what?"

His lashes swept down, shielding his eyes in the dim overhead light that was just a bare bulb going bad. "I was caught off guard when you kissed me at the lake."

My eyes widened. What was happening right now?

"I didn't regret it. I didn't dislike it. I just never thought you were...you were into me like that." He laughed again, but this time it was self-conscious, unsure. "Well, that's a lie. Sometimes I wondered. I wish I hadn't freaked out afterward. I wish I kissed you back. I wish... I wish I kissed you at the pool." His shoulders rose and his gaze lifted. "Because I'd been wanting to do that for a while now."

"What?" I repeated dumbly.

Sebastian didn't look away. "I don't know when it happened—when I started seeing you, *really* seeing you. Actually, you know what? That's a bald-faced lie. I do know. I fell in love with you the moment I heard you say something ridiculous to your dad. I just didn't know what that meant—what I was feeling. And it took years for me to figure out what I was feeling meant. It wasn't until you started seeing Andre. That's how I figured it out. I was... Damn, I was *not* happy. I didn't like him. Thought you could do better. Didn't appreciate how he was always touching you."

All I could do was stare at him.

"I fooled myself for a long time. I told myself that I was being so hard on him because you're my best friend. But it wasn't just that. Whenever I'd see him kissing you, I wanted to lay him out cold. When I saw that he was at your house, I wanted to interrupt. Make sure you had no time alone." He laughed once more. "Actually, I did that quite a bit."

Sebastian *had* done that. Many, many times he'd come right through the balcony door unannounced, and sometimes it had been so, so awkward. Andre used to get so mad, especially when Sebastian would plop his butt right down on the bed and not leave.

"But when you broke up with him, it wasn't just relief I felt. Hell no. I was *happy*. When I heard you and Abbi out here talking about breaking up with him, I remember thinking, 'Now's my chance.'"

Everything in me stilled. *Everything*. "But...but you were with Skylar—"

"It's why I broke up with her. She was right about me caring more about my friends than her, but it wasn't the way she thought. It was because I cared more about *you*," he said. "I thought about you the way I should've been thinking about her."

My lips parted.

"But I never believed for a second you felt the same way. I didn't want to risk ruining our friendship." Sebastian leaned close again, his head not very far from mine. "When you kissed me, I... Hell, I panicked. Kind of feel like a coward now. I should've said something to you. I can't go back and change that, but I want you to know that I didn't regret it. I regret not being the one to do it."

Sebastian took in a deep breath. "I wanted to talk to you about this that night. That's why I said I needed to talk to you. And looking back, I should've told Skylar she could wait. God, I wish more than anything I'd done that, because... because I don't think you'd have been in that car. Who knows what would've happened? But I like you, Lena. You know that." There was that self-conscious laugh again. "I... Well, I *really* like you and I wish I had kissed you by that pool. I wish I'd told you how—" he cleared his throat "—how badly I've wanted to kiss you for a long time. How I don't look at you as just one of my friends."

Was this a dream? It had to be, because this felt like one. These were the words I'd lived for what felt like forever waiting to hear.

"I think… I think I know how you feel, but I don't expect you to say anything right now," he said, his eyes finding mine again and searching intently. "I just needed you to know."

I stared at him, unable to fully process what he was saying. I mean, I got it. I did. He was telling me that he'd wanted to kiss me. Had been wanting to. That he *liked me* liked me. And had for a while. I was shocked, stunned into silence. I'd hit the jackpot of fantasies coming true, but now? Now? When I was so undeserving of having what I so badly wanted handed to me on a silver platter? Now, when one of my best friends was dead, and three more friends along with her, because I…I didn't stop them?

I shook my head. "Why…why now? Why would you—" My voice cracked. "Why would you wait until after *that*, after everything that happened, to tell me this?"

"I shouldn't have waited."

"But now is, like, the worst timing in the history of timing." I lowered my feet to the floor and stood, having to put space between us. The abrupt movement caused pain to lance across my ribs. "Really bad timing, Sebastian."

"Or it's the best timing," he fired back, watching me walk around the chair. "And you know what? Waiting is too risky. There's no bad time to tell someone you love them."

Sebastian loved me. Like *loved me* loved me? There was no way. This wasn't happening now. Not when it should've happened *before*.

I started backing up toward my door as he rose and followed. My back pressed against the door. I reached behind me but froze as he stalked around the chair.

Stopping in front of me, he planted a hand on the space beside my head. "The only better time to have told you this was the moment I realized I felt this way," he said, lowering his head to mine. My heart turned into a jackhammer. "I've had a million moments since then."

"I can't even process this right now." My voice was thick, my eyes wide as I stared up at him.

"You don't have to. I just needed to get it out there." Sebastian leaned over, pressing his mouth to my temple. My heart thundered as I closed my eyes. "What does waiting do? None of us are promised a tomorrow. We learned that, didn't we? We don't always get a later." He kissed my temple again, then pulled back, his eyes finding mine. "I'm done living like we do."

CHAPTER NINETEEN

Normally I would've been on the phone with my friends immediately. The conversation with Sebastian was a five-alarm-fire-level emergency that I needed to hash out until I was just repeating myself over and over again, talking in circles.

But things weren't normal anymore.

I wanted to call Abbi and Dary. I'd almost done it Sunday morning, but as I'd stared at my phone until my vision blurred, I couldn't get up the nerve to do so. It didn't feel like something I should do. I seriously doubted they wanted to hear about my boy drama, or whatever it was that had gone down with Sebastian.

Sitting on my bed Monday night, nibbling on my fingernail like it was dinnertime, I had other things on my mind.

I'd been cleared to return to school tomorrow. There was no fighting it, even though I knew if I told my mom I wasn't ready, she would contact the school. But that would mean she'd call off work. There was no way she was going to leave me home alone right now, and Lori was back at Radford. That did leave my father, wherever he was, but she knew I wouldn't be okay with that. Her boss was being amazing with all of this, but I didn't want to put her job in jeopardy. So I would be going to school tomorrow. I would be seeing everyone. There was no more hiding.

Sebastian would drive me tomorrow morning and, oh God, I didn't want to think about him, because when I did, I thought about what he'd said Saturday night.

That's when I fell in love with you.

My heart skipped a beat.

I can't think about that. I tried to push what Sebastian said aside, but that was as successful as walking down the stairs with my ankles tied together. A shiver curled down my spine. I turned to stare at the world map above my desk. Several years ago, I'd taken a blue marker and circled all the places I wanted to visit one day. Sebastian had grabbed a red marker and joined in. A lot of the places were the same. We were thirteen or fourteen when we did that.

He'd been in love with me this whole time?

I squeezed my eyes shut and, for a few seconds, just for a couple of heartbeats, let those words he'd spoken seep through my skin, invade my muscles and tattoo my bones. My right hand curled against the center of my chest and my stomach dipped like I was on a roller coaster. In those seconds, I envisioned what it was supposed to be—what my life was supposed to be like.

Sebastian would tell me he loved me. We'd kiss, this time deeper and stronger than before. I'd kiss him back, and maybe we'd get caught up in the moment. Maybe things would go further, and it would be glorious and perfect. We'd go out on dates. Hold hands at school. Travel to parties together. Everyone would smile and whisper "About time" to one another. We wouldn't be able to keep our hands off one another and—

Reaching up, I swept my hand under my eyes, wiping away the wetness gathering on my cheeks. I scooted to the end of my bed and placed my feet on the floor. A few seconds passed and then I opened my eyes and stood. A sharp stab of pain shot out across my rib cage, snapping me back to reality. I drew in a shuddering breath.

Guilt settled heavily in my chest.

How could I even think about this kind of stuff? It felt so, I don't know, self-absorbed. Wrong. I didn't know how I was supposed to feel, how I was supposed to move on from this point, but I knew I didn't deserve something good like this.

Not now.

Maybe a hundred tomorrows from now.

But not now.

"Are you sure you're ready to do this today?"

I looked up from the kitchen table, brushing the crumbs from my Pop-Tart off the tips of my fingers. I hadn't been hungry but had forced myself to eat. The sugary breakfast coated my throat like sawdust. "Yeah."

Mom stood by the sink, dressed for work in a light blue blouse and black slacks. Everything about her was well manicured on the surface, but her eyes were weary. "If for whatever reason you start to feel ill or worn-out, you call me immediately. I will come and get you."

"I'm going to be fine." I stood, crumpled up the paper towel and tossed it in the trash. "Don't spend all day worrying about me."

"I'm your mom. It's kind of my job to do so."

A faint smile formed on my lips. "But I'm going to be okay. The doctor said I was healing and he doesn't expect there to be a problem."

"I know. I was there. But he also warned that up to fifty percent of people who've suffered a collapsed lung can have a reoccurrence."

"Mom." I sighed, but before I could say anything else, there was a knock on the front door. A second later, we heard it open. Heart thumping heavily, I turned toward the entryway.

"Hey," Sebastian called out. "It's me."

Mom smiled like the sun had just entered the house. Footsteps neared the kitchen and then Sebastian was standing in the doorway, hair damp and the worn cotton shirt clinging to his broad shoulders.

He looked good, really nice.

I smoothed my hands across my jeans, suddenly nervous for reasons that had nothing to do with going to school. Sebastian had come over on Sunday and hadn't mentioned the conversation we had Saturday night, but it was there when he looked at me, in every brush of his hand or press of his leg against mine.

"Mornin'," he said, striding into the kitchen. "You about ready?"

Nodding, I told myself to pull it together.

"I want you to do me a favor," Mom said as he walked

over to where I stood somewhat petrified in front of the sink. "Keep an eye on Lena."

"Mom," I groaned this time.

She ignored me. "I don't want her overtaxing herself. This is going to be a long day for her."

My eyes widened slightly as he draped his arm over my shoulders. The weight was minimal and he'd done it a million times before, but I shivered in response.

Sebastian felt it. I knew he did, because that half grin formed as he looked down at me. "Don't worry, Ms. Wise. My eyes will be glued to her."

Oh dear.

The urge to lean into Sebastian, to press my cheek to his chest, was hard to resist, but I stepped out from him and picked up my backpack. Slinging it on my shoulder did not feel good, and I needed to remember that next time. "We better get going so we're not late."

"The world is your oyster." Sebastian grabbed the armful of books that I would need to stash in my locker.

Mom followed us out the front door, stopping me before I went down the steps. She clasped my cheeks. "I love you," she whispered fervently. "Today is going to be a long day." Her eyes searched mine. "For a lot of reasons."

"I know." That burning knot of hysterical tears was back.

Slipping her hands off my cheeks, she turned and looked up at Sebastian. "I'm handing her over to you."

Handing me over? I made a face, but neither of them saw me.

"I got her," he promised, and there was a heavy meaning to those words, as if he was staking some sort of claim, accepting unspoken responsibility.

"Thank you," Mom said, patting his shoulder.

I barely stopped myself from rolling my eyes as I hit the walkway. "We should get going," I reiterated.

Chuckling under his breath, Sebastian came down the steps to join me. I waved goodbye to Mom and started across the driveway, through the tall hedges, toward Sebastian's house.

"You know," I said, shifting the bag on my shoulder, "you don't 'got' me, whatever that means."

Sebastian's long-legged pace put him in front of me. "Yeah, I do." He transferred his load to his other arm, opened the Jeep's back door and placed the books inside. "I've had you for longer than I realized."

My lips pursed as I glared at him. "I don't even know what to say to that."

"You don't have to say anything." His fingers slipped under the strap of my bag. I sucked in a soft breath as he lifted it off my shoulder. "You look good today."

Not expecting that, I blinked and looked down at myself. I was wearing an old shirt, jeans and flip-flops that were days from coming apart. "Really?"

"Yeah." He placed my bag in the back and closed the door. Facing me once more, he stepped out until his feet were nearly touching mine. I craned my head back as he looked down. "No bruises."

I almost didn't get what he was saying.

"They'd faded for the most part, but there was a little bit of it that was here." His thumb brushed along the left side of my jaw, causing my breath to hitch. His deep midnight-blue eyes flicked to mine. "It's gone now."

"It is?" I managed to say.

"Yeah." His thumb traveled the line of my jaw. "It was just a faint bluish color, but I saw it."

I shuddered.

His thumb skimmed my chin and coasted along my lower lip. His head lowered.

"Today is going to be rough," he rasped out, voice deeper than normal. "You're going to tire out physically..." His thumb made another sweep. "It's going to wear you out emotionally. The first day for me... Yeah, there are no words."

Everything inside me, every cell and muscle, tightened and loosened at once. It was hard to pay attention to what he was saying when he was touching me like this. Touching me in a way he never had before. In the way I'd always wanted from him.

"Sounds...sounds like you've been reading up on psychology again," I forced out, sounding breathless.

His lips kicked up on one side. "Or I've been talking and listening."

I tilted my head to the side, brows fitting together. I started to ask what that meant, but he suddenly pressed his lips to the corner of mine. It was brief—briefer than the one kiss at the lake—but it rocked me straight to the core.

"What are you doing?" I gasped out.

Stepping back, his heavy hooded gaze swept over me. "Doing what I said I was going to do."

A note was waiting for me the moment I walked into homeroom. I didn't even make it to my seat before the teacher waved me over and handed me a slip. A sympathetic look was etched into her heavily lined face. "You need to go to the front office, sweetie."

Sweetie? Pretty sure I'd never been called that in my entire high school career, but I nodded, took my note and walked right back out of class.

I kept my head down—when I walked in and out, when I was out in the hall, and even at my locker, where Sebastian had helped unload my books and get everything situated before kissing me *again*, on my cheek this time, and leaving to head to his class.

Everyone was staring, they were whispering, and when I made the mistake of looking up as I closed my locker door, a girl who'd never spoken to me my entire life had rushed up to my side, awkwardly hugged me and spewed out this rambling paragraph about how sorry she was for me and how glad she was that I was okay. I had no idea what her name was. I was pretty sure she'd had no idea who I was before the accident.

I'd been left standing there, utterly confused.

Now the note crinkled in my hand as I made my way to the front of the school and pushed open the double glass doors of the main office. One of the administrative volunteers was at the front desk, an older lady who had the brightest pink lipstick I'd ever seen on a person.

I approached the desk. "I was told to come to the office. My name is Lena Wise."

"Oh." Recognition flared in the rheumy eyes. "You stay right there and I'll let them know you're here."

Them? I stepped back from the counter, tensing. What was going on? I watched her shuffle down the narrow hallway that led to all the offices. I didn't have long to wait. A tall silver-haired man came out just a few moments later.

"Ms. Wise?" He walked up to me, extending his hand. "I'm Dr. Perry. I'm with the team that has been brought in due to the recent events."

Oh.

Oh, *dammit.*

"Let's step back and chat for a few minutes, okay?" He moved aside, waiting. Not like I had much of a choice.

Swallowing a sigh, I trudged down the hall and followed Dr. Perry into one of the meeting rooms usually reserved for parent meetings. The kind filled with stupid motivational posters of kittens clinging to ropes, talking about teamwork.

I dropped my bag on the floor and eased into the hard plastic chair as he walked around the desk to sit across from me. An obvious Father's Day gift—a mug proclaiming his greatness—sat on the desk next to a closed file that had my name scribbled along the tab.

"May I call you Lena?" he asked.

I nodded, shoving my hands between my knees. That didn't feel good on my arm, so I pulled my arm up and laid it on the table.

"Perfect." He smiled faintly. "As I said, my name is Dr. Perry. I have my own practice, but I work for the school district, brought in as needed in certain circumstances where staff may be overwhelmed by the need for counselors." He fired off credentials at that point, and they were impressive. Undergrad at Penn State. Grad school at Brown University. A ton of certifications that were like a different language to me. Then the conversation turned to me. "How are you feeling about starting school?"

"Okay," I answered, crossing my ankles. "I'm…I'm ready."

He rested an arm on the table. "It has to be tough missing nearly two weeks and dealing with the deaths of your friends."

I jolted at the unexpected bluntness. He was the first to just put it out there like that. "I… It's been…" I blinked. "It's been tough."

"I can imagine. The deaths of four young, bright people who had their entire futures ahead of them is a very hard thing to grasp, to fully comprehend." His brown eyes were sharp as he spoke. "And it's more difficult for you. You were in the car with them. You were seriously injured, and according to your file, these injuries will affect volleyball? A lot has happened."

Tensing, I winced as pain shot across my ribs. I glanced at the door, debating on making a run for it.

"We're not going to go there today," he said softly. "You can relax."

My gaze shot back to him. "Today?"

"We're going to meet three times a week for the next month," he announced, picking up his Greatest Dad Ever mug. "I'm not sure if your mother mentioned that to you."

Mom had *so* failed to mention this part. Too irritated to speak, I crossed my arms over my stomach.

"Typically our sessions will be on Monday, Wednesday and Friday. Today is a little different, but we'll get together tomorrow and get on schedule."

Three days a week? Oh my *God*. I exhaled roughly as I looked up at the ceiling. "I don't think this is necessary."

He sipped his coffee. "It's necessary and you're not the only one that our team has been meeting with. You're not alone in this."

My gaze darted to him, and I wanted to ask who else he was meeting with. Was it Sebastian? That would explain why he was so incredibly on point with some of the stuff he'd been saying.

I didn't ask, because I figured he couldn't answer that.

"No one is going to judge you for meeting with me."

I wasn't so sure about that, since this was high school, after all, and everyone judged everyone for everything.

"And this is needed, Lena. You may not feel like it, and at first it may feel like it's doing more harm than good." His gaze was unwavering. "You got some stuff in there you're going to need to get out."

Clamping my jaw shut, I didn't say anything.

He studied me a moment, and I had this unnerving sensation that he saw right into me, gazing upon the *stuff* I didn't want to speak out loud.

"The guilt of living when everyone else has died is a heavy weight to carry, Lena, all on its own. Survivor's guilt is no joke. You're never going to truly get rid of that burden, but we can lessen it. We can make it bearable."

I exhaled softly. "How?"

"I know it doesn't sound possible now, but your life is still going to go on. You'll have tomorrow. Next week. Next month. Next year. You will eventually move past this."

I didn't see how that was possible. "I...I didn't expect this to happen," I whispered, briefly squeezing my eyes shut. "I know how stupid that sounds, but I never thought this would happen."

"It's not stupid, because no one ever does. No one ever thinks it will be them." When he paused, I knew right then he knew. *He knew.* My gaze dropped to the file in front of him, and my heart started racing. Had he spoken to the police? My mom? And when he continued, I wanted to get up and run from the room, but I was rooted to the chair.

"I know what happened."

CHAPTER TWENTY

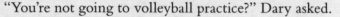

"You're not going to volleyball practice?" Dary asked.

"Not today." I didn't elaborate beyond that. Coach had caught me just after lunch, when I was at my locker. He'd asked if I would be at practice, and I told him that I still tired easily and my mom wanted me home.

That wasn't really a lie.

Coach then told me he expected to see me at practice next week, and I nodded. I had plenty of opportunity to tell him that I wasn't coming back, but I pushed it off to another day.

In other words, I chickened out.

Sebastian walked several feet ahead in the hallway outside the gym, his backpack slung over his shoulder, mine dangling from his fingertips.

"Not a bad view," Dary admitted to me in a whisper.

A tired smile tugged at my lips. There was no way I could deny that, but what I really wanted to do was crawl into bed and nap. I was drained.

On the other side of Dary, Abbi's fingers were flying across the screen of her phone. "He's being a real helpful guy, isn't he?"

Surprised, I looked over at her. Abbi hadn't been very talkative. Not in Chem or at lunch. Everyone else had been chatting. Like the girl in the morning, so many people had approached me throughout the day. I got so many hugs, so many well-wishes from people I barely knew. There were others who didn't approach me. Jessica and her friends hadn't, but I guess she wouldn't, since she'd been dating Cody. Skylar hadn't looked in my direction during class earlier.

But I got the distinct impression Abbi wasn't exactly thrilled with me, and there could be a ton of reasons for that. "Yeah, he's been really...helpful."

"Is that what they're calling it nowadays?" Dary joked. "When boys are into you, they're helpful?"

"That actually sounds like a nice way of putting it." Abbi's gaze was on Sebastian's back. "Has something changed between you two?"

I opened my mouth, about to tell them what Sebastian had told me, but I stopped. I was sure they didn't want to hear it.

Abbi's lips pursed as we stepped out the double doors. The sky was overcast, and the scent of rain lingered in the air.

Eyes wide, Dary glanced between us. "I was thinking maybe we could meet up for something to eat later? Like we...we used to do."

Like we used to with Megan.

"I don't know," I said hoarsely. "I have a lot of work to catch up on."

Abbi's half smile was bitter and her words sharp as we crossed into the parking lot. "Of course."

My gaze shot to her as my stomach dipped, and Abbi sighed. "Maybe next week you'll be better caught up?" she asked.

I nodded and replied with a quiet "Sure."

"Text you guys later." Dary quickly kissed my cheek and then Abbi's before darting off toward where she was parked.

Up ahead, Sebastian looked over his shoulder at me. He was almost near his Jeep and I knew he didn't have a ton of time, but I had to talk to Abbi. The question was bubbling up. I knew I needed to just keep my mouth shut, but I couldn't.

I stopped, angling my body toward Abbi's. "Can we talk for a second?"

Her brows rose as she slowly lifted her gaze from her phone. Her stare wasn't hostile, but it wasn't exactly friendly. There was a wall between us. "What's up?"

Drawing in a shallow breath, I asked, "Are you...mad at me?"

Abbi lowered her phone as she tilted her head to the side. For a moment, I didn't think she was going to answer. "Honestly?"

My heart turned over heavily. "We've always been honest with one another."

She looked up at the fat clouds and gave a shake of her head. "Let me ask you a question."

"Okay."

"What's going on with you and him?" She jerked her chin in Sebastian's direction.

"Nothing," I answered quickly. "He's just helping me out."

"Really? That's what you're going to say?" Her hand tightened on the strap of her bag. "Because I know he's not just helping you out."

"He's—"

"He told Skylar that he was into you," she interrupted, dark eyes hard.

I blinked. "He said *what*?"

"Skylar told Daniela that he admitted to liking you and that is why they broke up last spring," she explained, shifting her weight from one foot to the next. "That he wasn't getting back with her, because he couldn't do that when he had feelings for you. So are you telling me that you have no idea? After all this time you've been obsessed with him on the down low, you don't know he feels this way about you? That he hasn't been up front with you?"

"I…" I stepped back, my gaze finding Sebastian. He was tossing my bag in the back seat.

"I cannot believe you wouldn't tell me about that, especially since I know how you've felt about him. How upset you were when you kissed him and he seemed like he wasn't interested in that," she said, her voice cracking slightly. "I'm one of your closest friends and I'm *still* here. I'm *still* alive and you haven't told me about this—about something that I know is important."

Oh my God. My entire body jerked. I had not expected the conversation to be about this. "I just didn't want to talk about it. I mean, I did. I wanted to call you and Dary the moment Sebastian told me how he felt, but I haven't really been able to process it. What he said came out of nowhere and I don't even know if he really feels that way or if it's because of…because of everything that happened," I admitted in a rush. "And after what happened, it doesn't feel right talking about Sebastian like nothing happened."

"That's the thing, Lena. What happened didn't just happen to you. Yeah, you were in that car, and God only knows what you saw and went through. I have no idea. You know why? Because you won't talk to me about it. You won't talk to Dary—"

"I just came back to school." I swallowed against the feeling of razors in my throat. "It's only been—"

"It's been two weeks and three days since the accident. I know," Abbi shot back, her chest rising and falling heavily. "I know exactly how many days since Megan, Cody, Phillip and Chris have died. I know exactly how many days have passed since I thought you were going to die, too."

I sucked in a sharp breath. "Abbi—"

Her voice wavered as she said, "Do you realize that? That all of us thought you were also dead in that car? Or that you were going to die like Cody had in the hospital? That me and Dary and Sebastian—" she flung her arm out in his direction "—believed that? And then, when we find out you're alive, we hear you don't even want to see us?"

Tears blurred my eyes. "I'm sorry," I whispered, having no idea what else to say. "I'm sorry. My head… It's just—"

Abbi held up her hand. "A part of me can even look past you not wanting to talk. Can even understand your reluctance to talk about normal things. And I'm sorry. I'm not trying to be a bitch. I get that you've been through a lot. So have I. So have Dary and Sebastian and Keith and everyone at this damn school, but what I don't—" She closed her hand into a fist and looked skyward, counting to five under her breath. "What I don't understand is how you got in that car, Lena. How Cody could be that drunk and you still got into that car. You weren't drunk. I was with you right before you left and you weren't drunk, but you still got into that car and you let Cody drive."

I drew back as if I'd been smacked. I didn't know what to say at first and then the shock gave way to anger—red, burning-hot anger that erupted inside me like a volcano. "You and Megan got in the car with Chris and came to that party and you all thought he was messed up. You—"

"We thought he was on something. We didn't know definitely," she said, nostrils flaring. "And he didn't drive off the road and kill four people, did he? No."

My mouth dropped open. How could I respond to that? She was right, but it was also so damn wrong, because she was lucky—so lucky—that she was standing where she was and I was existing where I was.

"Hey, is everything okay here?" Sebastian appeared at our sides. His hand landed on the small of my back as his gaze focused on Abbi. His jaw was hard, stare unflinching.

"Yeah." Abbi breathed in deeply. "Everything is fine. I'll see you guys later."

Shoulders tensed, I watched her wheel around and stalk off toward where she was parked. Abbi had lied.

Nothing was fine.

When I got home, my phone was ringing from my backpack. I slipped the bag around, dug out the phone and saw that it was Dad.

"No way," I murmured, silencing the call. I didn't have the brainpower for that.

I dragged myself upstairs and spent the next hour or so working on homework, which meant I didn't get a lot done, because all I could think about was what Abbi and Dr. Perry had said. When Mom came home, I forced myself to go downstairs. She was just putting her purse on the table when I shuffled into the kitchen.

"How was school?"

"Okay." I sat down at the table. "Would've been better if I had a heads-up about having to meet with a psychologist at school."

Mom stripped off her blazer. "I didn't mention that because I had a feeling you'd get upset and I didn't want you to feel that way before you went back. Today was tough enough."

"I wish you'd told me so I would've been prepared."

She came around the table and sat in the chair beside me. "The school contacted me last week about the grief counselors, and I thought it was a good idea."

"I'm not so sure about that," I muttered.

Mom smiled faintly. "There are things you need to talk about that I wish you'd talk about with me but might be easier with someone else." She paused. "At least that is what Dr. Perry said."

Rubbing my brow, I closed my eyes. "Did you… Did you tell him what we talked about with the police?"

"I told him everything he needed to know," she answered. Her fingers folded over my left hand. "Everything you need to talk about."

I jerked my arm back and stood, latching on to the surge

of anger I'd felt earlier when I spoke to Abbi. "I don't want to talk about it. Why doesn't anyone understand that? Respect that?"

Mom looked up at me. "Because respect doesn't always mean doing what is right."

"What?" I spun around and grabbed my bag. "That doesn't even make sense." Turning away, I headed for the stairs in the hall, prepared to stomp my way all the way upstairs. "That really makes no sense whatsoever."

"Lena."

I didn't want to stop, but I did at the bottom of the stairs. "What?"

"I'm not mad at you."

My spine locked up.

Mom stood under the archway. The thin, well-worn blue blouse stretched at her shoulders as she crossed her arms. I thought about what Lori said about Mom doing okay since Dad left. If that were so true, then she'd be able to afford a new shirt even though she took extreme care of the old ones.

"I was angry at first. Relieved that you were alive and going to be okay, but angry because you made a bad decision. But I'm no longer angry. I'm upset because of what has happened and what you've had to go through, but I'm not mad at you."

Staring at her, I couldn't believe she was saying that. How could she not be mad?

She drew in a deep breath. "I just want you to know that. I think you need to know that."

I didn't know what to say. My knees felt like they were

going to cave. Mom wasn't angry, but it didn't feel right. She should still be pissed at me.

No consequences.

I hurried up the steps before she said anything else. My bedroom door slammed shut behind me. I holed myself up in the room, pretending to focus on homework and coming downstairs only for dinner because I smelled fried chicken.

There was no way I was going to turn down fried chicken.

It was a little after seven when I changed into sleep shorts and an old tank top. Dragging a quilt over my legs, I fully intended to get back to the school stuff, but I dozed off without even cracking my History textbook open. It was a restless nap, one where I woke every fifteen minutes or so, but the last time I peeled my eyes open, I heard a door close. I turned my head toward the balcony. A surprising burst of chilly air rolled across the bed.

Sebastian entered my room without a word.

Groaning, I pulled a hand out from the quilt and rubbed the side of my face. "You know, what you're doing is kind of like breaking and entering."

"Nah, I don't think so." He sat down on the side of the bed. "I'm actually just being courteous."

I lowered my hand, frowning at him. "How so?"

"You don't have to get up and open the door." He winked, and I hated that it was sexy. "I am only ever thinking of you."

Rolling my eyes, I shifted so my legs were pointing toward him. "Whatever. Maybe I don't want to see you."

"You could've just locked the door," he pointed out. "If you don't want to see me, that's all you have to do."

I could've. But I hadn't, because I wanted him to visit. I

wanted him to be here even though I shouldn't, but I wasn't going to admit to it. "You're impeding on my freedoms."

Sebastian tipped his head back and laughed. Loudly. My eyes widened.

"Shh." My head swiveled toward my closed door. "My mom will hear you."

"Pretty sure your mom knows I'm here every night."

That was pretty much what Lori had said. "But I doubt she knows you stay, like, forever."

"Probably not." He moved, stretching out on the bed, his head on the pillows beside mine. "Were you sleeping already? It's only nine."

"I was tired. Today was…" I trailed off. How in the hell did I describe today?

"It was what?" When I didn't answer immediately, he persisted. "It was like what, Lena?"

I sighed heavily, loudly and obnoxiously. "It was rough. I feel like I'm ninety years old. I needed a nap by third period. My ribs ached all day, and I couldn't take the pills the doc gave me, because I would've passed right out."

"And?" he asked when I went silent.

"And…it was just hard."

Sebastian didn't say anything, and I knew he was waiting for me to continue. Several moments passed and I tried again. "I was supposed to have Creative Writing with Megan. It was…" I swallowed hard. "Not having her in the class or at lunch was weird. I kept waiting for her to sit down at the table. Not going to practice felt wrong. Like I was forgetting something all evening."

"Same with the guys." Sebastian crossed his arms loosely.

"I expect to hear Chris throwing weights in the weight room. Phillip giving everyone a hard time. Cody standing next to me at practice."

There was just so...so much loss, so many things that would never happen again. I ran my finger along the edge of my cast as I let out a shaky breath. "I had to meet with one of the grief counselors."

"So did I," he replied. "I think half the senior class did."

I slid him a look. "I have to meet with that guy three times a week."

There wasn't a flicker of judgment on his face. "That will probably be good."

I wasn't so sure of that. "Did you talk with them? Like really talk?"

He was still for a moment and then nodded. "Yeah. It helped." His gaze met mine. "It will help you."

Except Sebastian didn't have the kind of guilt I needed to talk about.

"What was going on with you and Abbi after school?" he asked, rolling onto his side so he was facing me.

My shoulders slumped. The familiar crawl of tears was making its way up my throat. "Nothing."

"That wasn't nothing that I walked up on," he denied. "Looked like you two were getting heated with one another." Sebastian lifted his arm and gently curled his fingers around my chin. He turned my head toward his. "Talk to me, Lena."

My gaze dropped as the feeling of his fingers seeped into my skin. "She's...she's mad at me."

"Why?" he asked, sliding his fingers off my chin. They traveled along my jaw, sending a shiver down my spine.

"Because I've...I've shut her out," I admitted, closing my eyes. His hand was still on the move, fingers sifting through my hair. "I haven't talked to her." It wasn't the only reason why she was mad, but it was the only reason I could cop to, especially when he was touching me. "I didn't mean to. It's just... I feel responsible."

His hand stilled. "Lena, you're not responsible. You didn't get behind that wheel."

God, he didn't know. He didn't have a clue. I started to turn away, but his hand tightened. My eyes opened. His hand slipped from my neck, falling in the scant space between our bodies.

Sebastian was on his side next to me, slightly raised on his elbow so his body almost hovered over mine. There was something wholly intimate about our positions, like we'd done it a hundred times. And we had, but what he admitted Saturday night had changed things. This wasn't just two best friends lying in bed beside one another. He wasn't just the boy next door anymore. We couldn't go back to that no matter how we moved forward, and even though it was what I'd wanted for so long, it was terrifying.

"Lena," he whispered my name like it was some kind of benediction.

"I don't want to talk anymore," I said. "I...I want you here, but I don't want to talk."

Understanding flared. The look in his eyes changed, switching from concern to something wilder, sharper. He bit down on that bottom lip. Everything in the room changed in an instant. It was that extreme. One moment I felt like

I was on the verge of losing it and now I was standing on a totally different cliff.

He said he loved me—was *in* love with me.

And I'd been in love with him since…since forever.

I didn't feel like I deserved that. Like I'd earned this opportunity or second chance. That I should be experiencing the quickening in my breath or the sudden heat that swept over my skin and flooded my senses.

And maybe he didn't mean he loved me in that beautiful, endless way I read about in the books littering my room. The kind of love that was like a chain connecting two souls, an unbreakable bond that prevailed over the worst kind of circumstances, the most horrific decisions. He obviously thought he did, but people believed and felt all kinds of crazy things in the face of loss, but those feelings drifted away and lessened once life returned to normal and the pain of loss faded.

But right now, I didn't want to acknowledge any of that or what led us to this point where things were no longer the same between us. I didn't want to think. I just wanted to explore the heat building low in my stomach, the breathlessness in my chest that had nothing to do with my lungs or ribs.

Maybe it was going back to school today. Or it was the unexpected talk with Dr. Perry and knowing that he knew. It could've been the confrontation with Abbi and facing the fact that out of everyone, she knew I left that party…that party sober enough to…to *fucking* know better. It could've been the talk with Mom.

Maybe it was because Sebastian had said he loved me.

It was probably all those things rolled into one wrecking

ball of a mess, but couldn't I…couldn't I just, I don't know, pretend for a little bit? Play out the fantasy in my head? My pulse was all over the place as my gaze tracked over the sharp angle of his cheekbones, down to the scar in his upper lip.

I lifted my hand but stopped inches from touching him.

A small smile curled the corners of his lips up. "You can touch me if you want. You don't even have to ask."

I wanted to touch him, so very badly, but I hesitated. Touching him wasn't pretending, and how would I come back from *that*?

His chest rose with a deep breath. "I would love for you to touch me."

My breath caught.

Tentatively, I splayed my fingers across his cheek. A jolt of exhilaration rushed me when I felt the tremor that rocked his strong body. His jaw was almost smooth under my palm with just the hint of stubble. I slid my hand down, sliding my thumb along his lower lip. His sharp intake of breath elicited a shudder. He closed his eyes when I followed the curve of his upper lip, feeling the indent of his scar.

All these years, and I'd never touched him like this. Ever. I was lost a little in the moment, in the right now, as I coasted my hand down his throat. My fingers brushed over his pulse and I could feel it beating as wildly as mine.

I kept going.

Flattening my hand over his chest. He made this sound, this low gravelly groan that was part growl, and it was like taking a match to gasoline. A fire started. Emboldened, I went lower, following the taut ripples and planes. His muscles were hard, clearly defined like I always knew they were, like I'd always seen and only ever accidentally touched briefly.

But this wasn't brief.

I took my sweet time, tracing just a finger over his abs and then two fingers, mapping them out, committing them to memory.

I kept going.

My fingers drifted around his navel and lower, reaching the band on the flannel bottoms he was wearing. His body jerked again, bringing him closer. His thigh pressed against the side of mine.

This isn't right.

I shouldn't get to do this, but knowing that didn't stop me. Slowly, I lifted my gaze to his.

His eyes were blue as the deepest seas I'd never seen in real life but had circled on that map above my desk. Somehow our faces had gotten closer and closer during my exploration. Our breaths mingled together.

I closed the distance.

The contact of my mouth against his was just as shocking and electrifying as it had been the first time, maybe even stronger now. It was just the sweetest, gentlest of pressures. Only my mouth moving against his, and then his hand was on the nape of my neck.

I made a sound I'd never heard myself make before, opening my mouth to him, and whatever control Sebastian had, whatever was holding him back, snapped. Sebastian kissed me, *really* kissed me. My heart threatened to explode. His tongue slipped in. He tasted of mint and *him*. My hand moved to his hip and flexed, urging him closer, but he couldn't get closer. Not with my sore ribs and the bum arm.

But he kissed me, drank from my lips and mouth and my sighs. And he moved down, nipping at my lower lip, drawing out a moan, and he kissed his way down my throat when I kicked my head back, giving him more access. He licked and sucked, paying special attention to this spot just below my ear that had my toes curling and my hips twitching restlessly. Then he was devouring my lips once more, our tongues tangling and the only sound in the room was our panting breaths.

I had no idea how long we kissed. It went on for forever, and there was no faking or pretending each time we dived back into each other, wanting and silently begging for more. Friends did *not* kiss friends like this. They didn't clutch at one another like we were, my fingers digging into his hip and side, his hand a firm hold on my neck, unwilling to let me go even though I wasn't running.

And still, we kissed and kissed.

When his mouth finally lifted from mine, I pressed my forehead into his shoulder. Breathing heavily, I curled my fingers into his shirt. For what felt like an eternity, neither of us moved and then he shifted back down on his side, curling his hand over my hip. His hand moved, drifted up and down my back in long, smoothing strokes, and his breath danced warmly on my cheek.

And we didn't talk the rest of the night.

CHAPTER TWENTY-ONE

I stared at the stupid poster on the wall. It was a picture of skydivers holding hands and underneath in large print was one word: TEAMWORK.

Only a high school would have a poster of people willingly jumping out of planes as an example of teamwork. That wasn't the kind of team I'd want to be a part of.

Dr. Perry was waiting. He'd asked me a question. Like he'd done last Wednesday and Friday, and it was now Monday, the start of my second week back, and nothing and everything had changed.

This week's question was different from last week's. Then he'd just really focused on how I was adapting to being back at school and when I was planning to start going to volleyball practice even though I couldn't do anything. I'd dodged that last question, just like I dodged Coach Rogers. He'd asked how I was handling the morbid curiosity from the other students. And how I was in my classes. He'd talked about the accident. Not what was so obviously in my file, but about how hard it was to allow yourself to let go of the guilt of surviving and how important it was to move on.

This week, he asked if I'd decided when I would visit the graves of my friends, stating that doing so was important to begin the process of closure. I didn't want to answer the question, but I also kind of wanted to, because I wasn't talking to my friends about any of this, especially Abbi, who apparently thought I was a terrible human being, and I kind of thought the same about myself. I hadn't opened up to Sebastian. Not even after last Tuesday night—after we spent the time together really getting to know the feel of each other's mouths.

I ran the palm of my right hand over the edge of the chair's arm. "I can't think of them like that," I said finally, staring at the skydivers over his shoulder. They were all wearing different-colored jumpsuits, so they reminded me of a box of crayons. "When I think of Megan, I still think of her sitting in my room, talking about TV shows. The idea of going to a cemetery, where they are now, I…" I shuddered. "I can't."

Dr. Perry nodded slowly as he lifted his mug. The Greatest Dad Ever mug was replaced with one that had an image of Elvis Presley. "You haven't moved past the trauma of the accident. Until you do so, you won't be able to grieve."

My hand stopped moving and I curled my fingers around the arm of the chair.

"I can get you past the trauma. Do you want that?"

I lowered my gaze to him and drew in a deep breath. "I want, more than anything, to go back to the way things were."

"But you can't go back to the way things used to be, Lena.

We can never go back. You have to accept that, no matter what happens from here on out, your friends are not coming back—"

"I know that," I cut in, frustrated. "That's not what I meant."

"What do you mean?" he asked.

"I...I just want to be who I was," I forced out, and then it was like something deep inside me was unlocked, and a torrent of words spilled forth. "I don't want to be *this* me anymore. I don't want to think about *this* every waking moment, and when I do start to think about anything, *anything* else, I feel horrible because I shouldn't. I don't want to look at my mom anymore and see *that* look on her face. I want to be able to go back to volleyball, because I did...I did love playing, but I can't even think of doing that, because of Megan. I don't want to sit with my friends and constantly be worrying about what they really think of me. I don't want them to think that I don't understand the accident affected them just as badly. I want to be able to believe that Sebastian loves me and it'll be okay and I can love him back," I blurted out, having no idea if he knew what I was talking about, since I wasn't even sure I did. "I don't want to feel any of this. And I know it won't go away. I know when I go to bed later tonight and I wake up tomorrow it will be the same, but I don't want any of this."

His gaze sharpened. "Do you see a future for yourself, Lena?"

I fell back in the chair, wincing when I felt the stab of pain in my ribs. It wasn't often that my ribs still bothered me, but throwing myself around in a chair sure didn't feel good. "What do you mean?"

"Where do you see yourself a year from now?"

"I don't know." What did that even matter? "At college, I guess."

"Studying history and anthropology?" he clarified. "I talked to your guidance counselor. They filled me in on your interests."

"Yeah, that's what I'll be doing."

"Where do you see yourself five years from now?"

Annoyance flared. "What does this matter?"

"It matters because if you don't start working at this, you will still be dealing with this in five years."

My shoulders slumped. Five years was forever from now.

"Do you want to get past the trauma and the grief? Do you want to feel better than you feel right now?" he repeated.

Closing my eyes, I nodded even though I felt terrible about it, even though it felt so wrong to want to feel better.

"Then we have to get past the trauma to get to the grief, and I promise you, once we do that, you will feel better." He paused. "But you have to work with me and you have to be honest, no matter how uncomfortable the truth makes you."

I opened my eyes and his face blurred. "I don't...don't know if I can."

"This is a safe place for you, Lena. No judgment," he insisted quietly. "And getting better starts with rewinding time back to the party. It starts with you talking about what you remember and what you know happened."

"You're not hungry?"

Blinking, I slowly lifted my head and looked at Sebastian. He was sitting sideways in the seat beside me. One arm was resting on the table, the other hanging in his lap. Just the tips of his fingers touched my thigh. My body immediately reacted to his touch. A rush of warmth flowed over my skin, but my brain recoiled from the want and the need and the anticipation soaring through my veins. We hadn't kissed since last Tuesday, but he'd been at my house every night and drove me to school every morning even though I could drive myself. He sat with me at lunch and he touched me more, a little here and there. A brush of his hand on my arm or waist, a soft touch to my lower back or the nape of my neck.

And I thrived on those little moments even though I knew I shouldn't.

"What?" I said, having no idea what he'd just asked.

"You haven't touched your food." He glanced pointedly at my tray. "Well, if you consider salad food."

Salad? I checked out my plate with a frown. Yep. The plate of leafy greens was definitely a salad. I didn't even remember grabbing it when I was in the lunch line. That wasn't exactly surprising, though. After meeting with Dr. Perry this morning, knowing that on Wednesday I was going to have to rewind everything, my head was not where it needed to be. The morning had been a blur of going through the motions.

I was going to have to really, really talk about it, and I didn't know if I could. But Dr. Perry knew. Abbi suspected as much. It was all I could think about when I looked at my friends. It was all I heard in my head when Sebastian showed up at night and did his homework alongside me. It was what I saw when I spotted Jessica in the hallways between classes—

the girl who was back together with Cody. She never saw me, but I saw her.

Dary laughed now, snapping my attention back to the present. "I was wondering what was up with the salad. I don't think I've ever seen you eat one without a ton of fried stuff on it."

"I don't know." I looked across the table at Abbi. She, like Dary, had a slice of pizza and what appeared to be coleslaw on her plate.

Abbi's pizza was half eaten. She was sketching a rose in bloom on the cover of her notebook. She'd barely said anything to me in our Chem class and at the start of lunch. She wasn't ignoring me or anything like that. I wasn't even present enough to be ignored, to be honest.

I glanced around the table. It was a weird mixture now. Normally it would just be us—Abbi, Dary, me and…and Megan. There'd be other students we didn't know, but it was just us, really. Now it was us and Sebastian and several ball players.

And Keith.

He was sitting next to Abbi, as quiet as I'd ever seen him. He'd changed, too. He wasn't loud and in everyone's faces like he used to be. He still played ball, and I heard Abbi telling Dary during lunch this week, before Keith sat down, that he'd gotten reprimanded during the game last week for getting too rough on the field.

Right now his dark head was bowed, and every so often, he leaned toward her and whispered something to her and she'd respond.

Were they together?

I didn't know.

I hadn't asked.

Sebastian shifted closer, his knee pressing into mine. His voice was low as he asked, "Are you all right?"

"Yeah." I cleared my throat and forced a smile. "Just tired."

His eyes searched mine, and I knew he didn't believe me, and I knew I would probably hear about it later.

"Are you going to work at Joanna's this weekend, since you're not going to have a game or anything?" Dary asked.

I shook my head. "Um, no. Normally I wouldn't, because of volleyball."

"So you're going to go to the away game this weekend?"

I shook my head no again. Coach had given me space last week, but I knew that wouldn't last much longer. He expected me to show up today.

"Wow." Dary pushed her glasses up as she looked across the table. "I cannot think of a weekend when you didn't have a game and weren't working at Joanna's."

"Yeah." I watched Sebastian cut his roasted or baked chicken in half. He cut it up into slivers. "They've all been really understanding. They've been really good."

"Who?" Dary asked.

I cleared my throat. "Coach—Coach has been really understanding."

Sebastian took the pieces he cut up and unloaded them onto my salad. My eyes widened. Did he seriously just cut up my food like I was a two-year-old? "There," he said. "Now your salad appears to be almost edible."

"Still not fried," commented Dary, grinning. "But that

is possibly the sweetest thing I've witnessed in a very long time."

It was so ridiculous.

But it was sweet, because I knew it came from a good place.

The corners of my lips turned up as I reached for the fork.

"Are we having to hand-feed Lena now?" Abbi asked.

My head shot up as heat burned my cheeks. Abbi was staring at me, one eyebrow raised.

"Come again?" Sebastian said.

Abbi shrugged a shoulder as her gaze flickered to Sebastian. "I mean, she has to be driven to school. Can't go anywhere by herself. We have to watch what we say around her. So, I'm just wondering if we have to hand-feed her, too?"

I froze. Heart. Lungs. Brain. Everything.

"What the hell, Abbi?" Sebastian's voice sharpened.

Across from me, the hard look on Abbi's face cracked a little, only a fissure. Her voice was hoarse. "I just think it's a valid question and I can't be the only one wondering it."

"Abbi," Keith said, speaking loud enough for me to hear for the first time at lunch. "Come on."

Dary stiffened beside me.

"What? She's an adult, right?" Abbi swallowed. Her lower lip trembled as her gaze met mine again. "She can't speak up for herself? Can't step in and stop this?"

Flinching as if I'd taken a gut punch, I knew exactly what she was referencing. She wasn't talking about this conversation. She was talking about *that* night.

And I was done.

Standing, I reached down and grabbed my bag off the floor.

I heard Sebastian say my name, but I didn't stop. Straightening, I stepped back from the table and turned without saying all the words burning through my skin.

I hurried out of the cafeteria, mouth clamped shut so I didn't lose it. I had no idea if losing it meant screaming in rage or having a complete meltdown.

I made it halfway down the hall before Dary caught up to me, grabbing my good arm. "Hey, hold up," she said, forcing me to stop. "Are you okay?"

My gaze flipped to the ceiling. "I'm fine and I'm pretty sure Abbi's head would spin right off her shoulders if she heard you ask me that."

"Abbi is just being—"

"A bitch?" I finished for her, and then immediately felt bad. Closing my eyes, I shook my head. "No. That's not right. She's just…"

"She's just having a hard time dealing with everything." Dary squeezed my arm. "But she wasn't being nice in there."

I knocked the hair off my face as I glanced back at the mouth of the cafeteria. "Has she told you anything?"

"About what?"

"About me and that night—Keith's party."

Dary dropped her hand. "She told me about you and Sebastian kind of arguing and some stuff about her and Keith." She paused. "Why?"

Obviously Abbi hadn't talked to her about me. "I was just wondering."

"Is there something I should know about that night?" she asked.

Now. Now I could tell her what Abbi knew and she would

know why Abbi was so upset. But when I opened my mouth, I couldn't find the words.

A moment passed and Dary dropped her arm around my shoulders. "Everything is going to be okay again. I know it doesn't seem that way right now, but it will. It has to be."

I didn't answer, because I knew just because you wanted something so badly to be okay didn't mean it would be that way.

Dary rested her forehead against the side of my head. "I just want things to go back to the way they were before," she whispered. "We can't get Megan back—we'll never get her back—but we'll get ourselves back. I believe that. I really do."

CHAPTER TWENTY-TWO

Monday was literally one of those days that just wouldn't curl up and die.

By the time the last bell rang and I walked to my locker, I was already done with the day, and when I saw Coach Rogers striding toward me, I wanted to shove myself into my locker.

Stringing together an atrocity of F-bombs, I shoved my Chem book in and hoped that he wasn't coming to see me. That he was just out for a lazy afternoon stroll through the hallways, lulled by the sound of slamming metal doors and loud conversations.

I was pulling out my History text when I heard Coach say my name—my full name, because of course, it was going to be one of those days.

"Hey," I answered, shoving my text into my bag.

"You heading to practice?" he asked, stopping beside me.

Wishing I was far away from here, because I was so not

ready for this conversation, I shook my head as I zipped up my bag.

"I know you can't practice with those injuries, but I really want you at the practices, Lena," he said, and without even looking at him, I knew he folded his arms. "It would be good for you—for the team."

"I know, but…" I swallowed as I closed my locker door. "I can't."

"Are you not medically cleared to sit on a bench?" he replied, and I couldn't tell if he was being sarcastic or not.

Seeing the relatively bland expression, I was going to go with a nope. "I'm sure I'm allowed, but I'm…I'm not going to do the volleyball thing anymore."

His dark brows lifted. "You're quitting the team?"

Feeling my stomach sink, I nodded. "Yeah. I'm sorry, but with these injuries and getting caught up with school, it's just the best thing for me."

Coach Rogers gave a little shake of his head. "Lena, you're a valuable member of the team. We can—"

"Thank you for saying that." I shifted my weight from one foot to the next as a group of students skirted around us. "And I really appreciate all the opportunity you've given me, but I'm going to miss so many games and practices. I'm going to be completely out of it and it's for the best."

"If your arm comes out of that cast by the end of the month, you have all of October to play and any tournaments we might make it to," Coach reasoned. "You still have a chance to catch the eye of a scout. Remember how we talked about scholarships?"

"Megan would've gotten a scholarship," I said before I

could stop myself. "She wouldn't need it, but she would've gotten one. Not me."

Surprise registered across his face. "You have a good chance—"

"It's not what I want to do anymore," I cut in, taking a step back. Over his shoulder, I saw Sebastian approaching. I drew in a shallow breath. "I'm sorry." I stepped around him. "I've got to catch my ride."

Coach Rogers turned. "I think you're making a mistake."

If so, then I'd just tack that right next to the last one I made.

"If you change your mind, you come see me," he said. "We can make it right."

I wasn't going to change my mind, but I nodded and walked to where Sebastian was waiting.

Sebastian glanced down the hall, his gaze lingering on where Coach had been standing. "Everything good?"

"Yeah. Of course," I said, letting him take my backpack from me. "I'm ready to go."

His gaze flickered to mine and I thought for a moment he was going to say something else, but he didn't. As we walked down the hall in silence, I couldn't shake what Coach Rogers had said.

The twisting motion in my stomach increased. Had I done the right thing? I must have, because it was already too late if I hadn't.

I sat at the kitchen table that night, pushing peas around on my plate with my fork. I couldn't believe Mom still put them on my plate like I was five and thought I was actually going to eat them.

Mom had asked about my session with Dr. Perry, and I'd given her the general gist of what was going on. She then asked about Abbi and Dary, since she hadn't seen Abbi in a while. I'd lied, claiming Abbi was busy. Mom didn't ask about Sebastian, which for some reason made me think that she knew full well about his late-night visits but for whatever reason wasn't saying anything.

"Lori was thinking about coming home this weekend," Mom said, cutting into her slice of the meat loaf she'd had in the Crock-Pot all day.

"Really?" I stabbed my fork into the meat, hungry but not. "That's a lot of traveling for her."

"It is, but she wants to see you." Mom looked at me from across the table. "She's been worried."

A piece of my meat loaf turned to dust in my throat. "Is Dad still around?"

Mom stiffened just the slightest. "He had to get back to Seattle. I do believe he tried to call you and see you before he left."

I shrugged one shoulder. The funny thing about my dad? Nothing was stopping him from seeing me if he really wanted to. Yeah, I didn't answer his calls, but he could've come over. Mom would let him. So he could've seen me. I also recognized how backward it was that I was angry that he didn't try hard enough to see me when I didn't want to see him.

I was a hot mess.

"He's going to come back." Mom placed her glass back down. "Over Thanksgiving. We're going to have a dinner—"

"Like we're one big happy family?" I replied, admittedly snottily.

"Lena." Mom sighed, laying her fork down. "He is your father. He is a good man, and I understand that you have... unresolved issues with him, but he is, at the end of the day, your dad."

"A good man?" I couldn't believe my mom was defending him. "He left you—left us—because he couldn't deal with anything. Like, legit, *anything*."

"Honey." Mom shook her head as she put her arm on the table. "It was more than his business failing and us having money issues. Way more than that. I loved your father. Part of me still does and probably always will."

Pressing my lips together, my gaze flipped to the ceiling. Knowing what I always suspected, that Mom still loved him, just ticked me off more.

"There's something you need to understand about me and your father," she said, drawing in a shallow breath. "Your father—Alan—he simply didn't love me as much as I loved him," she said, dropping that bomb like she'd said nothing.

I gaped at her.

She focused on her plate, exhaling heavily. "I think—no, I *know*—I've always known that. All these years, he loved me. He genuinely cared about me, but it wasn't enough. Alan tried, he really did, and I'm not making excuses for him, but how he felt was just not enough."

I stared at her, unsure of what to say, because I...I had never heard any of this before.

"We married young, as soon as we found out I was pregnant with Lori. That is what people did back then." Then she dropped another bomb. "Your father didn't want to leave, Lena. He saw me—saw *us*—as his responsibility, and while you two were his responsibility, I wasn't. I wanted to be his equal and his partner, not his responsibility."

"What?" I whispered, nearly dropping my fork.

"I asked him to leave. It was me who initiated the separation." Her smile was sad, a little bitter. "I thought that confronting what I always knew, that what he felt wasn't enough, and asking him to leave might make him feel the way I did." Her laugh was like glass cracking. "I may be a grown woman, Lena, but every so often, we still believe in fairy tales. Asking him to leave was the last chance. That maybe he'd—"

"Wake up and fall in love with you?" I asked, voice pitched. Had she really believed that? I briefly squeezed my eyes shut. Had she thought that by asking him to leave, she'd get her own happily-ever-after like in a book?

Mom nodded. "I did. And looking back, there was a tiny part of me that knew you couldn't scare someone into loving you more. That's not how things work."

All I could do was sit there.

"I love him—unconditionally. But when I could no longer lie to myself and I could no longer let him lie to himself, I knew the marriage was over."

I sat back in the chair, hands falling into my lap. "Why… why didn't you tell us any of this?"

That faint, sad smile faded. "Pride? Embarrassment? When we divorced, you were still too young for that kind of conversation. So was Lori, even though she was a teenager. It's not something easy to talk about, to admit to your young daughters that you stayed with a man who didn't love you like he should've."

"But I…" But I'd always believed that Dad had just checked out and left. "You made him leave?"

"It was the right thing to do, and I know we should've been more honest with you girls, but…" She trailed off, staring out the window into the backyard. Her fingers folded on her mouth and she blinked rapidly. "But we don't always make the right choices. Not even when you're an adult and you're supposed to know better."

Like clockwork, the balcony door opened a little after eight. I wasn't napping. I was just staring aimlessly at my textbook, rereading the same paragraph for about the fifth time. Nothing was sticking in my head since dinner.

Sebastian grinned when he saw me. "Nice shirt," he said when he closed the door behind him.

"My shirt is awesome." It was an oversize black shirt with baby Deadpool on it.

He stalked toward the bed in a long-legged prowl and my stomach dipped crazily. "Yeah, but when you wear my old jersey shirt is better."

Flushing, I knocked a loose strand of hair back from my face. "I threw it away."

"Sure you did." He dropped into the computer chair, just like Abbi used to, when she actually liked me. "What have you been doing?"

"Nothing much." I watched him kick his legs up, planting his feet next to my hip. He was barefoot, always barefoot. I dropped my highlighter into my notebook. "You?"

"The usual. Practice." He folded his arms across his chest. "I also showered."

I cracked a grin. "Good for you."

Tipping his head back, he chuckled. "I live an exciting life."

My gaze flickered over him and our eyes met and held for a moment. A liquid heat slipped over my throat and into my chest, then spread much, much lower. Looking away, I took a deep, even breath. "So…um, my mom kind of dropped a bomb on me tonight."

"About what?"

"She told me why Dad left." I flicked the highlighter. "You know how I always thought he just checked out because he couldn't deal with everything?"

"Yeah." He dropped his feet onto the floor and leaned forward, fully invested. "That's why, right?"

I shook my head. "Come to find out, it's because he didn't really love my mom. Like he loved her but wasn't *in* love with her." I told him what my mom had said as I pushed the highlighter back and forth. "Crazy, right?"

"Damn." His brows were raised. "How do you feel about all that, since you and your dad…?"

He didn't need to finish the statement. I'd held a major grudge, obviously, after my dad had left. I lifted my hands up. "I have no idea. I still think I'm too shocked to be angry, you know? Like how did she keep that from us this long? But at the same time I feel terrible for her, because a part of me can understand not wanting to tell anyone."

And just not wanting to talk about it. That, I could totally understand.

"I got way too much in my head," I admitted. "Like it's just going to explode. Mom had basically let me and even Lori think Dad was just crap. I mean, he is still kind of crap, I guess, for marrying someone he didn't really, truly love, but... I don't know."

"Time to clear your head." He stood and walked over. Picking up my textbook, he closed it and placed it on my table.

"Hey," I said. "I was doing my homework."

"Uh-huh." The notebook, pen and highlighter joined my textbook. Then he sat on the bed, in front of me, one knee up and bent, pressing against my calf. "So it's Monday night."

"Yeah." I dropped my hands into my lap. "Thanks for clearing that up. I was so confused."

One side of his lips kicked up. "You know what that means?"

"I'd have a whole week before the next episode of *The Walking Dead* if it was on?"

"No," he replied drily.

I watched him plant his right hand next to my left knee. "Um. There's only four more days left in the week?"

"Well, yes. There's that." He leaned in just the slightest, and my heart rate sped up in response. The absolute crappiness of the day faded away. "But Monday night means something else, something far more important?"

"And that is?" My gaze dropped to his mouth briefly, and I felt the clench in my lower stomach.

His head tilted slightly to the side. "It's time for no more talking."

"No more talking?" I repeated dumbly as a flutter started

deep in my chest and moved south. Did he mean what I thought he meant?

"Yeah." He inched his upper body closer and I felt his breath dance across my cheek. "I've deemed Monday night officially No-Talk-Monday. And you know what that means?"

My right hand closed into a loose fist. "What?"

"We find better uses for our lips and our tongues."

Eyes wide, I coughed out a laugh. "Did you really just say that out loud?"

"Yes. Yeah, I did, and I don't take it back." He leaned in, and I jerked when his forehead rested against mine. "No shame in my game."

"I don't think you have any game."

"Oh, I have game," he replied smoothly. "So much you wouldn't know what to do with all of it."

A quiet laugh escaped me. "Sebastian—"

"This Monday's going to be different." His left hand found my right one. Just the tips of his fingers grazed my hand. "Can I show you how?" he asked, coasting his fingers up my bare arm, eliciting an acute shiver, stopping at the sleeve of my shirt. "Would that be okay?"

That would be *amazing*, but I…thought about what my mom had told me at dinner. Sebastian and I had been friends forever. Literally. I knew he genuinely cared about me, probably did love me, but did he *really* love me? I thought about how he drove me to school, worried about what I was eating and suddenly showered me with all kinds of attention. It wasn't exactly like Mom and Dad. I didn't get pregnant. But I did almost die. "Am I your responsibility?"

"What?" he asked.

"Do you feel like you're responsible for me?"

"In what way?"

What was I even asking him? "Forget it."

"No. I'm curious. What do you mean by that?"

Crap. I should've just kept my mouth shut. "I mean, do you do things for me because you feel like you have to because of what happened?"

"What? No. I do them because I *want* to."

That...that was the right answer, but it didn't change anything else. His forehead moved against mine, and that breath was on my lips now, and I wanted so badly to fall headfirst into this, to delve right in and deal with the eventual fallout later. "Is this smart?"

"I think it's brilliant." His fingers grazed over the loose sleeve of my nightshirt. "I think the last thing you need to be doing right now is thinking."

I seriously doubted Dr. Perry would agree to that, but then again, maybe he would. He'd talked about living and moving forward and facing the trauma, the grief, and no one made me feel like I was living as deeply as Sebastian.

Though I wasn't sure Dr. Perry considered making out as moving forward.

Drawing back, I saw a muscle flex in his cheek. His eyes searched mine. "You know how I feel about you."

My heart nearly came out of my chest. "Seb—"

"I love you," he continued, drawing his hand around to the nape of my neck, and my breath caught and my heart squeezed at those words. "I've been in love with you for years."

"Sebastian," I pleaded, finding myself close to tears.

"And I know things are twisted up in your head right now and I can only be right here, right next to you, while you untangle them, however long that takes." His fingers sifted through the wisps of hair. "But there is something I'm going to untwist for you right now. What I feel for you is real, has been real—"

My heart was pounding so fast it hurt. "I need to tell you something."

"You don't need to tell me anything."

Tears clogged my throat. "You don't understand."

"I don't need to." His thumb moved along my neck, comforting and energizing at the same time.

I shook my head as much as I could. "Why now?" I asked again. "Why—"

"Because we were too stupid to do it before and because we're still alive right *now*."

I don't know who moved first, if it was him or me or both of us at the same time, but our mouths came together in a clash. His lips. Mine. I tasted him, my fingers landing on his chest and my hand sliding up to his shoulder. And he kissed in a way that consumed me, lit a fire that burned through my skin, turned my muscles into lava and my bones to ash. There was tongue and teeth, and Andre had never kissed me like that. No boy ever had, and that was frightening and exhilarating all at the same time.

Sebastian doled out kisses like there was an endless supply and I had a high demand for them, and somehow, without knowing how, I was lying on my back, and he'd lowered me so gently, so carefully.

"My turn," he murmured against my mouth.

I didn't want to stop him.

Sebastian mirrored my explorations from last week. As his lips mapped out the curve of mine, his hand trailed down the center of my chest, over my stomach. The flutter was back in my chest, a pounding of wings that met my out-of-control pulse. His fingers slipped under my shirt, fingers splayed against my stomach.

He lifted his head, a question in his eyes, and when I nodded, a promise filled them, a promise I could barely look at because it was...it was almost too much.

I gripped him, tugging on the longer strands of hair, and his hand went up, his touch like a feather over my healing ribs, and his fingers kept moving. I gasped against his mouth, and he made this sound that had my back arching even though it put pressure on my ribs.

Sebastian let out a low, husky laugh when he pulled his hand away and I tugged his hair harder. "I'm not done."

Oh Lord.

His mouth moved over mine as those clever fingers of his went farther south, over the band of my sleep bottoms, stopping for only a heart-stopping moment. My entire body tensed in anticipation, and then his hand slipped between my legs. A sense of wildness invaded every pore. This was insane, completely crazy, but I didn't care. The pants were thin, and it was like nothing was between his hand and me. Every part of my body zeroed in on that hand and his fingers. Electricity zipped through my veins and—

A door closed in the hallway. My eyes flew open. Sebastian halted, lips above mine, hand *still* between my legs as his head turned to the door. I waited for it to fly open and Mom to either congratulate us or kill us. When neither happened and the door stayed closed, I relaxed a little.

"Oh my God," I whispered, heart now thumping for a whole different reason.

Grinning like a madman, his gaze shifted to mine and he raised his eyebrows. "That would've been awkward."

"You think?" I pushed at his chest with my right hand even though I wanted to pull him back onto me. "You should probably get going."

"Yeah." Sebastian chuckled as he rolled onto his side. "But first, I want to ask you to do something."

"What?"

"You know how we don't have a late practice on Thursday before the game?" he asked, and I nodded. "So I'll be home early, and Mom and Dad want to have dinner with my new girlfriend."

I froze. Did I hear him correctly? No way. But when I turned my head toward him and saw the smile, that sexy, heart-smashing smile, I knew I'd heard him right. A surge of conflicting thoughts and feelings swamped me. Elation was like a balloon lifting me up to the ceiling, but I was popped of all air before I could reach it. Guilt dug in with icy claws, latching itself deep to my chest.

"Girlfriend?" I whispered, sitting up so quickly pain lanced across my ribs.

He rose up on his elbow, grinning. "Yeah, I'm pretty sure that's what guys call girls that they kiss and want to do other things with..." His gaze became heavy hooded. "Girlfriend."

Oh my God.

How…how could I be doing this right now, lying in bed with him, making out and experiencing all of this, when Megan was just buried and she was dead because I didn't…I didn't do enough to stop what happened?

I wanted to peel my own skin off, because I'd never felt more gross, more selfish, than I did right then in my entire life. "No."

The playful grin slipped from his striking, almost too-beautiful face. "What?"

Pushing off the bed, I stood and backed away. "I can't… I can't be your girlfriend."

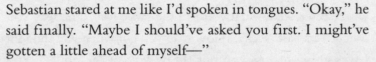

CHAPTER TWENTY-THREE

Sebastian stared at me like I'd spoken in tongues. "Okay," he said finally. "Maybe I should've asked you first. I might've gotten a little ahead of myself—"

"Yeah, I'm pretty sure you're supposed to ask someone if they want to be your girlfriend."

The corner of his lips quirked. "Will you be my girlfriend, Lena?" he asked in a sweet, teasing way.

My heart leaped in my chest like it was jumping on a trampoline. How long had I waited to hear that question? Years. Honest to God, *years*. And now he was asking, after everything that had happened?

I shook my head. "I can't."

"You can't what?"

"I can't be your girlfriend."

For a moment Sebastian didn't move, and then he sat up in one quick fluid move. "Are you being serious?"

"Yes." I walked around the bed, knocking a strand of hair

out of my face. I threw open the balcony door and stepped outside, welcoming the chilly breeze. I walked to the railing, squeezing my eyes shut when I heard his footsteps behind me.

"Okay," he said. "I'm so confused right now. You can't be my girlfriend?" When I didn't answer, he moved to stand beside me. "Is there someone else?"

"What?" I almost had to laugh. "No. There's no one else."

"Are you planning to leave tomorrow and never see me again?"

"No," I said, frowning.

"Then why can't we be together?" He angled his body toward mine. "What just happened in there tells me that you're interested—that you feel the same way. The way you touched me last week… How mad you got when you thought I was going to kiss you but threw you in the pool… You don't feel like that unless you want that person." His hand touched my lower back, and I fought the urge to lean into him. "Unless…unless it's just about feeling good? Is that all you want out of this?"

I could've said yes because that would've shut this whole conversation down, but I didn't. "No. It's not about that."

"Then what is this about?"

Running my hand over my cast, I couldn't believe I had to really explain this. "It just doesn't feel right. We get to move on and be happy? This soon?"

Sebastian was quiet for a moment. "But that's…that's life, Lena."

"Wow," I muttered, floored.

"What? Yeah, that sounded blunt as hell, but it's the truth. You can't stop living just because others…others died."

I understood that, but the thing was, he didn't get it. What I felt wasn't just survivor's guilt. I felt more rancid. More bitter. "It's not that easy."

"Yes." He curled his hand around my chin, bringing my gaze to his. "Yes, it is, Lena."

Exhaling roughly, I pulled away and stepped back. "You don't get it."

"You keep saying that." Frustration flared in his voice as he stared at me. "And I'm trying to get everything. To understand. To be patient. To be there for you. But you aren't talking about anything going on in your head. Not really. And you keep forgetting that I'm going through this right beside you. I know how you feel."

I snapped my mouth shut as I crossed my arms.

"What happened to our friends was a huge wake-up call for me. As cheesy as it sounds, there's no guarantee on tomorrow, or next year—"

"You tell me I need to move on! That I need to just deal with—"

"That's not what I'm saying! Not at all."

"You don't have to say it in those exact words, but the meaning is the same."

"Lena—"

"Oh my God, are you kidding me?" My voice was nearing code-red shrill level. "You're standing here like you're now doing everything you want to do, because you have this whole new outlook on life, and that's crap. You know that's *crap*."

"That's not crap." His voice was low.

"You don't want to play ball anymore, Sebastian. Right? You told me you don't want to do it."

His back went ramrod straight.

"What about that?" My hand curled into a fist. "You don't want to play football, but I bet a year from now you'll be doing it at college just because you don't want to face your dad. So don't stand there and act like you've changed so much since this accident, and grown so much, and faced all your problems head-on."

He lifted his head and a moment passed as if he was trying to collect himself.

"This isn't about football. This is about *us*."

"How can you even be thinking about *us* right now?" I demanded. "Our friends are dead. They *just* died. They're not coming back, and all you care about is getting laid—" I sucked in a sharp breath.

The moment I said it, I wanted to take it back. I'd gone too far.

Sebastian's eyes flared with shock and then his jaw locked down. "I can't believe you said that to me. I really can't."

I couldn't either. I really couldn't.

Swallowing around the knot in my throat, I willed my heart to slow down. "Sebastian, I just—"

"No." He held up his hand. "I'm going to unpack that statement for you real quick. And you're going to stand there and listen."

Closing my mouth, I stood there. And I listened.

"Our friends are dead. Yes. Thank you for reminding me that I lost three of my closest friends and almost lost my best friend—the girl I fucking love. I'm not trying to spend every waking moment thinking about it like you…and you know what? That doesn't make me a terrible person. None of them would've wanted that from us. Not even Cody, with his ego." He took a step toward me. "Their deaths do not mean that I die alongside them, or that I put my entire life on hold. Yeah, it's only been about a month and no one—*no one*—is expecting anyone to just get over it. But living your life and loving someone is not getting over it. That doesn't mean anyone is forgetting them. I can live my life and still mourn them."

I opened my mouth to speak, but he wasn't done.

"And how dare you insinuate that I don't care about them or that I don't think about them every damn day. What we were doing in there—" he gestured at the door "—it isn't a disrespect to them. And you know what, I am partially at fault for this. Obviously you're not ready for this. You're not in the right headspace and I thought that… I don't even know anymore, but I sincerely apologize for that. I'm sorry." His voice turned hoarse as he thrust a hand through his hair. "*What* I feel for you, *what* we were doing in there, *what* I want to do to you is not about getting laid, and I…I can't believe you would even think that about me."

I squeezed my eyes shut against the building tears.

"I'm not sure you can blame grief for that," he said, and I felt my heart crack. "Because no matter what has happened, no matter what is going on in our lives, you should know me better than that."

Those tears burned and no matter how hard I tried, the

tears snuck through. I lifted my hand to wipe at them. I stood for several moments before I opened my eyes.

Sebastian was gone.

I hadn't even heard him leave.

It was almost like he hadn't even been there.

I didn't go to school on Tuesday.

In the morning I told Mom I wasn't feeling well. She didn't ask the reasons why, which was good, because there were plenty. I had no idea if Sebastian had shown up to drive me to school. I'd turned my phone off, not wanting to deal with the world. Wanting nothing more than to hide.

If Sebastian never spoke to me again, I wouldn't blame him.

Staring up at the map above my desk, I knew I'd created a mess out of things with him. I wasn't being honest or open, telling him what I really felt or why my guilt was different from his. I wasn't being honest or up front with anyone, and I was a coward because of that.

I was just like my dad.

But I didn't want to be, so I lay there for hours thinking about *everything*.

It was a little after one o'clock when I heard my mom coming up the stairs. "I wanted to check on you," she said as she entered. "You obviously have your phone turned off and I wanted to make sure you were okay."

"Sorry," I murmured from my pathetic prone position on the bed.

"Where is your phone?"

I gestured at my desk with a limp hand and watched Mom

walk over and pick it up. She turned it on and tossed it on the bed by my legs.

"When you're not feeling well and staying home, you will never turn your phone off again. I have to be able to reach you." Her voice was stern, and her eyes sharp. "Do you understand?"

"Yeah."

Her shoulders tensed as she crossed her arms. "Lena, I know why you didn't go to school today."

"Mom," I groaned, rubbing my hand down my face. She probably thought I was ticked off about everything with Dad, though I still wasn't sure what to think about that.

She sat on the edge of the bed. "Sebastian stopped by this morning to take you to school. He looked like he had very little sleep last night and didn't seem surprised when I said you were feeling unwell."

My stupid heart swelled. He'd still shown up to take me to school even after I really, truly insulted him.

There was a pause. "Do you think I don't know Sebastian comes over every night?"

I covered my eyes with my hand.

"You two try to be quiet, but I can hear you talking sometimes. I haven't said anything because I think you need your friends right now, especially when I haven't seen much of Dary or Abbi," she explained. "And because I trust Sebastian."

I wanted to hide under the bed. "I trust you to make smart choices when it comes to Sebastian," she added, and I wasn't sure I believed her, because, truth be told, I obviously sucked at making good choices. "But I heard some of your conversation last night."

Oh *God*.

I winced.

"Lena," she said with a sigh. "The boy has cared about you from the first day he came over here, asking if you wanted to ride bikes."

"I know, Mom." I lowered my hand to the bed and looked at her. I'd done a lot of thinking as I lay in bed all morning. "I think... I think he does love me," I whispered, my lip trembling. "Like *really* love me, and I...I don't know if I'm ready for that now. I mean, I am. I've been waiting forever for him...but it all feels wrong now."

"Honey." Her breath was shaky as she leaned over me, clasping my hand. "You're going through a lot right now. And I know it's not just Sebastian. Coach Rogers called me this morning. He told me you quit the team."

"It just...wasn't what I wanted to do anymore."

"Is that the same way you feel about Sebastian?"

"It's not that. Not really. I just...don't deserve him... deserve *this*."

"Why would you say that?"

I shifted my gaze back to the map before looking back to her. "You know why."

Her eyes widened and shimmered with tears. "Oh, baby, don't say that. You do deserve happiness and a future and everything you've ever wanted. That one night is not going to define your whole life."

"But it defined Megan's and the others'," I argued. "When people talk about Cody, it will always be overshadowed by what he did. The same with Chris and with Phillip." And it would be the same about me, if everyone knew.

Mom squeezed my hand, and I could tell by the stricken look on her face that she had no idea what to say to me.

I pulled my hand free and sat up a little. "I just want to go back to that night and do things differently. I was being so stupid, obsessing over such stupid things. Everything I worried about before seems so pointless now."

"Baby, nothing you worried about before was pointless." Mom squeezed my hand again. "You're just looking at things differently now."

On Wednesday morning, Sebastian drove me to school. The ride was silent and awkward, and I couldn't do it again. I had to try to catch a ride with Dary after school, and tomorrow, I decided, I needed to do it myself. Needed to get behind the wheel of my own car.

To drive myself.

To take care of myself.

But as I walked from my locker to the administrative offices, I wasn't thinking about Sebastian or our fight or what Mom had admitted to. I knew what was expected from me in the next thirty minutes.

I was going to have to *really* talk today. I had to, because I needed to get it off my chest. I needed to say something, and I didn't know if it would change anything or make it better or worse when it was all said and done, but I just needed to tell someone in my own words.

My hands were shaking when I walked into the tiny room. The stupid posters were a blur. Dr. Perry was at the table waiting for me, a new coffee mug in front of him, but I was too nervous to read the words. I just knew it was new because it was orange, unlike the others.

"Good morning, Lena." He sat back in his chair, smiling as I shuffled toward the chair across from him. "I learned you weren't at school yesterday. Are you not feeling well?"

After dropping my bag on the floor, I sat in the chair, stiff as a board. "It was just a bad day."

"Care to elaborate?"

My first instinct was to say no, but that wasn't what these sessions were about. So I told him what had happened with Sebastian. Not all the details because, seriously, that would be way too awkward. When I finished, I already felt exhausted and emotionally spent, and I'd barely even really started.

"Do you think Sebastian is wrong for wanting to move on?"

"Yes. No." I wanted to bang my head off the table. "I don't know. I mean, no. He's not wrong. He gets to move on. He gets to—"

"And you don't get to move on?" Dr. Perry interrupted.

Shaking my head, I opened my mouth but struggled to say what he already knew. "Why should I get to move on?"

He placed his mug down. "Why shouldn't you?"

"Because it's my fault," I said, feeling sick.

"I think what we really need to do right now is for you to walk me through that night," he said gently. "Do you think you can do that?"

"Yes," I said. "I need to do this. To talk about that night." Tears filled my eyes and my heart pounded wildly in my chest. "I knew Cody was drunk and I...I could've stopped him. I wasn't drunk."

And then I walked him through everything that had happened that night.

I found myself standing in the driveway with Megan. I was done with the party. I had a headache stabbing me behind the eyes, and the music and shouting and laughter weren't helping.

I just wanted to go home, and I was so not looking for Sebastian to tell him so. Not after our talk/argument and the fact I hadn't seen him since Skylar showed up. I really didn't need to walk up on them in the middle of them practically eating each other's faces.

A heavy weight settled in my stomach.

God, I wished I hadn't said anything to Sebastian. Now tomorrow was going to be different, and there was no going back. No pretending that everything was the same.

I really wanted to go home.

"Where's Chris?" I asked.

Leaning heavily into me, Megan nodded to where Cody was bent over, one arm hanging on an open car door as he talked to someone. Her cousin Chris was standing beside him. "One of them is driving us home," she said slowly. "That's all I know."

Cody was leaving with us?

"I'm a bit trashed," Megan slurred after a moment.

"Really?" I replied drily, almost wishing I were in her shoes that moment.

"Just a little." Sighing, she wrapped her arm around my waist. "I love you, Lena."

I grinned as I pushed my damp hair out of my face. "I love you, too."

"Do you love me enough to carry me inside my house, pass my mom and tuck me into bed?" she asked, pushing away from me. She was momentarily distracted by the hum of crickets. "After we stop at McDonald's so I can get chicken nuggets?"

I laughed. "Maybe I can help you get nuggets, but not sure how to get you past your mom."

She giggled as she looked around, swaying slightly. "Wait... did you tell Sebastian you were leaving?"

"I have no idea where he is," I said, watching Cody and Chris head toward us.

She clapped her hands together, rocking backward. "Let's go find him."

"Find who?" Cody asked.

"Sebastian!" shrieked Megan, and I winced.

Cody dropped his arm over my shoulders. "Pretty sure he's with Skylar. Probably in the pool house." He squeezed me. "Thought I saw them walking into there."

The hole in my chest tripled. Cody could've been making it up, but it could also be true, and it...it also didn't matter.

Megan cringed. "All righty, then, let's not find him."

"Sounds like a plan," I said, stepping from under Cody's arm.

Yawning, Chris turned around and tossed his keys at Cody. They smacked off his chest and hit the ground. "Can you drive?" he asked. "I'm whipped."

"Yeah. Sure." Bending over, Cody swiped up the keys. "Next time give me a warning."

"There's the reason why you're the quarterback and not the receiver," Chris taunted. "No amount of heads-up will change that."

"Screw you," Cody shot back.

This was going to be the longest ride home ever.

"Hey, wait up!" Phillip came running around the side of the house, holding up the back of his swim trunks. "I'm leaving with you guys."

Megan sighed beside me. "And here I thought I'd snuck off."

I was guessing their talk earlier hadn't ended well.

"All aboard," Cody said, reaching for the driver's door and missing it. The handle snapped back.

"Hey," said Chris from the front passenger seat. "Careful, man. Some of us actually respect our cars."

"If you respect your car, why are you letting him drive?" Phillip smacked Megan's behind as he walked past.

She whipped around and nearly fell over, but I caught her arm as I watched Cody open the door, his movements odd and jerky. His face looked flushed in the car's interior light.

"Are you okay? To drive?" I asked.

"Why wouldn't I be?" He started to climb in behind the wheel.

I stopped at the door. "You look a little drunk."

His eyes narrowed. "Jesus. Are you *serious*? I had one drink."

I stepped back, surprised by his tone. "I was just asking."

"He's fine. Come on." Megan took my hand and leaned in, whispering in my ear, "I want chicken nuggets and sweet-and-sour sauce."

"Ew," I murmured, distracted. Chewing on the inside of my cheek, I tried to think of how many times I'd seen Cody with a drink. I knew I saw him with a bottle. Or was it a cup? I really hadn't been paying attention to him.

"Maybe I should drive?" I offered.

Chris groaned from the passenger seat. "If you want to leave now, just get in the car, Lena."

Phillip was climbing in the other side as Megan pushed in behind me. "I don't want to sit next to him," she whisper-yelled.

"I can hear you." Phillip slapped his hand down on the middle seat. "And I'd rather sit next to Lena anyway. She's nicer."

"*She's nicer,*" mimicked Megan in the whiniest voice I'd ever heard, her hands on my hips. "Hurry, Lena. I'm hungry."

"I'm *fine.*" Cody hauled himself up into the front of the SUV. He looked back at me, eyes bright in the light. "Seriously. I'm fine. I've driven this road a million times."

I wasn't so sure if he was fine or not, but the guys were staring at me and Megan was pushing me, going on and on about the ten-piece nugget meal she was going to murder.

"He's fine," Megan said, and then giggled. "I'm so hungry."

"Come on," Cody said, smacking his hand off the steering wheel. "You're being stupid. Get in the car."

I felt my face heat up. He was right. I was being stupid. I climbed into the car, smushed between Megan and Phillip. It took several moments to wiggle my seat belt out from under Phillip and lock it in place. The windows rolled down all around me as I dug my phone out of my purse and saw several missed texts from Dary.

Megan leaned over me and reached out, flicking her finger off the side of Phillip's face. "Hey, are you going to buy me nuggets?"

Leaning back, I checked out Dary's texts. She'd sent me a picture of a painting that looked like something a two-year-old could've done. Underneath it was the caption This is art? What am I missing?

"Baby, I'll buy you *two* nugget meals," Phillip told her. "And all the sweet-and-sour sauce you could ever want."

So romantic.

Megan sighed. "You know me. Know me well enough to know that sweet-and-sour sauce is the way to my heart. Why did we break up?"

I made a face at my phone.

The radio turned on, and when I glanced up, Chris's head was already lolling to the side. Cody was messing with the stations, flipping through them so fast I had no idea what the songs were.

Zoning Megan and Phillip out, I prayed they didn't try to start making out with me between them as I scrolled through Dary's texts. Another picture was of a dress, with Dary saying she was thinking about making one just like it. I got to the end of her messages and texted her back.

You'd look amazing in that dress. Heading home from Keith's. Call you tomorrow.

Cool air streamed through the windows, lifting the ends of my hair. I glanced up. It felt like we were going really fast, but I couldn't really see anything outside the car. I hit Send and then started to text Abbi so she didn't worry when she realized I wasn't there anymore.

Caught a ride with Megan. Didn't want to bother

"Holy—" Cody's words were cut off as the SUV suddenly jerked to the right, the movement so sharp my phone slipped out of my hands.

Someone—*Megan?*—screamed, and we were moving sideways fast. *Too* fast. Confusion swamped me. I couldn't breathe past the ball of fear and disorientation choking me.

Time...time slowed down and moved too fast, all at once. My arms flew up. I tried to grab the front seat, but I was suddenly in the air. Then we were slamming back down. The impact jarred every bone in my body. An earsplitting crack of thunder jolted the car. I heard glass break, shattering like fragile icicles. Shooting pain exploded along the side of my face as something slammed into my head—an arm, no *a leg*.

We were *flying*, air lifting us up, and my head snapped backward as the seat belt caught me, the material digging into my stomach and chest. A fire burned through me, and my throat was stinging.

Metal crunched—the roof. Oh my God, *the roof* gave way, and we were upside down and then upright, then upside down, and I was thrown back and forth, side to side. All I could hear was something...*something*, eating the car, tearing it apart, piece by piece. Red-hot pain erupted, blindingly white, and that was all there was. Pain. Terror. Flying. Screaming.

Then there was nothing.

TOMORROW

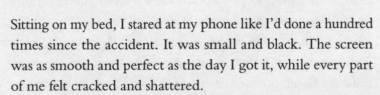

CHAPTER TWENTY-FOUR

Sitting on my bed, I stared at my phone like I'd done a hundred times since the accident. It was small and black. The screen was as smooth and perfect as the day I got it, while every part of me felt cracked and shattered.

I closed my eyes and breathed through the burn crawling up the back of my throat. The session with Dr. Perry killed me. Other than when the police had come into my hospital room, it was the first time I talked about what happened and actually gave those memories a voice.

I thought talking about what happened would serve like some kind of epiphany. That things would change. That I'd feel some sort of release. But talking openly about the accident, about everything leading up to it, just made me want to take a wire brush to my memories.

I'd known Cody shouldn't have been behind the wheel. I should've listened to that little voice in my head and that feeling in the pit of my stomach, but I hadn't. If I had, today would've been different. Tomorrow would be like all the better yesterdays.

I just hadn't thought anything would happen.

Opening my eyes, I saw my phone and the pressure in my chest tightened, reminding me of how it felt when I first woke up from the accident. Of course I'd used my phone—texted and called, but...

But there were still texts I hadn't looked at, voice mails I hadn't listened to. They remained on my phone, not forgotten but untouched.

I picked up my phone and opened my texts. I scrolled until I got to the dozen or so unread ones. All of them had come in after the crash. I opened them and read the OMG, I hope you're okay! messages. I opened up the numerous I'm so glad you're ok. Text me messages. I read them all, my brain completely empty as I clicked out of one and went to the next, until my finger hovered over Abbi's name and the goofy picture of her wearing a panda hat.

I didn't even know where she got the panda hat.

I opened her message and slowly scrolled up. The last text from her was the Wednesday after the accident.

Why don't you want to see us? We miss you and we're worried about you.

The breath I took scorched my throat. Did Abbi know I hadn't had my phone while in the hospital? Did that matter? I hadn't wanted to see my friends and I hadn't even checked her messages in over a month. It didn't even matter if she did at this point.

I kept reading and I saw the texts from that Saturday night. It was just two of them. Where are you? And PLEASE TEXT ME BACK NOW.

The text before that was from before I left the party. It was a selfie that she'd taken of us and sent to me. Our cheeks pressed together and both of us smiling. Over our heads, I could make out part of Keith's face.

Dumbly, I backed out of her texts and then I scrolled back up to Sebastian's. Swallowing hard, I opened up his texts and made my way to the ones I hadn't read. His started off just like Abbi's.

Where are you?

There were several more messages, and I could easily see him firing them off, one after another.

You didn't leave without coming to get me?

Okay. Please text me back. I'm starting to freak out. Someone said there's a really bad accident not too far from here.

Come on. Answer your phone. Please.

My heart thumped heavily in my chest. I knew his voice mail was one of the many that sat unheard on my cell.

Closing his texts, I scrolled back down. My thumb hovered over Megan's texts. I could see that the last text she ever sent me was an attachment. I already knew what it was. A picture of a volleyball that she'd drawn a face on. She'd done it after practice one day. No idea why, but that was Megan. She just did things.

A huge part of me wanted to read through her messages, but I couldn't handle it—reading her words, seeing what used to be and now what could no longer be. I tapped out of the texts and went to my voice mails.

I listened to them.

The missed call from Lori happened after Mom must've called her. In her message, she told me she was coming and that she loved me. She'd sounded okay, calm even, as she spoke. It sounded nothing like Abbi's message that had come that Saturday night when she had been looking for me, or Dary's message the following Sunday. I could barely make out what Dary had been saying.

There were more messages from friends I saw every day at volleyball practice, and other messages from people I hadn't spoken to since we shared a class last year. They were the voices of strangers, but their messages were all the same.

I could barely see the delete button when each message came to an end. Tears filled my eyes and my hand was shaking as I got to the last one I'd skipped over. It was a message from Sebastian, from that Saturday night.

Every muscle in my back locked up as I hit the play button. There were only a few seconds of silence and then I heard his voice.

"Answer your phone. Come on, Lena. Please pick up your damn phone." His voice was hoarse with a panicked edge after a pause. "You're not in the car. God, please tell me you're not in that damn car. Call me and tell me you're not in that car."

The message ended. Dropping the phone, I pressed my palms to my eyes. Sébastian sounded like he did when I first woke up in the hospital and saw him.

He sounded destroyed.

Because he knew when he made that call, deep down he had to have known at that point, that I wasn't going to call him back. That I was in that car along with Cody, Phillip, Chris and Megan.

My hands felt damp as I dragged them down my face. Everything inside me felt raw and bruised. One night had irrevocably changed all of our lives. One choice had altered the course of what we all were supposed to become.

What would I have done differently that night if I'd known there was no tomorrow? *Everything.* I would've done everything differently.

CHAPTER TWENTY-FIVE

Pumpkins were on front porches. The tree in the backyard had turned burnt orange and red, as had the maples lining the streets and surrounding the school. Halloween decorations plastered the windows of the shops in town.

Homecoming banners filled the hallways at school. Excitement buzzed in the classrooms and the cafeteria as talk of dancing and parties and dresses consumed the senior class.

The air had turned chillier. Long sleeves and cardigans replaced tank tops, but I was still wearing my flip-flops. I would until snow kissed the ground.

I was preparing my application for early decision to UVA.

Two weeks ago the cast had come off my arm. There was only a twinge of pain in my ribs every now and then, and I was able to sleep on my side now. I was breathing normally. Only a little over two months since the accident and...

And people were already forgetting.

Life was moving on.

Talking to Dr. Perry about what happened the night of the accident, how I'd suspected Cody had too much to drink but still got in the car, had lessened some of the suffocating weight I carried but not all of it.

When I told him that I had finally listened to the messages and read the texts, he'd told me that was progress. I was making some of the right steps, but there was still no sudden awakening or clarity after rewinding the night of the accident and actually forcing myself to come face-to-face with the decisions I'd made.

I'd had two choices that night.

And I'd made the wrong one.

Dr. Perry had said, in the session on Wednesday, "Some people may try to say or may even believe what happened that night in August cannot be blamed on anyone but Cody because he was behind the wheel. They may even say that all of this has nothing to do with blame, but that's not the actual case. Do you know why?"

"Why?" I'd asked.

"Blame isn't about making someone feel terrible about their actions, and it's not about hurting the person's feelings. Actions and inactions have consequences. If we did not accept responsibility or blame for them, then we'd be at risk of repeating those actions," he'd explained. "Everyone who was there, who saw you all leave, who knew that they had been drinking, and even the parents who allowed the drinking to occur. But it is also partially your fault."

Partially.

Not completely.

But *partially.*

Partially didn't feel any different from completely, but what he said at the end of the session, what he'd reiterated the following Friday meeting, was that I was not the only one who was partially responsible. And it stuck with me.

It wasn't like things changed. Like there was some magic switch thrown and I was suddenly okay with everything. If anything, things were more real, the memories sharper and more clear.

But then, after that Wednesday session, the nightmares started.

I was back in the car again, being thrown side to side. Sometimes I dreamed that I was in the driveway and I hadn't gotten in the car, but I knew what was going to happen to my friends. It felt like my feet had been cemented to the ground, and I kept telling myself to go get someone, to warn everyone that they were about to die, but I couldn't move. I was frozen until I woke up, gasping for air. Many nights I came to, throat raw, with Mom clutching my shoulders. Only then would I realize I'd been screaming.

Dr. Perry had been right. I guess those fancy degrees attached to his name had a lot to do with it. I was still traumatized from the accident, from the memories I kept to myself, and talking about them pushed the accident to the forefront of my thoughts.

And I did a lot of talking.

The session on Friday and the following Monday were basically lessons in exposure therapy. Rewind. Relive. Each time it got a little easier to say the words I needed to, but by the next Friday, something finally clicked into place.

My friends were dead.

They really were dead, and no amount of guilt was going to bring them back. Nothing was ever bringing them back or undoing what strangers and friends alike now thought of them. Nothing was stopping the suits being brought against Keith's family or the pending legal charges. Nothing was stopping the lawyers from contacting me and Mom every other week.

At the end of that session, my face hurt from the tears I'd tried not to let fall but couldn't stop. I had to hide my face throughout the rest of the afternoon because it was so obvious that I'd spent the morning sobbing.

Dr. Perry had been so right about grieving.

I hadn't truly begun the process, so blinded by the trauma of the accident and consumed by the burning guilt. I hadn't let any of them go. Hadn't even truly begun.

Those days, those weeks, were hard. Focusing on classes became difficult for a whole different reason. I missed them— missed Megan and her hyperactivity, missed Cody and his arrogance, Phillip and his sarcasm, and Chris and his goofiness.

And I missed my friends who were still here. I missed them terribly.

Dary was still desperately trying to make everything normal, and Abbi hardly spoke to me at all.

Seeing my friends start to move on while I was still stuck on the cliff, half dangling off, wore on me. They were racing ahead, while I was still on the first leg. Dary and Abbi talked about the homecoming dresses they'd bought over the weekend, a trip I'd been invited to but had begged off. They were so...normal, so everyday, and I was so not, because I was stuck in the welling grief that I was just now experiencing.

And, oh God, I missed Sebastian so much.

Things were rough between us. He was around, but things weren't like they had been. He still sat at our table at lunch and talked to me. He didn't ignore me or pretend that I didn't exist, but every interaction with him was superficial. His guards were up, walls intact.

Nothing was the same.

I'd hurt him.

I'd hurt myself.

And he didn't even know the full extent of it.

My heart had felt like it was going to fall out of my chest when Skylar had shown up at our table on Monday. He was sitting with Griffith and Keith, who was, like usual these days, right beside Abbi. I once tried to ask her if they were seeing each other, and she'd just shaken her head at me like I should've already known.

But at that moment I wasn't thinking about it, because I could hear Skylar's laughter and Sebastian's deeper chuckles and that drew my attention.

That's when I fell in love with you.

Sebastian had nodded at something she said, and then slowly his head turned in my direction. Our gazes had met, his shadowed, and then he looked away, his jaw clenching down hard. Skylar laughed again.

He said he loved me, but it appeared he was also moving on. Moving right back to Skylar, and her pretty smiles and clean conscience.

After school on Tuesday, I was dragging myself across the parking lot out to my car. I'd gotten there late that morning, so I was all the way in the back of the lot, near the football field. The sun was out, warming what would normally be a cooler autumn day, and I was thinking about how this was perfect weather for practices. Coach Rogers liked to have us run on the track at the end, and it was so much easier when you didn't have the hot summer sun beating down on you.

But I wouldn't be joining them after school for that run. I didn't miss those practices, but I did miss the game. Funny how I used to convince myself that the only reason I played was because of Megan. I knew now that it wasn't true.

I sighed and picked up my pace. I was about halfway across the parking lot when I heard my name called out, a breeze catching Sebastian's voice. I turned and saw him jogging toward me. He was dressed early for practice, in tights with nylon shorts over them.

My heart rate kicked up as I squinted up at him. "Hey," I croaked out.

"Hey." His arms were at his sides. "So, I had a question. I wanted to ask at lunch but forgot."

"Okay?"

"Are you going to homecoming?" he asked.

Caught off guard, I knew I was gaping at him. Was he seriously going to ask me to go? After what I'd said to him? After not really talking to me for almost a month? But if he was asking me, no matter how unexpected it was, I couldn't say no. I wouldn't, even though I had no business going to a dance when I...

Swallowing the rancid guilt, I shook my head. "No. I don't have plans to."

His blue eyes narrowed slightly. "It's your senior home-coming. Last one."

"I know." Really, it just *felt* like it was my last year to play volleyball and to go to homecoming. But it wasn't. Not for me. But for Megan and the others, it had been.

"So you're just going to stay home?" He glanced over his shoulder briefly, and then his gaze settled on me.

I knew right then that he wasn't asking me to the dance and heat blasted my cheeks. Of course he wasn't. Why would he? I cleared my throat. "Yeah, I'm staying home."

Sebastian stared at me.

"Is that all you wanted to ask me?" I asked, glancing away from his eyes and then focusing on his shoulder.

"Yeah." Sebastian started backing up toward the school. "I was just curious." He started to turn and then looked over at me. A moment passed before he said, "I'll see you later, Lena."

"Bye," I whispered, watching him turn around and jog off. That had been our longest conversation in weeks.

I'm in love with you.

Standing in the parking lot, I squeezed my eyes shut. A car honked nearby.

He'd loved me, and I'd…I'd damaged our friendship and ended a possible future for us…before it even began.

Dary leaned against the locker beside me. Her polka-dotted bow tie matched the blue-and-white suspenders she wore. "You have to meet with Dr. Perry today?"

"Yeah." I pulled out my History text. "I only meet with

him Monday and Friday this week and next. Then I think I'm done with him in November."

"That's good news, then?"

I nodded and closed my locker door.

I guessed it was good news. I mean, either Dr. Perry thought I'd be in a better headspace by then, or his time he could dedicate on me was simply up. I knew in one of his follow-up calls with my mom he'd mentioned that I might benefit from outside, continuing therapy, but I was pretty sure Mom's insurance didn't cover that and we really didn't have the money to spend on it.

Hopefully, I would be better by then.

But that was a bridge I wasn't crossing yet.

"Can I ask you something?" When I nodded, she said, "What's going on with you and Sebastian? I've been wondering for weeks now, but you always get all weird when he's brought up, so I haven't said anything."

I hitched the strap of my bag over my shoulder. "Nothing is going on."

"Really? Because he was all Lena, twenty-four hours a day, seven days a week, and then all the sudden he's not sitting next to you and I haven't seen you guys really talking."

"He's just busy. So am I," I lied as I turned.

Dary walked beside me as I made my way to the front of the school. "So, I've heard a rumor," she said, speaking each word carefully. "I debated on telling you, because I didn't want to upset you, but I also didn't want you to be blindsided if it's true."

The muscles in my back tensed. She could be referencing *so* many things. "What?" We stopped at the end of the hall, by the wall of really terrible art projects that I had no idea why anyone would showcase. "What rumor?"

Dary bit down on her lip as she shifted her weight from one foot to the next. "I heard… Well, Abbi heard this and then told me, so—"

"Wait. Abbi heard a rumor and told you but not me?" Exasperation raised my voice.

"Yeah." Dary sighed.

"She couldn't have just told me?"

"She could've, but you two aren't exactly best friends forever right now, and I think she knew I'd tell you," Dary reasoned, and then pointed out, "And you also aren't really making much of an effort to repair that broken bridge."

I opened my mouth to disagree, but Dary was right. I wasn't doing much of anything. "Okay. What did she hear?"

"She was hanging out with Keith after practice—"

"Are those two together?" I asked.

Dary raised a shoulder. "Who knows? I think they are, but Abbi doesn't want anyone to know, because, well, you know how Abbi is, but they are going to the dance as dates even though she's driving with me. You're being a loser who's not going at all, but I know Keith asked her." She took a breath and rushed on. "She was hanging out with Keith after practice and Sebastian was with them. Skylar was there, too. Not *with them* with them, but she was there."

My heart splattered.

"Abbi overheard Skylar and Sebastian talking about homecoming. She said it sounded like they were going together." Dary looked uncomfortable. "Abbi said she couldn't be certain from the bits and pieces she heard, but that's what it sounded like. And the last you opened up about him, you said he'd told you he loved you. So I thought you just needed to know."

My mouth opened, but I didn't have any words, because this shouldn't be a surprise to me. Even though it felt like my chest had just been stomped on by a combat boot, I was the one who'd pushed Sebastian out and away.

No wonder he'd asked me if I was going. Now he could go with Skylar and not worry about me seeing them, all dressed up and perfect together.

"That's nice," I murmured, blinking rapidly.

"Seriously? That's all you have to say?"

I nodded numbly. "Yeah, I think it's good for him—for them," I lied. That was the best I could do right then.

It was all I could do.

CHAPTER TWENTY-SIX

"How did it feel going back to work this weekend?" Dr. Perry asked Monday morning, like he did every Monday morning.

It was the last week of October. Homecoming was this weekend. The big game. The big dance. Normally I wouldn't have started at Joanna's until middle or late November, but since I wasn't playing volleyball, I'd decided that at least I could go start making money again.

"It was okay." My arms were wrapped around my knees. "A little weird, being back. Felicia, one of the other waitresses, had made a cake for me. It was nice."

"Chocolate cake, I hope," he said, and smiled when I nodded. Today there was no mug. Only a silver thermos. "Did you do what I asked you to over the weekend?"

Pressing my lips together, I shook my head.

Infinite patience filled his expression. I didn't understand how he did it. "How have things been with your friends?"

He'd asked the question every Monday, because every Friday one of my "assignments" was to open up to my friends, and every weekend I couldn't work up the nerve.

I loosened my grip on my knees. "Dary is the same. She just wants everyone to be normal, you know? She just wants us all to be friends. It's not like she wants to forget about Megan or any of the guys, but I...I don't think she wants to think about it anymore. So it's hard to think about dragging it back up."

"Talking about what you're dealing with isn't dragging it up," he said, and I wasn't sure I agreed. "And Abbi?"

"She hasn't said anything about me not being drunk since the first time, but she barely talks to me." Sadness poured in like a torrential downpour, because I missed Abbi as much as I missed Megan. I couldn't bring one friend back, and I had no idea how to fix things with the other. "I don't know if I told you this, but I...I brought up how she came to the party with Chris and had thought he'd already been drinking." I shifted, uncomfortable. "She said it wasn't the same because no one died when she was in the car."

"Well, it's often hard for people to admit that they, too, have made potentially life-altering choices when they did not receive any consequences for them. It is even more difficult for people to look at themselves and acknowledge that they are not perfect, that at times in their life they have also been *that* person. That they, too, have made decisions that could've ended disastrously."

Dr. Perry crossed one leg over the other. "Some people are simply lucky. Some are not. But some learn, even when they didn't suffer. They see situations like yours, and it serves as a painful wake-up call that they could've been where you are, which creates a lot of internal conflict. That's hard to recognize. It's always easier to point out the flaws in others while ignoring your own." He lightly drummed the end of his pen on the table. "Then you have those who never learn a lesson in their life, but they will be the first to cast judgment."

I nibbled on my nail. "But their judgment is on point, though. I could've walked away. I could've tried to get the keys from Cody. I could've gone back to the party and found Keith or Sebastian or—"

"Yes, you could've done that. You could've *not* caved to the pressure from your friends and decided that you were not going to ride with him. You might've been able to convince Megan to stay behind. You might not have, and that accident still would've happened. You may have gotten the keys from him or he may have ignored you and still gotten behind that wheel." He paused, sighing heavily. "Cody had quite a bit of weight on you. You can't know you would've been able to get those keys, or if he would've hung around while you went and found someone else."

"But I could've tried," I whispered, dropping my feet onto the floor.

"You could have, Lena, but you didn't. What you did do is ask him if he was okay. You didn't listen to that little voice inside you that told you differently when he answered, but..." He sighed. "I'm going to be really honest with you right now. Is that okay?"

I wrinkled my nose. "Have you not been honest this whole time?"

A brief grin appeared. "You made some bad choices that

night. You fully understand that, and you accept that. You're not deluding yourself. You haven't created a revisionist history of events. You could've convinced yourself that there was nothing you could've done, but you haven't. You know what happened, and what could've happened but didn't. That's never going to change. You're going to have to learn to live with the decisions you've made, accept them, learn from them, grow from them and become a better person because of them."

Scrubbing my hand over my face, I was glad I hadn't worried myself with mascara this morning, because it would've been all over my cheeks by now. "But how do I get to that part where I accept the decision I made? That I become this magically better person? When I stop feeling like the worst human being on the planet?"

"You're not the worst human being on the planet."

I shot him a droll look.

He arched a brow as he lifted a hand. "Most big changes happen slowly...and, also, all at once."

"That makes no sense."

"One day you will just realize you've made it through this part of your life and you've accepted what cannot be changed. That is when you've moved on. It will feel like it happened suddenly, but in reality, it's been a work in progress."

My eyes narrowed. "That's not exactly helpful."

Dr. Perry smiled in a way that said one day I wouldn't hold that same opinion. "A good place to start is opening up with those you care about."

A burst of panic lit up my stomach.

"You have a choice. Either continue the way you have

been with them, always worrying about what they'd do if they found out. We know that's exhausting, and it's already hurting your friendships." He was right. "Or you could open up to them."

"But what…what if they hate me?" I asked.

"Then they never were truly your friends in the first place," he replied. "They may be mad, at first, and even disappointed, but when someone is truly a friend—truly cares about another person—they accept them for all their flaws."

I started nibbling on my finger again. I wasn't sure what I'd done was something that could be considered *just* a flaw.

"How are things with you and Sebastian?" he asked.

A heavy sadness hit my veins. I thought about how I saw him with Skylar the other day, the rumor that Dary had heard, and I shook my head, because that wasn't important. He'd come into Joanna's for lunch on Saturday, after practice, like he used to do before…before everything. He'd ordered pie and milk, but it wasn't like it used to be.

"It's not that great," I said finally. "I want to tell him, but I think, what if he hates me afterward? I know you say he was never my friend if that happens, but he *was*. He was my best friend, and what I did…"

Dr. Perry's steady gaze met mine. "There's something I want you to understand. You did not kill your friends, Lena. You made a poor decision that night. They made poor decisions that night, too.

"You did not kill them."

After classes I closed my locker door and slung my backpack over my shoulder. Dull pain flared down my arm, but

I barely winced as I pivoted around and started down the hall. Faces were a blur. They'd been a blur all day as my session with Dr. Perry repeated over and over.

Since I'd already known that I hadn't technically killed my friends, Dr. Perry's parting words really didn't put me at ease. I didn't drink and drive that night, but I hadn't done everything in my power to stop Cody. So I wasn't legally responsible. I hadn't *technically* done it.

I was, however, morally responsible.

Which I was discovering was a heavy weight to carry, because how did you shed that kind of culpability? I wasn't sure you ever could.

But I was willing to try.

I hadn't gone to lunch, my stomach too twisted up in anxious knots from what I planned to do. Dary had texted while I was hiding out in the library, and I'd told her I was fine, just had to study for an exam.

I knew what I needed to do when I got home, and the mere thought of it made me want to hurl all over my shoes. Maybe that was why, as I came down the stairwell and hit the main hall heading out to the parking lot, I stopped by the closed double doors to the small gym. Maybe I was procrastinating. Maybe it was something else.

Peering through the small windows, I felt the muscles in my stomach clench as I watched the girls run sets across the court. Coach Rogers stood by the net, calling out commands. The walls and thick doors muted most of his deep voice. There were only a few more weeks in the season. I'd been paying attention. The team had had a good year and they would most likely make it to the semifinals.

I should be in there.

The moment the thought finished, I squeezed my eyes shut against the sudden wave of regret. I could've played the last couple of weeks since the cast came off. I could've—

I could've done a lot of things.

But it was too late for that. I'd made my choice to leave the team, and I couldn't go back on that, even if I did miss playing. When I was out on the court, my brain had shut down. I hadn't obsessed over Sebastian. I hadn't stressed over Mom or worried about my absentee father. I'd just been out there, focusing on the ball—on my team.

"I can play again," I whispered, and my body jerked. Surprised, I opened my eyes. The team was over by the bleachers. I *could* play again. Try out for a college team. I might not make it, but I could try. I could—

The sound of footsteps pulled me out of my thoughts. Hand tightening on the strap of my bag, I stepped back and glanced down the hall.

It was Keith.

I hadn't seen him all day. He was dressed like he was coming back from a banquet, in dark trousers and a button-down white shirt. His gym bag was on his shoulder, football cleats dangling from one of his hands.

Our gazes connected and his footsteps slowed. "Hey," he said, glancing at the doors beside me. "What are you up to?"

Having no idea how to explain what I was doing, I shrugged. "You heading to practice?"

"Yeah." He stopped in front of me, and there was no way I could miss the slight red rimming his eyes. "I had a meeting thing with my parents and...and the lawyers. Took most of the afternoon."

My stomach dropped as I remembered that Keith was dealing with a whole different set of consequences from that night. How could I have forgotten about that? "How...how is everything going with that?"

Lifting his free hand, he scrubbed his fingers over his head. "It's not... Yeah, it's not good. Our lawyer is advising them to take a plea deal. You know, a fine and community service to avoid jail time." He drew in a deep breath, dropping his hand. "There's the civil suits, you know?"

I nodded, unsure of what to say.

"Can I ask you something?"

"Sure," I said.

A muscle flexed along his jaw as he looked away, and then his gaze found mine once more. "Why didn't you join the suits? You were hurt pretty bad. You were in that car."

Not expecting that question, I floundered for words. "I...I just didn't think it was the right thing for me to do." And it wasn't. I hadn't been drinking that night. I should've been sued myself. "I just don't want to be a part of it."

He nodded slowly and a long moment passed. "My parents aren't bad people. They let us drink at home because they thought it was safer. That we wouldn't be out there driving..." I knew all of this. "Cody could've stayed with me. He knew that we had an open-couch policy. Everyone could've stayed. That was the agreement. Have fun, but don't drive if you've been drinking." Keith cursed under his breath. "Cody knew that."

My chest constricted. His parents weren't bad people. They

were people who, I guessed, just didn't think things through. They were good people who'd made a series of bad decisions when it came to allowing everyone to hang out at their house. "I know."

"I don't know… I don't know what's going to happen." His shoulders slouched. "I mean, they're going to lose the farm, the orchards, everything." He looked over my shoulder, shaking his head. "I don't even know why I'm going to practice. Like, what's the fucking point? Shit."

"I'm sorry," I blurted out.

A flicker of surprise crawled across Keith's face, and then it was washed away with disbelief. His mouth moved as if he was about to say something, but he didn't. I knew then. I knew right then that he couldn't understand why or how I was apologizing, and it hit me with the force of a speeding truck.

Keith was just like me.

He blamed his family.

He blamed himself.

He didn't see the point in doing the things he did before.

He felt these things even though, at the same time, he wanted to defend his family and himself. It wasn't fair, because Keith hadn't done anything. He didn't deserve this, but he…

He was *just like me*.

I never saw it until this moment. I knew Abbi had realized it already, but because I was so caught up in my own guilt, my own pain, I never saw Keith. I never saw Abbi or Dary. I never saw Sebastian. I never saw this entire school grieving. I saw only myself.

Keith dipped his chin. "I've...I've got to go." He side-stepped me. "I'll see you later, Lena."

"Bye," I whispered, turning as he walked away. I watched him go and I stood there long after he disappeared from view. A hundred different thoughts were racing through my head all at once as I started walking down the hall, but one question stood out among all the others.

Was I a good person who'd just made a bad choice?

Out on my balcony, I paced back and forth as I waited for Sebastian to get home from practice. He hadn't texted, but I'd messaged him as I sat in my car after class and asked if he'd come over. My heart had been pounding the whole drive home. He hadn't come to my room since that night.

It was a little after four when he texted back and said he would come, and while I'd been able to breathe a little easier, I was now a nervous mess.

Tugging the sides of my cardigan together, I walked to the end of the balcony and peered around to the front of the house, my breath halting in my throat. His Jeep was now out there. My gaze flicked up, and I saw a light on in his bedroom. When had he gotten home? I had no idea. Practice could run for hours.

As I stood there, I wished I hadn't eaten the entire plate of spaghetti for dinner, because now I felt like hurling.

I figured I'd talk to Sebastian first, because I'd known him the longest. And, well, he'd said he loved me. I'd probably ruined that with the harsh crap I'd spewed at him, but he deserved to know what happened.

And so did Abbi and Dary.

They'd be next.

I just had to get past this conversation.

The light flipped off, and I gasped out a little squeak, but I couldn't move. I stood at the edge of the stairs that led into the backyard until I saw the back door open and Sebastian walked out onto the brick patio.

Even from where I stood in the failing light, I could tell he'd taken the time to shower. His hair was wet, slicked back in a way that highlighted the sharp, high cheekbones. He was wearing a pair of jogging pants, the kind that hung low on the hips, and a thermal.

God, he was breathtaking, and I wished he hadn't stopped to take a shower and instead smelled of sweat and had dirt and grass staining his skin.

Who I was kidding? I'd still find him stunning.

Sebastian crossed the patio, stopped at the edge and looked up. He appeared completely frozen for a second, possibly realizing that I'd been out there waiting for him.

Then he walked up the side of the house and passed through the gates, and my pulse was all over the place. He came around the corner and then started up the steps.

Only then did I move.

Edging backward, I clasped my hands together. His head crested the top and then he was right in front of me, towering over me, his sea-blue eyes guarded, as they had been since the last time he'd been here.

His eyes held mine. "I'm here."

"Can we…go inside?" I asked.

Sebastian's gaze darted to the door and he hesitated—and

it hurt, because he'd never hesitated—but then he nodded curtly.

I walked to the door and opened it, letting him in before he changed his mind. From there I went to the bed and sat on the edge. Sebastian took the computer chair.

"Keith said he saw you right before practice," he said.

"We…we just chatted for a few minutes."

Sebastian waited, and when I didn't say any more, a muscle popped out in his jaw. Mouth dry, I focused on the map as I blurted out the stupidest possible thing ever to come out of my mouth, which was saying something. "How are things with you and Skylar?"

Silence and then, "Is that why you wanted to talk to me tonight? About her?"

"No," I said immediately. "Just ignore that. I don't even know why I asked."

"Of course not," he muttered.

I flinched. "I need to tell you something. Well, I need to first say I'm sorry for what I said to you that, um, that last time you came here. That wasn't right."

"No," he replied. "No, it wasn't."

I winced but kept going. "I know what we were doing wasn't about… It wasn't about getting laid." I flushed hotly. "And I know you miss your friends as much as I do, and I shouldn't have insinuated otherwise."

Sebastian didn't reply, so I shifted my gaze down to him. He was watching me intently with those eyes, his head tilted slightly. Then he spoke.

"It took you a month to apologize?"

"It shouldn't have. I've wanted to before now, but…" I

swallowed hard. "I don't have a good excuse except that I've been working to get my head sort of straight with Dr. Perry, and I just need to tell you the truth. And I don't know how you will feel afterward. You might walk out of here this time and really never speak to me again. You might end up hating me." Tears clogged my throat. "But I need to tell you something."

A change came over Sebastian. Since I knew him so well, I could see it. A wall dropped, and he leaned forward, resting his forearms on his knees. "I could never hate you, Lena."

My heart shattered into a million pieces at the almost brutal sweetness of those words. He had no idea. None. He could hate me. That was real. But I took a deep steadying breath anyway and said, "When I got into the car the night Cody was driving, I…I wasn't drunk. I could've stopped him. I didn't."

CHAPTER TWENTY-SEVEN

Sebastian didn't move. He didn't speak for the longest moment. His steady gaze didn't leave my face as he finally said, "What happened that night wasn't your fault, Lena."

"I am partially at fault," I said, using Dr. Perry's phrasing. "That's why I haven't talked about what happened this whole time. I could have stopped Cody. I should have. But I didn't."

He straightened, that muscle flexing along his jaw again. Another pregnant pause that stretched my nerves thin. "Tell me what you need to say, Lena."

My lips moved without sound at first, and it took a couple of seconds for me to get the words out right. I wanted to do what Dr. Perry had told me to do: to rewind and start from the beginning, no matter how hard it was.

"After you and I... After we talked at the party, I went and hung out with Abbi and Keith. They were having an intense conversation. I don't know about what. It was kind of like they were arguing and flirting at the same time. I sat with them for a while but didn't drink anything. Just water and I think… No, I'm sure I drank a Coke. Then it was getting late, and I just wanted to leave."

That night, sitting on the chair beside Abbi, I had been thinking only about Sebastian, about him and Skylar disappearing, having no idea that in a matter of hours, none of that would matter.

I took another gulp of air and didn't look at him, because he knew why I hadn't come to find him like I'd promised. "Megan was ready to go home, too. She was hungry and wanted chicken nuggets. I don't even know how Cody ended up leaving. Megan and I were walking with Chris and then Cody was just there. Chris was pretty messed up. Someone said he'd been drinking since that afternoon, and he said he was too tired to drive. Cody took the keys, and he seemed fine at first. I swear he did. But I remember seeing him reach for the handle of the driver's door and miss it."

Closing my eyes, I spoke through the rawness. "I asked him if he was okay to drive and he said yes. He actually seemed kind of annoyed about the question. I didn't want to get into the car. It was instinct, I guess. I was just standing there, and then Chris was telling me to get in the car and Megan was pushing me and Phillip was joking around like he always was and Cody said he only had one drink that night, but I knew…*I knew*…that wasn't the case. He said he was fine, though, and I…I didn't want to be *that* person, you know? The one who makes a big deal out of nothing."

Tears pricked my eyelids. "But I guess I became a different kind of person, because I should've tried to stop him. I knew he'd had more than one drink. His face was flushed.

I shouldn't have gotten in the car, because he wasn't okay to drive, and God…it happened so fast. I texted Dary and was about to text Abbi where I was. The radio was on. Music was playing. I remember wind coming in through the windows. I remember thinking that we were going fast and then I heard Cody shout and Megan scream. And that…that was it." I let out a shaky breath. "So, you see, I could've done something. Stopped him. Stayed behind. Driven the car myself. I just did the wrong thing, and I'm…"

I didn't know what else to say.

I was done, and I wanted to slip off the bed and hide under it, but all I could do was sit and wait for the anger and the disappointment. Part of telling him was dealing with how he felt afterward.

Slowly, I opened my eyes and looked at Sebastian.

His face was pale and tight. His hands were on his knees, his knuckles bleached.

"You…you remember the accident?"

I nodded. "Up until I lost consciousness. Something hit me in the head, but I remember the car hitting the tree and flipping. I remember the car rolling. It…it was the scariest thing I've ever experienced. I thought…" I trailed off, because Sebastian had to know what I thought.

I'd thought I was going to die.

"Jesus." He closed his eyes tight. Then he said, "I knew."

"What?" I breathed.

He leaned forward again, the chair creaking under his weight. "I've always known you weren't drunk that night."

"I don't understand."

His hands slid off his knees. "I think I've only seen you

drunk once, and that wasn't at a party. It was when Megan dared you to drink the bottle of wine your mother had forgotten about in the cabinet. You were too trashed to walk upstairs and Megan had to come get me to carry you to bed."

A watery smile pulled at my lips. Damn Megan. I'd forgotten about that messy wine-induced horror show. "I got so sick."

"Yeah, you did." He tilted his head, his own smile sad. "And as soon as I got you upstairs in your bedroom, I then had to carry you to the bathroom, where you turned into a volcano of vomit."

Oh gosh.

Sebastian had held me up with one arm around my waist, and Megan had scooped strands of hair back from my face. That was two years ago.

It had also been the first and only time I'd gotten drunk.

For some reason I never thought that Sebastian even remembered that.

"I know you don't drink more than a couple of mouthfuls, and unless you decided to change it up that night, I knew you couldn't have been drunk," he said.

"So…" I wet my lips, stunned. "So you suspected this whole entire time that I was sober and got in that car anyway?"

Sebastian nodded. "I didn't know if you really remembered the accident or not. You said you didn't, and since you wouldn't talk about it, I figured you didn't have solid memories of it. Knowing that you do, though? Hell…"

I was thunderstruck.

His gaze held mine. "I probably would've gotten in the car."

"What?" My entire body jolted, and I started to stand, but my knees went weak.

"I probably would've done the same thing," he said. "Shit. I know I would've. I would've taken Cody for his word, and I would've gotten in the car just like you did. I don't even know if I would've thought about it as much as you had."

"No. You wouldn't have. Sebastian, you would've stopped him. You—"

"I'd been drinking that night and had been planning to drive you home," he interrupted, collapsing back in his chair. "I told you that before. I could've been Cody. I know I could've been. Drink a couple of beers, think I was fine and then get behind a wheel. I cannot even count how many times I've done that."

I started to say it wasn't the same thing, but it was, and I didn't know what to say or do. I was expecting him to be furious and disappointed in me, but his expression showed none of those things, and neither did his words or actions.

He got up, walked over to the bed and sat next to me. He didn't say anything. He didn't need to at that moment.

I realized as he stared at me that he really had known the truth this entire time. He'd known I could've done better, I should've, but he also had been honest with himself. He knew he'd been in that situation himself and had made bad choices, but, as Dr. Perry said, he'd gotten lucky. He'd never had to pay the consequences for those decisions.

It didn't make what he'd done okay.

It didn't make what I'd done okay.

But he wasn't judging me, and he had never judged me. This whole entire time I'd been so afraid of what he would think of me, and he already knew. He knew and was still there for me. He *knew* and *still* said he loved me.

My shoulders lowered centimeter by centimeter. "You don't hate me? You're not disgusted or dis—"

"Stop. I could never think those things, Lena. Not about you."

A wave of relief rose, tinged with a deep sorrow that started loosening its razor-sharp claws. My voice was thick when I spoke. "But how? I'm so disgusted with myself. I h–hate myself."

"You made a mistake, Lena." He leaned in closer. "That was what happened. You didn't kill them. You made a *mistake*."

A mistake that cost people their lives.

I shuddered, lifting my hands to my face. Smoothing my palms over my cheeks, I willed the wetness gathering to go away, because I was tired of crying.

"Lena," he said, voice low and rough. "Come here." Sebastian extended his hand.

I was moving before I gave thought about what I was doing. My hand folded into his, and when he hauled me into his lap, knees on either side of his hips, my arms went around his waist.

He clasped the sides of my face and, without saying a word, he kissed my cheek once and then twice, and he kissed away each tear that fell, and a heartbeat passed.

I broke. Ripped right open.

He made a sound in the back of his throat and then pulled my face to his chest. Tears streamed down my face, dampening the front of his shirt within seconds. His arms swept around me and he held me tight, held me close as I cried for Megan, for the guys, for Abbi and Dary, and for myself.

We lay side by side in bed, our faces separated by only a few inches. It was late, well past midnight, and the morning was going to come soon enough, but neither of us were sleeping. We had whispered to one another after the tears had subsided. I told him about the guilt, how it weighed on me, about how I wanted nothing more than to go back to that night and make different choices. I told him about the nightmares and how my mom knew the truth, how disappointed I knew she really was but wasn't saying. I admitted to wishing I hadn't quit volleyball. I told him how I talked to Keith today and what I realized. I even told him about Abbi.

Sebastian listened.

"Are you going to talk to them?" he asked. "Abbi and Dary?"

"I need to." My arms were folded against my chest. "It's not going to be easy, but I need to." I shifted my legs. "Has Abbi said anything to you about the accident?"

"No. Nothing beyond what everyone else has said. Nothing about you." He inched closer. "Abbi has gotten really close with Keith, and I think she's helping him deal with everything on his end." He reached over the small distance and hooked his fingers around a strand of my hair that had fallen across my cheek. "What's going on with Keith is so different. No one blames you or your family. They don't know what you told me, and even if they did, I think most people would understand you made a mistake."

A deadly mistake.

"But with Keith, everyone knows his family furnished

the alcohol. They were the adults, and it's really tearing his family up," Sebastian explained quietly. "No one is really saying anything to Keith, but he's having a rough time. Not to sound like an ass, but he's letting his friends help him and…"

"And I didn't," I finished, feeling gross. I hadn't really even thought about what Keith was going through.

Sebastian trailed a finger over my cheekbone, drawing my gaze back to him. Something, I wasn't sure what exactly, had changed between us. It was almost tangible, and I think it had happened when he kissed away my tears and held me through the worst of them.

"You really not going to homecoming this weekend?" he asked.

The change of subject made me think of Skylar. "What about you?"

"Was going with some of the guys."

"Not Skylar?"

His brows shot up. "No." He laughed. "Why would you think that?"

I felt my cheeks heat. "You guys have been getting chatty again."

"We've always been chatty," he replied drolly. "She's actually going with someone from Wood."

"Really?" Surprise flashed through me. "I heard that you two were talking about homecoming."

One of his eyebrows rose. "We talked about it, but not going together." His gaze searched mine. "She knows I'm not going back there with her, and you should know that, too.

Just because things…didn't pan out the way I hoped doesn't mean I'm going to play someone else."

Things panning out had to do with me. I knew that.

Sebastian smoothed his thumb over my jaw. "There's always prom."

I liked how he said that. "There is prom."

He was silent for several moments and then said, "Thank you for tonight."

I frowned. "You're thanking me?"

"Yeah." His hand slid down to my shoulder and he squeezed. "You've been carrying this around and you're not doing that by yourself anymore. You've told me. You're going to talk to Abbi and Dary. You're really not alone in this anymore."

A tired smile tugged at my lips. "Shouldn't I be thanking you, then?"

"Nah. I didn't do anything. I just listened."

But that was incredibly powerful.

"It's all you," he added.

Sebastian was sort of right. A lot of it was me.

My sleepy smile spread. Tonight…talking to Sebastian, was big, because either I could let what I'd done wreck me or I could learn to live with it.

That was the only choice I could make at this point, and I had to make the right one this time.

I was going to.

CHAPTER TWENTY-EIGHT

Dr. Perry was so ecstatic with my progress Wednesday morning he gave me an assignment. Two, actually, not counting the talk I needed to have with Abbi and Dary.

"There are two things I want you to do," he said. "Both are incredibly important to the grieving process. First off, I want you to dedicate one day a week to grief."

My brows pinched. "Like, the whole day?"

"Not the whole day, unless you feel like you need that," he clarified. "It can be just an hour or several hours. What I want you to do on that day is spend time remembering your friends. Look at old pictures, visit their social media accounts if they're still available, write about them. I want you to think about them, remember them and process those feelings. Do you think you can do that?"

I could. It would be hard, especially looking at their pictures and seeing their last posts, but I could do it.

"Grieving them isn't an easy thing to do, especially for you.

Mainly because you feel a responsibility toward what happened. And it's never easy grieving the deaths of those who ultimately played their own role in their deaths." He rested his arms on the table. "I see a lot of anger and uncertainty when working with families of those who have overdosed. What you need to remember, at the end of the day, is that these people were your friends. No matter what happened, you cared about them and you are allowed to grieve them."

Nodding slowly, I said, "I can do it."

"What day?" he immediately followed up.

"Um." I wrinkled my nose. "I could do Sunday evenings?" I also thought Sunday evenings were kind of depressing anyway.

"Sounds good. The second thing I want you to do is actually a commitment."

I raised a brow.

"By the end of the year, I want you to visit their graves."

My stomach immediately tumbled at the thought.

A sympathetic look filled his eyes. "I know. When you see their graves, it'll be very final, but I think that for you, it's necessary. You were unable to attend their services. Visiting their grave site may do more for you than just providing closure."

Pressure clamped down on my chest, but I nodded. "I can do that."

Because I had to.

Because I had made the decision to not let the choices I made on August 19 define my life or wreck it.

I was full of nerves at lunch, but I forced myself to eat what I think was lasagna but just looked like a lump of cheese and hamburger meat. Sebastian was back to sitting next to me, but his back was turned. He was having some deep conversation with one of the guys about the best hydrating drink or something. Keith was listening.

It was the perfect opportunity.

"So, um, I was wondering if you two wanted to grab something to eat after school?" I asked Abbi and Dary, sounding as awkward as if I was asking someone out on a date.

Dary's eyes immediately lit up behind the glasses. "I think that would be great." She glanced over at Abbi. "I don't have plans."

"I don't know." Abbi was peeling apart her lasagna with her fork. "I don't think I'll be hungry."

Dary's shoulders deflated.

I was prepared for this. "We could go to the smoothie place," I suggested, knowing Abbi could never turn down a fresh smoothie. "We don't have to go to a restaurant or anything like that."

Abbi's face was hard, but her gaze lifted to mine. My lower lip trembled as I leaned forward and whispered, "Please. I really want to talk to you guys."

Her jaw softened, and I held my breath, because I really thought she'd shoot me down, but then she nodded. "Okay."

Relief almost swept me out of my chair while Dary clapped like an overexcited seal. "Thank you," I whispered to her.

Abbi didn't respond, but she nodded, and that was something. That was enough for now.

Smoothies in hand, we found one of the booths in the back of the small restaurant. Abbi sat across from me and Dary.

I'd gone with Old Faithful—a simple strawberry smoothie. Dary was more creative and went for something that had peanut butter in it. Abbi ordered a mango.

If Megan was here, she would've bypassed the smoothie and gone straight for the flatbreads, claiming she was doing it for the protein.

Dary had been chatting since we sat down, and the moment she quieted, Abbi asked, "So why did you want us to come here?"

I'd stopped with the straw halfway to my mouth. "Does there have to be a reason?"

"No," Dary replied at the same time Abbi said, "Yes."

Abbi elaborated a second later. "You haven't wanted to do anything with us for months, so I'm figuring there's a reason."

"That's not entirely true," Dary stated gently.

"Maybe for you, but I've barely seen anything of her." Abbi slurped down a mouthful of smoothie.

"Okay." I held up my hand. "I deserve that. I haven't been a good friend in the last couple of months. I know that. That's why I wanted to talk to both of you today. I...I wanted to talk about the accident. About what happened that night."

Dary dropped her arm onto the table. "You don't have to." Twisting toward me, her eyes were already shining. "We don't have to do this."

"But I do." My gaze found Abbi's. "I need to get this off my chest."

And then I did.

I told them what I had told Sebastian, and it was easier simply because this was the third time I rewound that night, and it was less painful to bring myself back to that place.

But it wasn't easier to look Abbi or Dary in the eye. I made myself do it, because Abbi already knew the truth and Dary might've also suspected it, but I took that bitter weight of silence and I laid it out on the table between us, hoping that they would understand where my head had been since the accident but never once expecting forgiveness or acceptance.

As I spoke, Dary had pushed her glasses up and had covered her face, and I felt her shoulders tremble every so often. Continuing when I knew it was getting to her was like walking on heated shattered glass.

"I've been trying to work through all of that," I finished, feeling sapped of energy. "And I know me dealing with my guilt isn't a justification for shutting you guys out, and I...I don't even expect you guys to be okay with it. I just needed to be honest."

Abbi wasn't looking at me. She'd stopped when I got to the part about asking Cody if he was okay to drive. She was fiddling with the straw, her lips pressed together.

My throat burned. "I'm just so sorry. It's all I can say. I know it doesn't change anything, doesn't rewrite what has happened, but I'm so sorry."

Dary lowered her hands. Her eyes glistened. "I don't know what to say."

"You don't have to say anything," I said, feeling shaky.

She wiped at her cheeks. "You know, I suspected this. I mean, I knew you didn't drink a lot, and I've always wondered why you weren't the one who was driving, but I... It sucks to be in that situation. To not want to piss everyone off but do the right thing."

Abbi remained quiet.

"I should've done the right thing," I said.

Dary's breath shuddered out of her. "Yeah, you should've."

Sitting back, I dropped my hands in my lap. What could I say beyond that? Beyond the truth? I'd known going into this that I might lose Dary, like I was sure I'd lost Abbi.

Then Abbi finally spoke. "You made…a mistake. A big freaking mistake," she said, still staring at the bright yellow drink. "But that was *all* you did. You made a mistake."

My breath caught. What I felt I couldn't quite describe. It wasn't exactly absolution, but it was something powerful.

Dary looked at me, her cheeks damp. She didn't say anything, but a moment passed, and she leaned over, resting her head on my shoulder. A tremor coursed through me, threatening to take over.

"Okay," Dary said hoarsely. "All right. So, I would like some french fries right now, and this place doesn't sell them."

A watery laugh escaped me. "French fries sound perfect."

Abbi shook her head, causing the two thick braids to swing at the sides of her neck. "You just drank an entire smoothie and you want fries?"

"I need salt right now. I need tons of salt."

Abbi rolled her eyes.

"You know," Dary said, lifting her head off my shoulder, "I still love you. I just want you to know that."

Tears raced up my throat and I beat them back but didn't trust myself to talk, so all I could do was nod.

The subject at the table changed, and by the time we walked out of the smoothie shop, it was almost normal. *Almost* like it was before.

But I still needed to talk to Abbi one-on-one before they searched down the fries.

I stopped by my car. "Abbi, can you hold on a second."

Waving goodbye to Dary, she twisted around and faced me. Like when we were inside, some of that wall was down. Not a lot. But some.

"I know things are still weird between us, but I wanted to ask you about your parents. How is everything with them?"

Abbi opened her mouth and I braced myself for a snarky or snide response, but she said, "Mom hasn't been 'working late.'" Added air quotations with the last part. "And they're not arguing nearly as much anymore. I don't know if she's admitted to something or not, but I guess they're trying to make it work."

I leaned back against my car. "That's good, right?"

"Yeah. I guess so. At least we don't have to listen to them try not to kill each other." She knocked a braid back over her shoulder.

"I'm glad to hear that. Really."

She nodded again and then took a deep breath. "I need to tell you something, okay?"

I tensed. "Okay."

"I'm sorry about what I said to you about riding with Chris when he'd been drinking and it not being the same. I know it was, and you were right... I just got lucky." She swallowed hard. "And I really am sorry for saying that to you. I shouldn't have."

I briefly closed my eyes tight. "It's okay," I said, because it was.

"I...wasn't mad about you getting in that car. I mean, I was mad. I think anyone would be mad at first. But what pissed me off was the fact you shut me out. You shut all of us out."

"I know," I whispered. "I did."

"Do you have any idea how that made us feel? I didn't know how to help you. You wouldn't let me or anyone else in to even try to figure it out, and that's what really made me angry. I lost Megan, and it felt like I lost you, too."

"I'm sorry. I didn't mean to do it. I just—"

"I get it. Your head wasn't in the right place, and I...I should've done what Dary did. Given you space. Given you time." She dipped her chin. "So I am sorry for that."

"You don't have to apologize." I stepped toward her. "I don't want any more apologies. I just want things to be...to be okay between us."

"Me, too." Abbi then popped forward and hugged me. It was quick, not like they used to be, but it was better than nothing and it was a start. She stepped back. "I have to get going, but I'll text you later and you'll answer, right?"

"Right."

Abbi gave me a quick smile and then she was walking away, and I kind of wanted to cry. But these tears would've been so different from the ones from before.

So different.

Wednesday evening Sebastian was sitting on the bed, listening while I told him what had gone down that afternoon with Abbi and Dary, and then I told him what Dr. Perry wanted me to do.

"It's been a big week or so for you," he said when I finished.

I was sitting next to him, cross-legged with a pillow thrust in my lap. "It has."

"How do you feel after talking to them?"

Shrugging, I held the pillow tighter. "Better. Relieved. At least now they know everything. I know it doesn't change anything, and I know they are both disappointed, but it's out there between us now and, yeah, it's a relief," I repeated.

"I get what you're saying." He cocked his head to the side. "Sometimes disappointment is worth the truth." As he poked the pillow, a small grin played across his face. "You know, that night we got into it, you said something that was true."

My brows rose. "I don't think I said anything that was true."

"No. You did." He pulled the pillow out of my lap and put it behind him. "You were right about me not telling my dad about football."

Oh. Hell. I'd forgotten how I'd thrown that in his face. I'd probably blocked it out.

"I talked to my dad."

I jolted. "Seriously?"

"Yep." He peered at me through thick lashes. "It didn't exactly go over well."

Popping up on my knees, I scooted closer to him. "What happened? Tell me *everything*."

A brief grin appeared as I plopped down right in front of him. "I talked to him about a couple of weekends ago, actually. There's really not much to tell. I was just honest."

"And you're just now telling me?" I smacked his arm. "Sebastian!"

"Hey." He caught my hand, laughing. "We weren't exactly

being real talkative with one another, and you were dealing with other stuff."

"True." But I felt bad, because I should've had my head out of my butt long enough to have been there for him. I couldn't change that, but I could be here for him now. "So what did he do?"

"He flipped out. Said I wasn't thinking straight and that the accident had my head messed up. But I told him the truth—playing ball just isn't something I'm that into now." He lowered our joined hands to his knee. "I explained that I'd been feeling this way for a while."

"Wow."

"He didn't speak to me for a straight week." Sebastian laughed while I cringed. "But he seems to be trying to accept it. He's talking to me at least, and I think Mom has been working on him."

I squeezed his hand. "This is huge."

"Yeah," he murmured, biting down on his lower lip. "Looks like Dad won't enter a downward spiral because of it, so that's good."

Grinning, I asked, "So now that you've officially decided to not do the college-football thing, what school are you thinking about?"

"God, there's so much more opportunity now," he said, his gaze drifting over my shoulder, to the map above my desk. "May stick around and do community college for a year, or maybe I'll apply to Virginia Tech or—" his blue eyes fixed on mine "—UVA." The hollows of his cheeks turned pink as I gaped at him. "Or somewhere else. Who knows? I've still got some time. Anyway," he said, stretching out on the bed. He tugged on my hand. "Want to watch a movie?"

I studied his profile for a moment and then nodded. "Whatever you like."

The answering grin warmed me, and I let him pull me down so I was lying next to him. I reached over, grabbed the remote off the nightstand and handed it to Sebastian. He started flipping through the free-movie section.

"Hey," I said.

He turned those beautiful eyes to me.

"I'm proud of you. I just wanted to say that. I'm really proud of you."

The grin turned into a blinding smile that stayed on his face the rest of the evening.

CHAPTER TWENTY-NINE

Joanna's was dead on homecoming night, so much so that Felicia all but shoved me out the door at nine that evening.

After hanging up my apron, I made my way outside and climbed into my car. The drive home was quick, and once I was in my driveway, I checked my phone and saw a text from Dary of her and Abbi in their pretty dresses, under a flowery awning. They were totally rocking the awkward couple pose, with Abbi's arms wrapped around Dary's waist from behind. I'd messaged them both earlier in the evening, telling them to have a good time. Dary had texted back immediately with a heart and smiley face. And a half an hour later after that last text, Abbi had texted back with a simple message that chipped away at the heaviness in my veins.

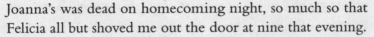

Wish you were here

That was a start—a *great* start—at repairing our friendship. And I wished I was there because I would've had fun with them, but I planned on doing something tonight I hadn't done in a while.

Read a book.

And I couldn't wait.

I was going to read while eating at least a half a bag of Fun-yuns. Maybe even an entire bag. I wasn't going to beat myself up for not going tonight. And I wasn't going to think about Sebastian at the dance, most likely being surrounded by girls.

Sebastian had swung by last night, after the game. There'd been no kissing or talking about the accident or about his dad. We'd just studied together.

I had no idea where things were going to go for us or where we'd end up, if we were together or apart. There would probably always be a part of me that would want more, but I was thrilled to have my best friend back. That was... That was good enough.

I climbed out of the car, then walked to the front of the house and reached for the door, but it opened before I even touched it.

Mom stood in the doorway, motioning me in. "Come on. Hurry up."

Frowning, I hurried inside and stared openmouthed as Mom took my purse from me. "What's going on?" I looked around, half expecting to see my father lurking in the dimly lit hallway.

"Nothing." Mom smiled, taking my hand as she pulled me into the living room. Then she picked up a bundle of cloth-ing and all but shoved it at me. "Go upstairs to the bathroom and change into this."

"What?" I looked down at what I was holding. Looked

like my oversize thermal and a pair of my black leggings that I was almost positive Mom must've washed while I was at work, because they had been dirty and lying on my floor. "I'm so confused."

"Don't ask questions. Just go do it." She ushered me toward the stairs and I let her practically shove me up the steps. "I'll be waiting for you in the hall. You have fifteen minutes."

I stopped outside the bathroom and barked out a surprised laugh. "Why? This is weird and you're—"

"Get in the bathroom," Mom ordered with a grin. "Or you're grounded."

"What?" I gasped out another laugh. "Have you lost your mind?"

Mom folded her arms. "I will drag you in there and change you myself."

"Oh my God. Okay, okay."

Taking the bundle of clothing, I went inside the bathroom, having no idea what she was up to or why I had to change right now. Did I smell that badly of fried chicken tenders? I'd barely worked up a sweat at Joanna's, but I took a quick shower anyway, like I always did when I got home. I'd kept my hair up in a bun, so I didn't have to mess with drying it. Changing into the clothes, I discovered the bundle had included a pair of thick socks. I rolled them on, tugging them up my calf.

Mom was waiting for me in the hallway.

"Are you going to tell me what's going on yet?" I asked, pushing up the sleeves on my thermal.

"Nope." She pivoted around. "Follow me."

Beyond curious, I followed her back downstairs and to the kitchen.

"Put these sneakers on." She motioned at the pair by the door. "And then go outside."

"I'm a little freaked out at this point." I slipped my sneakers on. "Like I'm about to walk into a trap."

"Now, why would I do that to my daughter?"

I shot her a look over my shoulder but opened the door anyway and came to a dead stop.

Sebastian was waiting outside on the patio Mom never used anymore, dressed like me with the exception of the leggings. He had on sweats and a slouchy gray knit hat. Over his shoulder, I thought his backyard looked brighter than normal, but then I saw what he held in his hands.

A corsage—rose petals in a vibrant, dewy red and in full bloom, sprinkled with baby's breath and fresh leaves.

I dragged my gaze to his.

A shy smile tugged at his lips. "Since you didn't go to homecoming, I thought we'd do something better."

My brain completely emptied of all thoughts.

"Be good." Mom passed both of us a long look. "Have fun."

With wide eyes, I turned back to Sebastian as Mom closed the door behind us. "I thought you were going to homecoming."

He shook his head as he walked over to me. "Nah. We can always do prom, right?"

We. The way he said that... "Right," I whispered.

"May I?" he asked, and in a dumb daze, I held up my arm. He slipped the corsage over my left hand and secured it to my wrist. "Looks good on you."

Blinking rapidly, I gave a little shake of my head. "Thank you."

"You can't say thanks yet." Taking my hand, he led me off the cracked cement, toward the gate between our yards. "So, I came up with something I thought would be much better than a dance."

With a knot in my throat, I followed him, absolutely stunned.

"I've actually been wanting to do this for a while and figured this was the perfect chance." He pushed open the gate and tugged me through. "What do you think?"

My mouth was hanging open as I took in the sight in front of me. Twinkling lights were hung from the shed to the trees, casting a soft glow on the narrow yard. In the center, several feet away from the patio, was a tent. A light flickered inside it.

"Camping?" I whispered.

Sebastian let go of my hand and shoved his hands into his pockets as he nodded. "You remember doing this when we were younger?"

"Yeah." Of course I did. "Every Saturday night. Either your dad or mine would come out here and set it up for us."

"We'd make s'mores." He nudged me gently with his shoulder. "Until that one time you caught your hair on fire."

"I didn't catch my hair on fire!" I laughed, and it was a real, deep laugh that shocked me into silence. When had I last laughed like that?

"I stand corrected. It was only a few strands. Same thing." He leaned into me this time, and I turned slightly, dropping the side of my head against his arm. "We're not roasting s'mores tonight, but I got the next best thing."

"What?" My voice was hoarse.

"You have to wait and see," he answered. "It's a surprise."

"Another?"

"Another."

Oh God.

Lifting my right hand, I rubbed my palm over my eyes. A slight wetness clung to my lashes.

"You okay?"

"Of course." I pulled it together as I stepped away and glanced at the back door. "Where are your parents?"

"They're doing date night. They'll be home later."

"And they know about this?"

He chuckled. "Yeah. Mom wanted to hang around and take pictures of us standing in front of the tent, since she feels she got cheated out of the senior homecoming pictures."

Another laugh burst out of me, shaking my entire body, and as the laugh faded like ashes in the wind, I saw Sebastian staring at me in the glittering lights.

"I missed that sound," he said, angling his body toward me. "Your laugh. I missed it more than I even realized."

Feeling a little breathless, I brought my gaze to his. "Me, too."

"Good." His eyes searched mine and then he exhaled heavily. "Ready to check out the tent?"

Toying with a string of baby's breath on the corsage, I started to follow him when suspicion suddenly blossomed, and I stopped to look up at Sebastian. "Did you...talk to Felicia?"

He grinned, hands still shoved into the pockets, obviously pleased with himself. "Maybe."

"You did!" My eyes widened. "That's why she let me go home two hours early. When did you do it?"

"Thursday night I swung by and asked," he said, eyes glimmering in the low light.

"And obviously you talked to my mom."

He nodded once more. "A couple of days ago. She said, and I quote, 'You're such a sweet boy.' Not that I needed to be told that."

"You *are* a sweet boy."

Chuckling, he peeled back the flap of the tent. "You first."

I toed off my sneakers, then ducked inside the tent and was able to stand straight. Sebastian wasn't able to as he stepped inside, so he knelt beside me as I inhaled the musty scent, immediately swamped by memories of the long summer nights spent in a much smaller tent.

There was an air mattress on the ground, along with two sleeping bags and a comforter I vaguely recognized from Sebastian's house. Pillows were stacked at one side of the mattress. A little LED lantern sat on a plastic folding table. A pile of food waited in the corner—chips, sodas, Tupperware containers and even a bag of Funyuns.

That was pretty much when I knew I would forever be in love with Sebastian.

Sebastian reached over to the pile of food, picked up a container and popped the lid open. "Mom made s'more brownies."

My mouth watered. "S'more brownies? That sounds like heaven."

"They are amazing." He put the lid back on and picked up another. "The last time she made them, I ate so many I thought I'd vomit."

I laughed as I watched him open another lid. That one had strawberries and pieces of watermelon in it.

"Cut them up myself," he said, sitting down on the edge of the mattress. "I think I deserve a pat on the head for that alone."

Grinning, I patted the top of his knit cap and then looked around the tent again. Emotion closed up my throat. This was amazing, perfect and so incredibly thoughtful.

I kind of wanted to cry. "This is…"

"What?" Sebastian looked over at me.

"Thank you." I dropped down on the mattress beside him. Leaning over, I clasped his cheeks. "Thank you so much. I never expected you to do anything like this, and I know I don't—"

"Don't say it." He folded his hands over my wrists. Our eyes met. "There will be none of that tonight. At all. It's just you and me and a ton of calories waiting to be consumed. Nothing else. No past. Nothing."

I just stopped thinking. Right then. Right there.

And I just *acted*.

Closing the distance between us, I kissed Sebastian on the lips, throwing not just the welling gratitude behind it but also everything I felt for him. There wasn't a moment of hesitation from him. One hand moved to the nape of my neck and he moved off the mattress, onto his knees in front of me. His mouth was soft and hard all at once, and when my lips parted, he deepened the kiss.

He was the one who eventually pulled away, and when he spoke, his voice was deliciously thick. "We should probably start eating."

"All righty." I would've agreed to almost anything at that point.

We broke apart and started rifling through the bags of

chips and containers. While we ate, we talked about utterly nothing important, and it was *glorious*, because it had been so long since I could just…just *be*. Since I could talk about my favorite show or the books that were in my room, yet unread, and listen to Sebastian go back and forth on what he'd like to study in college without my mind being caught up in the past.

Once I was stuffed and Sebastian was closing up the bags, I asked, "Are we really going to sleep out here?"

Sebastian chuckled. "Hell yeah." Craning his head back toward me, he raised his brows. "Unless you're not comfortable."

"I'm comfortable," I said. I was and wasn't at the same time, because being out here all night with him wasn't anything like when we were kids.

His lashes lowered. "You sure about that."

"Yes." I scooted down. "I'm just curious to how our parents are okay with this."

"They trust us."

I snorted.

Sebastian crawled up the length of the mattress and stretched out on his side. "I want you to know I don't expect you to stay here all night," he said. "You can hang out for however long you want and leave whenever you want."

Easing down next to him, I hadn't imagined in a long time that I'd find myself spending the night in a tent again. When we were kids, I wasn't picturing him shirtless or thinking some of the things that were crossing my mind now. I rolled onto my side, facing him. I had no idea how long I would stay, but I knew deep down, no matter what I decided about tonight, Sebastian would be okay with it.

No expectations.

Except one.

I felt my cheeks heat before I even got the question out of my mouth. "Is it... Is it okay if I call myself your girlfriend?"

The smile that raced across his striking face nearly stole my breath. "I've been trying to call you my girlfriend since I realized I liked girls."

Happiness bubbled up, and I didn't let anything stamp it down. Nothing. Stretching across the tiny space between us, I placed my hand on his chest, above his heart. His hand folded over mine. Courage rose, pushing me to take a big step, to allow myself to do it.

I kept my eyes open as I said what I'd wanted to say for so many years. Words that, for a while, I thought I no longer deserved. "I love you," I said. "I've been in love with you for as long as I remember."

Sebastian moved instantly.

One hand cupped my cheek, and then his mouth was on mine and we were kissing. There was nothing artful about these kisses. Our lips and mouths crashed together. He tasted of chocolate and salt, and when the kiss deepened, he shifted even closer.

He worked one arm under me, and we were fused together, chest to chest, hip to hip. When he rolled me onto my back, he followed, and our hands were needy, slipping under clothes, skin to skin in a heady rush.

My hands roamed the length of his back and his sides.

His hand traveled down my hip, over my thigh. He hooked my leg around his waist, bringing us even closer together, although I hadn't thought that was possible. His shirt came off, then mine. And then we were truly skin to skin in a way we'd never been before.

Acute shivers raced over my skin as the small, rough hairs of his chest brushed against me. Unbridled sensation pounded my senses.

"This wasn't why I did this tonight," he said, his voice unlike I'd ever heard before. "We don't have to do anything. We don't—"

"I know." Curling my hand around the nape of his neck, I opened my eyes. "I know."

I tugged his mouth back to mine, and this time when we kissed, there was something different about it. It was uninhibited and more…more *purposeful*, and I felt wild in the most wonderful way. I had no idea where tonight would go, where we would end up, but I trusted him. He trusted me.

"I love you," I whispered against his mouth.

Sebastian made this sound, this rugged and deep sound against my mouth, as his hips settled between my legs and his chest was once again pressed into mine. He moved, and I was falling, swimming, drowning in sensations.

And I lived.

I loved.

And it was okay, more than *okay*.

It was beautiful.

It was *living*.

CHAPTER THIRTY

Brown leaves floated from nearly bare limbs, falling down to the ground silently. It was the Wednesday before Thanksgiving, and on Monday I had my last session with Dr. Perry.

I had my assignments.

I'd been following them dutifully.

I took Sunday evenings to truly remember my friends, and God, that had not been fun at first. Since the accident, I'd avoided looking at their Facebook and Instagram accounts or any of the pictures I had of them. I hadn't read their old messages on my phone or their emails.

The first Sunday I'd lasted for only a half an hour before I tossed an old photo album aside. I didn't cry. I had no idea why, especially since my eyes were their own water park at that point. The second Sunday night, when I went to their social media accounts, I'd lost it. Seeing their last posts killed me.

Megan had posted about *Dance Moms* that Saturday afternoon. That had been what she was thinking about, having no idea she'd die later that night, and I think that was what messed with me the most. None of us had even the tiniest of ideas that our lives were about to be irrevocably altered.

Cody had an Instagram post from that night before, a picture of him holding a red cup, smiling into the camera. He was with Chris. Both of them so bright and so happy. I focused on their smiles, because that was what I needed to remember.

Phillip had shared a video of pranks being pulled with the caption "LMFAO." Those were his last words on the internet. *LMFAO.*

The worst part of seeing their accounts was scrolling through all the messages left on their pages after the accident. All the words of mourning and sorrow, the #RIPs and the shock left in the wake of their deaths.

It broke me all over again.

I'd spent most of the evening sitting on the couch eating chocolate, wrapped in my mom's arms and talking about them. I woke the following morning expecting to feel like crap, but I'd felt a little better.

A little lighter.

But I still hadn't gone to their graves yet.

When I left the room with the lamest motivational posters ever, the smile Dr. Perry had given me was as real as any of the ones from the past, but it had been a little different.

There was confidence in this smile.

Not hope or approval but *confidence.* In me.

Confidence that I would find closure and some semblance of peace. Maybe I had already found some of the latter. Right now I was more peaceful than I ever could've imagined.

Sebastian was sitting in the old Adirondack chair, his feet propped up on the railing. I was sitting sideways in his lap, my legs wrapped over the arm of the chair. A soft chenille blanket was dropped over us.

We were reading.

Together.

And there was something so nerdily perfect about what we were doing that I might've fallen in love all over again.

Closing the paranormal book I was reading, I lowered it to my lap and looked at Sebastian. He had his concentration face on. Brows furrowed together. Lips pressed in a thin line. It was cute. Beyond cute. He was reading a graphic novel, and he held it open with one hand. His other arm wrapped around my waist, under the blanket. His fingers moved continuously against my hip, drifting in a slow circle, as if he was letting me know that even though he was focused on the novel, he was fully aware of me in his lap.

I wanted more attention, though.

Pressing my lips against his smooth cheek, I grinned when I heard him snap the novel shut. His arm tightened around me. "What are you doing?" he asked.

"Nothing." I kissed the hard line of his jaw.

He turned his head toward mine. "I like this idea of nothing, then."

I kissed him on the lips this time and he returned the kiss in a way that made me wish Mom wasn't home.

Sliding my hand along his cheek, I pulled back just enough to rest my forehead on his. "What time is your dinner tomorrow?"

"Six. Are you sure you don't want to come?" His family was

going to his grandparents' house for their Thanksgiving dinner. "You're more than welcome to. They'd love to see you."

"I know." I dragged my thumb across his jaw. "I want to, but Dad is going to be here tomorrow. Mom would flip if I tried to be anywhere else."

He kissed the corner of my mouth. "True." Another pause so he could kiss the other side of my mouth. "I'm kind of surprised your sister isn't out here staring at us, drawing hearts in the air with her fingers."

I laughed. "It's only because Mom has her in the kitchen baking pies."

"I think we need to visit that kitchen," he said after a slight pause.

"I think you'll change your mind once you've tried my sister's baking." Looping my arm around his neck, I rested my cheek on his shoulder as he chuckled. "I'm not sure why Mom is letting her bake. Kind of feels like a punishment."

Another chuckle rumbled from his chest. "I'll bring you home some of my grandma's pie."

"Pumpkin?"

"Pumpkin and pecan."

"Mmm." My stomach grumbled. "That sounds amazing. Will you bring me some Cool Whip? Mom buys the generic stuff and it totally does not—"

The balcony door opened, and I lifted my head in surprise, half expecting to see my sister or my mom. But it was Dad. *Dad.*

It was my dad walking out of my bedroom and onto the balcony while I was sprawled across Sebastian's lap.

Holy hell.

My entire body jerked as I scrambled to stand up. I all but fell out of Sebastian's lap, nearly smacking my face on the floor after my legs tangled in the blanket. The last thing I wanted was for my dad, even if he excelled at the absentee-father gig, to walk in while I was sprawled in my boyfriend's lap.

Sebastian ducked his chin as he helped unwrap my legs from the blanket, and I knew he was hiding a grin, and I was so going to smack him upside the head.

Dad's hazel eyes moved from where I stood to where Sebastian was rising. "Your mother mentioned you two were seeing each other."

That was how he greeted me—greeted us.

I hadn't seen him, or talked to him, since the visit in the hospital, and that was the first thing that came out of his mouth.

I wasn't exactly surprised.

Sebastian walked around the chair, extending his hand toward my dad. "Hi, Mr. Wise."

My dad shook his hand, smiling faintly. "Sebastian, my man, good to see you."

"Same," replied Sebastian, moving his hand from my dad's to mine. Our fingers threaded, and he squeezed my hand gently.

Heat hit my cheeks. "I didn't know you were here. I thought you weren't coming until tomorrow."

"I just got here a little bit ago," he explained. "I was hoping we could have some one-on-one time while your mother and sister are busy destroying the kitchen."

Not entirely sure I wanted one-on-one time, I hesitated for a moment. Then I nodded, because I might as well get it over with. Dad wasn't going anywhere, at least not for the next day or so.

"All right." I looked up at Sebastian. "I'll text you later?"

His eyes searched mine as he continued to hold my hand. Concerned pinched his features. "You sure?"

"Yeah," I told him in a low voice. "It's okay."

Sebastian seemed reluctant, not that I could blame him. He knew the word *tense* didn't even begin to describe my father's and my relationship, but he lowered his head, pressing a kiss to my cheek. "Okay. I'll be waiting."

Saying goodbye to my dad, he headed down the stairs, leaving me alone on the balcony with my dad. With no idea what to say or do, I bent over and picked up the blanket to fold it.

Since my head had been so wrapped up in the accident and everything to do with it, I hadn't really given myself much space to mull over what my mother had admitted and everything it meant.

"How have you been doing?" he asked, leaning a hip against the railing.

"Okay."

"You and Sebastian are really an item?" He laughed as soon as he finished speaking. "Well, I'm hoping that's the case, considering how I found you two."

My cheeks flushed, and I fought the urge to point out that Mom had already told him, but I was done...done just being so angry, so torn. Although Dr. Perry and I had never talked about my dad, I knew enough to know that if I had to move on from the accident in August, I had to move on from, well, everything with my father.

"Yeah, we started, um, officially seeing each other not too long ago," I said finally, staring at the scuffed sneakers Dad was wearing. "I'm...really happy with him." A flicker of guilt shot through me like an arrow. Admitting happiness was still hard. Probably would be hard for a very, very long time.

"He's a good kid. Can't say that I'm surprised. Always thought that you two would end up together."

My brows rose. "Really?"

"Well, I *hoped* you two would end up together," he clarified. "Like I said, he's a good boy. He'll be a good man."

I shifted my weight from one foot to the next.

"You look a lot better," he said, swiftly changing the subject. "No cast or bruises. Standing up and moving around. I'm relieved to see that."

Holding the blanket to my chest, I looked up at my dad, *really* looked at him. He looked like he had when he came into the hospital back in August. A little older and a little more tired, but he had the same rigid posture. The conversation was still stilted.

To be honest, it had kind of always been like that. Growing up, Lori was Daddy's little girl. I was a mama's girl. Lori and I always took sides—in going to restaurants, to the zoo or amusement parks. She went off with Dad. I hung close to Mom. Dad and I just never really connected, and it wasn't all his fault. I could've answered the phone when he called, especially after Mom told me why he'd left. And he probably could've been a better dad to me and refused to back down when I was being a brat.

His eyes, the same as mine, held my gaze. "I've been worried about you."

"I'm doing better. I'm not...a hundred percent, but I'm doing better."

He smiled faintly, but the sadness lingered in his eyes. "I know you are. You're so strong and I don't think you give yourself enough credit."

"I don't know about that." I sat in the chair, placing the blanket in my lap. "If I was stronger, I probably wouldn't have ended up in the situation I did."

He seemed to consider that. "Maybe that part is true, but you had to be strong to get through this."

Pressing my lips together, I nodded.

"You're stronger than me," he said, and I jerked in my seat, surprised. Dad wasn't looking at me. He placed his hands on the railing and looked out over the yard. "You know something your grandfather used to say all the time that I hated? He'd always say 'Tomorrow will be better.' Every time I was mad about something or something bad happened, he'd say that. 'Tomorrow will be better.' I didn't hate it at first. Not at all. I lived that way for a very long time." Turning around slowly, he faced me. "Do you understand what I mean about that?"

I shifted my gaze to his sneakers again, silent.

"Every time something got hard or was broken or not what I wanted, I told myself it would be better tomorrow. It didn't make whatever it was easier. It didn't fix whatever was broken. If I was uncomfortable with something, or if I just didn't want to do it, tomorrow always came and I still didn't do it."

Closing my eyes against the sudden sting, I exhaled roughly.

"It's a nice sentiment, though, isn't it? Living life saying tomorrow will be better whenever something bad happens. Whenever we're filled with disappointment. But tomorrow is never guaranteed." He stopped to take a deep breath. "Baby girl, you learned that lesson far too young."

The four of us will always be the four of us.

No matter what.

We would no longer be four of us. Ever. Dad was right. I knew tomorrow was never guaranteed.

"We don't always get tomorrow. Sometimes it's not because of death. Sometimes it's the decisions we make for ourselves." He lifted his hand and scrubbed it over his face, a habit I realized just then that I'd picked up from him. "I hate that saying because that's how I handled things with you. Tomorrow I'd fix what's broken between us. But when tomorrow came, I never did."

My eyes started to sting. "I...I don't think I exactly made it easy for you."

"Doesn't matter." Tone gruff, he went on to say, "I'm your father. It's on me. Not you. So I want... I want today to be the tomorrow I kept putting off. What do you say?"

Dad extended a hand and for a long moment all I could do was stare, and then I let go of the blanket and laced my hand in his.

CHAPTER THIRTY-ONE

Sitting in my room, I held my phone to my chest as I stared at the map above my desk. The circles Sebastian and I had drawn all over blurred and each breath I drew in felt shaky and raw.

I'd finally done it.

I'd read Megan's texts.

There were a lot of them, since my phone was set to keep messages until I was forced to delete them.

The tears that had welled up and fallen had mingled with laughter as I read through some of her most random, non-sensical messages. I wanted to reach into the phone and see her one last time. The *real* her. Not a picture. Not a set of letters and sentences.

But I knew I couldn't

Memories would have to be enough.

Exhaling heavily, I placed my phone on my desk and plugged it into the charger. I wheeled back, turning the chair toward my closet door. It was cracked open, overflowing with clothes and books.

When I left school the day before, I had taken a big step. One not outlined by Dr. Perry but that I felt was one of the best ways I could honor Megan's memory, or at least do right by her.

And do right by myself.

I left the chair and padded over to the closet, my thick socks whispering along the floor. I opened the door and knelt down to push aside the crumpled jeans. Carefully, I shoved the stack of books against the wall and then leaned in. I reached blindly, knowing I found what I was looking for the moment my fingers brushed over them. With my prize in hand, I sat back and looked down.

My knee pads were scuffed from sliding across the gym floor, but they'd lasted me almost four years of playing volleyball. They'd last at least another year.

I'd visited Coach Rogers after class yesterday.

The season was over, but he knew of the different rec leagues that played throughout the year in the county. One was going to be starting up in February, and I was planning to go to tryouts, which meant I needed to get my butt back in gear, and Coach had set me up with a plan to make it happen.

I wouldn't land a scholarship, but I fully intended to do tryouts at whatever college I got accepted to. I was still hoping for UVA, and I still had a bit of waiting before I would find out if I got early admittance.

Tomorrow I would hit the gym at school, and I would willingly run the bleachers with these knee pads. And I would do it thinking Megan would be…would be *proud* of me.

But today wasn't over.

Today was just starting.

I sat in the Jeep, staring over the rolling hills, over the tombs and stone wings. Bare-limbed trees dotted the landscape. A faint dusting of snow carpeted the ground.

Winter had come fast and hard, spreading frost over the grass and icing the roadways. It was December 19, exactly four months from the day everything changed.

I hadn't planned it that way. Coming to the cemetery today was more of an accident. But now, as I sat in the warm Jeep staring out the window, I guessed it was kind of fitting that I ended up here on this date.

I swallowed hard as I stared out over the cemetery. "I found my knee pads today."

"I can't believe you can find anything in that closet," he teased, and a small grin cracked my lips. "I'm going with you tomorrow."

As I glanced over at him, my gaze immediately connected with his bright blue eyes. "You don't have to. I'm sure sitting in the gym or running up and down bleachers is the very last thing you want to do."

"If I didn't want to do it, I wouldn't offer," he returned. "Plus I'm not just there for moral support. It's very possible you'll fall and hurt yourself."

"Whatever." I rolled my eyes, my grin spreading an inch and then fading again as I focused on the silent tombs. I still struggled with accepting an offer of help, because that was what Sebastian was doing. He was offering to be there with me, *for* me, because he knew it would be hard, both physically and emotionally. Just like he knew what I was doing right now wouldn't be easy.

And I wasn't going to shut him out. One of the things I'd learned was that when someone offered you a hand, you took it. And sometimes it was hard to see that offer or accept it, but life was easier when you did.

"Okay," I whispered. Then silence fell between us.

Sebastian curved his hand over my knee. "You ready to do this?"

Dragging my gaze from the window, I nodded.

He was watching me closely. "We don't have to do this today. We can come back—"

"No. If I don't do this today, then I'll keep pushing it off till tomorrow and I'll never do it." I thought of my dad, of the once-a-week phone calls we now had and held each other to, even when neither of us had a thing to say to one another. Our relationship was truly a work in progress. "I have to do this."

"Okay." Leaning over, he slipped his hand around the nape of my neck and brought my mouth to his. The kiss was sweet and brief. He pulled back. "You look good in my hat."

Laughing, I touched the gray knit cap I'd grabbed from his bedroom. He was wearing a black one. "Really?"

"Of course." He tugged the sides down, straightening it.

My smile faded as my gaze shifted to the windshield. I inhaled deeply. A shudder worked through me, and I twisted back to Sebastian.

"You're not doing this alone," he whispered, eyes intent and body still. "I'm here. Abbi and Dary are here."

And my friends were. They were in the car behind us,

waiting for me to open the door and get out. Things had improved between me and Abbi. We were hanging out again, talking to one another like we were actually friends, and I knew that eventually it would be like it was before. I knew it in every part of my being. It just needed a little more time, because when I cut Abbi out, I'd really hurt her. Repairing that definitely took time.

Just like dealing with everything took time.

Living when others died wasn't something you just woke up one day and got over, even though sometimes it felt that way. Even when I realized I'd gone an entire day, or maybe two, without thinking about Megan or the guys. And sometimes I still felt guilty about that. And sometimes I still cried when I thought about everything they'd had to live for and all the opportunity that had been wiped away in a matter of seconds.

It just took time and family and friends and love to come to terms with the fact that life did move on. Life kept going, and you couldn't be left behind, living in a past that no longer existed.

But the other guilt I carried deep inside me? That was still a work in progress, harder to untangle and much messier. Working through my part in that night was the one thing that was going to hurt for a while. That was the one thing I was going to have to carve out of myself. And it was going to leave some scars behind. But I was learning how to live with my part in that night, my *silence*, and I was learning to live with the fact I was a lesson, not just for myself but for others.

My friends' pasts and futures had been erased in seconds. Mine could've been, too, and all those comments on the news articles could've been about me and, in some way, some of them were. I knew I could never go back and change anything about that night. I could only do *better*. I was alive—I was still here.

I knew I couldn't go back and start a new beginning. I couldn't rewrite the middle. All I could do was change tomorrow, as long as I had one.

Swallowing hard, I wrapped my gloved fingers around the door handle. Cold air rushed in as I opened the door and climbed out, gravel crunching under my booted feet.

I looked out over the cemetery, letting the brisk, snow-scented air fill my lungs. Car doors opened and closed all around me. Out of the corner of my eyes, I saw Abbi and Dary approaching me. A second later, Sebastian's fingers found mine, and I knew as I took the first step that while tomorrow was not guaranteed, never promised, there was going to be so much possibility.

★ ★ ★ ★ ★

ACKNOWLEDGMENTS

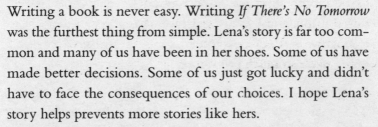

Writing a book is never easy. Writing *If There's No Tomorrow* was the furthest thing from simple. Lena's story is far too common and many of us have been in her shoes. Some of us have made better decisions. Some of us just got lucky and didn't have to face the consequences of our choices. I hope Lena's story helps prevents more stories like hers.

This book wouldn't be possible without my amazing agent Kevan Lyon. A huge thank you to my editor Michael Strother (why do I know so many Michaels?), the editorial team at Harlequin TEEN, my publicist Siena, and everyone at Harlequin who touched this book and had a hand in bringing it to life. Thank you to Taryn Fagerness, who is responsible for getting this book translated into many different languages. Thank you to Steph for being an awesome assistant and friend.

Sarah J. Maas—I love you. Thank you. Erin Watt—you guys are amazing. Thank you. Brigid Kemmerer—thank you and I don't know how we don't see each other more often. A quick shout-out to Jen, Hannah, Val, Jessica, Lesa, Stacey, Cora, Jay, Laura K. and Liz Berry, Jillian Stein, Andrea Joan and everyone in JLAnders. You guys rock.

You may have recognized a name in this book. Darynda Jones—the amazing creator of the Charley Davidson series and more. Thank you for letting me steal your name and for supporting an amazing cause in the process.

None of this would be possible without you, the reader. Thank you.

HQ Young Adult
One Place. Many Stories

The home of fun, contemporary
and meaningful Young Adult fiction.

Follow us online

 @HQYoungAdult

 @HQYoungAdult

 HQYoungAdult

 HQMusic